CODE

THEIR BOND IS UNBREAKABLE.

NAME

THEIR MISSION IS SECRET.

RASCAL

THEIR STORY IS UNFORGETTABLE.

DOROTHEA N. BUCKINGHAM

ISBN:

979-8-9996582-9-6 (paperback)

979-8-9996582-8-9 (e-book)

979-8-9996582-7-2 (Large Type)

Cataloging-in-Publication Data

Buckingham, Dorothea (Dee), 1949–

Code Name Rascal / Dorothea Buckingham. — First edition.

p. cm.

1. Women—Hawaii—Fiction. 2. World War, 1939–1945—Hawaii—Fiction. 3. Radar—History—Fiction. 4. Female friendship—Fiction. 5. Hawaii—History—20th century—Fiction. 7. War fiction.

I. Title: Code Name Rascal.

First Edition

Published by Sydney Press Kaneohe, Hawaii 96744 1-808-726-0271

For Jack

Anche in paradiso non è bello essere soli.

There is no greater torment than to be alone in paradise.
—Italian Proverb

Character List — Code Name Rascal

Caroline ("CJ") Delano

A firecracker New Jersey journalist, one of three women to graduate from Columbia School of Journalism, comes to Hawaii to marry the love of her life, (Joe Delano) and to set the Honolulu newspaper world on its ear. They marry on a Friday, the war starts on Sunday and CJ's career, her marriage, and her role as a woman all collide.

1st Lieutenant Joseph A. Delano, USMC

The love of CJ's life, Joe is a fireplug of a Brooklyn Marine who declared his opinions like dogma but had a hard time navigating the communication skills required in a marriage. Joe's and CJ's expectation of married life weren't defined, then the war happened, shattering any previous roles.

Lieutenant JG Lincoln W Armstrong, USN

Linc Armstrong, Joe's roommate at the Naval Academy for all four years, straight out of Wisconsin who believed in God,

Country, and anything topped with cheese, A PBY pilot with plans on being a doctor in his hometown of Madison.

Lieutenant Parker Holt, USN

Part of Honolulu's social elite, Parker, a Harvard trained medical doctor was assigned to Joe's unit. His childhood friend, Eve Russell is one of the most sought-after Hawaii bachelorettes, but Parker has no eyes for women.

Eve Russell

A Honolulu socialite, daughter of a prominent newspaper editor, Eve is accustomed to privilege but longs for purpose. Outspoken, sometimes for the sake of it, she stakes a claim on Linc.

Ruth Elliott

Quiet, thoughtful, married to a much-older Navy commander, Ruth has self-defined purpose in life: to be a mother and a good Navy Officer's wife, but instead she must learn to carry loss with dignity, and show a resilient face.

Commander Gordon Elliott, USN

Ruth's husband, Gordon, values family and the Navy and tries to balance his loyalties. His love for Ruth is firm, but their marriage is tested by their haunting grief and he struggles to save it.

Jane Meade Anderson

A Texas aviatrix, straight off the farm in Crawford, Texas. According to her flight students, Jane's the best instructor in the air, but when it comes to choosing a husband, Jane's instincts fell short and she must face a decision that was unheard of during the war.

First Lieutenant "Buck" Meade, USAAF

Buck was the first cadet Jane agreed to date. He didn't buy her flowers or chocolates; he bought her aviation magazines and seduced her with a vision to create an airline that would haul cargo and passengers… and its pilots would be all girls! But his talk was just that.

Chapter One
December 5, 1941

Wo Fat's Restaurant, Waikiki

CJ MARTINO WANTED it all, and she nearly got it, though not quite the way she expected.

Two days before the attack on Pearl Harbor, Carmela Jean Martino married Lieutenant Joseph Anthony Delano, USMC. She wore a yellow linen suit and her grandmother's pearl earrings. There was no cascading bouquet. No high Mass. No grand Italian reception. There were only Joe and CJ, the Justice of the Peace, and a dozing clerk as their only witness

It wasn't the wedding she'd dreamed of—walking down the aisle on her father's arm, wearing a gown with a ten-foot train, and Joe in his dress blue uniform. But it was the wedding of her choice.

When the judge proclaimed CJ and Joe "man and wife," Joe

kissed his bride, whisked her down the courthouse steps, and hailed a cab.

Joe opened the cab door, but CJ didn't get in. She was mesmerized, staring down the street lined with palm trees swirled with green and red Christmas lights, and a department store window display with Santa riding a canoe pulled by eight flying dolphins.

Joe took her arm, and CJ slid in, still pivoting her gaze from barefoot newspaper boys to arm-in-arm couples of men in tan linen suits and women in flowered sarong dresses.

There was a Salvation Army Santa in green plaid shorts and sandals. She thought, at least his bell and kettle were familiar.

She closed her eyes and inhaled the evening breeze perfumed with flowers instead of bus fumes.

Ten days before she was standing on a platform at Newark Central Station surrounded by family, hugging and crying, all there to see her off. Then she boarded a train to San Francisco, then a cruise ship to Honolulu.

CJ turned to Joe and whispered, "If this is a dream, Joe Delano, don't even think about walking me up." She leaned her head on his shoulder and smiled when she got a whiff of his Old Spice and the linger of a cheap cigar.

Joe lifted her chin and kissed her. "You ain't seen nothing yet. Wait until you see Wo Fat's restaurant! It's right out of Hollywood!"

CJ figured Wo Fat's would be a two-bit chop suey place like all the other hole-in-the-wall dives they ate at in New York's Chinatown, with Formica tables, cracked vinyl seats, and dog-eared menus. And when he told her that Linc was going to be there, she was sure it would be a nickel-a-beer dive.

But she had to eat her words when the cabbie pulled in front of Wo Fat's—it was an Imperial Chinese palace with floodlights scanning its low walls. All it needed was a moat.

"Isn't this top drawer?" Joe asked.

"You bet." She was sure it was top drawer enough to cost him a month's salary.

Joe took CJ's arm and strutted past a line of waiting couples dressed in tuxes and gown, straight up to an old Chinese man in a tuxedo, who was welcoming guests to Wo Fat's.

Joe introduced his bride. "PY, this is my wife, CJ."

PY smiled and bowed, and CJ thought she caught a glint in his eyes when he did.

"CJ, you Number One beautiful lady. Welcome to Wo Fat's, the finest Chinese restaurant in the world, and me, PY Chong, Number One cook."

CJ returned his bow and smiled.

"Don't let him fool you," Joe said. "PY is the owner and chief dictator here."

"Not dictator," PY corrected. "I am Emperor."

Joe started to tell PY they were meeting Eve Russell and Doctor Hold, but before he could finish, PY raised his hand. "They're already here."

PY waved to a man in red silk tunic and black trousers and said, "I saved you the best table. Ah Ching will show you."

As they walked through the garden of koi pond and brass statue cranes, CJ asked Joe, "A doctor? And who is Eve Russsell?"

"You're going to love them." Joe held her hand and the couple followed Ah Ching down a corridor of dark wood panels carved with swirling dragons, hanging red silk lanterns. When Ah Ching held back a beaded curtain, CJ gasped.

Light in the dining room glinted from crystal chandelier, gilded mirrors; it bounced off gleaming brass trombones and the sequins on the Chinese soloist's gown.

CJ held on to Joe as they snaked through the tables with long white tablecloths. There were waiters in tuxedoes and cigarette girls in slinky black gowns. If the folks at the bakery could only see me now! Vinny's daughters at a swanky Waikiki hotspot.

"There." Joe pointed to a table next to the dance floor. "There's Linc." Joe waved to him.

Linc Armstrong, a Wisconsin farm boy who believed in God, Country and anything topped with cheese, and Joe Delano, a fireplug of a Brooklyn Italian who declared his opinions like they were dogma and never laid his eyes on a cow—they were best friends and roommates at the Naval Academy for all four years. Linc looked tanned and his hair was streaked blond. Hawaii agreed with him.

Joe said, "The other guy is Parker Holt. He was our unit doctor when I first got here, and the gal next to him is Eve Russell."

"Are Eve and Parker and item?"

"No." Joe laughed. "For lots of reasons."

"What about Linc and Eve?" CJ asked.

Joe shook his head. "No one lassoes Eve Russell."

When they got to Linc, he hugged CJ so hard that he lifted her off the floor. "Gosh, it's good to see you."

"Watch it, Lieutenant. I'm a married woman now." CJ flashed her wedding ring.

"Damn, I'm so sorry I couldn't make the wedding. I tried like hell, but when the Navy calls. . ."

"I know. I know." CJ held up her hand to quiet him. "If the Navy calls, you answer."

Linc stepped back and eyed her head to toe. "You look great! What's it been? Two years?"

"Eighteen very long months since you two got shipped to Hawaii."

"How are your parents?"

"Adjusting." She shrugged slightly. "They're happy that Joe and I are married, but they're disappointed."

"No reception for 200 of your closest family?" Linc smiled.

CJ raised her eyebrows. "More like no cathedral high Mass."

The officer next to Linc stood and extended his hand. "Parker Holt."

Parker was handsome in an Ivy League kind of way—fine-featured, horn-rimmed glasses and hazel eyes.

The platinum blonde next to Parker introduced herself. "Eve Russell," When CJ extended her hand to Eve, Eve ignored it and instead blew a kiss to CJ with a flip of her wrists.

CJ pegged Eve as coming from money. She had a perfected society smile, penetrating blue eyes and understated diamond earrings, necklace and bracelet.

"You got one of the good ones." Eve motioned to Joe.

CJ turned to her groom. "I think he got a pretty good deal himself."

"Did Joe introduce you to PY?" Eve asked.

"He did," CJ answered. "PY said I was 'Number One beautiful lady.'"

Eve feigned offense, tossing her hair over her shoulder. "That PY! He should only say that about me."

"Oh, don't fret, my dear." Parker put his arm around Eve in mock consolation. "You'll always be my number one."

"Thanks, Park." Eve patted his hand and CJ read the gesture as more sisterly than anything faintly romantic.

CJ turned to Parker. "Joe said you were the unit doctor."

"If you're asking if I patched them up after bar fights and dispensed copious amounts of penicillin? Yes. I was." Parker smirked.

Eve raised a brow. "Must you be so crude?"

"It's from hanging out with Marines too long. They're a bad influence," Parker answered.

"Count your self lucky to be won over by Marines," Joe said.

Parker put his hand to his cheek. "Why Lieutenant, I'd be thrilled to be won over by a Marine. . . especially one with impressive credentials." Parker wiggled his eyebrows.

CJ replayed Parker's words. Did he mean what she thought he meant?

Joe said, "All I know I that Park was the best damn doc ever."

"I accept the compliment." Parker graciously bowed.

"Absolutely 100% agree," Linc said. "Park, you're one of the best, just not one of the most discreet."

"I'll have you know that even the Navy can turn a blind eye when they've got a Harvard-trained doctor in the clinic. Besides," Parker said, "Discretion is my specialty." He raised his glass toward Eve. "She can vouch for that."

Eve nodded. "My mother's still hoping we'll get married."

Parker put his hand to his heart. "We'll always have Valentine's Day."

CJ furrowed her brow. "Translation for those of us who are new to the game?"

Eve explained that every year, at his Valentine's Day Party, Parker proposes to her. "And if neither of us is married by the time we are forty, I'll accept."

"CJ, you've got to come to the party," Parker said. "It's the social event of the year."

"In some circles," Eve corrected.

"Yes, fairy circles." Parker kissed Eve's hand, then turned to CJ. "But enough talk about Parker. This is your night." She waved her hand toward CJ and Joe. "Tell us how you met."

"I got this." Linc raised his hand. "It was at a party after the Navy-Columbia game. Columbia wiped the floor with us."

"Navy never had a defense worth a damn," Parker said.

"Neither did Joe," CJ quipped.

"We all spotted CJ—Joe, Charlie Banks, Fritz Holbrook, and me. Who wouldn't? A dark-haired beauty with an attitude you could read from a mile away. But the rest of us had the good sense to recognize trouble when we saw it."

"The rest of you were cowards," CJ jibed.

"True." Linc conceded the point. "The first thing you need to know about these two is that Joe is a fierce Dodgers fan, and CJ worships the Yankees."

"She's a Yankee bully," Joe chimed in.

CJ cupped her hand to her ear and leaned toward Joe. "How many World Series have the Dodgers won?"

When Joe didn't answer, she formed a zero with her fingers.

"As you can see, CJ doesn't believe in second place." Linc cocked his head toward CJ and she nodded.

"On the train ride back to the Academy, Joe told me he'd met the girl he was going to marry. He was drunk, so I laughed it off."

"Drunk with love." Joe put his arm around CJ.

Linc shifted his eyes toward a couple walking toward their table. "Be on your feet, boys. Commander Elliot and his lady are headed straight for us."

CJ watched the older couple approach. The commander looked to be in his forties, with a ramrod posture, a pencil-thin mustache, and steel-grey eyes. Quite distinguished for an older man.

Linc and Joe snapped to their feet, Parker stood up slower, less enthusiastic to rise.

"Good evening, sir," Joe and Linc recited in perfect unison.

Commander Elliot nodded in response.

Eve jumped up and hugged the Commander's wife, kissed the air next to her cheek, then turned to introduce CJ. "She's a blushing bride of what? Three hours now?"

"Congratulations." Ruth extended her hand.

CJ guessed Ruth to be no more than twenty-five, but she

dressed like a matron in a maroon Chanel suit, a double-strand pearl choker, and a fox stole with its head and claws still attached.

"Is this your first time in Hawaii?" Ruth asked.

"It's my first time west of New Jersey."

"I'm sure we can get you into the swing of things," Ruth said. "I'll have someone from the Officers' Wives Club call you. I'm confident we can find a project you'd be interested in volunteering."

"That would be wonderful," CJ said, thinking that there was no way in hell she was joining a wives' club She wanted a job, not an afternoon covey.

"But I see you're already in excellent hands with Eve. Between Eve and her mother, you'll be well taken care of." Ruth turned to Eve. "Speaking of your mother, you and I need to talk."

"Some territorial warfare?" Eve raised her eyebrows.

"Can you meet me for lunch Monday? Coco's?"

"I can't wait to her what she did now." Eve smirked.

And as if on cue, Commander Elliot took his wife's arm, leading her away saying, "We should let these young people get back to their evening."

CJ looked over at Joe and Linc, shoulder-to-shoulder, rigid at attention, like the wet-behind-the-ears junior officers they were.

As soon as they left, Parker said, "It looks like the old man robbed the cradle."

"A three-star cradle," Linc added. "Her daddy's an admiral.

"How do you know that?" Parker asked.

"He was our Communications and Intelligence professor at the Academy. He was by the book and no mercy."

"And arrogant," Joe added. "You'd think he won the Great War from a communications desk, but the S.O.B. never saw combat." Joe was about to go on, but Eve tapped her glass with her knife. "Enough shop talk! We're here to celebrate CJ and Joe's wedding." She turned to Parker. "I think we need champagne."

"Mumm's '38?" he asked.

"Order Demi-sec," Eve added.

As Parker got the waiter's attention, Linc asked Joe who was watching the airfield.

"I've got the place locked up," Joe said. "All the planes are parked wingtip to wingtip, and I've got six sentries walking the perimeter." Joe lit his cigar and took a puff. "That airfield is wrapped so tight, no Jap can get near the place." He held the cigar away from himself and examined it as if he were admiring it.

"Scuttlebutt says they're planning an air attack," Parker said.

Joe scoffed. "That's ridiculous. How the hell are they going to fly in? From where? Carriers? We'd spot them." He turned to Linc. "That's why we've got PBY pilots for? Right, Linc?"

Parker said, "I'm just repeating what I heard from the brass."

"Exactly," Joe said, "And we all know the brass have their heads up their asses."

CJ squeezed Joe's thigh. It was the signal she used to tell him to calm down, but Joe kept on going. He asked Linc, "Have you ever seen a Jap carrier while you're flying patrol?"

"I've spotted a few Zeroes past Midway," Linc said. "So, there's got to be carriers out there somewhere."

"To hell with the carriers!" Joe jabbed the air with his cigar. "Truth be told, I'm not as worried about the Japs—it's the locals I'm worried about. I'm aiming my guns toward them."

Eve's eyes bulged. "Just be careful which locals you're aiming at."

"I'm not talking about the white ones," Joe said.

Eve stared at him. "Neither am I." She paused, then pulled out a silver monogrammed cigarette case from her purse.

"Look," Joe ranted. "It's not secret, there's 160,000 Japs on this island—and those are only the ones we know about."

CJ dug her fingers into Joe's thigh, squeezing it even harder, but he didn't stop. "It doesn't take a genius to figure out a few of them are rooting for the old country."

"Not all locals have pitchforks," Parker said. "Some of us, are beyond approach—There's a lot of money supporting the troops." He cocked his head. "Including local 'Jap' money."

The veins in Joe's neck bulged. CJ jabbed his ribs with her elbow, to no avail.

"I'm telling you there's a Fifth Column and the locals—white, Jap, I don't care—are a threat."

Eve leaned over for Parker to light her cigarette, as he did, she didn'. "Keep in mind, Joe," she spoke slowly, enunciating every syllable. "If it weren't' for the money these local families were pouring into to this. . ."

Linc interrupted her, "Eve, with the exception of one of us." He turned to Joe. "The military appreciates the support. Some of us don't know how to be gracious."

Joe scoffed. "I'm a Marine. I missed the diplomacy class at the Academy."

Parker laughed, "It if were up to me, I wouldn't give the lot of you a dime. It's my father whose squandering his money."

"And depleting your trust fund?" Eve quipped.

Parker snickered. "Neither of us will live long enough to spend our money."

"I intend to live a very long time," Eve countered.

CJ looked at each of them. "Will somebody tell me what you're talking about?"

Linc explained, "Between Eve's family and Parker's, they own half of Honolulu."

"I wouldn't say half," Eve said.

"Parker's family is in banking and real estate, and Eve's family owns the *Honolulu Advertiser*," Joe said.

But as Linc took out a paper from his pocket, the band struck up *Chattanooga Choo Choo*, and the trumpets and trombones blared. It sounded like every guest at Wo Fat's was singing along.

Linc raised his voice. "Please join me in raising your glasses to Joe and CJ." He almost shouted. "To my best friend. . ." His words were drowned out. "For years." He shook his head and cupped his hand to his mouth. "To CJ and Joe," he said, and sat down.

When the song ended, Joe asked Linc if he wanted to try the speech again.

"I'll pass. But." Linc raised his glass. "Here's to you both. May you live long and well. Enjoy your honeymoon." They toasted.

"Where are you spending your honeymoon?" Parker asked.

"The Kamehameha Suite at the Royal Hawaiian Hotel," Joe answered.

"Don't you just love the Royal?" Eve almost cooed.

"Actually, I haven't been there. We went from the ship to the Justice of the Peace," Cj answered.

"How virginal," Parker taunted, and CJ responded with a Mona Lisa smile.

Eve ignored Parker and turned to CJ, "CJ, you're going to love the Royal. They have the best bands. Harry Owens is playing there tomorrow night." She sat up. "What if we all go?" Her voice got lighter. "How about it, Linc?"

Linc exchanged glances with Joe. "We've got a big maneuver scheduled for this weekend. All hands on deck."

CJ wondered if Linc was telling the truth, or just looking for a way out of Eve's invitation, but then Parker said, "They even have the docs scheduled for mock casualty duty."

"Does that mean you're working, too?" CJ asked Joe.

"Yeah, I'm off on Sunday, and after that, I have a 72-hour pass."

CJ knew being married to a Marine would have its challenges, but she didn't expect Joe to work on the first day of their honeymoon.

"I don't know how you military wives handle life." Eve stubbed out her cigarette. "I could never tolerate it."

"You can't tolerate your soup served cold," Parker countered.

"I've got it!" Eve perked up. "If Joe's going to work, let's you and I go the newspaper."

"Tomorrow's Saturday," CJ said.

"Pops works six days a week, and on the seventh day, he's home calling the office every hour."

CJ smiled. "He sounds like a true newspaper man."

"I'll set up an appointment with him for ten o'clock."

"That would be swell."

Who knows? CJ thought. By Monday, she could be a cub reporter.

CJ was grateful and she appreciated the offer from Eve, but she was cautious. With one gesture she went from the evil sorceress to her fairy godmother. And as the night went on, she became more guarded, not for herself, but Linc, as she watched Eve lean into him as she spoke and the strap of her dress kept slipping off her shoulder. She couldn't keep her eyes off them as they danced and Eve leaned into Linc and he slid his hand down her back.

When Joe caught her staring at them, he whispered in her ear, "Linc's a big boy."

"He's a babe in the woods with that one."

"Hey, look at me," Joe said. "Linc doesn't need a big sister." He pulled CJ closer. "Besides, I should be the only man in the room for you."

CJ laughed and rested her cheek against his.

"That's more like it." He clenched her waist and dipped her back to the floor. She loved that he thought he was Fred Astair, but she held on for dear life, afraid he would drop her.

And for the rest of the night, the five of them danced, and drank, and laughed until the band played *Good Nights, Ladies* signaling the end of the evening, and the friends said their adieus and Joe and CJ drifted off to the Royal Hawaiian Hotel for their honeymoon.

Chapter Two
December 5, 1941

The Royal Hawaiian Hotel, Waikiki

THE ROYAL HAWAIIAN Hotel was painted a Pepto Bismal pink!

It was a garish Moroccan palace plunked in the middle of Waikiki. Pink turrets. Pink pennants. And busboys in pink Aladdin trousers.

"Isn't it incredible?" Joe puffed with pride.

"I've never seen anything like it."

CJ could understand how Joe could get caught up with the theatrics of it all, but Eve?

She told CJ she'd "love the Royal." Was it some kind of local icon?

A bellman led the couple through the Royal's lobby—pink Persian rugs and pink ottomans—to a birdcage elevator that opened to a second-floor atrium with French doors leading to a balcony overlooking Waikiki. CJ glanced at the potted palms and oversized rockers and wished she could explore the balcony's view.

Inside, the circular atrium was painted ivory with an ivory Persian runner down the hall—there wasn't a hint of pink.

The doors of each guest room were highly polished wood, carved with tropical flowers.

The bellman opened the door and pointed out CJ's luggage, which had been sent from the ship.

Their room was a kaleidoscope of fruit baskets, trailing orchids, and pink foiled wrapped chocolates set on silver trays.

CJ stepped out onto the lanai, twirling around with her arms raised in the air. "Joe, you've got to see this!" The moon striped the waves silver and sapphire. Beachboys strummed ukuleles, and jazz from the hotel ballroom floated on the breeze.

Joe stood behind CJ and wrapped his arms around her waist.

She pointed to a spotlight waving across the sky. "Theater opening?"

"Searchlights looking for Japs."

"No. Not tonight," she said. "Tonight, they're looking for the stars."

"Whatever you want, babe." He kissed the back of her neck. "I love you."

"I love you right back, Mr. Delano." She stroked his chin and traced her finger along his eyebrow.

Joe kissed CJ's hand, her mouth, and her neck. "I've missed you." He unbuttoned her jacket and slid it off her shoulders.

CJ loved being undressed by Joe. She remembered the first time he did—she'd watched him as he moved slowly, caressing every part of her and declaring his love to her.

Joe untucked CJ's blouse and unbuttoned it, gliding it off her shoulders.

She remembered the first time she ran her hand down his back. They'd been in his room at the academy, not in a grand room on the beach at Waikiki.

"Do you think we should have waited?" she asked.

"For what?" Joe unzipped her skirt, and it dropped to the floor.

"Our first time." CJ raised her arms, and Joe lifted her slip over her head. "It would have made our wedding night special."

"Do you remember the time at the boathouse?" Joe asked.

"The boathouse was stupid and dangerous." The academy security guard was making his rounds as they were stripping off their clothes.

"Remember the hike at the Potomac?" Joe said.

She remembered them wandering off the trail. Joe leaned her against a tree, lifted her in his arms, and she clasped her legs around his hips.

"There are hikes all over Hawaii." Joe traced the edge of her bra with his finger.

CJ grinned. "I like hiking."

Joe kissed the cleft of her cleavage.

It would be so easy not to stop, to just keep going, but she gently pushed him back. "I need a minute."

"Not tonight." He held her tighter.

She wriggled free. "I have to get ready."

"Please." Joe pleaded like a child.

CJ laughed at him. "We had a deal, Delano. And I know exactly what you're trying to do."

"Make passionate love to my wife?"

"You're trying to get me pregnant." She darted into the bathroom and slammed the door. "That's not going to happen."

Joe spoke to the closed door. "CJ, you know our children will be beautiful. They'll have my looks and your brains."

"Two years. That was the deal."

"Let's hope the boys will be taller than me," Joe said.

"Oh, Joe, you should see this bathtub. It's big enough for both of us."

"Let me in."

"Not a chance."

Joe knocked on the door. "Room service."

She laughed. "I don't want any."

When she finally opened the door, Joe stood stunned. "You're beautiful!"

CJ caught sight of herself in the mirror, hair disheveled, lipstick smeared and swaddled in a pink hotel bathrobe. "Love really is blind."

Joe carried her to bed. "You are so beautiful, babe." He laid her down and untied her robe. "I love you, CJ."

CJ ached for his touch, for the rhythm of their bodies.

He leaned over and kissed her. He cupped her breast in his hand and took it into his mouth, and she cradled her hands around his head and pressed him closer. "I love you, Joe."

He moved slower, lingering as he kissed her belly. She moaned as he lifted her hips. She'd missed making love with him—the smell of it, the sound of it—the total exhaustion after.

Joe spread CJ's legs and massaged her softness. He kissed her thighs, and she arched her back. He took her with his mouth, and she panted. She tried pulling him into herself.

"Wait." He pleasured her again. She writhed, grabbing his shoulders, sliding up until their faces met, then she reached down, took him in her hand, and guided him inside herself. When they fell back panting and sated, CJ knew that from that night forward, they would be husband and wife, for better, for worse, for richer, for poorer, in sickness and in health, to love and to cherish.

Until death do them part.

CHAPTER THREE
DECEMBER 6, 1941

The Royal Hawaiian Hotel, Waikiki

THE NEXT MORNING, CJ woke up to a note on Joe's pillow: *My darling wife, I'll be home by 6:30. Love you.*

He was at work on the first day of their honeymoon. How many times had she heard the joke at the academy? "If the Marine Corps wanted you to have a wife, they would have issued you one." But now, she was that wife.

She sat up and held up her hand to the sunlight, admiring her wedding ring.

She wished she could have had the wedding her parents wanted to give her. Before she left, she promised them when Joe finished his tour in Hawaii, they would go back to New Jersey and have a proper ceremony with eight bridesmaids, a flower girl, and a ring bearer. She laughed thinking that if Joe had his way, the ring bearer would be their son.

But all that would have to wait; it was years down the line. This morning was about meeting Eve's father and her chance at getting a job at a newspaper.

She called room service and asked for both the *Honolulu Advertiser* and the *Honolulu Star-Bulletin* to be delivered with breakfast. She pored over the papers while devouring fresh mango and papaya.

Both newspapers had solid circulation numbers and a good ratio of advertising to copy. A woman, Liz Townsend, had a byline at the *Advertiser*. CJ couldn't see that happening at the *Newark Star-Ledger* for years.

There were other differences between the Honolulu reporters and the *Ledger's*: They had names like Bingham and Dillingham, even a Twigg-Smith. There were no Bernsteins or Friedmans or Turtlebaums masquerading as a Turtle, let alone any Marconis, Marinos, or Morellis.

It wasn't so much the names of the reporters that jarred her as much as the choice of stories the papers put on the front page. The *Advertiser's* headline was "Willamette and University of Hawaii Football Teams to Square Off," and the *Star-Bulletin's* was "Football Titans Clash." She was used to headlines about crime, political corruption, the war in Europe, and the threat of Hitler.

The rest of the *Advertiser's* front page had articles about local elections and a proposed ferry service between islands. The only mention of the war in Europe or tension with Japan was a two-inch article tucked away in the entertainment section between an ad for *A Yank in the RAF* playing at the Varsity Movie Theater and the KGMB radio program guide.

The article read, "An unnamed source, assumed to be the FBI, recorded a conversation between a Tokyo official and the Japanese Consulate in Honolulu. The Japanese official ordered the local consulate to burn all secret documents."

She didn't understand why that wasn't splashed across the first page. Was it routine to burn secret documents in Hawaii?

She'd figure it out eventually, but her more pressing issue was deciding what to wear to the interview. She hadn't brought many clothes with her; the only business suit she'd packed was her navy-blue gabardine. She held it in the mirror. She'd pair it with her white silk blouse and her navy pillbox hat. It was a good look—professional yet feminine.

CJ assessed herself in the mirror. She tied and re-tied her blouse bow, and smoothed her jacket. Perfect.

Perfect, until she put on her shoes. They were the same Spectators she wore the day before—a steal at 60% off at Macy's, but they were a size too small and after dancing in them all night long, her ankles were so blistered she had to patch them with Band-Aids.

She gave herself one more look in the mirror, slung her purse over her shoulder, tucked her portfolio under her arm and announced, "Knock 'em dead."

CJ strode through the hotel lobby and asked the front desk clerk to call her a cab.

"*Honolulu Advertiser,*" she told the cabbie.

"You work there?" he asked.

"I hope so."

During the ride over, she tried reading the names of the Honolulu streets—Kalakaua Avenue, Piikoi Street, and Kapiolani Boulevard—but quickly gave up.

"Here you are." The cabbie pulled to the curb.

The Honolulu Advertiser Building, Honolulu

The *Advertiser* building was a green stucco Art Deco structure with twenty-foot brass doors and equally tall Palladian windows. She opened the door, matching her thumb to the smooth patch of brass worn down by countless hands before hers.

The lobby had a tile marble floor. A massive Information Desk took center stage. During the week it was probably manned, but it was empty that morning, and no one else was around.

CJ checked her watch; it was ten minutes to ten. She paced

the lobby, her heels clicking on the marble and her blistered ankles throbbing.

Five minutes of, and Eve still wasn't there. She wondered if Eve remembered their appointment or, worse, if she hadn't set up a meeting with her father.

She scanned the building directory. "Suite 620, Gordon Russell."

At three minutes of, CJ took the elevator to the sixth floor.

When she knocked on the door of the suite, no one answered. She tried again.

Of course, the secretary wouldn't work on Saturday—she gingerly opened the door. "Excuse me. I'm here to see Mr. Russell."

A muffled voice from an interior office answered, "Come."

Mr. Russell's office was flooded with light. Behind his desk were ten-foot windows with a view of Honolulu harbor. The office smelled of cigars and coffee. She glanced around as Mr. Russell buried himself in a report.

The photos on the wall were typical shots of old men posing with other old men, whom she assumed were local politicians and businessmen. She didn't spot any awards on the wall or the bookshelves. The *Newark Star-Ledger* had three Pulitzers.

Finally, Mr. Russell glanced up and motioned CJ to sit, then his head went down again, and she noticed he was slightly balding. He kept reading, ignoring her.

He was the perfect image of a newspaper owner—pinstripe suit, wire-rimmed eyeglasses, and properly knotted Windsor tie.

CJ shuffled the papers in her portfolio, putting the letter of recommendation from the Dean of Columbia's School of Journalism on top, then the letter from her editor at the *Star-Ledger*, and finally, the tear sheets from the three articles she'd written.

"Eve tells me you're a reporter." Mr. Russell abruptly closed his folder and looked up.

CJ startled. "Yes, sir. At the *Newark Star-Ledger*." She didn't mention she covered stranded cats and fussy dog shows.

"I'm familiar with the paper." Mr. Russell's tie was blue with a silver crest, and his cuff links were monogrammed.

He took off his glasses and looked her up and down as if she were a horse being bought for breeding. "What did you cover there?"

"General assignments." It was only a slight lie.

She handed him her portfolio, which he accepted with a polite smile. It took him less than a minute to scan it, then he handed it back. "I'm looking for a girl who can write obituaries."

"Obits?"

"With a 'slice of life' angle. You know the kind of thing—the professional accomplishments, businesses, fraternal organizations of the men, and for the women, what volunteer work they did and how many children they had."

"I can do that." Any high school kid with half a brain could.

"And if you work out, Miss Fixit can always use help."

Great. She could help write tips on how to unplug a toilet without getting a run in your stockings.

"Then are we agreed?"

"Yes, sir."

"Fine, then. Monday at 8 a.m. See Maude. She'll take care of you." Mr. Russell returned to reading his papers.

CJ sat, unsure the interview was over.

Mr. Russell looked up. "Do you have questions?"

"No, sir."

"Then, Monday morning. Eight a.m." She was dismissed.

On the ride down the elevator, CJ replayed her job responsibilities: Writing obituaries. It wasn't a job she'd submit to Columbia's alumni newsletter, but it was a foot in the door.

When the elevator doors opened at the lobby, Eve pounced on her. "How did it go?"

"Good." Good as it could be, she thought. "I start on Monday."

Eve hugged her as if they were long-lost friends. "You must be good! My father doesn't impress easily."

Good enough to fill a hole on the staff, CJ thought.

Gump's, Honolulu

Eve locked arms with CJ. "I know the perfect place to celebrate! The Willows! But first, I need to stop by Gump's. I have Christmas shopping to finish up." Eve led CJ out of the building. "Do they have a Gump's in New Jersey?"

CJ didn't know what Gump's was. "I don't think so."

"Have you ever been to the one in San Francisco?"

"The only time I was in San Francisco was the bus ride from the train station to the dock."

Eve walked CJ toward a hunter-green Packard. "The Gump's in San Francisco has a glassed-in restaurant on the roof, and their cheesecake is the best in the world."

No, Junior's in Brooklyn has the world's finest cheesecake, but CJ doubted Eve was a Brooklyn kind of girl.

Eve went on, "The Halekulani serves a divine chocolate torte, and the Alexander Young has the best macadamia cream pie."

"Thanks." CJ listened as Eve schooled her on what the "best" places in Honolulu.

Eve unlocked the door. "Get in."

CJ slid in on the leather bench. It was her first time in a car with a radio or a highly polished walnut dashboard.

Eve started the car. "And, before they take the Christmas decorations down, you've got to go to Hau Tree Lanai for Sunday brunch."

As they drove through Waikiki, Eve went on telling CJ what she considered to be the best sunset bar, the best Martinis, the best clientele. They drove through neighborhoods with names like Kakaako, McCully, Puiwa. They all looked alike—a few blocks of small shops, tenement homes, scrub grass playgrounds, and a gas station or two. But when they drove through Moiliili, CJ sat up.

It was a maze of alleys lined with flat-roofed buildings. Shop signs were written in Japanese characters. As far as she could tell there was a hardware store, a fish market and a grocery store with stacks of baskets in front of it, brimming with unfamiliar produce.

Shopkeepers swept sidewalks, and men sitting on produce crates played cards. It could have been Little Italy, except for the sake brewery and the pagoda-looking Baptist church.

The loudest sounds in Moiliili were the claps of wooden geta on the sidewalks. There were no Italian nonnas in black dresses haggling for a better price or elbowing each other to get to the head of the line. Instead, there were curved-over old women dressed in dark kimonos, and younger women toting their infants in cotton slings.

In New York, there was Little Italy and Chinatown, and the Hassidic Jews had their own neighborhood, but there was no Japan Town. CJ had never seen so many Japanese, and the sight of them unsettled her. Maybe Joe was right? There had to be loyalists to the Emperor among them.

Her question was soon answered and she flinched when she spotted a photo of Emperor Hirohito taped to a barbershop window. The photo was small, curled at the edges, and covered with years of dust, but there was no doubt it was the Emperor.

She heard Joe's warning. "With 160,000 on this island, it doesn't take a genius to figure out a few of them are rooting for the old country."

Eve pointed to a fabric store. "Mrs. Kimura is the best seamstress on the island. She did my gown for my Coming Out party."

CJ was more concerned about the photo of the Emperor.

Eve turned the corner on to King Street, and the world shifted from pagoda-looking churches to a row of elegant shops.

"Here we are. Gump's." Eve pulled to the curb.

Gump's looked like a movie set of a Spanish villa with its stucco walls, leaded glass windows, and a blue tile roof.

What was it with Honolulu's obsession with foreign architecture?

"Good to see you again, Miss Russell." A valet helped Eve out of the car, then an older woman in a black suit greeted her again.

"Alfred is expecting you," the woman said and she escorted Eve and CJ through the Gump rooms as if she were a museum docent.

There was the Dutch room, heavy with blue and white

porcelain, the Italian Room with cameos and leather handbags, and the Jade room where Alfred was waiting with his hands clasped at his waist and a staged smile pasted on his face. When he welcomed Eve with a slight bow, CJ remembered when she first learned the definition of the word "obsequious."

The Jade Room, appropriately painted in a subtle but shimmering green, was furnished with one long rosewood table surrounded by four chairs. Along the walls were lighted glass curios displayed jade sculptures.

"It's so good to see you, Miss Russell." Alfred pulled out a chair for Eve and then did the same for CJ. "What can I show you today?"

"Some jewelry for my mother," Eve said. "A Christmas present."

Alfred smirked. "Something youthful?"

"I think she'd like a lovely pair of jade earrings, don't you?" Eve set her purse on the table.

Alfred raised his finger behind a door concealed as a panel. "I have just the pair."

Eve told CJ that Alfred had been selling jewelry to her mother for years. "The more he kowtows to her, the more expensive the piece she buys." Eve removed her gloves, slid the table mirror toward herself, and removed her earrings. "I could use some ear glitz."

"Trying on earrings for your mother?"

"My mother's Christmas presents are on loan to her," Eve said. "Whatever I give her, she'll accept, smile and never wear again. By Easter, she'll toss them back at me, remarking on my 'garish' taste."

Alfred returned carrying a tray covered with a black silk cloth. He set the tray on the table and whipped off the fabric.

"These are the 'Stallion of Jade.'" He waved his hand over a pair of dangling earrings.

Eve crinkled her nose.

"Perhaps the accompanying necklace?" He held it up

The jade beads on the necklace were as big as bubble gum balls.

Eve dismissed them with a wave of her hand.

Alfred tried several more pieces before he unveiled a pair of black jade earrings set in platinum and a melee of diamonds. "Burma has the most exquisite black jade in the world." Alfred handed the earrings to Eve.

Eve hooked her hair behind her ear and put the jade earring to her ear.

"What do you think?"

"They're gorgeous." CJ didn't know jade came in black. The only jade she had ever seen were the ten-cent bracelets in Chinatown.

Eve tilted her head, allowing the light to catch the diamonds in the mirror. She adjusted the mirror a bit closer. "I'll take them."

She never asked how much they were.

CJ's Uncle Dario always said, "If you have to ask how much it costs, you can't afford it." But he'd been talking about a standing rib roast.

Eve turned to CJ. "Now, let's go before I buy something else. But first, the ladies' room."

The ladies' room was furnished with ivory silk chaises and rosewood chairs in front of a mirrored makeup table.

Eve sat at the table and emptied an arsenal of cosmetics from her purse. CJ had one lipstick in her bag—a neon yellow plastic tube with a red Woolworth's logo that she kept hidden.

Eve casually asked, "How long have you known Linc?"

"You mean Joe," CJ corrected.

"No, I mean Linc. You two seem quite close."

CJ recognized an interrogation when she heard it. "We are."

Eve blotted her lipstick. "What does he do?"

"He's a PBY pilot."

"I know that, but what does his family do?"

CJ knew the real question: Was Linc a corn-fed millionaire or an escapee from the farm.

"I don't know," CJ answered. "All the time together at the academy, it never came up."

"Can you tell me anything about him besides the fact he's got the cleft chin of a Hollywood star?"

"He's a nice guy."

"That's it?"

CJ nodded.

"You protect him like an older sister." Eve snapped the clasp of her bag.

"Maybe." CJ smiled. "But, I'm not older."

Eve smiled an equally disingenuous smile to CJ. "We should get going. Alfred's probably waiting at the door with my mother's earrings."

There it was, CJ thought, not "the best" conversation she could have had with Eve.

The Royal Hawaiian Hotel, Waikiki

When CJ returned to the hotel that afternoon, she settled on the lanai, sipping a Mai Tai and worrying that after her snit with Eve, that Eve would dissuade her father from hiring her.

If things at the *Advertiser* didn't work out, maybe she could pitch an article about life in Hawaii to the *Newark Star-Ledger*? It would be more than a travel piece on hula girls and dazzling sunsets. It could be an insider's look at the island—she could snap photos of Art Deco architecture, a faux-Moroccan castle, a sake brewery. After all, how many people in New Jersey had ever seen a sake brewery? Or women in kimonos and geta? But, when she thought about Moiliili, the photo of the Emperor in the Japanese barbershop chilled her.

At six-thirty that evening, Joe burst into the room with a bouquet of flowers peeking out from behind him. "Did you get the job?"

"Of course." She cocked her head and flung her hair. "Who wouldn't hire me?"

"Of course you did!" He presented the bouquet of jasmine, gardenias, and a white-starburst blossom that smelled like a clementine.

Joe leaned over and kissed her. "I'm so proud of you, babe."

Don't be proud of me, not for this. I'm just the obit girl. She promised herself she wasn't going to complain. All he needed to know was that his friend's father gave her a job. But somehow, "It's not a top-notch job," slipped out of her mouth.

"Any job you have is top-notch." He sat next to her and pulled her close. "Let me show you how proud of you I am." He slid his hand down her spine.

She gave him a nudge. "We have beachside dinner reservations."

"We can get room service later," he countered.

"I really want to see the sunset on the ocean." CJ stood and Joe grudgingly went along with the plan.

During dinner, CJ recapped her day starting with the interview with Mr. Russell, then Gump's and Eve's questions about Linc.

But, her tone changed when she talked about Moiliili. "It was so quiet," she said, "There was no yelling, no haggling."

"No Aunt Concettas accusing the butcher of thievery?" Joe joked.

"It was more than that. There was a photo of the Emperor in a barbershop window, and it scared me." She looked at Joe. "I couldn't help thinking about what you said last night about a Fifth Column."

"Trust me, CJ. We've got it under control. The first move they make, we'll pick them up."

Trusting him wasn't the point.

"Babe, you know if I thought there was the chance of any trouble, I never would have asked you to come out here."

Chapter Four
December 7, 1941

The Russell Estate, Nuuanu

DECEMBER 7, 1941, was a glorious morning of clear skies and gentle trade winds. The Koolau Mountains were shrouded with a cotton candy mist.

Eve and her father were sitting on the backyard lanai of the Russell estate. Their Sunday morning ritual was to have a leisurely breakfast together where she listened to him huff and grunt and curse every D.C. politician as he read the paper. When Eve was a student at Mills College, the memories of those mornings made her homesick.

Eve would have been a senior at Mills if her life had gone as planned. But that September, with a war threatening, her parents forbade her to return to California, afraid she would be stranded on the mainland for the duration of the conflict.

Eve poured herself a second cup of coffee, glimpsing the paper's headlines: "FDR Will Send Message to Emperor on War Crisis."

She lifted the coffee pot. "Could I top that off for you, Pops?"

He put down the paper and slid his cup to her. "Damn Roosevelt, he can't wait to get us into war."

"Two sugars?" she asked.

"Four."

She put in two.

He pointed to the sugar bowl. "I can count to four, Eve."

"Just watching out for you, Pops." She added another spoonful and slid the cup back to him.

"The man is sitting in the White House petting his dog while the world goes to hell. His dog has more sense than he does."

"That could be said about quite a few people." Eve tried to lighten the mood.

"Eve!" Eve clenched her jaw at the sound of her mother's voice.

Mrs. Russell was in the lower garden, tending her prize-winning roses, hacking off the less than perfect ones for bouquets to bring to the hospitals.

Eve didn't answer.

Her father eyed her. "Your mother's calling you."

Eve turned toward the house. "Ginger, Mother's calling you."

"You cause your own problems," her father said.

Eve shrugged. She knew her mother would soon emerge from

the garden in all her glory. The *Queen of the Red Cross.* First she'd see her mother's straw hat, then her French linen garden apron, and finally her basket of imperfect roses.

"You and your mother are two sides of the same coin."

The most certain thing in Eve's mind was that she was *not* like her mother.

"Eve!" Her mother paused at the top of the stairs. "Didn't you hear me?"

"Sorry, Mother." Eve assumed a suitably startled expression. "Did you want something?"

Mrs. Russell was out of breath. "I needed my *How to Grow Roses* book." She set her basket of Queen Victoria roses on the table.

"Where is it?" Eve pushed back her chair. "I'll get it."

"Never mind, it's too late." Her mother untied the ribbon of her hat. "I've already climbed the stairs." She tossed her hat on the chair next to Eve.

Eve stood. "I'll get the damn book."

"Eve, do not speak to your mother like that!"

"I apologize, Mother."

"You're quite adept at apologizing, Eve. It's responsibility that you have trouble with." Her mother pointed to the coffee pot and Eve kept her mouth shut, grit her teeth, and passed it.

Mrs. Russell angled the pot to the sun. "Remind me to ask Michiko to polish the silver for the Christmas party."

Eve nodded.

Mrs. Russell cocked her head and looked toward the pass between the mountains. "Did you hear that? Are they starting maneuvers at this hour?"

Eve definitely heard the planes, but she wouldn't give her mother the satisfaction of agreeing. "I didn't hear anything."

Mrs. Russell examined the creamer. "If Michiko starts tomorrow, she can have all the silver polished and we can get the crystal and china done next week."

"I'll let her know, Mother."

"Graham, did I tell you the Kahns are coming to the Christmas party?" Mrs. Russell asked.

"That's nice, Loretta." Eve's father was barricaded behind the newspaper.

"I think it's a bit overstepping."

"Didn't you invite them?" Eve reminded her mother.

"Of course I did, but I thought they'd know better than to accept."

"Because they're Jewish?" Eve challenged.

"You know that's not why!"

Eve knew the Kahns weren't shunned for being Jewish; theirs was a graver sin—they were outsiders, New Yorkers no less.

According to local society, Mr. Kahn owned a construction company that had "descended on Oahu like a vulture."

More planes swept through the valley, swooping and diving toward Pearl Harbor.

Mr. Russell checked his wristwatch. "Eight o'clock on a Sunday morning. This is outrageous."

"Parker told us a big maneuver was scheduled for the weekend," Eve said.

Her mother's expression brightened. "When did you see Parker?"

"I had dinner with him at Wo Fat's."

"Parker Holt is a fine man," her mother declared.

Yes, a fine man in search of a fine man for himself.

"His mother called me yesterday to RSVP for the party." Mrs. Russell was almost shouting over the thundering rumble.

The planes kept coming.

"She's bringing her niece with her." Her mother's words were drowned out by the planes.

"Eve, are you listening to me?"

The planes were so loud, Eve had to admit she couldn't hear her mother.

"I've arranged the catering with the Moana Hotel." Her mother raised her voice.

"Sorry, Mother. I can't hear you." Eve cupped her hand to her ear.

Mrs. Russell tossed her napkin on the table. "I can't even hear myself think!"

Mr. Russell slammed down the newspaper. "This is outrageous."

Eve kept her eyes on the sky. The planes kept coming. It was the biggest exercise she had ever seen.

Her father groused, "This is an abuse of the citizenry!"

"It'll be over in a few minutes, Pops." The last thing he needed was to get upset.

"I'm calling General Short." He pushed his chair away from the table and stomped toward the house. "Let's see how he likes his Sunday disrupted."

Eve looked at her mother. "Aren't you going to follow him?"

"He just needs to blow off steam."

The year before, on Thanksgiving, her father had his second heart attack. The doctor warned that the third might be "an invitation to the heavenly gates."

"Once he vents to General Short, he'll be fine," Mrs. Russell said.

Eve pushed her chair back. "I'm going in."

"He'll be fine." Mrs. Russell put her hand over Eve's with the subtlest of commands, and Eve complied with the order to sit.

Her mother continued, "This year, I'd like low floral arrangements for the tables. They're in all the magazines."

The planes kept coming. Eve could hardly hear her.

"Eve, are you listening to me?" Her mother asked. "I've arranged for the Alexander Hotel to do the catering—"

Eve's sister Ginger threw open the doors so hard they slammed against the side of the house. "It's the Japs! We're under attack!"

Eve blocked the sun with her hand and looked up. All of the planes were emblazoned with the Rising Red Sun.

"Get in the house!" Mrs. Russell grabbed her hat. "Hurry!"

Eve's legs wouldn't move.

Her mother screamed as she was running, "Eve!"

Eve was mesmerized. They kept coming. No one could withstand them.

"Eve!" Ginger's voice jolted Eve to move and she ran into the house, trembling, hugging Ginger for dear life.

Her father was on the phone and her mother was screaming, "Graham, we're under attack."

He cupped his hand over the phone. "Goddamn it, Loretta, I know that."

Mr. Russell pointed to the radio. "Someone find out what's going on," then he yelled into the phone, "What the hell am I paying you for, Hank?" Then, back to Eve. "Find out what's going on!"

KGMU was airing a Japanese language melodrama.

"Find KGMB!"

Mrs. Russell put her hand on her husband's shoulder. "Graham, calm down."

"It's the biggest story in history, and we can't get a paper out!"

KGMB was broadcasting the Sunday service of the First Baptist Church.

He paced as far as the telephone cord allowed. "Loretta, lay out my gray suit."

"I'll do it," Eve told her mother. "Pops needs you."

Mr. Russell raked his hand through what hair he had. "How many times did you reset the presses?" Then he waved his hand at his wife. "Lay out my clothes!"

"I got it" Eve ran up the stairs, listening to her father shout into the phone. "Did you call the *Nippu Jiji*? Ask Hiroshi if he'll let us print on their presses."

She could still hear him from her parents' bedroom. "Jesus, Hank, do I have to tell you everything?"

She laid out his gray suit, Yale tie, and monogrammed cufflinks, the whole time thinking that war was not possible.

She took a starched white shirt from the closet. For all the months her mother went to the Red Cross coordinating preparedness efforts, Eve mocked her and her mother's cronies for "playing at war" to keep themselves from being bored with Bridge and Mahjong—all their uniforms, their drawn-out meetings, their mock wounded—but they were right.

Mrs. Russell burst into the room. "Go downstairs," she told Eve. "Keep an eye on your father." Her mother bent over pulling out a pair of Mr. Russell's shoes. "Get socks." She pointed to the dresser.

"I've got to go to Headquarters."

Mrs. Russell pulled her Red Cross uniform out of her closet. "It's dangerous for your father to be alone."

So, now she was worried? Did it take a war for her to be concerned about him?

"At the first sign of chest pain, get him to a hospital, no matter how much he argues!" Then her mother took Eve's hands in hers. "Eve, you be careful."

When Eve told her father his clothes were ready, he shoved the phone at her. "Stay on with Hank. If anything happens, tell me. Immediately."

Eve took the phone. "Don't worry, Pops. Hank will take care of it."

"Hank couldn't find his own ass without a map."

Eve was sure Hank heard him.

Once her father was out of earshot, she asked Hank how things were.

"Bad," he said. "There's no way we're getting a paper out."

"Have you asked the *Star-Bulletin* if we could use their presses?"

"They'd be dancing on our graves if…" Hank's voice was lost in the yelling in the background.

"Hank? Hank?"

"Hold on, Eve. The pressmen are telling me they can jerry-rig something."

Eve pressed her ear to the receiver, trying to catch the conversation. She thought she heard the words "asbestos won't work" and "not the right paper size."

She was still listening when her mother and Ginger came down the stairs.

"Any news?" Her mother asked.

Eve shook her head. "Hank's talking to the pressmen, but it doesn't sound hopeful."

Mrs. Russell pinned her Red Cross nametag on her lapel. "Remember what I told you. No matter what, take care of your father."

"I love you, Sis." Ginger hugged Eve.

Eve stared at her baby sister in her Motor Corps uniform. Ginger was going off to war.

Mr. Russell hurried down the stairs, his shirt unbuttoned, his jacket and tie slung over his arm. He snatched the phone from Eve and cradled it on his shoulder as he buttoned his shirt. "I don't care how you do it, Hank. I'm on my way." He slammed the phone down, then eyed Eve. "Aren't you supposed to be somewhere?"

"The Hongwanji Mission. I need you to give me a ride."

"I can't. I've got to get to the paper."

"You can drop me off on the way."

"It's not on the way!"

"Pops, you have to."

"Then hurry up."

Downtown Honolulu

When Eve got in the car, Mr. Russell was fiddling with the radio dial. "I still can't get a damn thing."

"Let me try." Eve turned the dial to KGMU, but it was off the air, and so was KGXD.

"Jesus, did they hit the radio stations?"

Eve heard Web Ebley's voice; it was nothing more than static but as they drove down the Pali Road, KGMB came in clear.

Webley was screaming: "This is the real McCoy! Stay off the streets! Stay off the telephone! This is the real McCoy. Oahu is under attack!"

Then, at Jack Lane, traffic came to a standstill.

Mr. Russell slammed his fist on the steering wheel. "How the hell am I going to get to the paper?"

Ebley repeated, "This is the real McCoy! Stay off the streets!"

"I've got news for you, Web, the whole damn city is on the street."

Drivers were standing on their running boards, swiveling their heads, asking each other what was tying up the traffic.

"This is ridiculous." Mr. Russell got out of the car. "I'm getting to the bottom of this."

"Pops." Eve followed him as he headed straight for a Civilian Defense warden; it was their neighbor Jed Brewton.

"What the devil's going on, Jed?" Mr. Russell asked.

"They bombed downtown—Schuman Carriage, the palace, the phone company. All of Bishop Street is blocked off."

"What's King Street like?" Mr. Russell asked.

Jed told him the King and McCully neighborhood got hit. "The whole block's up in flames."

"What about Punchbowl?" Eve asked.

"Yeah." He nodded. "I can clear the street to get you to Wylie. After that, it's a crapshoot."

"I'll take it!"

Jed directed cars to move to the shoulder to make way for Mr. Russell. It was a good move. Wylie was clear until they got to Chinatown, where two firetrucks, police cars, and ambulances blocked Nuuanu.

"Not again!" Mr. Russell laid on the horn.

"Pops, calm down."

"Will you stop telling me to calm down!" He charged out of the car, barreling through the crowd, with Eve following in his wake. At the corner, knots of gawkers crammed against each other. A teenage boy sat on his friend's shoulders and yelled out, "Tamanaha's alive!"

Mr. Russell was questioning a police sergeant when Eve caught up to him. The cop flipped the page of his notebook. "We've got nine dead so far. Four boxers from Our Lady of Peace's team." The cop shook his head. "Half tonight's card was in there killing time 'til the fights."

"You got any names?" Mr. Russell dug his notebook out of his jacket pocket, ready to take down the information.

"I heard Freddy Higa's dead, but that's not confirmed. The only confirmation I've got is the shop owner."

"The name of the shop?" Mr. Russell scribbled as the cop talked.

"Cherry Blossom Saimin Stand."

Eve lost her breath.

Her mother sent her to the Cherry Blossom Saimin Stand for "the best yellow ginger lei in Chinatown." Mrs. Hirasaki would always have the order waiting, and when Eve paid her, Mrs. Hirasaki would give Eve a ginger candy as a good-luck charm.

"Anyone else?" Eve steeled herself against hearing his answer.

"The owner's wife's alive, I'm not sure for how long," he said. "Blood was shooting out of her like a geyser, but the little girl didn't make it."

Shirley!

Whenever Eve went to the shop, she and Shirley played a game. Eve would squat down and ask her what her name was, and Shirley would laugh and run behind the backroom curtain. Then, one day, instead of running away, the girl stood tall and said, "My name is Shirley."

Eve asked her, "Like Shirley Temple?"

She put her hands on her hips. "No. Shirley Hirasaki."

A second cop stepped into their huddle. "So far, we've got Hisao Uyeno, Paul Ianamine, Freddy Higa, Seiko Izumi—all dead. Masa Nagamine, Bunny Tokusato, and Toy Tamanaha are still alive—more or less."

Sometimes, the boys would be in the shop when Eve was there. They'd lean over pinball machines, cigarettes clenched in their teeth, swearing and banging the sides of the machines.

They couldn't be more than eighteen.

Eve chilled when she saw the shop. The front was smoldering. The folding chairs where old women strung flowers were strewn on the sidewalk. The bodies of boys were lined up—their arms splayed as if they had been dragged from the flames.

"Clear the way." Other boxers in Our Lady of Peace shirts

linked arms, holding back the crowd, clearing a path for their coach.

"Make way."

Bill Kim was a burly man with meat-hook hands and a lumbering gait, but when he saw the bodies of the boys, he dropped to his knees, cradled his head, and rocked. "Mother of God." He pounded his head on the ground. "Mother of God."

He rocked and prayed until his prayer became a wail.

Eve wanted to shield him from the crowd, to keep his grief from being seen, but she, too, watched him because he was doing what she could not.

CHAPTER FIVE
DECEMBER 7, 1941

Makalapa Housing

THAT SAME MORNING at Makalapa Military Housing, Ruth Elliot slid a tray of biscuits into the oven. She set the timer for eighteen minutes, so they'd be warm when Gordon got home from duty.

Then she poured herself a cup of coffee, grabbed the newspaper, and settled into an Adirondack chair in the backyard.

"Morning, Ruth." Their neighbor, Mac Reynolds, was sitting in his car in the driveway with the engine running.

His daughter Christina waved from the back seat. "Morning, Mrs. Elliot."

"Morning."

Sara pushed her sister away from the window. "'Morning, Mrs. Elliot."

Sisters. Ruth smiled.

Mac pointed to the empty carport. "Does Gordon have the duty?"

"He should be home any minute," she said.

"Morning, Ruth." Catherine Reynolds hurried out of her house, pinning her hat on her head, her purse swinging from her arm.

Ruth couldn't remember once when Catherine was on time.

"I'll say a prayer for you." Catherine waved.

Ruth had little faith in prayer but said, "Thanks," and returned to the newspaper. The headlines warned: "F.D.R. Sends Message to Emperor on War Crisis."

Ruth was fourth-generation Navy. She could read between the lines: war was inevitable. It was only a matter of time before Japan attacked Singapore. After that, Hong Kong and Burma would fall like dominoes, but the Brits, not the Americans, would defend them. She felt comfortable that the U.S. wouldn't get involved. It would never happen; Roosevelt was campaigning for a third term and knew any talk of involving the country in a war would guarantee his defeat.

But that morning, Ruth had more pressing matters—she hadn't started her Christmas shopping, and her gifts had to be mailed by the 12th if she expected them to make it to Virginia on time.

Hartfield's was selling cellophane Christmas wreaths for

twenty-five cents. Bon Ton's advertised a sale on quilted bath-robes for $3.99. She thought that would be perfect for her sister. In Susan's last letter, she complained about her Pablum-stained robe.

Ruth heard the rumble of planes. She checked her watch. Five to eight. Maneuvers were being scheduled earlier and earlier. She remembered when her family lived in Newport—or was it San Diego?—when maneuvers went haywire, and some flyboy dropped a bomb in the middle of the officers' golf course. Heads rolled.

The planes were coming in from the east—probably from Kaneohe Marine Base. Bombs exploded, antiaircraft fire sput-tered, and smoke billowed over the cliff facing Pearl Harbor.

She went back to the newspaper. Maybe she should get her sister something extravagant? Expensive perfume? A silk blouse? A robe was so practical, and with three kids under five years old, Susan deserved something totally excessive.

The planes kept coming. There were more of them than usual, flying lower and in tighter formations. Something wasn't right. They didn't sound right. They were too loud.

A few dogs barked. Some garbage cans rolled, and the umbrella on the Momsen's lanai got airborne.

The planes kept coming.

What a dog and pony show! Ruth assumed some heavy-duty brass from D.C. must be visiting Hawaii.

Then screen doors flung open. Men ran out of their homes.

"It's the Japs!"

More planes. Their guns clattered, digging up pieces of lawns.

"We're under attack!"

Men and women ran to the cliff overlooking the harbor.

An air attack wasn't possible. Everybody knew that.

She tossed the newspaper, ran into the house, and called Gordon's office. There was no answer.

Where are you, Gordon?

She hung up and dialed again—still no answer.

She checked her watch; Gordon should have been halfway home. But she knew he'd race back to the base once he figured out what was happening.

She called again, but there was no answer.

She ran to the cliff overlooking Pearl Harbor and squeezed in between her neighbors. Every gun at Pearl Harbor raged into action. Tracers streaked the sky through smoke billowing over ships. The noise was skull-splitting and the planes kept coming, dropping their bombs.

Evelyn Momsen touched Ruth's arm. Ruth barely could hear what she asked.

"Where's Gordon?"

"I don't know."

Evelyn handed Ruth her binoculars.

Ruth stood on her toes and leaned over the fence. She focused where the Communication Center was, but all she saw were plumes of orange flames, glowing white flashes, and more black smoke.

Gordon had to be safe. She knew it. The Japanese wouldn't waste explosives on random buildings. They wanted battleships.

From the cliff, she could see the *Arizona* and heard the orders blaring from the ship, "General quarters!"

Ruth watched the ship's hull rise like a breaching whale with the sailors on her deck tumbled into the flaming water. "Abandon ship!" With one final rise, the *Arizona* was underwater.

Then the *Shaw* exploded into purple and blue flames. The smoke teared her eyes, and the wind carried the smell of burning—like a cast-iron skillet left on the stove too long.

The biscuits! Ruth shoved the binoculars at Evelyn and ran home around Jeeps circling the streets, their drivers shouting into bullhorns. "All dependents evacuate immediately. Ready your evacuation."

Ruth raced into the house, grabbed her mitts and pulled the baking sheet from the oven. She tossed the tray in the sink, opened the back door, and instinctively flapped a kitchen towel, waving the smoke from the biscuits into the smoke of the attack.

She called Gordon's office again.

MPs blasted orders as they drove through the streets. "Evacuate now. No pets allowed. Repeat. No pets allowed."

Ruth dragged her evacuation suitcase from under her bed. She checked for her passport, health records, and Gordon's will, then grabbed a sanitary belt and some Kotex from the linen closet. She tried to remember if Kotex were included in the evacuation inventory lists. She could only hope they were, but she shoved more pads into her shoulder bag just in case.

She was out the door into a funnel of families rushing to the evacuation buses. An MP waved her to a bus parked under the banyan tree.

Her neighbor, Betty, held her baby in one arm and her three-year-old son with the other hand. Evacuation bags dangled from her arms, and a diaper bag was slung over her shoulder.

Tommy jerked away from his mom, screaming, "I want Rusty."

"Can I help?" Ruth asked her.

"Can you carry him?" Betty asked.

Tommy squatted on the ground, refusing to budge, but Ruth wrestled him in her arms and carried him, kicking and flailing.

"I want Rusty," he cried.

"I told you we can't take him!" Betty yelled.

"Dogs are smart." Ruth tried to soothe Tommy. "He'll be safe, and when we get to our new place, I'll call the MPs, and make sure someone's taking care of him." It was her first lie of the war.

Whether he believed her or just needed to, he reluctantly climbed the steps, taking one step at a time, two feet on each stair.

"Hurry it up." An MP waved his arms.

Ruth guided Tommy into a seat across from Betty. Tommy sat with his fists clenched; two rows up, a toddler clenched her baby doll.

Women herded crying children on the bus. They filled the seats and stood in the aisle until not one more person could fit. Then, a Marine banged the side of the bus, yelling, "Go! Go! Go!"

"I want Rusty," Tommy whimpered.

Ruth couldn't remember who was supposed to contact the Humane Society about establishing a procedure to evacuate pets or if it had ever been done.

"Rusty's okay," Ruth said. "I promise."

She watched Tommy unclench his fists and realized her own hands were shaking.

Ruth turned her back to the window, shielding Tommy from seeing the harbor where men were throwing hooks into flaming water and hauling up sailors whose bodies were slick with oil.

Their bus inched forward in a long queue for the ferry. Ruth had made this crossing countless times—for the commissary, the clinic. It was a ten-minute trip into Honolulu—but this was different.

When it was their turn, the bus lurched onto the ferry, and the ten-minute crossing felt like hours.

Ruth huddled over Tommy to muffle the wail of sirens.

At the Pearl City dock, ambulances idled, and fire trucks were lined up to board the ferry on their return to Ford Island. The whole pier was a bottleneck.

"It'll be okay," Ruth whispered to Tommy.

One more lie.

Shore Patrol directed traffic. Frantic. Yelling. "Go. Go!"

Their bus sped off the ramp and bounced on the road. But where to?

The plan was for Ford Island evacuees to go to the Honpa Hongwanji Buddhist Mission, but plans seemed to have gone to hell.

They sped on, out of the traffic, and onto the boulevard. Her loss of faith suspended, Ruth prayed to God to keep them safe.

A plane flew over. The driver yelled, "Incoming!" Prepare for impact!"

Ruth cradled Tommy in her arms.

"Put your head between your knees," the driver shouted.

Ruth silently finished the line she had heard for years—and kiss your ass goodbye.

She held Tommy tighter.

It was a quick pass of a few planes. Anti-aircraft fire.

Ruth threw her body over Tommy. She kissed his head and rocked him in her arms. "We're safe. I promise." She gave up counting her lies.

When it was over and they got back on the road, Tommy wriggled free from Ruth, squeezed between the women standing in the aisle, and climbed into his mother's lap.

Ruth turned her thoughts to the center, hoping it was open. She assumed that Mrs. Kanazawa would have attended Sunday services. Shimeji Kanazawa was a good woman but not adept at supervision. Ruth hoped that Eve was already there.

But what if civilian neighborhoods were hit? The hospitals? Her head spun. Was the Motor Corps ready? The Red Cross nurses? During all the Red Cross meetings, Ruth never truly believed an attack would occur. Details weren't critical. The plans were a routine military precaution.

Honpa Hongwanji Buddhist Mission, Honolulu

When the bus pulled into the Honpa Hongwanji Buddhist Mission, straight lines of Japanese girls, all dressed in white, stood in the parking lot. Shimeji Kanazawa was dressed in a formal coral brocade kimono, her hands were folded at her waist in front of her obi. On any ordinary Sunday, she would have been welcoming congregation members to the temple's services.

As the women exited the bus, the Japanese girls surrounded them, assisting them with their luggage. When Shimeji saw Ruth, she told her that the evacuation plan had changed. The University of Hawaii was a suspected target, and all families expecting to be housed there would be staying at the Hongwanji Mission.

"There are reports of paratroopers landing there," Shimeji said.

This wasn't a scenario. The plan failed. The enemy was supposed to attack by sea. There was no checklist for this. They'd expected to have hours to implement their plan.

Ruth glanced at the far end of the courtyard where Japanese teenage girls were jumping rope with American children. "How many evacuees do we have?" she asked Shimeji.

"140. Maybe 170 with your bus."

"What about supplies? Cots? Food? Medical provisions?"

Shimeji told her that Eve was on the phone, arranging for them.

She was relieved that Eve was at the helm. Eve would get things done.

We will get through this, she told herself. We'll get through this, and Gordon will be okay. She said it over and over again.

Chapter Six
December 7, 1941

The Royal Hawaiian Hotel, Waikiki

ON THE MORNING of December 7th, CJ opened her eyes to see Joe's face on the pillow. His body was curled toward hers. His dog tags hung from his neck, and his beard was a black stubble.

She smiled as she listened to him snore. She stroked his cheek to wake him, she wanted her face to be the first thing he saw. But he didn't budge. She kissed him hard, but he was unfazed.

She leaned over to read the clock. It was eight-fifteen. She wasn't going to let the first day of her honeymoon be wasted with Joe asleep. She was about to pounce on him when the telephone rang.

Joe moaned and opened his eyes. "I love you, babe." The phone rang again, and he rolled over to answer it.

He sat up, and CJ stroked his back. This was how it was supposed to be—lazy mornings, no alarms, no uniforms.

"Yes, this is Lieutenant Delano."

She tiptoed her fingers up his spine.

"What?" He threw off the sheets. "When?" Joe stood up. "How many?" He looked out the French doors toward Pearl Harbor. "Why the hell didn't you call me?" He cupped his hand over the mouthpiece of the phone and turned to CJ. "The Japs bombed Pearl Harbor."

The words didn't make sense to CJ. They were something you'd hear in a newsreel. She grabbed her robe and ran to the lanai.

"I'll be right there," Joe said. "And tell Snelling to open up the armory." He slammed the phone down, ran and stood next to CJ. "Look at them. And we kept saying the bastards didn't know how to fly!"

The planes looked like gnats diving into smoke with sparks of orange and white arching over the ships.

Joe gripped CJ's shoulders. "Babe, you've got to stay here!" He held her so tightly, it hurt her. "The hotel has a defense plan. Do not leave the hotel!"

Where would she go?

"God, CJ I never would have asked you out here if I thought this would happen. Never."

CJ covered Joe's mouth with her hand. "I know that."

"Promise me. You'll stay here."

"I promise."

Joe ran back into the room and pulled his uniform out of the closet. "If you need anything, call Eve Russell. She'll know what to do." Joe put on his trousers. "They've got a house in Nuuanu. Maybe you could stay with them?"

CJ handed Joe his socks.

"I should have never asked you to come out here." He put on his shoes, shaking his head. "It was a stupid idea."

"It was our idea—both of us."

He buttoned his shirt. "I promised your father I'd take care of you. And I bring you out in the middle of a war!"

"Joe, I'll be okay." CJ handed him his tie.

"I'll call you as soon as I can." He grabbed his jacket. "I love you, CJ." She stared at him as he walked out, the door shut, Joe disappeared, and CJ stared at the door. Her husband of two days was going off to war.

"Joe!" She ran out the door and down the corridor. "Joe!" She pressed her hand on the closed elevator door.

She thought about running down the steps, but she knew she'd miss him. She flung open the balcony doors and looked down at Kalakaua Avenue.

Where the hell was he?

Car. Buses. Bakery trucks. Milk trucks. Jeeps.

Joe had to be somewhere. She kept looking.

Damn. All the soldiers looked alike, packed in together, all headed for Pearl.

She spotted Joe in an open-bed truck.

She flailed her arms. "Joe!" Her voice cracked. The truck turned the corner and she lost sight of him.

She looked down at Waikiki. Boy Scouts stacked sandbags in front of buildings, and armed sentries patrolled building roofs. They were ready. They knew. They all knew.

This was war, and she had a front-row seat. This was a day that would change history and she should be reporting it.

She ran down the stairs to the front desk. The lobby was mobbed. There were guests dressed in pink hotel bathrobes, some in tennis togs, a few in church finery. All were demanding answers from any and every hotel employee.

She elbowed her way through to the front of the line, and told the clerk she needed to place a long-distance phone call. "It's to the *Star-Ledger* newspaper in Newark, New Jersey. I've got the number."

"I'm sorry, Ma'am. No overseas calls can be put through."

"I'm a reporter. I have to call my paper."

"I'm sorry. No overseas calls can be placed."

"You've got to have an emergency line."

"Ma'am, I can't put any overseas calls through. Governor's orders."

"You can't do this!" She slammed her fist on the counter.

The man next to her shoved her. "Let it go, lady." He leaned on the counter and ordered the clerk to call him a cab.

The clerk answered with the same, "I'm sorry, I can't do that."

CJ raced up the stairs to her room. She threw on clothes, stuffed her notebook and press badge in her shoulder bag and ran down the corridor, pinning her hat on as she did.

In the elevator, she composed her lead. "Sunday morning, December 7, 1941, the Japanese launched a surprise attack on Pearl Harbor."

When the elevator opened to the lobby, she was almost run over by a busboy pushing a Philco radio on a dolly.

CJ slithered by him and out of the front portico, where a valet stopped her. "I'm sorry, Ma'am. No civilians are allowed on the street. Governor's orders."

She stiffened. "I was just out here."

"Maybe, but you can't be out here now."

"I'm a reporter." She dug in her shoulder bag for her press badge.

"I'm sorry, only military and essential persons are allowed on the street." He put his hand on her arm, and she firmly shrugged it off.

There was no way she was going to let some pink-costumed valet deter her.

She scouted the lobby for a different exit. The beach! She could stroll down the beach and get to the park where the buses were. But, as soon as she stepped onto the beach, another bubble-gum pink valet stopped her.

"I'm sorry, Ma'am. No one can leave the hotel."

"Of course," she said and politely smiled.

She went back into the lobby fuming, watching waitresses in pink Victorian dresses circulating among the guests, offering them tea and biscuits. Incredible!

A waitress waved her hand over a pink linen-draped cart. "May I get you something to drink?"

"No, thank you." But the sight of her sparked a solution. There was a hotel kitchen, which meant there was an employee's exit.

She followed a waitress to the kitchen, pushed the swinging doors open, nodded to the staff as if she should be there, and walked straight out the exit door.

It took her a second to get her bearings. She was in a side alley lined with rubbish bins and broken-down dining chairs. If she walked to the front of the hotel, she knew she'd be stopped again. So, she walked down a narrow alley that led to the back of the adjacent hotel, where there were more rubbish bins and broken chairs, then she walked out to the street from there where she fell in line with a few nurses walking toward Kapiolani Park. At the park, there were tens of buses, first aid stations, and trucks hauling water tanks. She stood in a line for a bus with a sign for Pearl Harbor, but when she got to the bus door, an MP asked to see her I.D. so she handed him her press pass.

"Nurses only." He handed it back to her.

"I'm a reporter."

"Nurses only," he repeated and blocked her with his forearm, letting the nurse in uniform behind her board.

CJ walked to the other side of the lot and got in line for another Pearl Harbor bus, but this time, when the MP asked for her ID, she told him that she was a nurse but didn't have her I.D. with her.

"No I.D. No bus."

"Why would I lie to you?" CJ insisted. "I'm a nurse."

"Look, Ma'am. Why don't you go to the Red Cross tent? Maybe you can help out there."

There had to be a chink in the armor. Think! She put her hands on her hat and threw back her head. Think! Then, an MP tapped her on the shoulder. "Ma'am, are you looking for a nurses' bus?"

"Yes!"

He grabbed her elbow and led her to a bus that was driving away. He banged on the door. "I've got one more for you," and CJ jumped on.

CJ held on to the backs of the seats as the bus raced away. In the empty last row, she sat down, took her notebook out and began writing her report.

No, she couldn't use Pearl Harbor in the headline, no one knew where Pearl Harbor was, let alone that Hawaii was part of the United States. She had to go in for the emotional kill: "While the good people of Hawaii were on their way to church, the Japanese…"

She looked up; the story needed visual details. Don't miss what's in front of you. It was Journalism 101.

On the road, there were convoys of speeding trucks, buses, ambulances, and fire trucks. From what she observed, none of downtown Honolulu was bombed.

As the bus drove through Chinatown, the road went from a paved four-lane road to a two-lane street, past fields where there was nothing but scrub brush and a few shacks—then a dairy farm with grazing cows and ducks in a marsh.

The closer they drove to the base, the heavier the smell of smoke, but she didn't hear any planes or bombs, nor did she see any fires.

Maybe it was over.

She kept taking notes—a hand-painted sign for Sumida's Watercress Farm, a street marker for "Cane Haul Road."

Traffic got slower and slower then jammed to a halt. There were abandoned cars parked on the side of the road, and when

CJ pressed her cheek against the window, she could see the base gate, men running toward it, and MP's pinwheeling their arms, yelling, "Go! Go!"

Ford Island, Pearl Harbor

When her bus reached the gate, an MP yelled at the bus next to hers. "Who you got?"

"Welders and cooks."

"Dock 10. Go!"

"Who you got?" he yelled to CJ's bus driver.

"Nurses."

"Dispensary. Building 70."

CJ's bus jolted forward; the engine groaned. The air got thick, and CJ's throat stung with the tang of burnt metal.

CJ cupped her hand against the window as if it could help her see through the smoke. They passed warehouses and oil tanks, and trucks and buses going in both directions. Then her bus turned into the parking lot of the Ford Island Dispensary.

CJ went cold. Stretchers and bodies.

Out of the smoke, a corpsman pushed a wounded sailor in a wheelbarrow; the sailor's legs and arms dangled as the medic ran.

"Everybody out." The bus driver yelled.

The door slid open, and smoke poured in. A nurse boarded

the bus yelling, "Emergency room nurses, go to triage. Surgical nurses, third floor. The rest of you, do whatever you can."

Everybody was yelling and screaming. Orders. Cries for help. Cries of pain.

Her pulse hammered.

CJ watched the nurses get off the bus, but she couldn't move.

"Come on!" a nurse grabbed CJ's arm.

"I'm not a nurse," she said.

The nurse pulled CJ off the bus. "Follow me." She led her into the clinic, where she was hit with the stench of ether, urine, and blood.

"I need help here," someone yelled.

On the floor, stretchers lined both sides of the hallway, leaving a path between them barely wide enough to sidestep through. Halfway down the hall, a priest kneeled over a sailor.

"Help with the morphine." A nurse handed CJ a tray.

"I'm not a nurse."

"Do you have first aid training?" she asked.

"No."

The nurse turned to a corpsman. "Get her away from here! Put her outside."

CJ followed the corpsman as he treaded through bloody footprints down the hall. She held her breath and skirted the wounded.

Outside. To get away? To take a bus out of there?

"This way." The corpsman pointed to the back door that opened to a parking lot where wounded men were laid out on stretchers and parked like cars within the designated lines.

"Do you have any training?" A nurse asked CJ.

"No."

"Line Three." She pointed to the far-left corner.

Guns popped, and CJ crouched and covered her head.

"Now!" the nurse yelled. "Go!"

None of it was like the newsreels. There were no dashing doctors or blue-eyed nurses. No wounded clean in their hospital beds. There was nothing clean or heroic about it. There was a sailor with a head wound, another with a bandaged chest. Some were just oil-slick black bodies, maybe alive.

The nurse at Line Three held up a Flit Gun. "Can you work this?"

"A bug sprayer?"

"It's tannic acid." The nurse bent over a sailor. When she sprayed him, he wailed.

The nurse shoved the Flit gun back into CJ's hands. "You do it."

"But he's screaming."

"It's the shock of the cold."

Bile worked up her stomach. "I can't."

"It eases his pain! Now!" the nurse demanded.

The sailor's eyes were open, unfocused. CJ wanted to tell him she was sorry. She held the gun. Just spray him, she told herself. But she couldn't.

"Give me the gun!" The nurse snatched it and sprayed the boy as if she were attacking a horde of beetles. "You spray fast and move on!"

CJ followed her to the next sailor. Where the whites of his eyes should have been, they were red.

"Cover his eyes while I spray him." She handed CJ a washcloth.

The sailor moaned, but CJ did it. The nurse gave her the gun again and told her to move on to the next sailor.

Then the next.

And the next.

The Flit gun grew heavier, and CJ's fingers cramped from clutching it so tight, but she kept going. Just spray them she told herself. Fight every instinct to run.

She could see what the men wore when they were burned because their clothes melted into their bodies. Some were in undershorts, probably still in their bunks, others had uniforms charred to their skin.

The nurse told CJ to keep moving and skip the next man, pointing to the "X" on his forehead. "'T' for tetanus. 'M' for morphine. 'X' for dead."

His chest didn't rise. His mouth hung open and his eyes stared up at her.

The next sailor was a boy barely out of high school. He should have been thinking about fast cars and fast girls.

CJ knelt and held his head in her hands. His face was blistered, but his eyes were clear blue.

"It'll feel cold at first," CJ consoled him. "But after a minute, the pain will ease."

He smiled, and CJ slid her hand from under his neck. His skin came off in her hands.

She ran! Flinging the gun, her shoulder bag dangling. She didn't stop running until she got to the parking lot where she squatted on the curb with her hands over her ears. She took deep gulps of air. Mother of God, give me strength.

She felt a hand on her shoulder and screamed.

An MP leaned over. "Are you wounded?"

She shook her head no.

"Is your husband wounded?"

"My husband is Lieutenant Delano. He's safe," and she prayed to God that she wasn't lying.

"We need to get you out of here, Ma'am." He helped her to her feet. "I'm putting you on an evac bus."

"My bag." She pointed to it on the curb.

He picked it up, hailed down a bus, and yelled, "Evac?"

"Yeah!" the driver yelled, "Get her in!"

A woman in the first row helped her up the stairs, and CJ hobbled down the aisle to the last row.

The bus rumbled forward. CJ's hands trembled, and her legs shook.

The woman across the aisle gently handed CJ a handkerchief, gesturing to the blood on CJ's arm.

"It's not mine." CJ wiped the blood on her skirt.

She looked out the window—it was the same scene—buses, ambulances, wounded and dead, then she focused on her reflection and bitterly whispered, "CJ Delano, Ace Reporter who braved the bombs to report from the warfront."

CHAPTER SEVEN
DECEMBER 7, 1941

Honpa Hongwanji Buddhist Mission, Honolulu

THE BUS DRIVER turned off the main road onto an unpaved gravel path that was canopied by banyan trees so dense that they blocked the sun.

CJ looked out the window as she fingered her grandmother's pearl earrings. She craved her grandmother's embrace. She called CJ *"Mia Luna,"* her moon. I love you, Nonna.

The driver turned into a walled compound. The sign read "Honpa Hongwanji Buddhist Mission."

Women on the bus swiveled their heads, and children knelt in their seats, looking out the windows.

There were no trees in the compound; instead, there were gravel paths and rows of statues. The main building resembled the Taj Mahal, except for its purple onion-shaped domes and several purple spires.

The statues weren't of benevolent saints. There were statues of a dancing woman with eight arms, a mustachioed man with lightning bolts emanating from his head, and an ancient warrior with a drawn sword.

On the right side of the compound, there was a raked stone garden where American women huddled together on benches, looking like the refugees they were.

On the left, there was an open area where Japanese teenage girls played with American children.

The girls were dressed in white skirts and blouses with black sashes across their chests, like American Girl Scout uniforms, but the letters on their sashes were all in Japanese, as were their faces.

When the bus door opened, a line of Japanese women in kimonos formed a gauntlet.

"This is it, ladies," the bus driver announced.

Tentatively, the women and children shuffled off the bus. CJ watched as Japanese women bowed to the evacuees, guiding each family away with the help of the Japanese "Girl Scouts."

After the last evacuee got off the bus, the driver walked back toward CJ. "This is the end of the line, Ma'am,"

CJ told the driver she had a room in Waikiki and asked if he could drop her off.

"No can do," he said.

"You don't understand. I have a room at the Royal Hawaiian."

He shook his head. "No can."

"You don't have to take me all the way," CJ bargained. "If you let me off anywhere in Waikiki, I can walk to the hotel."

The driver stuck his head out the window. "I need help with this lady."

It took CJ a minute to recognize the white woman who got on the bus. The double-strand pearl choker jolted CJ's memory. It was Commander Elliot's wife, Ruth.

Ruth smiled as she came down the aisle. "CJ?"

"Yes." CJ explained that she wanted the driver to drop her off at the Royal, but Ruth told CJ that the Navy had taken over the Waikiki hotels.

"I'm in the honeymoon suite on the top floor. I doubt the Navy will be using that."

"The Navy took it all over, and their guests were moved out to other hotels."

"Do you know which hotel I'll be moved to?" CJ asked.

"You'll be staying here with the other military wives."

"I'm not a military wife." She had been married to Joe for two days. She was his wife, not a 'military wife.' "Besides, all my things are at the Royal."

Ruth put her hand on CJ's shoulder, smiling, as if she were a school teacher patronizing a truant child.

"We have a system to have them sent here. They'll be here by this afternoon."

CJ knew she wasn't going to win, and she limped off the bus, the pain in her ankles flaring, suddenly aware of her blisters.

Ruth led CJ to a bench on the perimeter of the raked stone garden. The gravel crunched as she walked. A Japanese woman bowed to her, smiling. CJ couldn't smile back.

Ruth motioned for CJ to sit on the bench. She didn't know why they were stopping because all the other evacuees were being escorted up the stairs to a wing off the right side of the temple. The walk toward the temple was immaculately landscaped, not a leaf out of place.

"What is this place?" CJ asked.

"It's a Buddhist mission," Ruth explained. "There's a temple, a retreat center, and a school."

"And it's an American evacuation center?" CJ couldn't reconcile this Japanese church servicing American families.

"Eve is a friend of Shimeji Kanazawa, the bishop's wife. It was Shimeji and Eve who convinced the Bishop to offer the mission as a Red Cross evacuation center. He was already letting us use the common room to give our First Aid lessons, so it wasn't that far a stretch."

"How many evacuees do you have?" CJ asked.

"At last count, we were at 160, and the buses keep coming."

Ruth must have noticed CJ staring at two Japanese girls in a garden, turning a rope so American children could jump. "They're YBA girls—Young Buddhist Association."

Ruth motioned a young girl over. "Could you go to the Donation Closet and get Miss CJ a pair of shoes?" Ruth turned to CJ. "Size?"

"Seven," CJ answered.

Ruth gestured to CJ's ankles. "I couldn't help but notice the blood stains on your nylons."

CJ felt even more foolish—she had worn heels to cover a war.

"You'll find the community to be quite welcoming," Ruth told CJ. "The temple is the only place that is off-limits. They set up a canteen in the south wing, and the north wing is the dormitory."

When the YBA girl returned, she held up a pair of saddle shoes to CJ. The last time CJ wore saddle shoes was at Saint Cecelia High School.

CJ took them. Her stockings were ruined—ripped at the toes, caked with blood.

"Do you want to go to the first aid station before you put them on?"

"I'm fine," CJ said.

"Well, there's the common restroom." Ruth pointed to a separate white stucco building. "Freshen up, then I'll take you to Eve's office. I'm sure she'll want to see you."

"Eve Russell?"

"Yes. She's the Assistant Director."

Of all the women in Hawaii CJ met since she arrived—Eve and Ruth—were both her guardian angels.

CJ stared in the restroom mirror. Her cheeks were smudged with soot and streaked with mascara. Her hat was gone. She emptied her bag; her notebook and press badge were gone too.

She scrubbed her hands raw until she rid them of any sign of blood or skin. She couldn't stop seeing faces of sailors. CJ told herself that next time she would do better. She'd be prepared. She would handle it.

Then a metal cart stuttered over the tile floor and she ducked and covered her head.

∽

Eve's office was spare. Wood boxes stenciled "Red Cross Evacuation Supplies" were piled next to her desk, behind her desk was a canvas cot squeezed in next to the wall.

CJ was surprised to see Eve in uniform and wearing no makeup. This unadorned Eve looked almost innocent.

"I tried calling the Royal, but you were already gone." Eve got up and hugged CJ. "Oh, CJ, before you got here, Joe made me promise that I'd help you settle in, but I wasn't counting on a war."

Two days ago, CJ would have resented the idea that she needed help.

"I appreciate that," CJ said, and she meant it.

"You're safe here. And I'll put you on the Red Cross roster so Joe will know where you are."

Joe thought she was at the Royal. She'd promised to stay put.

"Where are your things?" Eve asked.

"At The Royal," CJ said.

"Hmm. They should have put them on the bus with you when you evacuated." Eve furrowed her brows. "I'll have someone from the Motor Corps pick them up."

"I have a favor to ask you," CJ said. "My wedding corsage is on the night table. Could they make sure to pack it? I wanted to press the flowers and send them to my mother." When she heard herself ask for the flowers, CJ realized how trivial that sounded.

Eve was quick to answer, "My sister Ginger is in the Motor Corps. I'll ask her to do it. But first, let me give you the tour of the mission."

Their first stop was a temporary dormitory set up in a gymnasium. Japanese women sidestepped between the rows of cots, distributing piles of sheets, pillows, towels, and an orange that they placed on each cot.

CJ asked, "Where do I put my things when they come?"

"Under your cot. The rest you store in lockers in the south

wing. There's a children's playroom and canteen there too. The coffee is lousy, and if you don't like peanut butter and jelly, you're going to go hungry."

"After I get settled, what do I do then?"

"Then you sit around and wait until the military says you can leave, or the Japanese blow us to kingdom come."

Neither option appealed to CJ. "I'll go crazy if I sit around. There's got to be something I can do."

"Have you ever worked in a commercial kitchen?"

CJ laughed. "I guess Joe didn't tell you I grew up in my family's bakery."

"Well, Eriko could use any help she can get."

The mission's kitchen was twice as big as Martino's bakery. It had a walk-in fridge, two 20-foot prep stations, and a 24-foot stainless steel counter with four double sinks.

A YBA girl sat on the prep table, swinging her legs. Eve asked the girl to get CJ an apron then she introduced CJ to a Japanese woman wearing a pinstriped suit and T-strap heels. "This is Eriko Fujimoto."

Eriko's hair was tightly rolled in a French twist.

Eve turned to CJ. "Eriko, this is CJ Delano. She arrived on-island three days ago, married a Marine, and this is the start of her honeymoon."

Eriko hugged CJ, and CJ stiffened. She had never been touched by a Japanese person before. She hadn't even talked to one.

The YBA girl came back with an apron, and CJ slipped it over her head and tied it at her waist. How many times had she done this in the bakery?

"So far, I'd say you've had one hell of a honeymoon," Eriko said.

CJ was still getting used to Japanese people speaking English, let alone swearing.

"She's all yours, Eriko," Eve said. "Show her the ropes. I've got to go back to scabbing up supplies."

"How can I help?" CJ asked.

"Today?" Eriko huffed a breath. "Just stay alive!"

CJ instantly appreciated Eriko's humor.

CJ rolled up her sleeves. The kitchen hummed with low chatter in English and Japanese, the clatter of ladles against steel, the rhythmic slap of knives on cutting boards. The smells—rice, vinegar, canned tomatoes—weren't quite home, but they were close enough.

"We managed to get through lunch," Eriko said, "The next order of business are the babies. We need to come up with a baby bottle sterilizer. We have more babies than we can handle, and with the Manoa Evacuation Center closed, they just keep coming."

CJ spotted the answer. She walked to the fry station and held up the basket. "We can put water in the fryer and set the baby bottles in the basket, and *voila!* We have a sterilizer."

"I like the way you think," Eriko said, then she asked a few YBA girls to collect the baby bottles from the evacuees. "Make sure you label every single bottle with the mother's name, and don't forget the nipples." Then she asked the remaining girls to get out the rice cookers and wash ten pounds of rice.

CJ was impressed. Eriko was a get-it-done kind of girl.

"We need diapers," one of the YBA girls said.

"I've got this," CJ said. "My sister-in-law always ran short when she brought my niece to the bakery." She rummaged through the storeroom and grabbed a stack of clean kitchen towels. She held one up. "We just cut them in half."

Between Eriko and CJ, they organized the girls into a work assembly line that Henry Ford would have envied. The girls worked fast, chatting, but when the radio announcer came back on, there was quiet in the kitchen.

Most of the announcements were the same: stay indoors, stay off the phone, and don't drink the water. CJ hoped for news about Pearl. She didn't want to know about casualties or ships destroyed; she wanted to know that Joe was safe.

As the two women worked, Eriko asked CJ where her husband was stationed. When she answered, "Ford Island," Eriko lowered her eyes and nodded.

"Do you have any news about it?" CJ asked.

"Not really. My husband is a doctor at Queen's Hospital, and I heard that the wounded from Ford Island are being sent there."

She wondered if Eriko's husband could check if Joe were there. It was an absurd request, and she immediately put it out of her head. Joe wasn't hurt. If he were, she would have had a feeling about it. Wouldn't she?

"I was at the Ford Island dispensary," CJ said.

"Are you a nurse?" Eriko asked her.

CJ shook her head. "I'm a reporter. I snuck out there to see what was going on for myself."

"How bad was it?"

"I had no business being out there," she said, "I went out there to get the story and I ended up spraying the wounded with tannic acid."

"There are stories you don't write," Eriko said.

CJ didn't respond.

The radio announcement interrupted them: "Go to 30-240 Date Street. They have chili for police officers… The blood banks are running out of bottles… A beautician is asking her fellow hairdressers to donate shampoo bottles… That's shampoo bottles only, ladies… The blood bank cannot use bottles from hair dyes… Her phone number is 659."

There were more troubling announcements: "Japanese

paratroopers landed in Manoa… The Japanese poisoned the water supply… A captured Japanese pilot was wearing a McKinley High School class ring."

She tried to stop listening and throw herself into work. By mid-afternoon, she and Eriko had all the babies fed, diapers were doled out, sterilized bottles were returned to mothers, and the two women took a break sitting on stools at the stainless-steel counter.

Eriko opened a new pack of Lucky Strikes, tapped one out, and offered it to CJ.

CJ declined.

There were more announcements, and there was no work to distract CJ.

Filipino plantation workers attacked their fellow Japanese workers… A Japanese maid at Navy housing was a spy… Japanese fishing boats were sending signals to enemy planes.

"It's going to be difficult for us Japanese," Eriko said.

Eriko was right. What if the Japanese army landed? How could anyone tell friend from foe?

"Some of the wounded are refusing to have my husband treat them," Eriko said. "They scream at him not to touch them." Eriko took a long drag of her cigarette. "I understand it. We have the same faces."

CJ kept seeing the photo of the Emperor in the barbershop window.

At about 3:30, Eve swung open the kitchen doors. "Sorry I couldn't get down here sooner—it's a madhouse upstairs. We're up to 180 evacuees." She nodded toward the cigarette pack on the prep counter and Eriko slid it over without a word.

CJ wiped her hands on her apron. "Any news about Ford Island?"

Eve shook her head. "But I do have good news. My mother's invited you to stay at our house. It comes with a warm bed, a hot shower, and no line for the toilet."

It was a tempting offer.

"Or…" Eve circled her unlit cigarette around the kitchen. "You could stay here, head-to-toe with 180 women and children, and hope the toddler in the next cot doesn't wet the bed."

"When you put it like that, I accept."

"Is Ruth going too?" Eriko asked.

"Ruth the Dutiful? I'm working hard on her, but I doubt it." Eve lit her cigarette. "Anyway, the night shift's arriving, so you two need to do turnover."

"Did my things come from the Royal?" CJ asked.

"They're in Ruth's office."

※

Standing outside Ruth's office door, CJ could hear Eve's voice.

She couldn't make out the words, but Eve's tone was loud, sharp and insistent.

She tilted her ear to the door. A woman pacing the hall with a crying baby stared at her.

CJ shrugged. "You caught me."

The baby in the woman's arms squirmed and let out a fresh wail.

"I guess he doesn't approve of eavesdropping," CJ said.

"This is Peter." Her voice was tinged with exhaustion. "He's not approving of anything these days. He has colic and I've got to keep moving."

She paced down the hall. When she passed a third time, CJ said, "I have got a secret weapon for calming babies. Can I give it a try?"

The woman didn't hesitate. "Please. I would love it." She shifted Peter into CJ's arms and said, "I'm Alexandra."

"I'm CJ." CJ pressed Peter gently against her shoulder, murmuring to him. "Would you look at your eyes, Peter? Just like my husband's—big, round, and those lashes!"

Peter whimpered.

"Joe wants a son first," she told Peter. "Joe's my husband. He's already named our son Raphael. Can you believe that?" She gave Peter a soft bounce. "I said we should go with Ralph, or he'll never survive grade school." Peter quieted, his eyes riveted on CJ. "I want to name him Anthony—Joe's middle name—but apparently that's not happening either." She felt the baby relax into her arms.

"I'll tell you a secret, Peter." Her voice dropped. "When we move back to New Jersey, we're going to live in a two-story house with a big yard." Peter seemed to be listening. "It'll be close to the train station so I can work in New York. I'm going to work for the *New York Times*."

On her next pass by Ruth's office, the door was open and she could hear Eve: "Don't be such a martyr."

Ruth snapped back, "Eve, I'm responsible for the center. Not you!"

CJ turned around, to keep walking when Eve came out into the hallway. "Is this your luggage?"

CJ stepped into the office. "Yes."

Ruth slammed her pencil on her desk and glared at CJ. "What are you doing with that baby?"

"Helping his mother." It seemed pretty obvious.

"That's not your job. That's what the YBA girls are for."

CJ wasn't going to argue that the YBA girls had gone home over an hour ago, she just said, "Yes, Ma'am. I'll return him right now." She stepped out of the office, glancing at Eve and raised her eyebrows.

Eve told CJ to meet her in the parking lot. "I'll take care of your luggage."

CJ slid into the car ready to vent. "Well, I guess we know who doesn't love babies."

"Ruth's tired," Eve defended Ruth.

"There's tired, then there's junkyard dog tired."

"Cut her a break on this one." Eve started the ignition. "She deserves it."

Chapter Eight
December 7, 1941

The Russell Estate, Nuuanu

ALTHOUGH JOE HAD made it clear that Eve came from money, CJ didn't realize how rich Eve was until they drove up to the Russell's home—it was more of a mansion.

Eve drove past a high lava-rock wall into a curved driveway lined with royal palm trees. In the sunset, the white clapboard of the house shone amber.

Eve parked in the porte-cochere under an unlit brass lantern. The front doors were flanked by Palladian windows.

A dark-haired woman in a Red Cross uniform waved to them from the front door.

"That's my sister, Ginger," Eve told CJ.

CJ thought Ginger looked more like she could be her sister than Eve's. She was short, with curly-dark hair and "child-bearing hips."

"Thank God you're home." Ginger hugged her sister.

CJ lugged her bags to the foyer where Ginger took them and set them next to the telephone table.

"Blackout already?" Eve fingered the drapes.

"Mother had Joe-san put them up. And be warned, Mother's in full form."

"Two martinis to the wind?" Eve asked.

"Can you count to four?" Ginger rolled her eyes. "She even has a full set of butcher cleavers on the coffee table ready to protect our virtue from enemy invaders."

"Maybe I should have stayed at the center," CJ kidded.

"Don't worry," Eve said. "My mother only butchers people with words, and typically, I'm the target."

CJ walked into the living room. It took a minute for her eyes to adjust to the darkened room. For the grand size of it, there wasn't much furniture. Two long sofas were flanked by club chairs, and a grand dining room table in front of the French doors was set with china and crystal for twelve. In the corner of the room, next to a painting of Diamond Head almost as big as the real thing, was a grand piano.

Eve turned to Ginger, "Did Joe-san run out of black-out curtains?" She pointed to the back wall of French doors bare of any curtains.

"No, these are the 'rules of Martial Law according to Loretta

Russell.' Mother claims if she has to sit in the dark, she insists on fresh air."

The view from the windows was of the Koolau Mountains.

Eve led CJ into the living room. "Mother, this is the friend I called you about."

Mrs. Russell sat up and waved to CJ. "Come in."

Mrs. Russell was a much smaller woman than CJ imagined; she expected a substantial matriarch. But Eve's mother was fine-boned and fair-skinned with clear blue eyes and platinum white hair drawn back in a perfect chignon.

"Thank God you're safe." Mrs. Russell's diction had the curl of someone who had been to finishing school.

"This is CJ Delano," Eve introduced her.

"Delano? My husband is one generation removed from Franklin Delano Roosevelt, although he's loath to admit it. Are your husband's people from the Hyde Park Delanos?"

CJ wanted to say her husband's people were from the Brooklyn Delanos, that Joe's father was a butcher, and that he was one generation removed from Ellis Island. Instead, she said, "I doubt it."

"Her husband is a lieutenant in the Marine Corps." Eve volunteered the information as if it would make a good impression on her mother.

"Have you heard from him?" Mrs. Russell asked.

"Not yet," CJ answered.

"What am I thinking? Of course, you haven't," Mrs. Russel said. "Have you been at the evacuation center all day?"

"I have."

"Then make yourself at home. What can we get you?" Mrs. Russell turned to Ginger as if to signal her.

"Anything but donuts and coffee." CJ smiled.

"I could use a Scotch on the rocks." Eve turned to CJ. "Are you interested?"

"Make mine neat," CJ answered.

CJ listened to the way the women spoke to each other. Every word was restrained; for sure, the rules of civility didn't give way to war. If it were CJ's house, her mother would be in tears, hugging the breath out of her and thanking God and all the saints who protected the family from harm.

Mrs. Russell asked Eve, "How are you managing at Hongwanji?"

"We had a few setbacks."

A volley of gunshots popped and CJ flinched.

"Someone's going to get killed," Mrs. Russell shook her head. "Every man out there is armed with his high school pistol. You should have seen the ragtag crew of defense wardens who showed up at Headquarters. They were shooting at any sound they heard! In broad daylight!" She huffed. "I'm certain they killed every stray cat in Honolulu."

Ginger carried in a silver tray of crackers, cheese, and drinks. Eve pushed aside the butcher cleavers so Ginger could set the tray down.

Another volley of gunshots unnerved CJ more than the first had.

Mrs. Russell told Eve, "I asked Ginger to get your father's pistols out of the attic, but she refused. I'd get them myself if I could climb up there." She turned toward the butler's pantry and pointed to the attic access. "I think he was at Yale the last time he fired them."

CJ picked up on the oh-so-subtle Yale reference. It was all subtle with them—the perfect humility of old money with frayed Oriental rugs and the club chairs that were patched on the arms. None of the furniture looked new; it all looked like it had been handed down at least two generations.

"God knows what else is up there," Mrs. Russell continued. "I don't think anyone's been in the attic since Grandmother Russell died."

CJ was trying to reconcile the fact that she was sipping drinks, eating cheese and crackers in a luxurious home, while that morning, she was surrounded by dying men.

"How were things at Motor Corps?" Eve asked Ginger.

"Mostly, I drove donors to the blood bank, and they kept asking me if I knew anything about Pearl."

The polite chatter among the Russell women almost angered CJ. She missed her family. She wanted to fall into her mother's arms and have her stroke her hair and kiss the top of her head.

"What about Headquarters, Mother?" Eve asked.

"We're doing the best we can." Mrs. Russell sighed. "We have 18 days of supplies in the food bank, and according to General Short, all of Oahu will be out of food in one month."

One month? All CJ could think of was one day—just stay alive and hope Joe was safe.

"Shh!" Ginger put her finger to her lips. "Anyone hear that?"

CJ was stock-still, listening. It sounded like gravel coming down a chute.

Mrs. Russell waved toward the French doors and asked Eve to see what was going on.

Eve looked out the doors and scanned the sky. There was another muffled rumble. "My God, they're back."

Ginger yelled, "Everybody under the table!"

"They're headed for the house," Eve said.

"Hurry!" Ginger tugged on her mother's arm and pulled her up.

Mrs. Russell struggled. "I can't get under there."

CJ was sure she was going to die in a stranger's house. Joe! What would Joe do without her?

The floor shook, and the windows rattled.

"Mother, you've got to get under the table!" Ginger took her mother's arm and Eve pulled a chair away from the dining table. "Grab the seat, Mother, and kneel down. From there, you can crawl. Hurry!"

A crystal glass tumbled off the table.

"I can't do this." Mrs. Russell grabbed the table's edge.

"Kneel down," Ginger said.

"Now, Mother!" Eve yelled.

The plane was close, and CJ stood, watching the two sisters push their mother under the table.

I'm going to die, she thought.

"Come on, CJ." Eve waved for her to get under the table.

CJ followed, curling herself into a ball, looking up at the bottom of the table. It wouldn't be worth a damn if the house were bombed.

There was a barrage of fire.

CJ closed her eyes. I love you, Joe.

"God, protect us," Mrs. Russell prayed.

Another explosion. The lights flickered, and the chandelier swung. The next explosion was not as loud as the first.

CJ braced for a third, but there wasn't one. There were volleys of guns, distant sirens and the smell of smoke—but no more explosions.

Ginger was first to speak, "I think it's over."

CJ doubted the Japanese would come back with only one plane.

None of the ladies moved until they heard the warden's call, "All clear," and slowly, cautiously, they crawled from under the table, and looked around the room checking for any damage.

Mrs. Russell tucked a few loose strands of hair behind her ears. "This is too much for me, girls." Her hand trembled. "I'm going to bed. If I die in my sleep, so be it." She stopped at the bottom of the staircase. "Don't wait up for your father, girls. Who knows if he'll come home tonight?"

Eve whispered to Ginger. "Pops may get killed, but 'Don't wait up. Who knows if he'll come home.' Spoken like a true wife."

"Stop it," Ginger said.

"She didn't even try to call Pops."

"This isn't the time, Eve," Ginger said.

A sporadic volley of gunshots interrupted them, then the wails of fire truck sirens.

The three of them sat stunned and silent in the living room until Ginger admitted she wasn't keen on sleeping in her room alone.

"Do you want me to sleep with you?" Eve asked.

"What if we all bunk right here?" Ginger suggested and she and Eve turned the living room into a fortress of blankets and pillows, then Eve lined up a service bar of gin and whiskey on the floor and CJ fiddled with the radio dial until she could get a station. The reporter confirmed there was a plane shot down over the Nuuanu neighborhood. There were no civilian casualties and the pilots were killed in the crash.

Eve raised her drink and condemned every Jap pilot to die.

Around midnight, the radio went off the air, and the only sound was the occasional warning yelled by an air raid warden patrolling the streets, then the front door opened.

"Pops!" Eve ran to the door. "Pops!" She wrapped her arms around him. "You okay?"

"Fine." He stepped back from her, laid his briefcase on the telephone table, and handed Eve the special edition of the *Advertiser*. "Take a look."

The headlines read, "Japanese Paratroopers Land in St. Louis Heights and Manoa!"

"One of the paratroopers was shot," Mr. Russell said.

"Good." Eve kept reading.

"No. Not good." He shook his head. "There were no paratroopers. There was a Japanese Civilian Defense warden at his post. He was in a tree, armed with a rifle, and another warden shot him."

"Is he okay?" Eve asked.

"He's alive."

"Oh, Pops." Eve laid the paper on the telephone table. "How did you find out it wasn't true?"

"General Short called me. He said there was enough chaos

being promulgated without me causing a panic. If I had been in his office, I'm sure I would have been standing at attention, clicking my heels."

"I'm sure other papers made mistakes," Eve consoled.

Mistake? CJ thought. He just announced to the whole world that the Japanese had landed. Didn't anyone check the facts? Heads would roll at the *Star-Ledger* if that had happened.

"It'll be forgotten," Eve consoled him.

"Eve, we're a laughingstock."

Eve changed the subject. "Pops, I have a friend staying here. CJ Delano. You met her."

"Delano?"

"CJ. She's the girl you hired yesterday."

"Yes. The obits girl."

And that was the reality of it, CJ thought. She was the "obits girl." Nothing more. Nothing less. But she was an obits girl who checked her facts.

CHAPTER NINE
DECEMBER 8, 1941

McCully/King Street, Honolulu

THE FOLLOWING MORNING, CJ was showered, dressed, and waiting for Mr. Russell in the foyer at 7:30 a.m. "Good morning, sir."

"'Morning." He put on his hat, picked up his briefcase, and opened the door for CJ. "It's a hell of a day to start a new job."

She followed him to the car. He told her, "I called one of the editors at the *Star-Ledger* on Saturday. A Mr. Spina."

CJ held her breath.

"He praised your coverage of the dockworkers' strike." Mr. Russell opened the door of his black Cadillac for CJ. "He sends his regards."

In between firing and hiring a male reporter, Mr. Spina had given her a shot at a story, but as soon as a guy was hired, she went back to covering dog shows.

"Before we get to the paper, I have a few stops." He started the car. "I didn't say anything to the girls last night, but one of our neighbors was killed. Alice White. It was about ten last night. A rogue plane came through Nuuanu. But they shot the S.O.B. down."

CJ was very aware of that plane.

"Their son was at Stanford when Eve was at Mills." Mr. Russell turned right on Dowsett Avenue as he speculated about what would happen to the two younger girls since their mother died.

The only deaths CJ was thinking about were her own and Joe's.

He stopped at 370 Dowsett, a Dutch Colonial with a sweeping circular drive. It looked untouched, but as Mr. Russell pulled over, CJ saw the side wall of the house had collapsed. It could have easily been Eve's house.

"Alice was a good woman. God knows she didn't deserve to die like this." He turned to CJ. "I want you to write a good obit on her. Talk about her Red Cross work, how many children she had—you know what I'm talking about."

"Yes, sir."

"And pay attention to all the civilian dead. Find out about them—but no melodrama. They deserve to be remembered." He pulled away.

"Do you know how many civilians were killed?" CJ asked.

"The last estimate I heard was forty."

"How about the military deaths? How do I deal with them?"

"You don't!" he barked.

She thought his tone was a bit of an overreaction until his frustration became clear.

"Under Martial Law, we can only report what the military tells us. We can't report anything about the dead or wounded other than the facts they give us."

Got it, she thought. He didn't want any more calls from General Short, but she had a question about the civilian workers killed on base. "How do I handle that?"

He kept his eyes on the road. "Good question. I'll get Maude to get the ruling on that. If you have any questions, ask her. If she doesn't know the answer, she knows who does."

As they drove down Pali Road, the houses became more modest. At the bottom of the hill, there were shops, a cemetery, and a Catholic church where nuns, in their habits, were sweeping up rubble in the yard.

Mr. Russell told CJ, "The Military Governor is censoring every word we print. I had one of my best reporters at Pearl during the attack. Liz Townsend. She's got five years of war correspondence experience. She turned in a solid story—photos, facts, and interviews, but the censors cut it all."

A woman reporter covered the attack—and he called her

one of his best reporters. Maybe a gal did have a chance at the *Advertiser*?

"Liz is top-notch. You could learn a lot from her."

Did that mean he was grooming her for a reporter's slot?

"She's at McCully, covering the fires." He turned off King Street to McCully. CJ smelled the smoke. Two blocks later, she saw the source. The homes on the street looked like the bungalows "down the shore" in New Jersey—small, asphalt-shingled houses that were built on stilts

On one side of McCully Street, there were burned-out homes, charred telephone poles, and blackened furniture stacked on the curb. On the opposite side, the houses were untouched: a milkman was delivering milk, and a man in a workman's uniform carried his lunch pail to his car.

Mr. Russell parked and told CJ to wait for him. She assumed he was going to find Liz and bring her back to introduce her to CJ. Five minutes passed, then ten, and he hadn't returned, so she decided to do some investigating herself. She eased the door open carefully not to bump the bicycles and the headboard stacked at the curb.

The windows of the house they parked in front of were shattered, and canvas awnings were no more than threads.

A few people wandered among the houses.

CJ continued down the street. The curb was jammed with

soaked couches, broken dishes, twisted lamps, and tackle boxes. It would have made a good photo for the story.

She shooed away a rooster and squatted down and picked up a Bang-Up comic book and a wall calendar from a mortuary service. Then she reached for a shiny red cookbook with gold letters, "The Chinese Christian Church Ladies Cookbook."

How strange. A Chinese Christian church. She hadn't known such a thing existed.

She leafed through the dog-eared pages, marbled with grease. There were handwritten notes in Chinese and a *Honolulu Advertising* clipping of a boy being awarded a Service Ribbon from the Boy Scouts was tucked in one of the pages.

"CJ." Mr. Russell's voice startled her. "This is Liz."

Liz was older than CJ expected. Maybe 50? She had Brillo-gray hair stacked on her head like a bird's nest. She wore khaki slacks—not a skirt—carried a worn leather shoulder bag and had a no-nonsense gait.

Liz extended her hand. "Liz Townsend." CJ labeled Liz as not suffering fools. "What do you have there?" Liz jutted her chin toward the cookbook, and CJ handed it to her.

"Interesting." Liz read the clipping about the Boy Scout.

CJ said she could imagine meals cooked from the book's recipes for holidays and large family gatherings.

As Liz perused the book, a rippled photo of a bride and groom fluttered to the ground.

"This is perfect." Liz picked up the photo, then stashed it and the cookbook in her satchel. "It tells the whole story."

Yes, the cookbook did tell the whole story, but it wasn't hers to take.

The first thing she could learn from Liz: Thou shalt steal when it suits you.

Liz turned to Mr. Russell. "Boss, if you could send a photographer out, I'd appreciate it. If Joel Brewton's available, could you send him? The kid's got a good eye."

"I will," he said wiping soot from his eyeglasses.

"I'll be back in the office in an hour or so," Liz said. "Good to meet you, CJ." She turned and walked away.

"Pay attention," Mr. Russell told CJ. "Read her story and see what she can do with a few facts." As Mr. Russell walked, he pointed to a school building. "That's Lunalilo Elementary."

It was a large white cinderblock building. Several windows were burned out, the doors were charred, and the front lawn was littered with desks, chairs, and books.

"The Cadillac dealership on Bishop Street was hit, the phone company and the palace. I can understand that. But schools?" He shook his head. "It's unconscionable."

On the drive through downtown, CJ stared at the overnight

transformation of Honolulu. The Christmas lights were gone. Department store windows were boarded with plywood, and soldiers and Boy Scouts built sandbag walls in front of government buildings and offices. Honolulu had become a military encampment. Barbed wire was strung around the parking lot of the *Advertiser* building, sandbags walled the front entrance, and armed sentries paced the rooftop.

When Mr. Russell asked the parking lot attendant how things were progressing, he said, "We got all the windows covered, and as soon as Civilian Defense delivers another load of sandbags, we can line the emergency exits."

Across the street, Marines were erecting tents on the Iolani Palace grounds. At the sight of the Marines, CJ thought of Joe. He was okay, she told herself. He had to be, she reassured herself. But that didn't stop her from wanting to run across the street and ask the Marine in charge if he knew Joe. She knew it was foolish, and she doubted anyone would know Joe, and even if he were hurt, would they tell her?

The Honolulu Advertiser Building, Honolulu

When Mr. Russell and CJ entered the *Advertiser* lobby, he instructed CJ to report to Maude. "She's a little rough on the edges, but if she takes you under her wing, you'll be among the chosen few."

For some reason, CJ pictured Maude as a buxom blonde in stiletto heels and a low-cut dress. But the only thing she got right was that Maude was buxom. However, her generous cleavage had sagged to her waist several decades ago.

"Maude McCauley." Maude leaned over her desk and offered CJ her hand.

"Nice to meet you, Ma'am."

"I'm Miss Fixit or Maude. Don't call me Ma'am."

Maude's hair was haphazardly braided on her head in a lopsided swirl.

"Take a seat." Maude pointed to the chair in front of her desk.

A photographer walked by and slung a camera over his shoulder. "I'll be at Lunalilo School."

"Bring me back some gut-wrenching shots, Joel. Burned desks, blown-out windows, kids walking around what's left of their school. Got it?"

"I'm on it."

Maude fumbled through piles of papers on her desk. "Did the boss tell you that you'd be helping me with the evac lists?"

CJ didn't respond; she assumed Maude was talking to the photographer.

Maude looked up. "CJ, are you with me?"

"Yes. I mean no," CJ blurted. "I mean, Mr. Russell told me I'd be doing civilian obits. He didn't tell me anything else."

Maude handed CJ a stack of forms. "The Military Governor asked us to publish the names of every evacuee and the center they're in. The Red Cross will collect the information, but we have to organize it and print the updated list every day. There are lots of husbands who don't know where their wives are, and this will give them a chance to connect before they're evacuated."

"Evacuated? Do you mean before they're deployed to the war?"

"Not the military. Their families are being evacuated back home," Maude said. "As long as we don't have a second attack, we should be able to knock this list out in a week. But your priority is the obits. And since this is your first assignment, Mr. Russell wants to see your work himself. Have them on his desk by 3:45."

"Understood."

Maude handed CJ a letter with the *Advertiser* logo on it. "The letter authorizes you to drive any car in the reporters' pool. Keep it with you. After a while, the guards will know who you are, and you won't have to show it, but these days, they're hyper-vigilant.

"This week, you'll be chained to your desk to get all the obits done, but next week, you've got to get out there. 'Man in the street' type stuff.'"

So, she was already being considered for other assignments?

"Where do I work?" CJ asked.

"The pit." Maude pointed to a beige-painted room filled with desks. "Snatch a chair with a pillow. Your backside will thank you."

CJ smiled.

"You may not be smiling by the end of the day. My last obits girl quit after a week. She was from New York City. She couldn't adjust to the way things are done in Hawaii. She was too pushy, and my contacts shut down on her."

How different could Hawaii be? Besides, writing obits was nothing more than getting the facts: Who died? When? And where will the funeral be?

Maude took a pack of Pall Malls from her desk drawer and offered CJ a cigarette.

"Too early for me." CJ waved her hand.

"What's special about doing business in Hawaii?" CJ asked.

"You show deference." Maude lit her cigarette. "You're humble."

"You want me to be humble? Are you serious?" Mr. Spina ended every morning meeting at the *Star-Ledger* with, "Get out there and fight for your story, and I don't care what you have to do to get it."

"I'm serious as a heart attack." Maude took in a deep inhale. "In Hawaii, it's about who you know and how you treat people."

"So, how exactly do I act humbly?"

"Don't try any East Coast ramrod tactics. You thank your contact for talking to you, and you apologize."

"Apologize for what?"

"Anything. You're sorry you're bothering them. You know they have important work to do. It's raining. It doesn't matter. Don't interrupt them either. None of this talking over people crap.

"Now, normally, I'd tell you to start making calls to Queen's Hospital, but they're running around like ants—the military sent hundreds of overflow wounded—and then there's the civilian casualties."

"Are they mostly defense workers?" CJ asked.

"No. Civilians in the wrong place at the wrong time. Remember, CJ, this is a small island. When you talk to people today, chances are good they may have family that somehow suffered. Be respectful and be humble."

"Okay." Working for the *Advertiser* was going to be far different than the *Star-Ledger.*

"Now, get to work." Maude pointed to the pit.

The pit at the *Advertiser* was just like every other newspaper's. It was a cavernous room crammed with desks that were cluttered with typewriters, legal pads, and overflowing ashtrays. There was a dictionary on a stand in the corner, a bank of telephones was on the back table, and on the wall over the phones was a blackboard that had been written on and erased so many times that it looked like a smeared gray cloud.

CJ poured herself a cup of coffee. She smiled at the line of cracked and stained cups next to the Pyrex coffee urn that probably hadn't been washed in months—if ever.

She set her coffee down on her desk, emptied the ashtray, pulled a pencil out of the top drawer, and started her calls. Her first call was to Queen's Hospital; her second was to the Coroner's Office. Then, she called the smaller hospitals and mortuaries.

Among the civilian dead, there was a three-year-old girl who was playing outside with her brothers, a twelve-year-old girl standing on her porch, and an infant being fed by her mother. She tried not to think about them; she told herself not to imagine their faces.

At about eleven o'clock, a swarm of men ran into the pit and claimed typewriters. They banged out their stories, yelling out who would cover what information.

Deadlines. The lifeblood.

Bylines. The prize.

There were multiple reports of simultaneous Japanese attacks on the Philippines, Guam, Malaysia, Singapore, Hong Kong, and Wake Island.

Before coming to Hawaii, the world as CJ knew it stopped at California. The only thing she knew about the Philippines was that every Lent, the nuns would give each child a donation box to help save the poor there. Sure, there was the Orient and the Pacific Islands, but they weren't real to her; they were places she read about in *National Geographic*.

CJ worked through the morning, making calls and being put on hold or told to call back. By noon, she had collected information on six people who died of natural causes and twelve civilian dead.

She needed a break from hearing about the dead, and at lunch, she walked toward City Hall, being stopped several times by MPs ordering her away from the public buildings. The only park bench she was allowed to sit on was near a statue of a Hawaiian queen.

When she got back to the office, Maude summoned CJ with the curl of her finger.

"Eve Russell called you." Maude handed CJ a note. "Let me give you a tip: I wouldn't let it get around that you and the boss's daughter are pals. And I wouldn't let it out that you live there. Got it?" Maude held on to the note a few seconds more than she should have.

"Got it."

By the end of the day, CJ had written twenty-three obituaries.

Fifteen were civilian casualties of war, and of those, nine were children.

At 3:40, CJ stood in front of Mr. Russell's desk, clasping her obit copy to her chest.

"Let's see what you have," he said.

She handed him the obits and watched him slash through every entry with a red pencil.

Obits were a simple fill-in-the-blank assignment. It was impossible to do a lousy job!

Mr. Russell took off his glasses and laid them on his desk. "As of this afternoon, gatherings of over ten people have been declared illegal, no matter what the event. Weddings. Funerals. Christmas services."

"But they have to be buried." It was a half-question.

CJ told Mr. Russell that Hosoi Mortuary had such an overflow of bodies that they negotiated with a local restaurant to store bodies in their freezers.

"I have no idea what's going to happen," he said. "They seem to be making up the rules as they go along." He paused. "But as far as your writing goes, good job. The little vignettes you wrote—you have a talent for human interest stories."

She said, "Thank you, sir." But she was afraid he had her pinned to write sentimental copy squeezed between ads for wheelchairs and hearing aids.

"It doesn't sound like you mean it."

CJ chided herself for having a face that always telegraphed what she was thinking.

"Covering the war is my goal," she said.

Mr. Russell smirked. "Yes, the cub reporter's dream." He opened the bottom drawer of his desk and took out a bottle of Scotch. "There are lots of ways to cover the war." He took out two glasses and set them on the desk.

And she knew how she wanted to cover it—shoulder to shoulder with the men reporting it, not interviewing women huddled over kitchen tables—and not running away, sobbing on a curb.

"They're going to bury 1500 sailors in Nuuanu Cemetery. It's going to be a three-star dog and pony show for the Department of War. Covering that will tell a different side of war."

He filled the glasses and handed one to CJ. "I was at Yale during the First World War. I enlisted to be a correspondent the day after graduation, but the Army, in its infinite wisdom, sent me to Fort Bliss, Texas, for the duration. The closest I came to combat was witnessing bar fights between cowboys and soldiers. But I had a classmate who was a war correspondent in France. He was a tough son of a bitch. A South Boston Irishman." Mr. Russell downed his drink. "After the war, he killed himself. A lot of war correspondents did."

He held up the bottle as if to ask CJ if she wanted another drink, but she shook her head no.

"I had another buddy who was a correspondent at Verdun. He told me that twenty years after the war, he still saw the faces of the dead."

CJ flashed the face of the sailor whose skin slid onto her hand. She smelled the charred bodies. "I was on Ford Island the day of the attack."

"Do you live on Ford Island?"

"No. I was staying in a hotel in Waikiki and snuck out there to get the story." She looked down, twisting her wedding ring. "When I got there, it was nothing like the newsreels. There were so many wounded. I couldn't handle it." Her eyes welled up and she gritted her teeth to keep from crying. She wasn't going to have her boss think she couldn't cover the hard stories. "It toughened me," she said. "I'll be ready for it the next time."

Mr. Russell put his drink down. "I just told you that men who were trained to deal with covering war couldn't handle it."

But Liz Townsend was out there, and when she was at the dispensary, she saw other women at the dispensary who didn't crumble.

"I'd say you've got good instincts as a journalist to get yourself out there…and a hell of a lot of grit. But as a father of girls your age, I'm not sure I'd want you out there."

"Liz Townsend was out there," CJ said.

"Liz has been covering the war in Europe for the last two years, and before that, she covered the Spanish Revolution. The reason she's in Hawaii is because, as you put it, she 'couldn't handle it' anymore. She came here to get away from war."

"I know Liz didn't get to where she is now overnight," CJ said. "I'm ready to put in my time."

"If that's the life you want, CJ, then go for it. Just be aware, it's a choice that comes with a heavy price." He handed her the afternoon edition. "But Liz can write more than war stories, she can turn in a solid human interest pieces too." He handed her the afternoon edition of the paper. "Take a look at her coverage of the McCully fires."

CJ glanced at the article. It was a front-page story about a soaked, dog-eared cookbook from the Chinese Christian Church. In her piece, Liz imagined the recipes in that book being used to make holiday meals in a house that was now gone.

"It's a nice angle," he said. "Learn from her."

Lesson Two from Liz: Watch your back.

Honpa Hongwanji Buddhist Mission, Honolulu

While CJ was having her first day at the *Advertiser,* Eve was at the evac center. When she arrived that morning, Ruth was in the courtyard surrounded by several Japanese women—all of them in Western dress; there wasn't a kimono in sight. Their words were a blur of English and Japanese. The consistent English words Eve heard were F.B.I., shoot, and spy.

Eve asked Shimeji to interpret, and Shimeji explained what had happened in her own home: At about 2 a.m. there had been a knock on the door. Two Honolulu Police Department officers demanded that Bishop Kanazawa go with them. They were respectful, Shimeji said, and told him he would probably be back home in an hour.

"At least they gave him time to dress," Shimeji added, "Some of the other men were taken away in their bedclothes."

Then, each woman, in turn, told her own story. The details varied, but the facts were the same: In the middle of the night or the early hours of the morning, their husbands had been taken away for questioning. Some were "arrested" by the F.B.I., others by the Honolulu Police Department, and all the women had been assured that their husbands would return home within an hour.

But none of the men came back.

"They are all good men," Shimeji said. "Kutsunai-san's husband is a bank president, Ishii-san's husband is a professor at the university, and Mori-san's husband is a lawyer."

"I'm sure they'll be back today." Ruth explained to the women that the questioning was routine, that information had to be gathered from all sources, and that the first place to start would be the community leaders

Mrs. Ishii came forward. She was a tall woman with an erect posture. "I asked if I could follow my husband to where he was being taken, that I would wait for him in the car, and when the questioning was over, I could drive him home. The police officers laughed. One of them said, 'That'll be a long wait.'"

"Sometimes things take longer than expected," Ruth said,

Eve glared at Ruth. "Those men deserved respect," then she turned to Shimeji. "I'll call my father to see what was going on, and as soon as I find something out, I'll let you know."

As Ruth and Eve walked to the office, Ruth defended the questioning. "Eve, it's a routine procedure. They'll detain them, question them, and let them go home."

"Detained?! Is that what you call it? They were nabbed in the middle of the night." Eve quickened her pace to get away from Ruth.

When they got to Eve's office, Eriko was sitting at the desk, crying, clutching a crumpled tissue.

"Not Hiroki, too!" Eve said.

"This morning." Eriko nodded. "They banged on the door so loud, it woke up the boys, and they came out to see what was going on. The police ordered Hiroki to go with them, and when he asked to change from his pajamas, the policeman went into the bedroom and watched him." Eriko sobbed. "My husband is a proud man."

Eve snapped at Ruth, "Is this what you call 'routine?'" Eve dialed the telephone. "I'm calling my father."

The conversation was brief. Eve nodded and listened. She took notes and assured him, "I'll take care of it, Pops. I love you."

When Eve hung up, she announced, "300 Japanese, 100 Germans, Italians, and Austrians have been picked up. Anyone with a foreign passport. One of the men was my father's shoemaker!"

"Is he a foreign national?" Ruth asked.

"How the hell should I know?" Eve threw up her hands. "He's from New York. Is that foreign enough for you?" Eve opened the top drawer and pulled out a set of keys.

"You need to calm down," Ruth said. "Just take a minute and listen to me. They need to do what they're doing."

"And the way they're doing it?" Eve flared.

"I admit, it could have been handled differently, but if you look at it, it's the logical thing to do."

Eriko's words were simple. "The logic is, if you're Japanese, you are the enemy."

Eve pulled her purse off the bookshelf. "Here's the logic, Ruth. Mr. Petrelli has been my father's shoemaker all my life. His wife is a hairdresser at the base. She was taken too and they have an eight-year-old daughter who has been left alone in the house after her parents were 'detained,' as you call it. How's that logic for you?"

"I'm sure they'll have Family Welfare Department pick up the girl."

"Judas H. Priest, Ruth! Do you have a heart beating in you? You're going to put her in Child Welfare!" Eve turned to Eriko. "I'm going to the Petrelli's house to pick up the girl and take her to the Sisters of the Sacred Hearts convent. Pops already arranged for her to stay there until her parents are released. I don't know how long I'll be gone. If I'm not back by noon, call my father again. He should know more by then."

Ruth's tone was apologetic. "Eriko, I'm sure your husband is safe."

Eriko bristled. "And as soon as he comes home, he can explain to my son that being Japanese is now a reason to be arrested."

Chapter Ten

December 8, 1941

The Russell Estate, Nuuanu

WHEN CJ AND Eve got home that night, Mrs. Russell told CJ
that she had just missed a call from Joe and that he would call back
at ten o'clock.

"Did he say anything else?" CJ asked.

"He was quite gracious," Mrs. Russell said. "He thanked me for
opening our home to you."

CJ could tell Mrs. Russell was pleased with Joe's gratitude, but
she was more interested in how he was. "How did he sound?"

"Quite robust."

CJ wanted to hear more than "robust." She wanted Mrs. Russell
to tell her that Joe was safe and unharmed and that he loved her.

That afternoon, the entire Russell family gathered for an early
dinner. Ginger rushed in at the last minute, just in time to beat the
4:30 curfew.

CJ drifted in and out of their conversation. She tried imagining Joe at work but had never seen his office. She couldn't picture him at his desk, who was with him, or what he was doing. And while CJ was lost in her own thoughts, Eve fumed about the incarcerations.

"For God's sake, Pops? Your shoemaker?" Eve huffed. "And pastry chefs from the Halekulani? What were they going to do, bake secret messages in their tortes?"

"I heard they picked up Mr. and Mrs. Preiss. Of all people!" Mrs. Russell said. "Graham, you need to print that. People should know what's going on."

"Loretta, I've got military censors breathing down my throat. We can't put out a weather report. Do you think they'll let me report detentions?"

Mrs. Russell said, "Reverend Kennedy's wife told me he can't schedule any weddings or funerals. No memorial services. Nothing. Can you imagine?"

"If there are no funerals, what's going to happen to the bodies?" Ginger asked.

"They're being stored in mortuaries until further notice," Mr. Russell told Ginger, sparing her the full truth that some were being stored in restaurant freezers.

CJ was undone, but she pretended to be strong, all the while aching to hear from Joe. She wanted to be able to call her family.

She wanted to go back to Ford Island. She wanted to prove herself. She wanted to tell the story of the war.

All of Hawaii was a war zone. Children played in playgrounds, running around trucks and tanks. Pet dogs were being recruited for military security. Truth and rumor flowed, and the Military Governor dictated daily life.

All through dinner, CJ listened to the litany of restrictions, sneaking a look at her watch every few minutes and calculating how long it would be until Joe called.

At eight o'clock, with everyone else listening to the radio in the blacked-out living room, CJ excused herself and went to her bedroom. At five minutes to ten, she padded down the stairs in the dark and huddled on the floor in front of the telephone table.

Ten o'clock came and went, and Joe hadn't called. Ten fifteen. Ten thirty.

She put the phone in her lap and her hand on the receiver, ready to pick it up on the first ring. Wait fifteen more minutes, she told herself.

At ten-forty, Joe called.

"CJ?"

At the sound of Joe's voice, CJ cradled the phone. "I love you, Joe."

"I love you, too, babe."

"Are you okay?" CJ blurted.

"Perfect," Joe said.

"Are you sure?"

"I'm fine."

"Don't lie to me, Joe." She held the phone tighter.

Joe laughed. "I didn't think being accused of lying would be the first thing out of your mouth."

"I'm sorry," CJ said. "I love you."

"You're sorry you love me?" Joe mocked her.

"Stop joking. It's not funny."

"I'm fine, CJ. I'm safe and unhurt, and my men are all good." Joe's tone quieted. "I even got a telegram out to my folks telling them we're both okay, and I asked them to call your parents." He paused. "I don't know if I can face your father ever again. I told him I'd keep you safe. Look babe, I never saw this coming—"

"Stop," CJ said.

"If anything happens to me, Linc has my—"

"I'm not listening to you."

"You've got to be ready if it happens."

"I'm not listening."

"You know all wives are being evacuated," he said. "You'll be home soon."

"I'm not going anywhere," CJ said.

"You won't have a choice."

"I want to see you."

"I have no idea when I'll get off base."

A guy yelled at Joe. "Come on, Delano. Cut it short."

"What's going on?" CJ asked.

"The line for the phone is a mile long. We get two minutes each, that's it."

"Joe, I've got to see you."

"I'd never let you near the place, CJ."

"I'll camp at the front gate. You know I will."

"No one should ever have to see what happened."

Someone else yelled, "Delano, my watch says your time's up."

CJ whispered, "I was on Ford Island on Sunday."

"CJ, what did you say? I couldn't hear you."

"Nothing."

"I love you, babe. Take care of yourself."

"I promise."

Joe hung up, and CJ sat on the floor, cradling the phone to her chest. It was almost eleven p.m. in Hawaii. 5000 miles away, it was four a.m. in New Jersey. Her father would be finishing up the bread dough. At six a.m., her mother would walk down the steps to the bakery. She'd put on her apron, then kiss her fingers and tap the picture of Saint Honore hanging on the wall.

"Good morning, Patrone."

Saint Honore was the patron saint of bakers.

"Pray for us and keep us safe," she would say.

But she knew that even if her mother prayed to every saint in heaven, there were no guarantees of safety. CJ headed back upstairs to bed.

Ten minutes later, the phone rang. It had to be Joe; she grabbed her robe and hurried downstairs. But when she answered the phone, the call was from the 7th Army Air Command for Mrs. Russell.

"Do you mean Mr. Russell?" CJ asked.

"No, Loretta Russell."

She wondered why the Army would call Mrs. Russell in the middle of the night. She went upstairs and rapped on their bedroom door until Mrs. Russell answered.

"The 7th Air Command is on the phone for you. Not Mr. Russell."

CHAPTER ELEVEN
DECEMBER 9, 1941

The Russell Estate, Nuuanu

THE NEXT MORNING, Mrs. Russell held court at the breakfast table. "I received a call from General Davidson last night." The Cheshire cat would have envied her grin. "He asked me to recommend the names of 50 girls between the ages of 18 and 25 who would be interested in being candidates for a secret Army Air Corps unit. They must be intelligent, physically fit, and come from good families. And he's leaving the selection in my hands."

Mrs. Russell continued, "All the volunteers must be willing to be sequestered on a military base, although they wouldn't have to stay there every night. My first calls will be to Mrs. Miller and Mrs. Frost."

"They're a bit past 25," Eve joked.

Mrs. Russell held her coffee cup mid-air and glowered at Eve. "I'm referring to Sarah and Maili."

"Sarah might do it," Ginger said.

"What about you, Ginger?" her mother asked.

"Me?" Ginger raised her eyebrows. "I'm quite happy at the Motor Corps." She looked at Eve and grinned. "What about Eve?"

Mrs. Russell's answer was quick. "I don't think the requirements suit Eve."

"In what way is that, Mother?" Eve asked.

"Let's not discuss this now."

"What do you think, Pops?" Eve asked her father, but her eyes were locked on her mother.

"Eve, this isn't a sorority project. You can't quit when you get bored."

"What do you say, Pops? Do I have it in me?"

Mr. Russell answered, "I think the war will be over before they get any women's unit together."

Eve turned to her mother. "I am officially volunteering, Mother. How about you, CJ? Want to join up with me? Do our part for the war?"

Before CJ could answer, Mrs. Russell explained that all military dependents were being transported back to the States. "No one under orders to evacuate may be considered."

CJ said, "I heard about families being evacuated, but I thought it was only those who wanted to go."

"No," Mrs. Russell said, "The first ship leaves Thursday."

"What if I don't want to leave?" CJ asked.

"That's not an option, dear," Mrs. Russell said.

Mr. Russell raised his index finger. "Actually, if I can designate CJ as an 'essential person' at the newspaper, she won't be required to leave."

"Would you do that?" CJ asked.

"I'll look into it," he said.

Eve turned to her father. "So, Pops, are you going to look into getting me into this secret unit?"

"I have to side with your mother on this one," he answered.

Eve threw her napkin on her plate. "Thanks for the support, Pops."

Mrs. Russell talked over Eve. "This is exactly what I'm talking about. You're still throwing tantrums like a three-year-old."

She pushed back from the table. "Please, excuse me. I'm going to my room to throw a tantrum."

Mrs. Russell apologized to CJ, "I'm sorry you had to witness that."

So was CJ.

Ginger followed Eve.

"You may as well go too." Mrs. Russell waved her hand at CJ.

Eve was lying on her bed. "Did you hear him? He always takes her side. And she'll take any side that's against me," Eve said.

"That's not what I heard this time," Ginger said.

"What exactly did you hear?" Eve's tone was sharp.

"I heard a man trying to please two strong women without getting stomped on."

"Stomped on? So, I'm a bull?" Eve turned to CJ. "What do you hear, CJ?"

CJ weighed her answer before she spoke. "Eve, do you honestly want to join this unit?"

"What I want to do is to go back to Mills."

CJ thought she could lighten the mood with a joke. "I'd like to be working at the *New York Times,* but we can't always get what we want."

Eve didn't appreciate CJ's humor. She shot back, "Thank you, Miss High and Mighty."

"Sorry," CJ said.

Eve turned to Ginger. "You know there's no way I can get through this war living with Mother."

"What about volunteering for the Red Cross on an outer island?" Ginger said. "Kauai has a big unit."

"And you think Mother's going to allow that?" Eve sat up and mocked her mother's voice. "Oh, yes, Mrs. Wilcox, my daughter did request volunteering on Kauai, but I'm afraid I need her here in Honolulu." Eve cocked her head and aped an overly broad smile.

"You're right," Ginger agreed.

"Honestly, I'll pay the Army room and board if they'd let me join."

CJ said, "I don't think it works that way."

"Parker told me if he gets deployed, I can live in his bungalow. Then I'd have a place of my own, at the beach, without my mother."

"Well, let's hope Parker gets deployed," Ginger said.

"You know that's not what I want," Eve said. "I've just got to get out of this house."

Honpa Hongwanji Buddhist Mission, Honolulu

That morning at the evac center, Ruth was at her desk at six a.m. At nine o'clock, there was a knock on the door.

"Come in!" Ruth barked, still jabbing at her notepad. "All right! I'll take twelve—but I expect the rest by Friday. And don't tell me you'll try. Get it done." She slammed the phone down.

The door creaked open.

"With that tone, maybe I shouldn't come in."

She caught her breath. "Gordon!" She crossed the room in two strides and threw her arms around him. Her whole body locked against his.

"I love you, Ruth." He held her shoulders and stepped back. "Let me get a good look at you."

She laughed and spun around like a runway model.

"You look exhausted."

"You don't look so good yourself!" she countered. "In fact, you look like hell." Her perfectly squared-away husband sported a wrinkled uniform and mud-crusted shoes.

"Forgive me. I'm an idiot," he said and brushed her hair back from her forehead. "You've never looked so beautiful."

There was another knock.

A YBA girl opened the door. "Miss Ruth, the man from Sanitation Laundry is here. He's asking about the diapers." The girl looked from Ruth to Gordon.

Ruth told her, "Miss Eve can take care of that."

"I already looked for her but I couldn't find her."

"Check the storeroom."

The girl nodded and ducked out.

As the door clicked shut, Gordon's voice changed. "We need to talk."

The phrase had a tone. A signal. She braced herself for the news.

"I'm being deployed."

How could that be? Comm officers don't deploy.

"When?"

"You know I can't say."

"Where are you going?"

"Ruth, please don't ask me."

"You know I'll find out."

"Not this time."

Gordon had deployed before—Cuba, Hong Kong, and Singapore—and typically, the officers' wives' club had the information before the command issued its statement. But she knew this time was different.

"You owe it to me, Gordon. Where are you going?" She wasn't backing down.

Gordon hesitated.

"Australia."

"Australia." She exhaled. The British wouldn't let anything happen there.

"There's more," he said, "The Navy is evacuating all dependents."

"I know." She waved her hand over a stack of papers on her desk. "That's the list of the first evacuees."

"Have you read it?"

"I've been a bit busy."

"Your name's on it, Ruth."

If her name was on it, she knew Gordon must have put it there.

"The first ship is for widows and pregnant women." She knew what was coming next.

"Your father called Admiral Kimmel, and Kimmel put you on the list himself."

Not Gordon. Not her father. Admiral Kimmel!

"You know I hate that sort of thing." Ruth heard it all her life. RHIP. Rank has its privileges

"Your father doesn't want you to be here alone," Gordon said.

"My father? Not you?"

"I admit it. I don't want you alone either."

There was a second knock on the door, and the same YBA girl came in. "Miss Eve's not in the storeroom, and the laundry man needs to talk to someone in charge."

"Tell him to wait in the parking lot. I'll be right there."

The girl left.

"Isn't there anyone else these people can go to?" Gordon's voice had an edge to it.

"Is there anyone else who can go to Australia?"

"Ruth, listen to me. You need to go home. If you don't want to stay with your parents, stay with your sister."

"With her three kids and Richard?"

"Why not go now? What's the difference? You'll be evacuated anyway. Who knows, maybe they'll send out more ships next week, and you'll be gone then?"

"I will go when I'm slated to go."

"I could rest easy if I knew you were safe," Gordon said.

"So, this is for your sake?"

"We all think this is best for you."

"We? Am I part of this 'We?'"

"Ruth, do you understand? Your father called Admiral Kimmel for a favor."

She understood exactly. Her father never asked for favors, he never granted them, and he judged men who did from his high moral horse.

"Your mother knows a doctor at Georgetown Hospital who is supposed to be the best pregnancy specialist in the country. She could arrange for you to see him. Maybe it's a simple thing?"

"Simple? Our daughter died!"

"I lost Grace, too, Ruth."

"And the other two?" Maybe Gordon didn't count miscarriages.

"Staying here won't bring Grace back."

"That was unkind!"

"Ruth, please go home. Let your mother take care of you."

"She'll parade me around to all her friends, 'Poor little Ruthie. She can't hold on to a baby, and when she does, it dies.'"

"Stop it, Ruth!"

Another knock on the door.

Ruth yelled, "Not now!"

"Okay," a faint voice answered from outside the door.

Gordon took Ruth in his arm. "I lost a daughter, too, Ruth."

"It's not the same." It was Ruth who carried her, felt her grow inside her, felt her move.

"All I'm asking is that you let someone else take care of you."

"If I go home, I feel like I'm abandoning her again."

Gordon's tone was soft. "I don't want to lose you, too."

"Lose me, too?" She pushed him away. "I'm not the one going off to war!"

"Who's being unkind now?"

Ruth buried her face in her hands. "I want it all to go away…"

"Maybe we can try again," Gordon said.

"For another miscarriage? Or a stillborn baby?"

"We'll get through this, Ruth. We'll have our baby."

She couldn't see how.

"We'll figure it out. Please, go home."

Ruth knew she would be evacuated sooner rather than later. She'd live with her parents in D.C. and she'd let her mother take her to the pregnancy specialist, because that's what good wives and daughters do.

She took a deep breath. "You're right."

"I love you, Ruth."

Love wasn't the issue.

"I can pick you up tomorrow to drive you to our quarters," he said.

"The Red Cross has buses scheduled for evacuees to go home and pack," she said. "The Makalapa bus is scheduled for the morning."

"Don't take the bus. I can pick you up. How about noon?"

"I should be on the bus with the other wives."

"Don't be stubborn, Ruth. Maybe we can sneak in an hour or two just for ourselves."

Time alone with him…the last time before he leaves.

"The limit for luggage is two full-size suitcases and a shoulder bag," he said.

"I know. I have all the orders on my desk."

"If we go together, I can help you pack."

"Fine."

She never needed help packing before, and things were not fine. She knew it and Gordon knew it. But what were her choices? Have her father call Admiral Kimmel? To say what? Thanks for the favor, Admiral, but my daughter's declined.

She never had a choice.

CHAPTER TWELVE
DECEMBER 9, 1941

Honpa Hongwanji Buddhist Mission, Honolulu

AFTER RUTH DEALT with the Sanitation Laundryman, she called Mrs. Russell to tell her she was leaving. Mrs. Russell didn't seem surprised, "I'm so glad you're getting out on the first ship. You deserve it."

Ruth cringed at the words "deserve it." She said, "We need to discuss appointing the new Director." She assumed it would be an easy transition and Eve would step up, so she was shocked when Mrs. Russell said, "I'd like to appoint Eriko Fujimoto as the Director."

"Eriko?"

"She'll be an asset as a liaison to the Japanese community. How are her administrative skills?" Mrs. Russell asked.

"Good."

"Does she get along with the staff?"

Ruth began her answer slowly. "Eriko's husband has been detained. No one can locate him, and she has two children at home. I'm not sure she's the right candidate at this time."

"Of course she is," Mrs. Russell insisted. "And being the Director of the Hongwanji Evacuation Center will only facilitate Hiroki's release."

Maybe there was some truth to that, but Ruth doubted it.

"Do you think she's capable of managing the center?" Mrs. Russell asked.

"I suppose."

"So, you have no reservations about her?"

"No, but Mrs. Russell, Eve knows every businessman and tradesman on the island. She gets things done in one phone call."

"Good. Then it's settled," Mrs. Russell said. "I'll call Eriko this afternoon." And she hung up.

✍

Eve was in the Community Room inventorying sheets when Ruth told her she would be evacuated on Thursday.

"That's great!" Eve hugged her. "First ship out! You must have a godmother pulling strings for you."

"My father called Admiral Kimmel. I'm not proud of it."

"Come on, Ruth, everybody does it. Don't be so self-righteous."

Eve's words stung. Ruth had called her father self-righteous all her life.

"You've had a tough year," Eve said. "How long has it been? Six months?"

"It'll be nine months on Christmas."

The Russell family were among the few civilians at Grace's memorial service.

"Ruth, go home."

"I have other not-so-good news." There were no words that would soften the blow. "Your mother appointed Eriko as the center's director."

At first, Eve didn't react, then she smiled. "Of course, she did."

"I'm sorry," Ruth said. "I assumed…"

Eve waved her hand dismissively. "My mother is nothing if not consistent. And, honestly, can you picture me working directly for her?"

When Eve first told stories about her mother, Ruth wondered why Eve would paint such a vindictive portrait. But the more she was exposed to Mrs. Russell, the more she wondered how Eve could tolerate her mother's vengefulness.

Eve clapped her hands together. "Let's get the office ready for Eriko!"

Chapter Thirteen
December 10, 1941

The Russell Estate, Nuuanu

THE NEXT MORNING, the first thing Mr. Russell said to CJ on the drive to work was that Liz Townsend was ill and wouldn't be at the paper.

Still steaming about the cookbook Liz had taken, CJ couldn't care less about the woman's health.

Mr. Russell continued, "Now, I don't have anyone to cover the burial at Nuuanu."

CJ held her breath, hoping he would offer it to her.

"It's a big human interest piece," he said.

Human interest, true, but it was going to be a front-page story.

"Do you think you can handle it?" he asked.

"Absolutely!" This was her shot. "Should I contact Liz about the details?"

"No, call the Protocol Officer at Pearl Harbor. He'll tell you all you need to know. There's a military phone directory in the pit."

The phone directory was on the back table, sandwiched between a pile of military binders.

CJ found the Protocol Officer's number, and with a bit more digging, she found the number for the Marine Corps Military Police at Ford Island. Joe's office! And as soon as she finished with the Protocol Officer, she called Joe.

A Private Shelling answered the phone in typical military form. He stated his name and unit, smashing it all into one word, followed by a "May I help you, sir?"

When CJ identified herself as Joe's wife, the private asked her how she was. She found it a bit odd, but charming. She told him she was fine, and he answered, "I'm so pleased to hear that, Ma'am."

When she repeated the conversation to Joe, he said, "Shelling's a nice kid, and he's a good admin secretary."

"I have news," CJ said. "There's a Memorial Service for the Pearl Harbor dead at Nuuanu Cemetery. It starts at 11:30 a.m., and Mr. Russell asked me to cover it. I was wondering if…maybe… if you could sneak away for a bit to see me?" She pushed. "Just five minutes. It's a Memorial Service. I'm sure your CO will give you permission."

Joe hemmed and hawed until CJ wore him down.

"I'll work something out," he said.

Nuuanu Cemetery, Honolulu

CJ had never been to a military funeral before, let alone one of this significance. She stood at the crest of the hill of the cemetery, notebook in hand. The Protocol Officer told her he expected 700 attendees. From her vantage point, she could see a bird's eye view of Honolulu, and in the distance, the hulks of burned-out ships still smoldering at Pearl Harbor.

Dignitaries streamed onto the grandstand. CJ recognized Mayor Petrie. To his left was a woman she assumed was Mrs. Petrie, and to Mrs. Petrie's left was Mrs. Russell. CJ asked the staff photographer to get a shot of all three of them. She also requested a long shot of the rows of wooden crosses marking the newly dug graves, and a close up of the word "Unknown" on one of the crosses.

The air was heavy with the smell of upturned dirt and the lei draped on each cross. The sun was intense and the heat was sweltering. Her makeup dripped down her cheeks and she could almost feel the humidity curl her hair.

She wished Mr. Russell could have told her she was going to Nuuanu at breakfast, instead of in the car on the way to work.

She would have worn the yellow polka-dot dress just on the chance that she'd get to see Joe.

She looked around. There were Marines in the Color Guard, several senior officers on the grandstand, but no other Marines that she could see.

She scanned the parking lot. But no Joe.

A Mormon elder opened the service with an invocation. He was followed by a welcome by the mayor and the color guard.

She took notes, swiveling her head between the podium and the parking lot, searching for Joe.

There were speeches from Admiral Sandley and Justice Roberts. CJ half-listened. She asked the photographer to get shots of the Gold Star Mothers, a few of the Red Cross volunteers, the Girl Scouts, the YBA girls, and the McKinley High School band.

As Justice Roberts finished his speech, CJ spotted Joe. He was walking straight for her. She waved, but he didn't wave back. She ran toward him, then stopped short, embarrassed when she realized the Marine wasn't Joe, then she double-backed toward the ceremony where the Captain of the Honolulu Fire Department tapped the microphone as the Oahu Girl Choir took the stage. The captain introduced Malia Kamekea, the daughter of Lieutenant Kamakea, a member of Fire House Number 4, who lost his life at Hickam Field fighting fires.

Malia was to sing *Mai Poina Iau.* The English translation is "Don't Forget Me."

CJ told the photographer, "Get a shot of her singing, and if anyone on the grandstand starts tearing up, make sure you get it."

The longer the program went on, the more CJ doubted Joe would show up. During Mayor Petrie's closing remarks, she was convinced he wasn't coming.

The mayor thanked the veterans of World War I for building 250 wooden crosses and the Boy Scouts for painting them. He also acknowledged the gravediggers who worked through the night to prepare the ground.

CJ mentally sketched out her piece. "They all mourned—the Garden Club who collected backyard flowers for the bouquets, the wounded in wheelchairs giving witness to their comrades, the Red Cross Gray Ladies standing in for the families of the dead.

Over one thousand grieving families would receive telegrams from 'a grateful nation.' They would hang a gold star pennant from their window and mourn a son whose body was buried in Hawaii, not knowing if his remains would ever be returned to them."

She was lost in thought when she saw him. "Joe!"

She ran up and threw her arms around him. But he kept his arms at his sides. Maybe he wasn't supposed to hug in uniform?

Joe stepped back, held CJ by her shoulders and, in a carefully controlled tone, asked, "What were you doing at Pearl during the attack?"

She stalled for time. "What do you mean?"

"Private Shelling was the MP who found you. He said you were hysterical."

That's why Shelling was so familiar with her on the phone.

She wriggled her shoulders from Joe's grasp. "I was not hysterical."

"But you were there? And I find out about it from one of my privates."

"I told you I was there the first time you called. It's not my fault you didn't hear me."

"You knew I didn't hear you? And you didn't bring it up again?"

"Because I knew you'd be angry."

"Damn right I'm angry."

"Joe, it was the biggest story of my life. I wasn't going to stay in a hotel."

"You could've been killed."

"But I wasn't."

Joe rubbed his temples. "Don't you get it? It's my job to protect you. If anything happened to you, it would have been my fault."

"No! It would have been *my* fault. I'm the one who went out there. It was my decision."

"Look, CJ, I didn't mind you working until we started a family, but war reporting?"

"You didn't mind!" What the hell was he thinking? "I'm not one of your Marines you can order around. I'm a reporter. I wanted to get the story!" She wasn't backing down.

"What was your angle going to be? Dying sailors?"

"My angle? I went out there to tell the true story."

"You are not a reporter here. You're my wife!" He turned to walk away.

She put her hand on his shoulder. "Joe."

He shrugged it off and kept walking.

"Wait. Please, Joe." She struggled to keep her voice steady. "I don't want to make a scene. Please, don't go."

Joe turned. "The first thing I did after Shelling told me you were out there was to talk to my CO. He got your name on the next evac ship."

"I'm not going anywhere," she said. "I'm staying right here and covering the war."

"What are you going to do when the MPs come? Tell them you're CJ Martino, and no one tells you what to do?"

"It's who I am!"

"I love you, CJ, but don't you ever get tired of fighting?"

"I'm not a military wife!" She wasn't backing down.

Joe shook his head. "I'm not sure you're a wife at all."

"What's that supposed to mean?"

"You only think of yourself."

"What am I supposed to do? Consult you on everything I do?"

"Exactly. It's called marriage."

CJ wasn't going to give in. "I'm staying in Hawaii." Maybe she was pushing too far, but she was arguing to win.

"Let the MPs deal with you," Joe said. "I've got to get back to work."

CJ watched him walk to his car. She almost called out to him, but she had her pride, and she stood there and watched him careen out of the parking lot.

The Honolulu Advertiser Building, Honolulu

When CJ got back to the *Advertiser*, she banged out her article like she was pounding out a fight—slamming keys, flinging the carriage return.

Let Joe try to stop her. She was going to stay in Hawaii, she'd write, and she'd become the best damn reporter the island had ever had.

She turned in her copy to Mr. Russell, braced for the critique. She expected him to say that it wasn't objective. Too emotional. Maybe it was. Maybe she had let her feelings bleed into the page.

But how could she not? 2500 men were dead—sons, brothers, lovers, fathers.

When Mr. Russell told her that her piece was "professional yet compassionate," she was elated. It was exactly what she wanted to hear, but she kept echoing the caveats of her female Columbia professors: Don't let them pigeonhole you in soft piece. Heartstrings and handkerchiefs. Men don't write them. Why should we?

She knew they were right, but she was discovering that she loved writing them.

CHAPTER FOURTEEN
DECEMBER 11-12, 1941

Honpa Hongwanji Buddhist Mission, Honolulu

THE FOLLOWING DAY at Hongwanji, Ruth finished off the last of her reports, grabbed her purse, and waited for Gordon in the parking lot.

Gordon was fifteen minutes late. He was never late, but she told herself that these were extraordinary days.

She leaned back on the garden bench, put her face to the sun. She would miss Hawaii. Miss the weather, the flowers, but most of all, she'd miss her visits with Grace and she hoped her sister would help her through that grief. She imagined herself going to D.C. with Susan seeing the National Christmas tree, going to a *Messiah* concert, shopping at Garfinkel's. She was looking forward to late-night talks sharing things she only could with her sister.

When a government car pulled up in the parking lot, Ruth

sat up. The car stopped, but it wasn't Gordon driving—it was his secretary, Mrs. Keller.

Mrs. Keller leaned over and waved. "Get in, kiddo. The Commander's busier than a one-armed paper hanger, and I volunteered to take you to Makalapa."

Ruth got in and Mrs. Keller ceremoniously lifted a napkin from a basket. "Just in case you missed my coconut muffins. I made you a fresh dozen."

"Is Gordon okay?" Ruth asked.

"He's fine. Just busy." Mrs. Keller leaned over the basket to hug Ruth. "When I heard the news that you're going home, my prayers were answered. You need to be pampered, not taking care of everyone else all the time."

But it was Mrs. Keller who was the angel of caring. When Ruth came home from the hospital after Grace died, Mrs. Keller visited her every day, bringing movie magazines, office gossip, and her famous coconut muffins.

"The Commander said we've got to be out of the house by noon. So, tell me what you need me to it. I'm pretty good at following orders."

"That's not what I hear from Gordon." Ruth smiled. "You've got him thinking he works for you."

Mrs. Keller shrugged off the remark. "Commanders come and

go, but your husband is one in a million. He's a real gentleman. I'll miss him."

"Miss him?" There was something in the tone of Mrs. Keller's voice.

"They all get transferred eventually."

Ruth wasn't sure that was what Mrs. Keller meant.

During their drive, Mrs. Keller filled Ruth in on the news at the Communication Center, mixing wedding bell news with classified information. Lieutenant Bennett married the blonde nurse from Oklahoma the night before he shipped out. The code breakers were working around the clock, sleeping on cots, and smelling like they hadn't showered in days. Truth be told, they were walking around like zombies, until the *Lex* went out to sea. "That's when they got crazy and ran around like chickens with their heads cut off."

Ruth had no idea how many security breaches Mrs. Keller had just committed.

Makalapa Housing

When they arrived at the Makalapa gate, an armed guard inspected their identification cards and the letter authorizing Ruth's entry into the housing area.

Makalapa looked like a ghost town. No cars or bicycles were

on the streets. No women pushed baby carriages along the side-walks. The playgrounds were empty.

A fine layer of ash blanketed the buildings, and as Ruth stepped out of the car, the acrid scent of smoldering ships from the harbor gagged her.

The handrail on her front porch had a coating of soot, as did the doorknob, the living room floor, and the kitchen counters. In the kitchen sink lay her tray of burned biscuits.

Mrs. Keller placed her hands on her hips. "I see I've got my work cut out for me."

Ruth didn't want Mrs. Keller to clean her house, but she was relieved to be left alone to pack.

She proceeded to her bedroom. Gordon's uniforms were missing; he had likely taken them to his office, sleeping there on a cot. No wonder he'd been so disheveled the last time she saw him.

Ruth picked up the invitation for a Christmas tea at the Kimmel's home off her dresser. Just days ago, it had seemed so important.

She began packing from the closet. Most of her winter clothes were in storage, but it didn't matter; she and Susan wore the same size. Susan could loan her coats and sweaters. She sifted through her drawers, packing her "good" jewelry and all essential papers. She wanted to pack a few photo albums, but space was limited.

The only item left was the Lynch family christening gown, stored on the top shelf of Grace's closet.

She stood at the threshold of Grace's room, her hand hovering over the doorknob. Months had passed since she last entered. It still felt like trespassing.

The first time Ruth entered Grace's room was a month after her passing. When she did open the door, she felt as barren as the room.

Before Ruth came home from the hospital, Gordon had cleared everything out. The crib, the changing table, the rocking chair—he donated them all to the Welfare Closet.

The luminescent stars that he pasted to the ceiling were scraped away, and the whimsical stencil of the Cow Jumping Over the Moon was painted over.

Ruth stepped inside, reluctantly. She took the cardboard box off the closet shelf as if it were a sacred relic. Sitting cross-legged on the floor, she lifted the lid and held up the embroidered lace gown. Bringing it to her face, she inhaled deeply, searching for a trace of her daughter. There was no scent, no lingering essence.

She remembered the nurse carrying Grace into her room, cradling her head with reverence, as if Grace was merely sleeping.

Ruth had expected Grace's lips to be gray, but they were pink. Her skin was rosy and a soft ginger fuzz crowned her head. But

Grace's eyes were closed, and Ruth always wondered what color they were.

She folded the gown carefully, smoothing it before placing it in her suitcase. It was a piece of what should have been—a ceremony never held, a future unfulfilled.

Honpa Hongwanji Buddhist Mission, Honolulu

When Ruth and Mrs. Keller returned to the Hongwanji Mission, Ruth extended an invitation for coffee—a gesture of politeness more than desire. She had so much to do and she was still reeling from the emotional toll of packing Grace's gown.

"I'd love to, but you know how the brass are with staff cars," Mrs. Keller replied, her tone light. "They'll probably check the mileage."

"And the gas gauge, too," Ruth added, managing a smile.

"For sure!" Mrs. Keller laughed, then her expression grew solemn. She opened her purse and handed Ruth an envelope. "The Commander gave me this with orders not to give it to you until I was about to leave." She gently took Ruth's arm. "God bless you, Ruth. You've been a joy to know."

Ruth tucked the letter into her pocket and lined her luggage up on the driveway. A YBA girl assisted in carrying them to her office. Once alone, Ruth opened Gordon's letter.

My dearest Ruth,

We received orders to ship out this morning. By the time you read this, I'll be gone. I know you understand why I couldn't say anything.

I wish I could hold you in my arms right now. Ruth, I love you more than you will ever realize. Be gentle with yourself, fair lady. Let yourself be cared for at home.

I haven't told you how much I admire your courage through your grief. Your heart is stronger than mine. I could not have a life without you.

Ruth, without Grace, we must love each other more strongly. If it is meant that we travel this life alone as husband and wife, let it be. It's enough for me. Perhaps, in time, it will be enough for you.

And now, I take your love with me,

Gordon

The sweetness of Gordon's words made them harder to bear. The one thing she wanted to give him—children—was not hers to give, and yet, for him, she was enough.

⁓

At nine o'clock the following day, a clerk from the Department of War delivered the first list of wives to be evacuated. Ruth scanned it; her name wasn't on it. She re-read it again noting that all the women on the list were married to enlisted men. Perhaps the officers' wives were on a separate list? But her name wasn't on that list either.

She called the Navy Evacuation Officer and asked if he could check a name for her. "Ruth Elliott," she said. "Commander Gordon Elliot's wife."

She heard him rustling papers.

"No, Ma'am. There's no Ruth Elliot."

"Try Ruth Lynch." Admiral Kimmel might have forgotten her married name.

"No. No Ruth Lynch either."

"I'm sure that Admiral Kimmel put her name on the list himself," Ruth said.

"Perhaps you should call the Admiral's office," he said.

But, when she did, a clerk answered the phone with, "Admiral Nimitz's office."

"I'm sorry," Ruth said. "I was trying to reach Admiral Kimmel's office."

"This is now Admiral Nimitz's office," he repeated.

"May I have the number for Admiral Kimmel's office?"

"Ma'am, Admiral Kimmell has been relieved."

Of course, Ruth thought. The Navy needed a scapegoat, so they offered Admiral Kimmel's head to Congress.

Ruth asked the clerk, "Could you check if the Admiral received a message about either Ruth Elliot or Ruth Lynch?"

"With all due respect, Ma'am, I have other priorities."

"I'm calling from the Red Cross Evacuation Center," Ruth said. "Mrs. Elliot was supposed to leave today, but—"

"I'm sorry, Ma'am. I can't help you." He hung up.

A few hours later, Eve knocked on Ruth's door. "Are you ready? I've got your bags in the car."

"I'm not being evacuated," Ruth said.

"Why not?"

"My name's not on the list."

"I thought Kimmel put you on the list."

"Kimmel's been replaced," Ruth said.

As usual, Eve seemed unfazed. "Can your father call the new guy?"

Ruth shook her head and a faint smile showed. "No. Even if he did, it's too late."

"The Navy owes this to you," Eve insisted. "It's not fair."

Ruth smile deepened, tinged with irony. "Eve, it wasn't fair that I was on the list to begin with."

"Why don't you get onboard anyway?"

Ruth laughed. "Stow away?"

"Why not?"

"Moby Dick. Billy Budd and me." Ruth stacked the papers on her desk, slid them into a folder, and stood. "Instead, what if the two of us drive out to the dock and help these ladies board?"

"Fine." Eve shrugged. "But once we get to the dock, you might regret not trying."

"I do love you," Ruth said. Even though Eve had no grasp on reality, she was occasionally amused by the world Eve lived in.

Honolulu Dock

When they got to the dock, the mood was somber.

Buses and ambulances jammed the pier. Corpsmen carried the wounded on stretchers, pushed them in wheelchairs and hefted their bags.

The air stung with stench of diesel mixed with sea breeze.

On the gangway, mothers loaded down with luggage clutched their children, elbowing their way through the gangway turnstile, pushing to the head of the line as if there were limited space on the ship.

Ruth expected an orderly boarding, everyone helping each other. But the reality would be chaos. The ship would be blacked out, zigzagging to dodge enemy torpedoes, overcrowded with the wounded and widowed. They would need each other.

Once everyone was on board, Ruth told Eve she didn't want to go back to the evac center.

"Okay. Where to?"

"I want to see Grace."

Eve checked her watch.

"Do you think we can make it back by curfew?" Ruth asked.

"Even if we don't…" Eve stared into the distance. "We've got the Red Cross car. If we get stopped, we'll say we're on assignment."

Chapter Fifteen

December 12, 1941

Schofield Barracks Babies' Cemetery

DURING THE DRIVE to Schofield, Eve told Ruth that she was leaving the Red Cross because she had volunteered for a secret Army unit.

"You? Army? Discipline?"

Eve turned to Ruth. "It's brilliant. The Army is going to pay me $120 a month to live away from my mother!"

"Do you know where your quarters will be?"

"The coconut wireless says either Shafter or Bellows."

"Are you allowed to tell me what you'll be doing?"

"I have no idea." Eve's answer was as flippant as her so-called commitment to the mission. "And I don't care. All I know is that my mother won't be able to contact me."

"Such patriotism!"

"I only hope the uniforms will have some style to them."

"I trust you'll have yours tailored."

"Mrs. Ige in Moiliili will be my first call."

"And your second?"

"To Parker to stock the bar at my quarters."

❧

It was almost noon by the time they got to Babies' Cemetery

Each time Ruth visited, she read the bronze lettering on the gate: "A Place of God's Angels."

What kind of God snatches infants from their mothers?

"I forgot how peaceful it is here," Eve said.

Ruth remembered Eve's family huddled under black umbrellas during Grace's memorial. It was an act of kindness she would never forget.

"It is beautiful," Eve said, and she was right, somehow, despite the perfectly cast shadows of headstones for children, it was a place of peace.

Ruth gestured to the headstone to the right of Grace's. "This is Nicholas Maldonado," she introduced him to Eve. "And to the left is Mary Conrad."

"A pleasure to meet you." Eve bowed slightly.

Ruth appreciated Eve's willingness to play along with the fantasy.

"Sometimes, I imagine them playing tag or pushing each other on swings. I always picture Grace as a carrot-top redhead and Mary as having long blonde hair."

"Grace is definitely a redhead," Eve agreed with a grin. "And she's stubborn and bossy."

Ruth raised her eyebrows. "Eve, we're talking about my daughter, not yours."

"You're right," Eve said. "Grace is proper and well-mannered but not prissy like Mary. Mary worries about getting her clothes dirty. And then there's poor Nicholas, with these two girls, he doesn't have a chance."

Ruth ran her finger over the top of Grace's stone. "There are times I picture myself driving Grace to ballet lessons, and on the night of her recitals, Gordon and I are sitting in the front row. When Grace comes on stage, Gordon scoots down and takes her picture."

"He'd definitely do that," Eve said.

"Gordon said he wanted enough children to field his own basketball team."

"It may happen," Eve reassured.

"I'm not sure he wants that anymore."

"What do you mean?"

Ruth had Gordon's words memorized. "He wrote me a letter. He said, 'If it is meant that we travel this life as husband and wife, let it be. It's enough for me. Perhaps, in time, it will be enough for you.'" Ruth looked at Eve. "You see? He doesn't want children."

"That's not what he said. He said it's enough just to be married to you." Eve took Ruth's hand. "You know he loves you."

"In his own way."

"Would it be enough for you if it were only you and Gordon?"

"I'm going to see a pregnancy specialist when I go home to D.C."

Eve's tone softened. "When do you think you'll be evacuated?"

"Maybe two months?"

"And in the meantime?"

"I'll go back to the Hongwanji."

"To 18-hour days and suppliers who don't come through?"

"It'll keep me busy."

"I have a better idea." Eve perked up and Ruth readied to hear the scheme.

"Why don't you stay at my house?" She clapped her hands. "It'll be great! Ginger and CJ are there. And you know my mother loves you!"

Ruth had dealt with Mrs. Russell enough to know that, living under the same roof with Mrs. Russell, she would be at her beck and call from day one. "I don't think so."

"Think about it. You'd have privacy, and Lord knows Michiko makes the best chicken on island."

"I don't know if I can deal with your mother right now."

"She'll be at Red Cross Headquarters all day, and at night, she'll regale you with her heroism. How bad could that be?"

"Let me think about it." As they walked back to Eve's car, she weighed the offer, well aware of the spider web of obligations Loretta Russell could weave.

The Russell Estate, Nuuanu

By the time Eve pulled into the Russell's driveway, it was five minutes before curfew.

"Okay," Ruth said. "I'll take you up on the offer. I'll stay at your house for one week, and if it doesn't work out, I'll go back to the evac center."

"I knew you'd come to your senses! It'll be grand!" Eve said

Mr. and Mrs. Russell, CJ, and Ginger were at the dinner table when Eve and Ruth walked in.

"Ruth!" Ginger said. "What are you doing here? I thought you were evacuated?"

Ruth responded with a flippant "typical military mess-up" remark, and Eve immediately announced that Ruth would be staying at the Russell's. Then, she turned to her mother and said, "If it's okay with you, Mother."

"Of course." Mrs. Russell's delight was apparent.

"I can't tell you how much I appreciate that," Ruth said.

Mrs. Russell preened. "It's my pleasure."

"While you're here, you can share the guest room with CJ," Mrs. Russell said.

"First give me ten minutes to tidy up before you see it!" CJ said.

"CJ won't be with us long," Mrs. Russell cooed. "She joined the WARD."

Eve looked at CJ. "I thought you couldn't because you're being evacuated." Then she looked at her father. "And you were trying to get her designated 'essential,' weren't you?"

Mrs. Russell explained, "The good news is that General Davidson opened eligibility up to military officers' wives, and CJ volunteered."

"What about the job at the paper?" Eve asked.

"Your father couldn't get me designated as 'essential.'" CJ glanced at Mr. Russell. "And there was also the matter of salary. The highest the paper could offer was $65 a month. I don't mean to appear greedy, but the $120 a month at the WARD is more than Joe makes, and if I put it away, we could have a down payment on a house in a year."

"I hope the war won't last a year," Ginger said. "Sean Harrison told me Lloyd's of London is giving twenty-to-one odds that the war won't last six months."

"Too bad Sean can't give odds on proposing to you," Eve quipped.

"So says my older, unattached sister?" Ginger raised her eyebrows.

"Ruth, what about joining the WARD too? We could be 'The Three Amigos'—CJ, Eve and Ruth." Eve rainbowed her hand in the air as if it were a movie marquee.

"I doubt Ruth would be interested," Mrs. Russell opined. "The military girls who are volunteering are junior officers' wives. I'm sure they wouldn't even consider accepting a senior officer's wife." Mrs. Russell looked at Ruth. "Besides, I could use your talents better at Red Cross Headquarters. I could have you the director of something by tomorrow."

"Thanks, Mrs. Russell, but my plans for the next few days include sleeping in and reading dime-store novels."

"Nonsense! I already have a project for you. War or no war, I'm determined to have the Red Cross Christmas Fundraiser this year. And if there's anyone who could pull it off, it's you."

Ruth glowered at Eve with a chilling *I told you so* glare.

"There's no thinking about it," Mrs. Russell said. "It's done."

Ruth's response was rash. A surprise, even irrational, but she said, "Actually, I'd like to volunteer for the WARD."

"My dear, you'd be the only senior officer's wife there."

"I'll keep that fact to myself."

Eve draped her arm over Ruth's shoulder. The irony wasn't lost on Ruth—she had just joined the WARD for the same reason as Eve.

CHAPTER SIXTEEN

DECEMBER 12, 1941

Little Robert, Fort Shafter

ON THE FIRST day of WARD training, a military bus zig-zagged through Honolulu neighborhoods and military housing picking up women who volunteered for the WARD. It wasn't the crowd CJ expected. To her, they looked like the Junior League lunch set dressed for an afternoon of bridge. They wore white gloves, carried alligator handbags and wore hats with feathers that fluttered as they exchanged gossip.

The military wives also wore hats and gloves, but their suits were off-the-rack, and their shoes showed signs of wear.

When the bus entered the Buckner gate of Fort Shafter, an MP waved them in, and they rode by the base theater, gymnasium, and rows of barracks before dipping into a low, muddy flat of Quonset huts and clapboard buildings surrounded by a moat of red clay.

The women tentatively got off the bus. Their heels sunk an inch deep into the sludge, and the feathers on their hats were still since no trade winds wafted through the flats.

CJ, Ruth, and Eve got off the bus together. CJ gravitated toward the military wives while Eve huddled with a bevy of Honolulu's elite who displayed too much enthusiasm for CJ's taste.

"Good morning, ladies." A skinny, red-haired soldier called them to attention. "My name is Lieutenant Tom Connor. May I be the first to welcome you to the Women's Air Raid Defense Unit." He motioned the women toward a corrugated tin shed that teetered over a cinderblock foundation. "This is your training center. It is Building 307, but you will refer to it as Little Robert."

A chubby brunette sporting a burgundy beret leaned toward her friend and, in a loud stage whisper, said, "I wonder which part of Robert is little?"

Lord, help me, CJ thought. I'm never going to make it with this crowd.

The lieutenant continued, "The surrounding inconspicuous area will be referred to as the Industrial Flats."

CJ thought "inconspicuous" was a generous description of the cluster of dilapidated buildings joined by a duck walk maze of wooden pallets.

"Ladies, please follow me." And like children trailing the Pied

Piper, the women followed, their heels catching on open grate steel steps that led to a Quonset hut perched as a second-floor addition over a concrete building.

"Come through." Connors slid a metal door open and the women filled into an anteroom with blacked-out windows. "Step all the way through, ladies."

When they crammed together shoulder-to-shoulder, CJ, who'd never been claustrophobic in her life, panicked, surrounded by well-doused, expensively perfumed women.

The lieutenant warned, "The light in the training room is bright. Give yourselves a minute before stepping in." CJ thought his warning was condescending. How bright could it be? But, when he opened the door, it was like the light of heaven blinded her.

She stepped in, moving with the swarm, into the heavenly gates of fluorescent lights. Blinking against the glare, she spied an army of men hunched over their desks, a bank of phones on a side wall. Other soldiers pushed mail carts down the aisles, tossing manila envelopes on desks. On the balcony, men tended to teletype machines and copied notes onto blackboards.

"Please move to the front of the room and sit in the row of chairs in front of the dais," the lieutenant said.

CJ and Ruth side-stepped through the rows of desks manned by soldiers cradling phones on their shoulders and cigarettes between their teeth. CJ and Ruth sat in the back row. Eve floated to the front where her cronies were clustered.

A few young officers and a barrel-chested sergeant sat at the dais; standing behind them was an older officer.

Lieutenant Connors stood at the podium and began his welcome, "You forty-four volunteers who…"

Forty-four? So, Mrs. Russell didn't get her fifty volunteers.

Connors continued, "To qualify as a WARD, you must pass a modified Army fitness test, an intelligence test, an eye exam, and, most importantly, you will swear never to reveal the existence of this unit.

"Your pay is $120 per month. Housing, dining privileges, and uniforms will be provided for you."

At the mention of $120, several women turned to each other and smiled.

"There will be times you will be sequestered in quarters or restricted to base. You will work shifts of four hours on and four hours off for a 24-hour cycle, followed by twelve hours off."

A woman in the front row said, "That's absurd."

The lieutenant dropped his smile. "If that concerns you, Ma'am, I suggest you leave now." And she did.

Connors went on, "Army Intelligence will investigate you and your family. You will be required to pass a security clearance of Level 2. This is one of the highest clearances allowed."

CJ wondered if being the daughter of immigrants would deny her clearance.

A soldier sitting at the dais coughed and tapped two fingers on his jacket's epaulet.

"Ah, yes." Connors flipped pages of his notebook and read, "All WARDs will be given the courtesy rank of an officer. As such, in the event of your capture by the enemy, you will be treated as an officer according to the Geneva Conventions."

A woman in a red suit with a diamond brooch as big as a baseball, raised her hand.

Ruth whispered to CJ, "That's Cornelia Fort."

CJ shook her head. She had no idea who Cornelia Fort was.

"She's Eve's friend. She owns a flying school in Honolulu."

CJ thought Cornelia looked more like a Barbizon model than a pilot.

Cornelia was direct. "Lieutenant, are we commissioned officers or not?"

"You are uniformed civilian employees with all the rank and privileges of an officer."

Cornelia's voice was smooth, cultured, and stinging. "I will take that as a no."

Lieutenant Connors announced, "The Women's Air Raid Defense is a unit proposed by Brigadier General Howard C. Davidson, Commander of the 14th Pursuit Wing. It is modeled after the British women's radar girls." Connors turned toward the general.

General Davidson had gray hair, clear blue eyes, and an approving smile. CJ would have cast him in a movie as a church vicar, not a soldier. But when he spoke, he offered no comfort.

He stepped up to the microphone, and after cursory thanks for their volunteering, he began in earnest, "Ladies, during the last nine months, over 20 of our pilots have been killed in routine training flights."

He picked up a newspaper from a stack on the table and read the headlines: "Twelve Army pilots killed in Plane Collision."

Then the next newspaper: "Navy plane crash. Four dead. Six dairy cows killed." And the next: "Pilot Killed at Kahuku. Army Planes Collide." He tossed the paper on the table. "And the press never hears about the near misses."

The general clasped his hands behind his back. "On Thanksgiving night, one of our scout bombers crashed at Bellows Beach to avoid a mid-air collision with another bomber. The pilot and crew of the plane that ditched were killed, adding seven more men to the death toll." He paused. "Ladies, these are not cold numbers. These are men with wives and children, mothers and sisters."

He stepped from behind the dais and walked to the front. "On the night of December 7th, six fighters from the aircraft carrier *Enterprise* were flying to Ford Island. Although the word of the inbound planes was broadcast, their appearance after the attack triggered panic.

"We didn't recognize them as our own and we shot them down." He took a deep breath. "We killed three pilots, and a fourth is still in the hospital. Not only did we shoot down our own planes, but one of them crashed in a civilian community, endangering hundreds of civilians in the Nuuanu neighborhood."

Eve turned around from the front row and caught CJ's eye; it had to be the plane that flew over the Russell's house.

"The last radio transmission from that pilot was: 'Do not attack. We are American.'"

Davidson paced back and forth. "I want you ladies to think about men like Ensign William Fleece, age 23, who was killed when his observation plane collided with an army pursuit plane. I want you to mourn Marine Lieutenant Richard Empie, who was killed in a crash near Waimanalo.

"I suspect the military wives among you may think, 'These are training accidents. They happen all the time,' and you are right. However, these accidents could have been avoided if we had an effective radar system—and you will be part of that system.

"So, when you are training, moving plastic arrows over a map, I want you to remember that each of those arrows is a plane crewed by a man like your husband or your brother."

Davidson returned to the podium. "Ladies of the Women's Air Raid Defense, this is the first time in the history of the United States that women will officially replace active-duty combat soldiers without a mandate or approval of Congress. There are many naysayers who doubt women can take up the banner. But you will prove them wrong. We will succeed and we will save the lives of our fighting men."

The women spontaneously stood and clapped.

"I wish you well." The general left the area.

Lieutenant Connors took the mike. "Ladies, joining the WARDs is a serious commitment. The Army is investing significant resources in training you, and we will entrust you with high-level security information. The program will be rigorous. You will be scrutinized closely and there are many who assume you will fail.

"Before you begin your training, be certain you will commit. If you have any doubts, feel free to leave and on behalf of the United States Army, we sincerely thank you for your consideration."

Connors gestured to the room's exit. "There are coffee and donuts in the break room to the left. This is a good opportunity for you to make your decision. For those of you who choose to stay, there is a table with sign-up sheets for bunkmates for quarters at the back of this room. The quarters will have four women to a bungalow. If you know you'd like to live with someone, sign up now. If not, you will be randomly assigned."

❧

Eve, Ruth, and CJ were signing up for shared quarters when Cornelia Fort and another woman joined them. Eve introduced Cornelia to the girls as her school mate, a pilot and the owner of a flight instruction school in Honolulu.

CJ couldn't picture Cornelia knowing a wrench from her diamond brooch.

Cornelia introduced her friend, "This is Jane Meade. She's another instructor pilot."

Jane looked like a pilot. Her resemblance to Amelia Earhart was undeniable—dirty blonde hair cut in a bob, finely chiseled features, and a handshake that could bruise you.

Jane chuckled. "It's been a while since I was an instructor."

"Ha." Cornelia scoffed. "Me, too. I'd love to have a student."

Eve furrowed her eyebrows. "I'd think a flying school would be bursting at the seams with students now."

Cornelia shook her head. "I'm completely shut down. Martial Law grounded all civilian flying, but my operating costs continue. So, when your mother called me and told me I'd be flying in WARD and they would pay handsomely, I jumped at the chance."

Eve apologized. "Do you think you'll join anyway?"

"No, I applied to a Women's Auxiliary Ferrying Squadron the Army's starting up. They're going to deliver aircraft from factories to bases."

"That sounds perfect," CJ said.

Cornelia nodded. "It's in Delaware." She paused. "I was hoping I could fly here, but…"

"My mother lied to you." Eve rolled her eyes.

Cornelia put her hand on Eve's shoulder, smiling. "We all know your mother, Eve."

"What about you, Jane?" Ruth asked. "Are you considering the ferrying squadron?"

Jane scoffed. "My husband would never hear of me joining the squadron."

"Which brings me to my favor," Cornelia said. "When I thought I'd be joining up, Jane and I planned to bunk together. She doesn't know any of the other volunteers, so I thought you could take her under your wing?"

Ruth, CJ, and Eve exchanged glances. "Welcome aboard," Eve said.

⚘

A buzzer signaled the end of the break. Eve, Ruth, CJ, and Jane sat together in the first row. Once all the women had settled, Lieutenant Connors introduced Sergeant Augustus Cranston.

Cranston's belly strained against his buttons; he looked over the recruits. "The Army—that means me—has six weeks to turn you ladies into reliable assets. You'll report for duty at 0700 sharp. Seven days a week. If you're late, you're out. If I find your attitude lacking, you're out. If I don't like the way you look at me, you're out."

CJ didn't flinch. She'd worked under editors who barked louder and carried more clout than Cranston—or so she thought.

"Tomorrow you'll face a battery of tests—medical, physical, intelligence, spatial aptitude. Some of you won't make it past lunch."

CJ was already cultivating a distinct dislike for Cranston.

Cranston droned on about uniforms, ID cards, and punctuality. Almost every sentence he uttered ended with the phrase, "you're out." It was as if he threw down the gauntlet at CJ's feet.

Chapter Seventeen
December 13, 1941

The Russell Estate, Nuuanu

AFTER THE GIRLS signed up for bunkmates, Lieutenant Connors released them at noon. Eve and her friends took off for an afternoon of unbridled shopping while Ruth and CJ boarded the military bus back to the Russell estate.

CJ stared out the window as they drove through Honolulu. The exterior wall of the Honolulu Telephone Company had been blasted away, making it look like a life-size dollhouse with operators working at their boards.

Barbed wire was coiled on the beach—just days before, she and Joe strolled there in the moonlight. Now, both the beach and Joe were off-limits.

She'd called Joe's office every day since their fight at the cemetery and every day Private Shelling said the same thing, "The lieutenant is out of the office. He'll call you when he returns."

He never did.

When Ruth and CJ got back to the Russell's house, Ruth went to the kitchen to tell the housekeeper they were home, and CJ called Joe from the foyer telephone.

She asked to speak to Joe, and Shelling recited the same apology. "I'm sorry, Ma'am, the lieutenant is out of the office. I'll let him know you called."

CJ thanked him, picturing Joe standing right next to him mouthing, "Tell her I'm not here."

Ruth walked through the living room carrying a tray of tea and cake, and like a hotel waitress, she asked, "Tea for two on the lanai?"

CJ opened the French doors for Ruth.

Ruth set the tray on the table. "Michiko made mango bread this morning."

"Michiko?" CJ asked, almost drowned out by the chatter of begging mynah birds.

"The Russell's housekeeper."

The two of them settled on the lanai, and CJ swept her arms full circle. "Look at this place. I'd give anything to live in a house like this."

"Really? I see you living in a brownstone in New York."

"I couldn't imagine raising kids in the city," CJ said. "My real dream is a Dutch Colonial in New Jersey. It'll have a big backyard where Joe will build a treehouse for our children. And, of course, it'll be near a railroad station so I can catch a train to Manhattan."

"To shop?"

"No!" CJ reared her head. "To work at the *New York Times.* I'm going to be their first gal editor."

"You certainly know what you want."

"That's what Joe says." CJ helped herself to a piece of mango bread.

"How's Joe doing?" Ruth asked.

CJ looked down at her plate. "I don't know. We had a humdinger of fight." She jabbed at the bread with her fork. "He found out I went to Ford Island the day of the attack."

"Weren't you staying at the Royal?"

"I was. But, right after Joe left for Pearl, I snuck out on a nurses' bus from Kapiolani Park. I had no idea where it was taking me, but I knew it had to be close to the action.

"When the nurse found out I had no training, she put me out in the parking lot to help with burned sailors. They were lined up on their stretchers and parked, like cars in their stalls.

"I remember holding a boy's head." The smell of blood and ether arose unbidden. CJ felt the boy's flesh slide on her hand. "I don't remember much after that until an MP helped me onto an evac bus. I didn't know it then, but the MP was Joe's clerk, and he told Joe about me. So, when I saw Joe at the cemetery, he'd already found out and he was furious."

"The private told him? Not you? Where did Joe think you were?" Ruth asked.

"He told me to stay at the Royal."

Ruth sipped her tea.

"When I saw him at the memorial, we argued, and I made it clear that he married a reporter, and I wasn't one of his Marines that he could order around—that I could do whatever I wanted. Then he stormed off and we haven't spoken since."

"That was quite a declaration." Ruth's voice had an edge of judgement. "Have you tried calling him?"

"A hundred times. And all I get is Shelling saying, 'The lieutenant is out of the office,' or 'The lieutenant will call you at his first opportunity.' But he never does."

"Did you tell him what happened when you were out there?" Ruth tilted her head and jutted her chin.

CJ jutted her chin too. "He didn't give me a chance."

"So, all Joe knows is that you went out there to make a name for yourself."

CJ bristled. "You make it sound so crass." What did Ruth know? She had no right to judge her. Ruth had no idea what it was like to start a career.

"But that is why you went out there, wasn't it?"

CJ stared at Ruth—the self-righteous officer's wife who had never worked a day in her life. "Do you know how hard it is for a girl to make it in the newspaper business?"

"That's not the point," Ruth said. "From Joe's perspective, he left you in a safe place at the Royal. He did everything he could to protect you, but then he finds out from his clerk that you put yourself in the middle of the attack. "

"I didn't need protecting!"

"But you did."

"You don't understand!"

"Don't get angry with me, CJ." Ruth pronounced every syllable precisely.

"I'm sorry. I'm really sorry." All the fight left her and CJ teared up. "I call him four times a day but he won't talk to me. He's got to understand."

Ruth's expression softened. She put down her teacup. "I think I know a way he'll speak to you. Come with me."

CJ followed Ruth into the foyer, wondering at Ruth's shift from judgmental to helpful.

Ruth picked up the phone, asked CJ to dial Joe's number, and took the receiver back before Private Shelling answered.

"Good afternoon, Private. I'm calling for…" Ruth spotted a pack of cigarettes on the telephone table. "Colonel Philip Morris.

The colonel needs to speak with Lieutenant Delano about a discrepancy in the weapons inventory."

CJ tried to hear Private Shelling's response.

"Yes. A discrepancy in the armory." Ruth was curt. "Yes, the colonel wants to speak to him now!" Ruth handed the phone to CJ. "I guarantee Joe will take this call, and he'll be standing at attention when he does."

A minute passed. CJ worried that Ruth's scheme might make things worse. Then Joe answered, "This is Lieutenant Delano."

"Joe, it's me. Don't hang up!" CJ blurted as fast as she could.

"CJ, I can't talk now."

"Please, listen," CJ pleaded. "Private Shelling was right. I was at the dispensary, and he did get me to an evac bus, but I wasn't hysterical. I was scared, and I was horrified. I went out to Pearl thinking it would be like the newsreels, but it was the most horrible thing anyone could imagine. I couldn't handle it, and I ran until I collapsed on the curb. That's when Shelling found me."

She waited for Joe to say something. "Joe?"

"CJ, all I could think of was what could have happened to you." She could hear the frustration in his voice.

"Maybe what I did wasn't so bright," she said. "I'm really sorry. But next time, I'll do it differently."

"The next time?" Joe fumed. "Jesus Christ, CJ. There's not

going to be any next time. You're not coming out here ever and next week, you're getting on that ship home."

"Actually, I have an exemption." CJ closed her eyes, waiting for Joe to explode, but he didn't, instead his tone was civil, almost too civil. "Mr. Russell got you exempt?"

"No," she said. "I got a job with the Army. Lots of military wives are doing it. Even Eve's doing it."

"Eve Russell?"

She scrambled for words. "You know if Eve's family's letting her do it, I'll be safe." It was a good argument.

"You're sure Eve's doing it?"

"Absolutely."

"What kind of job is it?" Joe asked.

"I think I'll be relaying messages from one base to another," she said.

"Where is it?"

"They haven't told us, but I can tell you the pay is $120 a month." She thought the money would strengthen her argument. "We can save up for a house faster."

"But you're still going to evacuate when you get called, right?"

Instead of answering him, she said, "Remember Commander Elliott's wife? Ruth? You met her at Wo Fat's. She's joined up, too. She's standing right next to me, if you want to ask her about it."

Joe snickered. "Was she the one who came up with the story about the discrepancy in the armory?"

CJ felt the tension ease. "Maybe." She tried to sound coy. "I was desperate to talk to you, and she was sure it would work."

"It worked all right."

CJ thought she heard a smile in his voice. "So, you're okay with this Army job?"

"Will you still work for the newspaper?"

"I don't know. I'm going to try." CJ paused. "But, Joe, I promise, no matter what I do, I won't do anything to put myself in danger."

"Promise me."

"I love you, Joe."

"Promise?"

"I swear."

Chapter Eighteen
December 14

Little Robert, Fort Shafter

ON THE SECOND day of training, the recruits showed up dressed for calisthenics. For Ruth, that meant wearing a starched blouse, knife-creased shorts, and her double strand pearl choker.

Eve wore tennis togs. CJ borrowed a Punahou Field Hockey shirt from Ginger, and Jane wore her Friendship Flight School T-shirt.

When they arrived at Little Robert, their area was reconfigured with twelve card tables, each with four chairs. In front of each chair was a three-ring binder the size of a Manhattan phone book. Around the perimeter of their area were stations set up labeled Spatial Recognition, Auditory Retention, Mathematics, Physical Strength, and more.

Sergeant Cranston marched in, his shoes clicking on the floor, his back straight and his face unsmiling. All he needed was a swagger stick.

"Good morning, ladies." Cranston adjusted the microphone on the podium of the dais.

"Good morning, sergeant," the recruits responded in a singsong.

"I will begin each morning with the news of the day. He picked up a clipboard off the table and read, "Yesterday at 1400 GMT, Japanese torpedoes sunk a freighter 270 miles east of here."

Eve leaned into Jane and whispered, "GMT?"

"Greenwich Mean Time. 1400 means 2 p.m. I'll explain later."

Cranston lifted his clipboard and flipped over the first page. "Fifty miles from where you ladies are sitting right now, the Army transport *Royal T. Frank* was sunk. There were 29 dead and 33 survivors." He tossed the clipboard on the table. "Let me repeat that, in case you ladies didn't hear me the first time: An enemy submarine hit and sank an Army transport ship less than 50 miles offshore. Had you been sitting on the beach, you could have seen it. Ladies, it is not a question if the Japanese will return—they are here."

Cranston made eye contact with each recruit. "On the day of the attack, we had a radar system in place. Had we utilized it properly, we would have had a heads-up on the attack, but we didn't.

"There's a chink in that armor, and the chink is the human

factor. Radar is a tool. It is a source of information, but without the human element to interpret radar signals, it is useless. That, ladies, is your job. Plotting the information.

"There are men in Washington D.C. who are convinced that women can't cope with the stress of plotting. They say women don't have the capacity to concentrate for hours on end. You must prove them wrong."

Cranston held up a manila folder. "Ladies, if you open the manual in front of you, you will find several packets of forms. May I direct you to the top one. It contains your last will and testament."

Eve darted her eyes to Ruth.

"Don't worry. It's routine," Ruth whispered. "Gordon does one at every new duty station."

Eve widened her eyes. "But I intend to live forever."

Cranston went on. "While you are filling out these forms, I will come around to each table, assigning you collateral duties."

Cranston read the headings on the blackboard next to him: Aviation, Operations, Administration, First Aid, Meteorology, and Other Duties.

He tapped the board with his pointer. "Operations is in charge of personnel records, inventory, mail delivery, keeping the laundry area clean, and the girls out of trouble.

"Filters will handle IFF, distress calls, and divergent echoes."

A recruit at the front table raised her hand. "What is IFF?"

Cranston glared at her. "If you make it through the next few weeks of training—and it's doubtful you will—you'll find out then."

CJ's dislike of Cranston simmered.

Cranston continued, "'Other Duties' means you'll do whatever I tell you to do."

He walked from table to table, followed by a private pushing a cart of files. As they approached, the private asked each woman for her name and then pulled a file from his cart.

CJ watched Cranston lord himself over the recruits. She was convinced his rhetoric about wanting to prove the brass wrong about women was pure malarkey and that, in fact, he agreed with them.

Cranston started with Eve. "You, Hollywood, get that hair tied back or cut it off."

Eve immediately hooked her hair behind her ear.

"You have Meteorology," Cranston said.

Jane was next. Cranston stared at her Friendship Flight School shirt. "Pilot?"

"My husband's a fighter stationed at Wheeler." For the last two years as a military wife, Jane got used to that question referring to her husband, not herself.

"I mean you."

"I was," Jane said.

"At Friendship?" Cranston jutted his chin toward her T-shirt. She nodded.

"Okay, Amelia Earhart, you've got Aviation."

When Cranston got to Ruth, his demeanor changed, and his tone modulated. "You, Mrs. Commander, you've got Operations."

Ruth didn't flinch. She stared directly at him as if she knew Cranston was "old school Army," and he wasn't going to play his game with a senior officer's wife.

"Thank you, sergeant." Ruth nodded as she would to an underling.

CJ was next.

"Jersey girl?"

CJ took it as a challenge. "Newark."

"You've got First Aid, Jersey."

CJ's throat clenched. She couldn't do First Aid, not after the Ford Island Dispensary. "What about Administration?" she said. "I'm good at Admin."

"What about you do what I tell you?"

"I have experience in Administration," CJ persisted.

"Great, Jersey, then you can take care of both of them."

Asshole.

Cranston returned to the dais and ordered the recruits to form into lines at each testing station. "Pair up with each other and move through the stations quickly. If you fail two or more of these tests, you will be dropped from training."

Jane and CJ paired up. "Goddamn asshole," CJ muttered.

"Excuse me?" Jane looked at CJ.

"Cranston not you." CJ tilted her head toward him.

"Ignore him."

She wished she could.

The two started at the Math station, where Cranson hovered over them. When they completed their math tests, Cranston asked the tester for Jane's score. The same thing happened when they went through the Spatial Acuity testing.

"What's with the special attention?" CJ whispered to Jane.

"I have no idea."

The girls continued to the next stations without Cranston looming over them. Then they got to the Auditory Retention table, where a tester tapped out a rhythm with drumsticks, and the recruit was supposed to repeat it.

When it was Jane's turn to be tested, Cranston stood next to the table with his arms folded across his belly.

The tester tapped out a pattern: Three taps, then one tap, then two.

Jane repeated it.

Cranston told the tester, "Do it again. Faster."

He did, and Jane repeated the pattern perfectly.

"Mix it up more," Cranston ordered.

Jane locked eyes with Cranston and tapped out the pattern precisely without looking at her drumsticks.

"Good job, Amelia," Cranston said. "Sam trained you well." He walked away.

"Sam?" CJ asked Jane.

"Sam Hutchinson owned the flight school at Friendship."

"Is that a good thing that Cranston knows him?"

"It could go either way."

While CJ and Jane were sailing through their tests, it wasn't so easy for Eve. She zipped through the Spatial Acuity test, but it was all downhill after that. She failed the math and basic science tests, and while Eve could float across the dance floor in a man's arms, she struggled to repeat the rhythms that were tapped out. However, her colossal failure was at calisthenics.

After she grunted out ten sit-ups, Sergeant Cranston said, "Give me ten more, Hollywood."

She managed two, then collapsed in tears.

The only respite from the testing was when Lieutenant Connors announced that all military housing, including Wheeler Field where Jane and Buck lived, had been reopened.

"Tomorrow, after training, all of you ladies who are returning to base housing will be bussed to your homes. Tonight, please pack up all your belongings from your temporary living quarters and bring them with you. We will store your luggage for the day and assist you if need be."

Jane had been hoping Wheeler Field wouldn't reopen for at least another week. She dreaded facing Buck. The night before the attack, she and Buck agreed to divorce. Somewhere between the salad and the tuna casserole, Buck put his fork down and said, "That night at Jawbone's was a mistake."

When Jane asked what he meant, he said, "We should never have got married."

He was right. She knew it, her parents knew it, even the guys at the flight school knew it, but she'd been too proud and stubborn to admit it. So, when they finally admitted that divorce was a good decision, Jane felt the shackles fall off her.

But that was before the attack. Before war. Things were different now. How could she divorce a man going off to combat?

All day long, she was distracted, imagining different scenarios and conversations with Buck. There wasn't going to be an easy way around any of it, and there was no way to avoid it.

After training that day, Eve, CJ, Ruth, and Jane gathered in the parking lot.

Eve was whining about flunking every test but the blood test. "And I'm not sure I got that right."

"You'll get through," Ruth said. "We'll all help you."

"Did you see me doing pushups?" Eve asked.

"You just need to get stronger," Jane told her.

"Stronger, smarter, and be able to tap dance to dots and dashes."

CJ reached for her hand. "We'll all get you through!"

"I can't get dropped. I'll die before I give my mother the satisfaction of seeing me fail."

CHAPTER NINETEEN
DECEMBER 14, 1941

Little Robert, Fort Shafter

SUNDAY, DECEMBER 14TH, marked one week of Hawaii at war. The shock of the attack was still raw, and the fear of a second invasion was heavy in the air.

Martial Law had been declared, military courts took over, curfews were imposed, and private lands were seized. All citizens were fingerprinted, registered, and given an ID card that they were required to have with them at all times, and everywhere there were lines. Lines for groceries, lines for buses, lines for getting in line, but the longest line was for gas ration cards. The *Advertiser* reported it was half-mile long.

After several people passed out in the heat, the city built temporary shelters and contracted musicians to entertain those in the long queue.

Then there were the soldiers and sailors who stood in equally long lines to "climb the steps" to Chinatown brothels, and while they waited, they could get a shoeshine from grammar school-boys, or get lured into tattoo parlors, or studios to have their picture taken with fifteen-year-olds dressed as hula girls.

Life was a series of lines and rules. You couldn't buy a drink, a roll of film, or make an overseas phone call. Saturday and Sunday were workdays. You could just about get to church.

December 14th was the second Sunday in a row that CJ missed Mass, but Sunday was an ordinary training day for the WARDs.

The last time she went to Mass was at the cathedral in Newark when her mother asked the pastor to give CJ a special blessing for her safe travel to Hawaii. She was thinking about her mother when Sergeant Cranston tapped the microphone. "Good morning, ladies. My first announcement is for those recruits who will be returning to your homes on base. Ladies, make sure your bags are clearly labeled with your name and address. After training today, your things will be loaded on buses earmarked to go to different bases. Pay attention to which bus you board!"

No matter what Cranston said, or how he said it, it just made CJ detest him more.

"Now for the news of the day: Yesterday on the island of Niihau, a Japanese pilot hiding since the attack was captured by a Hawaiian resident, Mr. Ben Kanahele.

"After Mr. Kanahele wounded the pilot and was severely

injured himself, Ben's wife attacked the pilot and killed him. Hawaii Representative Farrington will award Mr. Kanahele a Purple Heart and the Medal of Merit."

"Of course," CJ grumbled. "The wife kills the enemy, and the husband gets the award." A few heads turned. She may have said it a bit louder than she thought.

"Do you have an opinion you want to share with us, Jersey?" Cranston challenged.

CJ looked him in the eye, and with a mocking deference answered, "No, sergeant."

"Good, then we will continue." Cranston read from a teletype report. "This morning, 50 miles west of Necker Island, a Japanese sub attacked an American freighter."

Cranston rolled down a map of the Hawaiian Islands. "There are 137 islands in the Hawaiian chain. Necker is in the northwest quadrant." He tapped at it with his pointer. "Midway Island is the northernmost tip. The Big Island is the most southern.

"The main islands are the Big Island." He tapped the map. "Kahoolawe." Another tap. "Maui, Lanai, Molokai, Oahu, Kauai and Niihau." Tap. Tap. Tap.

"Nihoa, Necker, French Frigate Shoals, and Kure are also among them."

From where CJ sat, she could make out about six islands. The others looked like pebbles tossed across the ocean.

Cranston circled the entire chain with his pointer. "And every one of these islands provides the Japanese with a perfect staging area to attack. That's 1500 miles, and it's all your territory."

CJ tried to calculate the distance between Maine and Florida, but she had no head for that kind of detail.

Cranston stepped away from the map. "On the morning of December 7th, two hours after the first attack, the radar operators at Opana Station tracked the Japanese planes flying in a northerly direction. But the Army and Navy, in their infinite wisdom, disregarded that report and ordered its planes to search for them in a southerly direction because that followed conventional military strategy.

"When the fury of the day died down, the radar reports were re-examined and were verified to be accurate—the enemy flew north. It was then that many skeptics became believers.

"Ladies, you are an integral part of the radar system and knowing where to plot is central to your duties. For the rest of the day, you will study, memorize, and draw maps of the islands. Pair up. Study the map together and test each other."

CJ and Jane paired up. Ruth paired with Nancy West, another military wife, and Eve was paired with a gal CJ didn't recognize.

"This is Sarah Miller," Eve introduced her to CJ and Jane. "We went to Punahou and Mills together."

CJ eyed Sarah. She stood out from Eve's friends—no makeup,

her hair pinned back with a plastic barrette, and a deeply tanned and freckled complexion.

"She's another recruit who was bamboozled by my mother," Eve said.

Sarah laughed. "I was shopping at Gump's and ran into Mrs. Russell."

CJ thought the last place Sarah would have shopped would be Gump's. She pegged Sarah as a farm girl who'd be more comfortable in boots and overalls than a Gump's ensemble.

"I'm sorry my mother pressured you into this," Eve said.

"Honestly, Eve, I was happy to run into her. I was planning on calling her to see if she could arrange an interview with your father."

Eve turned to CJ. "Sarah's a newspaper writer, too. She was the editor of the Mills College paper and had her eye on a job at the *San Francisco Chronicle* after graduation." Eve introduced CJ as being a graduate of the Columbia's School of Journalism.

Sarah mocked a deep bow. "All hail, Columbia."

"Thanks." CJ returned the bow. "It wasn't easy playing in the good old boys' playground."

"CJ worked at the *Advertiser* for a bit," Eve told Sarah.

"Why didn't you stay?"

"I'm a military wife subject to evacuation, and Mr. Russell couldn't get me an exemption."

"Did you hear that Liz Townsend is leaving?"

"Where's she going?" CJ asked.

"Back to Europe to cover the war for the *Stars and Stripes*."

CJ wondered if she had stayed at the *Advertiser*, if Mr. Russell would have made her a full-time reporter, and maybe that would have made her eligible for an exemption.

"She's not leaving for a few months, but I thought I'd get my name in now. Between the Mills degree and my mother and Loretta Russell playing bridge every Tuesday, I think I've got a good chance."

"This is Jane Meade. She's a pilot," Eve introduced Jane to Sarah. "And this is Ruth Elliott," Eve said, "her husband is a Commander in the Navy."

Ruth extended her hand. "Yes, I'm the one who's neither a pilot nor a reporter, and this is my partner, Nancy West, another 'neither pilot nor reporter' married to a Navy man."

Eve smiled. "My mother was grooming Ruth for big things at the Red Cross."

"But I'm a WARD now—and as of today I am out of Eve's house and back into Makalapa housing."

"So, Jane, you'll be going home as well?" Sarah asked.

"Maybe not." Jane waved her hand dismissively. "It's a long story."

The short story was that Jane intentionally left her bags at her evac center, hoping to delay her return home by one more desperate day.

At the end of the training day, Jane admitted to Lieutenant Connors that she forgot to bring her things on the bus.

The lieutenant's solution was simple. "Bring them tomorrow."

After training, the girls were huddled in the parking lot, chatting, when a Navy officer walked by. "Ruth?"

"Paul?"

"Fancy meeting you here," he said.

Ruth introduced him to the girls. "This is Paul Hastings. I've known him longer than I've known Gordon." She rested her hand on Paul's arm. "And if it weren't for Paul, Gordon and I would have never met."

CJ squinted to read Paul's name tag. "Commander Paul Hastings, Communications and Intelligence Headquarters."

"When my family was stationed at Newport, my mother invited Paul to several Sunday night dinners. She seated him next to my sister Susan, hoping they would strike up a romance, but to no avail. Then one night, Paul brought a classmate of his named Gordon to offer him up to my mother—and it was love at first sight—between me and Gordon."

"Gordan was a cradle robber," Paul said. "But Admiral Lynch wouldn't allow Gordon to date his sweet little Ruth for a year. The next year they were married."

"What about you and Susan?" Eve asked.

"I kept getting invited to dinner and sat next to her Sunday after Sunday. We even faked a bit of a flirtation for her parents."

"Faked?" CJ asked.

"My sister was secretly dating a Yale man," Ruth said. "Paul covered for their New Haven trysts."

"So, Paul, it was you who should have ended up with Ruth?" Eve joked.

"Some might say that." He turned toward Ruth.

CJ thought that Paul and Gordon may have been the same age, but Paul seemed younger, more jovial, and much more handsome.

"Have you heard anything about Gordon?" Ruth asked Paul.

"You know I can't say."

Ruth pointed to Little Robert. "I've got Level 2 Security Clearance."

"Don't tell me you're one of Daddy Davidson's girls?"

"We all are," Ruth said.

Eve scoffed, "For a secret unit, it seems everyone knows about us."

"I work in Intelligence. We know everything." Paul grinned.

"And I'm going to find out what he knows about Gordon." Ruth led him away from the girls.

CJ watched how easily Ruth laughed around Paul. She seemed almost flirtatious.

∾

"Okay, Hastings, what do you know about Gordon?" Ruth asked him.

"The last I heard, he was in Nanchang, near the East China Sea."

"He told me he was going to Australia."

Paul shrugged. "That's all I know, Ruth."

Ruth reached into her purse and pulled out a notebook. "Here's my number. Call me if you find something out."

Paul looked at the paper. "I have this. It's your number at housing."

"They opened Makalapa today." Ruth pointed to the military bus. "See that golden chariot? It's my ride home."

"How much stuff do you have?"

"Two evac bags and a satchel."

Paul looked at his watch. "Why don't I drive you? It's better than lugging all that stuff on a bus."

"What about curfew? By the time you drive me home and get back to your base…"

"Ruth, I have a Communications Center pass."

"Of course." Ruth tilted her head. "I forgot how much you Comm gods get away with."

Paul pointed to his car, a red Ford convertible.

"You always lived well," Ruth said.

"I live the bachelor's life, my dear."

"Ah, the Hastings motto: The cost of a wife is the rest of your life."

Paul threw Ruth's bags in the back seat. "I did come close to getting married once, but that, as they say, is a story for another time." He got in and started the car. "Do you remember Tyler Dumas?"

"The tuba player who lived in the BOQ next to Gordon?" She remembered how Tyler practiced in the courtyard. "The first time Gordon kissed me, Tyler was playing *Hail to the Chief.*"

"In a different world, it could have been me you kissed that night." Paul kept his eyes on the road. "Eve may be right. Sometimes, I think I missed the boat."

She knew Paul was kidding, but the remark still made her uncomfortable. "We would have been a disaster together."

"Maybe."

Ruth changed the subject. "I wonder whatever happened to Tyler."

"Whatever it was, I'm sure he was called up by now," Paul said.

"I bet he has five kids and they all play tuba." Ruth tried to lighten the conversation.

Makalapa Housing

When they got to the house, Paul brought in Ruth's bags. Ruth thanked him with a smile and a cautious hug.

"I wouldn't mind being invited for one of your home-cooked meals. You make a first-class beef Wellington."

"Beef's a bit of a luxury these days," she said.

"I know a chef at the O'Club who might accidentally find a roast for me," Paul suggested.

"I'm sure you could pull that off." Ruth took a step back. "The next time I have a dinner party, I'll let you know. But don't count on it. Daddy Davidson's going to have us sequestered."

"Sequestered?"

"Absolutely."

"Then this will have to be our *adieu*." Paul stepped toward Ruth, hugged her a bit tighter than a friend should, and kissed her on the lips.

Ruth's eyes widened. She stepped back and put her hand to her mouth.

"I'm sorry, Ruth," Paul stammered. "That was completely out of line."

"Is that what you call it?" Her voice trembled.

"I'm sorry," he said. "I would never do that to Gordon."

"To Gordon?" She started to close the door, but Paul held it open.

"Ruth, please, could we pretend this never happened?"

"Leave." Ruth slammed the door.

Shaken, she sat on the couch and took off her shoe. "He could never do that to Gordon?" She hurled the shoe against the wall; it left a black scuff. "Couldn't do it to Gordon!" The second shoe hit the credenza and knocked over a porcelain bird. "Damn it."

She slouched back and thought of all the times Gordon would kid, "Watch out for Hastings, he has his eye on you."

She should have taken Gordon seriously.

"Oh, Gordon. Where are you?" She picked up her wedding photo off the end table. "Could you really be in China?" She ran her finger across his face. "China." She whispered to the photo of him. "Wherever you are, please don't do anything heroic. I'd die if I lost you too."

Chapter Twenty
December 15, 1941

Little Robert, Fort Shafter

ON THE FOURTH day of training, the dais was replaced with a giant linoleum map teetering on wooden horses. Around the map were four chairs on each side. Behind that row was another row of chairs.

As Eve slid into one of the front-row chairs, she asked Ruth, "Is the tall, blonde, and handsome Paul Hastings available?"

"Actually, he's totally captivated by someone he's been in love with for years." Ruth didn't explain that that someone was Paul himself.

"Pity." Eve shrugged. "He would have made an interesting distraction."

Once all the girls took their seats, Lieutenant Connors made an announcement. "Good morning, ladies. The news of the war is dire. Last night, Kahului, Maui was shelled by a Japanese sub, and there has been a marked increase in the presence of Japanese aircraft in the islands.

"As a result of the impending threat, the area of West Loch, adjacent to Pearl Harbor, has been evacuated. All farmers and ranchers have been moved inland, and all businesses, schools, and churches have been shut down. This is a radical but necessary action."

Connors paused. "As a result of this threat, your training, initially slated for six weeks, has been reduced to two."

There was a chorus of murmurs. What? Two weeks! He's got to be kidding.

"At the midday break, you will be issued uniforms, helmets, and all your necessary gear. Your rank insignia and bars will be issued next week at the latest.

"Furthermore, you will not discuss your training with anyone. In Britain, women radar plotters are subject to imprisonment for divulging any information about the radar system. We will not be so severe at this point."

CJ waited for some consolatory statement, but there was none.

"Your training will immediately shift to plotting." Connors motioned to Sergeant Cranston to take the microphone. "He will guide you through the intensified pace. Do well, ladies, and good luck."

Cranston began with the news of the day. "A Jap Zero was

spotted off the coast of Waikiki. Three Japanese subs attempted to break through the net at Pearl Harbor. All three eluded capture." Cranston tossed his clipboard on the table. "I'm not wasting my breath with the rest of this. It's more of the same. We're in a deep mess, and it's time for you ladies to step up.

"The plotters you are replacing are needed at the front. They will train you during your first week in the tunnel. After that, you will be on your own."

You're on your own—his words struck CJ. This wasn't a drill anymore. To quote Web Ebley, "It's the real McCoy."

"Next week, you will be manning the actual board, shadowed by an experienced plotter. If you have any doubt whatsoever that you will not be able to rise to the call, don't waste our time training you and leave now."

No one moved. No one spoke.

"Let's begin." Cranston took his place at the northwest corner of the map.

"In front of each of you in the first row is what looks like a miniature shuffleboard cue. It is your plotting rake. Pick it up." Cranston tossed a red plastic arrow in front of CJ. "Jersey, use your rake and slide your arrow three feet forward."

CJ stood and leaned over the map as far as she could.

"Stand up straight! When you do this for real, they'll be pilots in a balcony who need to see the plane's flight path, not you with your ass in the air."

CJ kept her temper and propped the rake flush against the arrow. She gave it a push. The first few inches were fine. Then, the arrow veered to the left.

"Do you know what straight means, Jersey?"

"Yes, Sergeant." She tried to straighten it.

"You're off course, Jersey."

With every correction she made, the arrow zigzagged wider.

"What are you doing wrong, Jersey?"

She knew any answer she offered would be turned against her. "I don't know, Sergeant."

"Don't ramrod the thing! Slide it!"

She squeezed the cue and slid her arrow forward, flinging it off the board.

Cranston motioned to the arrow on the floor. "There, ladies, is an example of a colossal failure."

CJ muttered something unintelligible.

Cranston nodded toward CJ. "And that attitude gives credence to the belief that women are too emotional to learn how to plot."

CJ snapped back, "I thought it was your job to teach me."

The room went silent.

Cranston smiled. "Okay, Jersey, I'll teach you. Pick up your rake and hold it like a billiard cue." He demonstrated.

CJ felt her pulse pound in her neck. She told herself to keep her mouth shut and mimic his pose.

"Angle the rake lower and slide the arrow to Lanai," Cranston said.

She took a guess which island was Lanai and got it right.

"Good job. Now, slide it to Kauai."

She got that right, too.

"Now take it to Midway."

She froze. She remembered that Midway was either the most southern or the most northern island. She took a chance and slid it south.

"I said Midway, goddamn it. The Japs know where to find it. You better find it, too."

She pushed her arrow to Niihau.

"Midway, Jersey! The Japs are already there," he yelled. "Find it!'

The third time, she got it right.

"Congratulations, Jersey, while you had our pilots floundering in the wrong direction, Oahu was attacked."

CJ seethed. Angry. Mostly at herself.

"Sit down, Jersey." He tossed an arrow at Eve. "You're up next, Hollywood. Take it to Kahoolawe."

Eve had no problem knowing where Kahoolawe was. She'd memorized the island map in sixth-grade geography. She slid the arrow straight to it.

"Good. Now French Frigate Shoals."

Once more, she was right on target.

"Maui."

Maui was a cinch for her.

"Hmm." Cranston put his hands on his hips. "You surprise me, Hollywood. I didn't think you had it in you."

Cranston called on three more recruits before turning the training over to actual radar plotters. "These men will be among the shadows that will train you. Learn from them. Ask them questions. Listen to them. They are your mommy and daddy, and they have much more patience than I do."

CJ couldn't have agreed with him more.

For the rest of the morning, the girls slid arrows to islands, correcting their mistakes, asking the shadows questions, and becoming better with each attempt.

At the end of the morning session, Lieutenant Connors directed the girls to pick up their uniforms in the adjacent room.

Eve leaned over to look at the uniforms—blue serge with red piping—laid out on the table. "Not great," she told CJ, "but at least they're not brown."

"Next in line," a soldier called.

"What size is this?" Eve lifted a jacket from one of the piles.

"Either small or large."

CJ picked up a jacket from the other pile. "And this?"

"Small or large," he answered.

Eve and CJ held up two jackets against each other. "They look the same," CJ said, checking their lengths and shoulder widths.

"Just take one," Eve said. "I'll have Mrs. Kimura tailor them for us."

"By Monday?"

"For me? She'll have them tonight if I ask."

They moved down the line, picking up a cap, and insignia. Eve picked up a pair of rubber boots as if they were yesterday's trash.

The clerk said, "The boots are to be worn over your saddle shoes. The gas masks and helmets attached are never to be out of reach."

CJ tried on the cap in the mirror. It was going to take a card of bobby pins to get her hair under it.

Moiliili

When they got to Mrs. Kimura's, Eve asked CJ one more time. "Are you sure you don't want her to tailor it for you?"

"Positive."

"Your funeral," Eve said as she got out of the car. "I'll only be a minute."

"For a fitting?"

"Mrs. Kimura has my measurements on her Rolodex."

Of course she does, CJ thought.

Mrs. Kimura waved at CJ from the shop window with her tape measure hanging around her neck and a tomato pin cushion bracelet on her wrist.

CJ waved back as if she were in kindergarten, waving to her friend across the room, and then Mrs. Kimura and Eve disappeared behind a flower-printed curtain.

CJ leaned her head back. All she wanted was a hot bath. A romantic tryst with Joe wouldn't be bad either. Maybe once she lived in quarters, Joe could visit, and the girls would look away for an overnight guest?

CJ sat up and looked around. Back to reality, she thought.

The Japanese language theatre marquee was blank and the photo of the Emperor was gone from the barbershop window.

There were more changes. All Japanese lettering was painted over in black. An American flag flew in front of Yoshimura's Produce Stand, and "We are loyal Americans" was painted on the hardware store window in broad-stroked white letters.

It had to be done, CJ rationalized.

Chapter Twenty-one
December 15, 1941

Wheeler Housing

WHILE EVE AND CJ were at Mrs. Kimura's, Jane was on a military bus to Wheeler Housing. When the bus stopped in front of her house, Jane remembered the first time she saw it.

The housing officer had joked, "If the termites stop holding hands, the whole house will collapse."

Jane suspected he told the same joke to every new resident.

But there was truth to his kidding. The front porch steps bounced, and the handrail was striated with termite tunnels.

"Here you are, Ma'am. WH 391." He got out to help her, and despite Jane's refusal, the driver grabbed one of her bags and followed her into the house.

When she stepped inside, Jane flushed with shame. A pyramid of Primo beer bottles was on the kitchen counter, take-out boxes were strewn on the floor, ashtrays overflowed, and a stream of ants crawled over the dirty dishes in the sink.

She expected no different from Buck.

The driver set Jane's bag on the floor. "Looks like you've got your work cut out for you."

"I suppose I do." She smiled.

As soon as he left, Jane flung open the window and tossed beer bottles in the trash.

The refrigerator was stocked with four six-packs of beer. The milk was sour, the lettuce was wilted, but there were still steaks in the ice box and potatoes in the crisper.

She took out the steaks to thaw and was tackling the dishes when she saw Buck's car pull up. He was in his khakis, not a flight suit, and was carrying a briefcase, not a helmet bag.

Her first thought was that there must have been a formation. Why else wouldn't he be in his flight suit?

She watched as he walked up the porch steps. What was she supposed to do? Say "Hello?" Hug him? Keep her hands in the dishwater?

The kitchen door swung open—she kept her hands in the sink.

Buck seemed surprised to see her. "I didn't think they'd be letting the wives back so soon." He looked around the living room. "If I knew you were coming, I would have cleaned up."

"I'm sure you were working night and day." Jane dried her hands on her apron, and Buck stepped toward her, then he retreated and Jane was relieved.

He laid his briefcase on the counter and took off his cap. Jane noticed a bruise around his left eye.

"I'll help you clean up," he said.

"I have steaks thawing." She went on with the charade of normalcy.

"I'm going to change," he said, not looking at her.

When he came back into the kitchen, he took some folders out of his briefcase. "I've got some papers for you to sign." He handed them to her.

Jane read the folder's label: Survivor's Benefit Forms.

"Does this mean we're staying married?" she asked.

"It doesn't make sense not to." It was simply a matter of fact.

The top sheet of the packet was a request to have his body sent to his parents in Pittsburgh, where he would be buried in the veteran's cemetery.

"You need to sign here and here." He held pages back for her to sign.

As she did, Buck asked, "Do you know what you're going to do when you get back home?"

"I'll probably go back to Friendship." She handed the paper back to him.

"Those guys are too green for you."

"What do you mean?"

"You like to push your students," Buck said.

Jane trod carefully. "I push my students to perform their best."

"But there are some of us who can't live up to your expectations."

And there it was. It wasn't her expectations that he didn't live up to. It was him—Buck Meade. He knew how to talk a good line, but that doesn't work in the cockpit.

"I gave it my best," Buck said.

"I'm sure you did." She looked out the window, fixed on the neighbor boy riding his bike on the sidewalk.

"What does that mean?" She heard it in his voice. Buck was ready for a fight.

Buck would never have made it through the program if she hadn't pushed him. She made flashcards of procedures and tested him during dinner. She made him juggle a ball while reciting systems. She even rolled toilet paper on the living room floor to simulate a runway.

"It doesn't mean anything," she said.

"It's your fault I joined the Army." Buck dug his cigarette lighter from his pocket and flipped it open.

They'd had the same argument ten times over. "You could have said no."

He flipped the lighter again, swung it closed, and flipped it again. Click. Jane stared at his hand.

"I could have been home walking a beat in Pittsburgh if it weren't for you."

Let it go, she told herself.

"My father had connections." Another flick of the lighter.

When Jane met Buck's father at the wedding, she thought he was a stern man, and his mother was overly deferential toward her husband and son.

Jane told Buck that the day after the attack, she called her parents to tell them that she and Buck were safe.

"Because you know it all? And you knew I was safe?"

Tread lightly, she told herself. Anything she said was going to get him to flare.

"When I was at the evac center. I volunteered to contact all the squadrons to make sure the husbands were okay, and—"

"You called my squadron?" His voice tightened. "What else did they say?"

"The Officer of the Day told me you were unharmed." She smiled, hoping to break the tension by telling him that the ODO told her that Buck had a new call sign.

"My call sign hasn't changed."

"They told me it was 'Shoots' and I asked him if you had shot down Zeroes?"

"How the hell could I shoot anything? There was nothing to fly." He flicked the lighter. Again and again. "For Christ's sake, it was a goat rope out there. Everybody was screaming. Nothing but smoke and strafing. The Japs wiped us out."

"Any fatalities?"

"Todd Sterling." Another flick of the lighter.

"The new lieutenant? How'd he get a plane?"

"He jumped into another guy's plane. The CO should have pulled his ass out. But he let him go and the kid got himself killed. The CO should have stopped him, and I told him so. He couldn't take it. We argued, and he assigned me to the *Lex*. So, now, I'm an Air Laison officer flying a desk. Me on a ship with 2000 sailors."

Something was off about Buck's story.

"Maybe you could talk to the CO? See if he'll take you back."

"What the hell is wrong with you? Do you think I can walk into a ready room and say, 'Here I am,' and they'll give me a seat?" Another flick of the lighter.

"You're right." Jane wanted to keep the peace, just for one more night, one more week, or however long it took before the *Lex* sailed.

"You think you know everything. You're just like Sterling. And it got him killed."

She'd hit a nerve, but she didn't know which one. "Buck, I didn't mean anything."

"You never do. Holier than thou, hot stick Jane Anderson, the next Amelia Earhart." He stormed back to the bedroom.

Jane dreaded the thought of sharing a bed with him that night. She planned on staying up to read and fall asleep on the couch. No fighting. No shared bed. But Buck came out of their room carrying a duffle bag and a pressed uniform. "I'm going move into the BOQ til we sail." He looked at her as if waiting for her to ask him to stay.

She had no intention of stopping him.

"I'll arrange to get the car to you," he said.

"Thanks." She nodded.

He stopped at the door, his hand on the knob and turned to her. "I have one favor. If I get killed, tell my parents I was a good officer and a good pilot."

One more of Buck's illusions.

CHAPTER TWENTY-TWO
DECEMBER 16, 1941

Little Robert, Fort Shafter

IT HAD BEEN three days since CJ heard from Joe. She thought their call had ended well, that things were patched up, and he would call her. But he never did.

At Little Robert, Cranston was reciting the news of the day. In Hawaii, the Japanese shelled Hilo and Nawiliwili, and in the Pacific, they were on their way to Borneo, Hong Kong, and the Philippines.

None of it was good.

Cranston stood on the north side of the map. "When you are on the board at the tunnel, you will be plotting two to six planes at the same time.

"Your day will begin with a security identification. At the top of your shift, Oscar will tell you the color of the day. For example, today, the color is amber."

Eve scribbled notes in her marble tablet.

"When Oscar radios a position to you, he will begin with the number of planes he sees in the flight." Cranston paused as the recruits took notes.

"For example, if he sees one plane, he would say: 'One. Amber,' followed by its coordinates." He pointed to the numbers on the edge of the map. "If he says, 'One. Amber. Two Four,' it indicates 24 on the north/south lines."

Cranston slid the arrow to that point. "Do you all see 24, ladies?"

Heads bobbed.

Cranston moved to the horizontal edge of the map. "Oscar will continue. To keep our example, it might sound like: 'One. Amber. Two. Four. Henry. Nine Two.' Henry means horizontal, and the Nine Two means 92 on the grid. So, you are at point 92 on the east/west grid. Got that?

"But the first thing you do is to identify yourself to Oscar."

A hand was raised. "Who is Oscar?"

Cranston sighed. "Let's take it from the top. The men at the radar station use the code name Oscar. The code name for you, the WARD, is Rascal. At the end of each communication with Oscar, you will say 'Over.'"

Eve had watched enough movies to know that.

"Oscar will report the coordinates of your plane every five

minutes. You will plot these points using the colored arrow. The sequence of colors is red, blue, and green." He asked the recruits to repeat the sequence.

In unison, they repeated it.

Cranston placed a red, blue, and green arrow in an evenly spaced straight line. "See the line of the arrows? It's the plane's flight path. With experience, you'll be able to tell the plane's approximate speed and any irrational change of direction will alert you."

Eve was overwhelmed. She had a hard time remembering numbers, and graphs were her downfall.

Cranston said, "Since you were the ace of the base yesterday Hollywood, let's start with you. After Oscar has identified himself, you say, 'Oscar, this is Rascal. Can you read me? Over.'"

Eve replied, "Oscar, I read you. This is Rascal."

"Try again, using the exact words. 'Oscar, this is Rascal. Can you read me? Over."

Eve stammered. "Rascal…no, I mean Oscar, not Rascal… Oscar, I can read you." Eve stopped. "Sergeant, can you repeat the phrase?"

"Hollywood, get your head in the game. 'Oscar, this is Rascal. Can you read me? Over.'"

Eve answered, "Oscar, this is Rascal. I read you loud and clear. Over."

"Okay, a bit of an ad-lib, but I'll let it go for now."

Eve knew once she got flustered, there was little chance of her recovery.

"Next, Oscar will give you the coordinates like, 'Rascal, this is Oscar. One. Amber. Two. Four. Henry. Nine. Two."

Sweat beaded on Eve's forehead.

"Got it, Hollywood?"

She nodded.

"Now position your arrow on the coordinates."

Eve couldn't remember if the horizontal or vertical coordinates were first. She moved the arrow to the wrong coordinates.

"Henry means horizontal. Do it again, Hollywood."

Eve told herself to calm down. She could do this. East/West coordinates are horizontal. H as in Henry. She got that, but she forgot the numbers. Eve stared at the board.

Cranston repeated, "'One. Amber. Two. Four. Henry. Nine. Two. Do it."

Eve looked at a WARD on the other side of the board. The WARD moved her eyes to the left, as if she were giving Eve a hint.

No, thought, Eve, the WARD's just looking at something else and slid the arrow right.

Cranston yelled, "This is the last time. 'One. Amber. Four. Seven. Henry. Nine. Two!' I'm going to be saying it in my sleep."

Eve panicked. "I can't." She turned to walk out.

"You walk out, Hollywood, and you're out of the program."

CJ held Eve's forearm. "Sit down."

CJ stood and picked up Eve's rake.

Cranston repeated, "Rascal, this is Oscar. One. Amber. Four. Seven. Henry. Two. Six. Over."

CJ plotted it exactly.

Cranston looked at the WARDs on the board. "Oscar will give you coordinates for each plane at five-minute intervals. Let's assume it is five minutes later. 'Rascal, this is Oscar. One. Amber. Four. Seven. Henry. Two. Six. Over."

Those were the exact coordinates Cranston just called.

"Oscar, this is Rascal. Can you repeat those coordinates? Over."

"Good instincts, Jersey." Then he said, "Rascal, this is Oscar. One. Amber. Four. Seven. Henry. Two. Six. Over."

CJ put the blue arrow next to the red one.

"Let's say another five minutes have passed, and Oscar says, 'Rascal, this is Oscar. One. Amber. Four. Seven. Henry. Two. Six. Over.'"

CJ put the blue arrow next to the red and green ones.

"Jersey, what happened to your pilot?"

"I don't know, sergeant."

"I'll tell you what happened. If Oscar repeats the same

coordinates for fifteen minutes, the plane is down and the pilot's likely dead."

CJ clenched her jaw.

Cranston tossed his rake on the map. "Ladies, we will now take a ten-minute break to mourn the death of Jersey's pilot."

You sadistic son of a bitch.

During the break, CJ didn't get the support from the girls that she expected.

Jane told her she was goading Cranston.

"Me?"

"The more you goad him, the more he'll ride you," Jane said.

"I was sticking up for Eve." CJ looked at each of the girls. "I didn't notice anyone else step up to help her."

"You're playing right into his hands," Ruth said. "He's looking for a scapegoat, and you're handing him your head on the platter."

"Is that what you think, too?" she asked Eve.

Eve looked at CJ, but didn't answer.

"Fine!" CJ said. "The next time you need help, I'll let you hang."

Quarters M-15, Fort Shafter

When Joe called her that night, CJ ranted, "He's a bastard, and I'm the only one who's got the guts to call him on it."

"It's an old game," Joe said. "He's fishing for someone to make an example."

"And I'm the fish!?"

"Babe, you're the great white whale."

She gripped the receiver tighter. "I am not going to let him bully me."

"Agreed," Joe said. "But don't make yourself a target in the line of fire."

"First I'm a whale. Now I'm a target."

"Prove him wrong. Do your job, not Eve's, Ruth's, or anyone else's. And whatever crap he throws at you, you say, 'Yes, sergeant,' and keep your smart-ass attitude off your face."

"Yes, sir. Yes, sir. Three bags full," CJ mocked.

"You got it," Joe said.

"Baa, baa, black sheep." She jutted her chin as if Joe could see her do it. "Is that what you want from me?"

"I want you to start playing his game his way, and you'll end up the winner."

She was sick of playing by the Good Old Boys' rules.

Chapter Twenty-three
December 17, 1941

Little Robert, Fort Shafter

DAY SIX BEGAN with Cranston strutting in, clicking his heels and swinging his arms. He stepped to the podium, lowered the microphone and tapped it. "Let's begin with the News of the Day." His voice was somber, and his speech was unusually slow.

"During the battle of Singapore, the Japanese sunk the Scottish steamship *Vyner Brooke*. The 22 Australian nurses and 60 Australian and British soldiers who survived washed up on Banka Island and surrendered to the Japanese.

"The nurses set up a medical station to aid the island villagers and injured Japanese. Three days later, the Japanese lined up all the surviving soldiers and shot them. When the nurses realized what was happening, they ran but couldn't escape. The women were raped, then were ordered to walk into the ocean, where soldiers, lined up on the beach, gunned them down. The sole survivor, Nurse Vivian Bullwinkel, was picked up by a friendly transport ship and reported the massacre."

Cranston folded his hands and put his tented index fingers on his chin. "WARDs, we need to defeat this enemy."

CJ felt a sense of fear and pride when she realized it was the first time Cranston called them WARDs, not ladies.

"Your training will become more complex. Train with a focus on the mission.

"When you are on the board, you will plot several planes at a time," Cranston continued. "Oscar will be relaying you information on three or four planes simultaneously. Each plane will have its own arrow, and each arrow will have a rod attached, enabling you to slide a number tag to it." He demonstrated sliding an identification number tag on a post attached to a red arrow. "That number identifies a particular plane. The additional weight of the identification marker will make the arrow easier to control."

CJ thought the post looked like a restaurant reserved sign.

"There will be times during a squadron training session that you will be hearing constant strings of vectors from Oscar. You listen and implement without question. You focus on that one vector. You do not breathe, you do not blink, you do not think."

CJ echoed his words: You do not think. All of her instincts

had to be shut down. There would be no question of why or what was going on. Just focus and implement.

Cranston held up a headset. "The headsets with mouthpieces attached are how you receive your coordinates from Oscar. Your shadows will assist you in putting them on."

CJ felt like she was being armed for battle.

She put on the headset and her shadow adjusted it and showed her how to switch the toggles on the hand receiver.

"Turn it slow, like it's a radio dial." The shadow demonstrated. "Sometimes, you have to fidget with it to get a clear signal."

CJ played with the dial, but all she heard was static. She started to panic: This can't be that hard. It's like tuning a radio dial. She worked faster but still nothing. She looked at her shadow and shook her head.

He urged her to slow down, but there was nothing.

Then he tried her headset on. He fiddled with the switches. His eyebrows furrowed; he examined the transmitter and slid his hand over the cord, stopping at a frayed knot.

He pulled a new headset from the drawer. "Try this one."

Good. It wasn't me, CJ thought. It was the cord.

The headset smelled like new rubber, the cord was clean and tightly woven. When she put on the headset, she heard a crackling voice.

"It works! But it's garbled."

"The transceiver hums as it warms up. Give it a minute." And one more time he urged her, "Slow down."

CJ gave him a thumbs up but she wanted to get on to business.

"The spotter will read the coordinates twice," the shadow said.

"Spotter?"

"Oscar is your spotter."

"I can hear him! Loud and clear!"

He nodded, unsmiling. "Now remove the headset, and we'll do it again."

It worked. She got it. She wanted to hug her shadow, but contained herself, bubbling out, "Shadow, may I ask your name?"

"Yes, Ma'am. Lieutenant Ken Berger."

"CJ Delano." CJ put out her hand.

Berger shook her hand perfunctorily and ordered CJ to put her headset back on.

For the rest of the session, she listened to Oscar's call with every cell of her body. She gripped the plotting rake tightly and maneuvered it with slow, perfect precision, and when the session was over, CJ unclamped the rake from her hand to see deep half-moon fingernail indentations on her palm.

❧

At lunch, the girls claimed a picnic table under the monkeypod tree. They were chattering away when CJ spotted the boys. "Linc! Parker!"

She introduced them to Jane and Ruth. There was an atmosphere of proper etiquette until Eve hugged Parker. "What brings you boys here?"

"We were in the neighborhood," Parker said.

"As on the same island?" CJ joked.

Linc held up a bag from Kau Kau Korner Drive-In. "As in the same neighborhood." He handed the bag to Eve. "Stuffed peppers and brownies warm from the oven."

"Who told you stuffed peppers were my favorite?" She opened the bag and inhaled the aroma.

"I may have let that cat out of the bag." Parker winked.

Eve pulled out the foil-covered plate of peppers. "You do know the way to a girl's heart." Then she took the brownie out of the bag practically caressing it. "Don't any of you expect me to share a bit of this." She dragged her finger over the frosting and licked it, eyeing Linc as she did.

CJ slid her hand under Linc's arm, marveling at Eve's sultry approach to the smallest gestures, but her mind was on Joe, not Eve's dramatics. "You wouldn't happen to have my husband hiding in your car, would you?"

"That would be a negative." Linc never took his eyes off Eve.

Eve held up the Kau Kau Korner bag. "In case you didn't know, tomorrow's plate lunch special is turkey with all the fixings."

"I'd say the ball is in your court," Parker said to Linc.

"I'd love to have lunch with you," Linc answered Eve.

"Darling, we are having lunch right now," Eve quipped.

"I mean, just the two of us on a proper date where I pick you up, and we are both charming."

Eve smirked. "Charming might be a challenge for me."

"What about lunch this weekend? I have Sunday off."

She put her hand to her chest. "Oh, I would love to, Lieutenant, but we're all moving into quarters on Sunday."

"I can help with that." Linc turned to Parker. "With the good doctor's car. What do you say, Park?"

Parker put his hand to his chest, mocking Eve. "Oh, I would love to, Lieutenant."

Eve cocked her head toward CJ. "Should we let them help us?"

CJ had been dreading how many "essential items" Eve would move to quarters. "Glad to accept the help," she answered.

Chapter Twenty-four
December 17, 1941

Makalapa Housing

WHEN THE BUS dropped Ruth in front of her house that afternoon, Catherine Reynolds was taking clothes off her line.

"Ruth." Catherine waved. "Mrs. Watt stopped by to see you."

Marie Watt was the wife of Admiral David Watt, Gordon's boss.

"Did she say what she wanted?"

"Just that she'll be back."

Ruth was relieved she missed Marie, but she knew she'd be back.

"Ruth, I never see you anymore," Catherine said.

"Busy." Ruth avoided the question. "You know how it is." Ruth scurried into the house, dumping her musette and gas mask on the counter before making a pot of tea.

She settled on the couch with her tea on the end table, her feet up, and a pillow tucked behind her head. She closed her eyes. Just for a minute, she told herself, but the hum of the ice box and the whirl of the ceiling fan lulled her to sleep.

About an hour later, the front doorbell rang, and Ruth woke with a start. She made out Marie Watt's profile through the front door curtains. She thought about ignoring her, but she knew Marie was persistent, and she would just be putting off an inevitable visit.

Ruth stood, pulled back her shoulders and put on her best smile. "Marie, please come in."

The admiral's wife sat in the wing chair, her back straight, her hands in her lap, and her legs crossed at their ankles.

"Can I get you something to drink?" Ruth hoped Marie would decline.

"No, thank you, dear. I just dropped by to ask you a favor."

Of course. Why else would Marie be visiting?

Marie began tentatively. "There's an ensign's wife whose newborn just died."

Ruth sensed where the conversation was going.

"Since you, you know…" Marie paused as if she were searching for the right words. "I was wondering if you could call on her…She's a young thing. Out here with no family, and her husband is deployed." Marie paused again. "It's so sad."

Ruth sat silently.

"She seems to be doing well," Marie said. "I saw her walking at a quick pace the other day."

Ruth remembered her mother's stinging order, "Walk with your shoulders back and your chin up so people won't think you're grieving."

"She's such a sweet girl, Ruth. I know you could help her get through this."

Marie couldn't imagine what that girl would be "getting through."

Getting through starts in the morning, when she'll wake, and the haziness fades and the memory sharpens, and she'll remember her child is dead. She'll "get through days," laying her hands gently on her belly, remembering when it held an unborn.

There will be days of impossible grief, and days she'll be looked at with pity. She will become a cautionary tale because "something went wrong with her baby, and it probably could have been avoided if she had taken better care of herself."

"I'm sorry, Marie. I just can't."

Marie almost gasped.

The silence stretched. Ruth looked down at the afternoon shadow cutting deep into the room.

Finally, Marie said, "Oh, I understand."

"I'm sure the chaplain can suggest someone to you," Ruth said.

"Of course." Marie clutched her handbag and stood, and Ruth slid her arm under Marie's elbow, gently leading her out the door.

"Ruth, I do understand," Marie said.

No, Marie, Ruth thought, you can't begin to understand the day your child dies and your own life stops.

Chapter Twenty-five
December 18, 1941

Little Robert, Fort Shafter

CJ WOKE UP to what she assumed was bombing from early morning maneuvers, but later at training, she found out it wasn't when Sergeant Cranston announced the news of the day. "At 2:10 a.m. this morning, a Japanese plane dropped four 550-pound bombs on the campus of Theodore Roosevelt High School."

CJ knew exactly where Roosevelt was. Eve had pointed it out as they drove from Gump's to Moiliili, and she remembered remarking to herself how bizarre it was that Hawaii had so many Moorish-looking buildings—especially a high school with a red and gold dome.

Cranston continued, "Codebreakers deciphered the Japanese plans to bomb the *California*, the *Texas*, and the two ships in the Ten-Ten repair dock. However, because of the total lack of visibility due to heavy cloud cover, it is now assumed that the pilots could not spot Pearl Harbor and arbitrarily dropped their bombs. The bombs left craters ten feet deep and thirty feet wide. A second plane dropped bombs in the waters of East Loch, at the mouth of Pearl Harbor.

"While the raid was a tactical failure, the Tokyo radio announced, 'a successful bombing of Pearl Harbor caused considerable damage to its fleet, with 30 soldiers reported dead and 70 wounded.'

"The planes flew low, eluding radar detection. Once they were spotted, the PBYs were deployed but never found them."

With the mention of PBYs, CJ thought of Linc.

"Ladies, next week you will be on the board, and it will be your job to prevent the success of the next attack."

CJ stared at the plotting board. She gripped her rake. Cranston's words echoed: It will be your job to prevent the success of the next attack.

"Let's get to work, ladies."

The first row of WARDs was paired with their shadows as the second row observed.

Midway through the morning, a clerk handed Eve a note: "Call the *Honolulu Advertiser* as soon as possible."

Another heart attack! Eve knew the stress of the war would get to her father.

Eve asked a second-row WARD to replace her and left to call the newspaper from Lieutenant Connor's office.

"Can you come to the paper now?" Maude asked Eve.

"The paper? Not the hospital?"

"Your father is fine," Maude said. "Wait a second… Mr. Russell, I have Eve on the line."

The conversation was short. Her father told Eve that Michiko was being evicted from her home by the Army and all of Iwilei was being evacuated.

"What do you expect me to do?" Eve asked.

"I want you to go out there and see what's going on."

"I'm in training. I can't just leave. Why can't Ginger go?"

"Your mother sent her to Kahuku to train a unit up there."

"Pops, I don't know if I can leave here."

"We owe this to Michiko. Just make it clear to your superiors that you have no option." He hung up. Typical Russell approach to life, Eve thought. Rules were made for other people.

Eve walked back to the board room and leaned over toward Ruth, who was sitting in the second row.

"Come with me," Eve whispered.

Ruth looked around the room. "Where?"

"Michiko's house."

"Now?"

Ruth was beginning to think that Mrs. Russell was right. Eve didn't have the character to join a military unit. Rules were mere suggestions to her.

Eve put her hand on Ruth's shoulder. "Ruth, I've never asked you for anything before."

Ruth raised her eyebrows.

"Okay, but this is different. It's important."

Ruth raised her eyebrows even higher.

"We won't be gone for more than 20 minutes," Eve pleaded. "I promise. No one will miss us. Cranston's gone, Lieutenant Connor's not in his office, and the shadows have no idea which WARDs should be on the board. Please, Ruth. The Army's evicting Michiko's neighborhood. She's scared."

Every sensible instinct warned Ruth not to go. But this wasn't about Eve. She weighed her friendship with Eve. Her stomach tightened. "Okay," she said. "Twenty minutes. Right?"

"No more," Eve said.

Iwilei

But as soon as Eve turned onto Dillingham Boulevard, traffic came to a standstill. "We should turn around and go back," Ruth said. "We'll never make it back in twenty minutes."

"We'll make it."

Ruth looked at her watch. "When?"

Eve drove down the shoulder of the road and made the next left onto Iwilei Road. There was still heavy traffic, but at least it was moving.

"We're almost there," Eve said.

"Almost?" Ruth pressed her lips together. She should have said no. "They're going to notice we're gone."

Eve kept her eyes on the road. Military trucks blocked the bridge near Chinatown.

MPs directed traffic, and soldiers strung concertina wire around the railroad station's ammunition depot.

That's it! Ruth realized. The ammo depot! If the Japanese hit it, all of Iwilei would go up in flames. The evacuation was to protect the residents. She rationalized the eviction—it was for their own protection.

"Damn." Eve smacked the steering wheel. They were caught in a snarl of a convoy driving out of the depot.

On the mountainside of the street, a motley crew of boys twirled signs in the parking lot of Kaumakapili Church. "Parking ten cents."

Eve pulled in.

"What are you doing?" Ruth asked.

"Trust me." Eve rolled down the window and told a boy she'd give him twenty-five cents if he'd let her drive out the other side of the parking lot. She held up a quarter.

"Fifty cents," was his answer.

Eve dug in her coin purse. "Thirty-five cents," she countered.

"Deal." The boys cleared a way and Eve was back on Dillingham Boulevard.

Ruth sighed.

"Don't worry. We're almost there."

"I doubt it," Ruth muttered.

When Eve drove onto Republican Street, she hit a caravan of cars and trucks creeping out of Iwilei. The trucks were packed to the gills with chairs, tables, and mattresses. She zigzagged through a maze of gravel alleys to Democrat Street, where the houses were two-story clapboard tenements. Work clothes and dried fish hung from porches. Young boys were pushing towers of chicken cages on dollies, women pushed sewing machines in wheelbarrows.

Eve spotted Michiko in her front yard helping a man, whom she assumed was her husband, load a mattress on a pickup truck.

Eve pulled over, and she and Ruth got out of the car. An old man raised his fist and yelled at them in Japanese.

"I'm sorry." A young woman pulled down the man's arm. "He thinks you're from the government."

As she explained, an MP with a .45 sagging from his belt asked Eve if the old man was giving her trouble.

"We're all fine," Eve said, and she and Ruth kept walking.

Michiko and her husband were tying a mattress to the roof of the truck.

"Eve! Ruth! What are you doing here?" Michiko wiped her hands on her apron.

"Pops was worried about you. What's going on?" Eve said.

"Early this morning, MPs came through the neighborhood and threatened they would take our houses if we didn't leave."

What were they going to do with their houses? Ruth thought. Make a bonfire?

A young boy came out of Michiko's home, helping an elderly woman down the porch steps.

Michiko pointed to them. "That's my son, Danny, and my mother-in-law, Saiki-San. My father-in-law is in the rocker."

The old woman stopped to talk to the old man sitting on the porch before descending the steps, putting two feet on each tread. When they got to the sidewalk, Michiko introduced her to Ruth and Eve, "This is my mother-in-law, Saiki-san."

The woman bowed, and Ruth and Eve returned the gesture.

The woman spoke in Japanese as Michiko translated. "My husband won't leave…he's a proud man…this is our house… our things."

"Okaasan, you've got it go." Michiko put her hand out to her mother-in-law.

As Saiki-san walked by her, Ruth said, "I'm so sorry."

"*Shikataganai*," Saiki-san answered. It couldn't be helped.

Maybe, Ruth thought, but this time, it could have been handled differently.

Danny helped his grandmother into the pick-up truck, guiding her hand to the door handle and lifting her to the seat. Then Michiko took a blanket and covered her mother-in-law's lap and legs. "My mother-in-law has never worn a dress before," Michiko said. "She's ashamed to show her legs."

Michiko's husband leaned over his mother. "I'll be back when I can. You decide what we're going to do."

"What did he mean what you're going to do?" Eve asked.

"My sister has a house in Moiliili. It's a small house, but she'll take us in and Kenji's parents too, but not my father-in-law's things." She turned to the porch. "My father-in-law was an officer in the Imperial Japanese Navy. He has medals, his sword, and a letter of thanks from the Emperor. He won't leave the house without them, and my sister's right to refuse to store them. If the FBI found them in her house, they'd think we are loyal to Japan and take the whole family away."

"What if you leave them in your house?" Ruth asked

"They'll be stolen. Some people are burying things in their backyards, but Kenji thinks looters are watching, and they'll dig them up."

"What are you going to do?" Eve asked.

"I don't know."

Ruth asked, "When did this all start?"

"Before dawn," Michiko said. "Jeeps drove through the streets. The MPs shouted for us to get out and people came out in their night clothes. Then the rumors started that they were going to take us to detention camps. Now my father-in-law is refusing to leave."

Ruth looked at the old man. She could picture her father and grandfather taking the same stand. She remembered her grandfather's officer's sword framed in a shadow box hanging over the mantle; her father's sword was framed in a glass box on the lowboy, and Gordon's hung from the wall in the living room in every house they moved to.

Ruth understood it wasn't the swords. It was their lives, their service, and their purpose. "We can take your father-in-law's things," Ruth said.

Michiko's face beamed. "Would you?"

"Of course. Right, Eve?" Ruth turned and nodded to Eve as if asking her to agree.

"I suppose." Eve's eyes bulged, belying her words.

When Michiko went into the house, Eve glared at Ruth. "You! Mrs. Intelligence Commander's wife, just what do you expect to do with Japanese contraband?"

"We've got to help him, Eve. Even Gordon would understand."

"I doubt it," Eve snapped.

"We can find a safe place." Ruth paused, as if trying to think of a solution.

Eve sighed. "Okay, but where?" Eve stared in mid-distance as if running through possible storage places. "What about the Hongwanji Mission?"

"That would put everyone there in jeopardy," Ruth said. "It can't be anywhere the FBI would search."

"What if I rent a storage locker?"

"I'm sure storage lockers are being searched," Ruth said.

"So, what do we do?"

Ruth's body sagged. She closed her eyes and deeply exhaled. "Not we," she said. "I'll tell Michiko I got carried away. We can't take any of it. There's just no place to hide it."

Then Michiko opened the front door of the house pushing a dolly loaded with wooden boxes with Japanese characters stenciled on them. A folded Imperial Japanese flag topped the boxes.

Eve stared at Michiko. "She's crying."

"Goddamn it," Ruth's voice cracked. "What the hell did I do?"

"It's done," Eve said. "We take it to my house."

"Are you serious?"

"We can put them in the attic. No one ever goes up there. It'll be fine," Eve reassured her.

"Are you sure?"

Eve dismissed Ruth's uncertainty. "Unless you can come up with another brilliant idea."

The Russell Estate, Nuuanu

Eve pulled the car around to the back of the Russell's house, and together, the women carried the boxes into the kitchen. Eve pulled down the attic ladder, and they lugged the boxes up the rungs.

Ruth was mesmerized. The Russell's attic was a sweltering kaleidoscope of rolled Oriental rugs, Louis Vuitton luggage, racks of winter clothes, Yale pennants—all smelling of mothballs and cedar.

Eve carried the flag to the far corner of the attic, folded it and put it in a white wicker pram tucked under a white coverlet, then she and Ruth stacked all the boxes behind a five-panel dressing screen.

After they had stashed it all, they went downstairs, pulled the attic ladder back up and swept the floor of any evidence.

When they were through, Eve asked, "Drink?"

"I need it." Ruth was still sweating from being in the attic.

Eve handed Ruth a gin and tonic and smiled. "Sweet, strait-laced Ruth Elliott, hiding enemy treasures."

"Two weeks ago, Ruth would have reported these things to

the FBI. There were procedures and protocols. Life was orderly, and choices were easy. Black or white. Friend or foe. God help me if Gordon ever finds out."

"I thought you said he'd understand."

"In theory, he'd understand why Mr. Saiki wants to keep them. And I think he'd want to help him too—but wanting to and doing it are two different things."

"Have you heard from Gordon lately?"

Ruth shook her head. "The last news was second-hand info that he was in China." She didn't say it was Paul Hastings who offered it.

Eve furrowed her brow. "We're not at war with China, are we?"

Eve's oblivion continued to be an unending surprise to Ruth. "No. We're allies," Ruth said.

"So, if he's in China, that's good. Right?"

Gordon being in China was far from good. "But China is at war with Japan," Ruth told her, but wasn't going to explain the history of the atrocities of war between them.

The front door swung open, and CJ dropped her gas mask and musette on the telephone table. "Where the hell were you two?"

Ruth sat up. "Did they notice we were gone?" She exchanged glances with Eve.

"No." CJ plopped on the couch. "Who'd notice? No one was there." CJ pointed to Ruth's drink. "I'll have one."

"Gin and tonic?" Eve asked.

CJ nodded.

"What do you mean no one was there?" Ruth asked. "Did we miss an exercise?"

"About 2 o'clock, Lieutenant Connor came tapdancing in flanked by two majors. He was 'yes sir-ing' it all over the place. The bottom line is that we are moving into our quarters tomorrow not Sunday."

"Did he say where our quarters are?" Eve handed CJ her drink.

"Somewhere in the hills of Shafter. All he said is that we meet at Little Robert as usual, and then the military buses will take us to quarters. Private vehicles will be allowed on base all weekend to move us in."

"All my stuff's at Makalapa," Ruth said.

"Eve, can you drive her out there?" CJ asked.

"I've got three gallons of gas for the rest of the month," Eve said.

"It's okay. I can take the base bus," Ruth said.

Eve rolled her eyes. "And spend all day waiting at bus stops?"

"Oh, yeah," CJ interrupted. "Connor reminded us to bring our own sheets, towels, toiletries, and anything else we can't live without for a month."

"Lord, I'll need a steamer trunk," Eve said.

"Eve, do you think you can fit all of your gear and me in the car?" CJ kiddingly asked.

"I don't think so." Eve was serious. "I'll ask Ginger if she can borrow Mother's car."

"By the way," CJ said. "Where did the two of you get off to this afternoon?"

"It's a boring story." Eve dismissed the question, knowing CJ wouldn't buy that answer, but hoping she'd let it go.

Chapter Twenty-six
December 19. 1941

Quarters M-15, Fort Shafter

IT WAS LATE Friday morning when the caravan from the Russell house arrived at Fort Shafter—CJ in Eve's Pontiac and Ginger in a Red Cross Motor Corps car.

The WARD's quarters were in the sector with other junior officers. Low-slung bungalows, each one brown and boxy, with screen porches and laundry lines in the front yard.

"There's Quarters M-15." CJ pointed to a bungalow with a front screened-in porch and a weed and gravel front lawn.

Eve cringed. "It's not exactly the Ritz."

"Nope, it's not." CJ forced a laugh. "But, if it doesn't suit you, you could stay home and live with your mother."

"Fine." Eve waved her hand. "It's a palace of freedom."

"Welcome home!" Jane opened the front door.

Eve walked in, gagging on her first whiff of mold, beer, and ghosts of cigar smoke, and turned toward CJ and said, "Remind me again that this a palace of freedom."

Ruth came out of the kitchen with an apron on, her hands in yellow rubber gloves and her hair covered with a red calico bandana. "I'm trying to get rid of the smell."

Jane was chipper. "A little elbow grease, and it'll be livable."

"Livable is a relative term." Eve put her hands on her hips and assessed the living room furniture—a splintered Papasan chair, a bamboo-print upholstered couch, and side tables concocted from ammunition boxes.

"And these?" Eve pointed to the yellow bug strips hanging from the ceiling that were pockmarked with dead flies.

In her best thespian trill, Ruth answered, "Silken Swords of Damocles."

Ginger walked in carrying two boxes. "Where do you want these?" she asked her sister.

"Right here." Eve said. "I packed chintz window valances, a lace tablecloth, and 'everyday' china," she told the girls.

"Did you pack any Lysol or Dutch Cleanser?" Ruth asked.

Ginger answered, "Michiko packed a box of house supplies for us. It's in the car with Eve's evening gown and tiara."

CJ was first to laugh.

"All right." Eve dodged the joke. "But you'll appreciate it when you see what I do with the place."

Jane stood in the middle of the living room. "Let me give you a tour of our new home." She waved her arms over the couch and Papasan chair. "This is the living room. To the left is one bedroom and the kitchen. To the right is the bathroom and second bedroom—that's the bedroom that catches the sunrise. And I've already claimed it."

Ruth looked at CJ. "'You want to share the other one?"

CJ nodded.

"That leaves me in the bedroom with the sunrises. I'll need a sleeping mask," Eve said.

"We all have our crosses to bear," Ginger said.

Ginger carried in Eve's suitcases, a satchel, an overnight bag, a makeup kit, and three hat boxes while Eve arranged throw pillows on the sofa.

In the other bedroom, Ruth helped CJ set up her things. The room was an adequate size with two single beds, two pressboard dressers, one window, and two small closets.

CJ noticed the saucers of water under each bedpost. "Thirsty beds?"

"They're for the centipedes. They crawl in the water and drown." Ruth's answer was nonchalant. "It's so they don't climb into your bed."

"Centipedes?" CJ felt her toes curl in her shoes. "Anything else?"

"Roaches, geckos, and the occasional scorpion." Ruth sounded almost amused.

"What? No locusts?" CJ pulled back the curtain and recoiled. The window screens were rusted, ripped, and crusted with grime and spider webs.

"The phone works!" Eve announced from the living room.

"Get off the phone and help me with your stuff," Ginger yelled from the bedroom.

"I wonder if we can call off base," Eve said.

"Eve!" Ginger came out of the bedroom to get her sister.

Eve told Ginger. "I think the room needs at least two fans, a few more throw pillows, and maybe a rug."

"Fine," Ginger acquiesced. "I'll bring the fans and pillows from the spare rooms, and there's probably a rug in the attic."

"The attic." The word caught in Eve's throat. "Don't bother going up there," Eve quickly retracted her request. "We don't need a rug. It'll just catch dirt."

"Do you want a rug or not?" Ginger's impatience was clear.

Eve called to Ruth. "What do you think, Ruth? Do we need a rug?"

Ruth came out of the bedroom. "I didn't hear you."

"I asked Ginger to bring a rug from home." Eve paused. "She said there was one in the attic she could get, but now that I think about it, a rug might just catch dirt."

Ruth had a flash of the white pram and the boxes stacked behind the screen. She stared at Eve. "Honestly, I think all a rug would do is give the roaches a place to hide."

"Then it's settled," Eve said. "No rug."

"Fine," Ginger said. "Next time, I'll bring two fans and some pillows. But right now, I'm going home, where I get to deal with Mother all by myself."

"There's a class of WARD recruits starting up next week," Jane offered.

"Then I'd have to deal with Eve!" Ginger hugged her sister and left.

⁓

The first night in quarters, the girls had chicken salad and coconut cookies, compliments of Michiko.

When it came time to clean the kitchen, Eve offered CJ and Jane her leftover scented paper to line their drawers.

CJ and Jane exchanged glances. "No thanks," CJ said, "but maybe Ruth does. She's on her knees in the bathroom scrubbing the tub." CJ was sure Eve missed the sarcasm.

Eve was headed to the bathroom when she was distracted by a knock on the front door.

"Our first guests!" Eve flung open the door for Parker and Linc. CJ glanced behind Linc, hoping against hope to see Joe.

Grocery bags dangled from Parker's arms, and Linc balanced a tower of boxes, topped with a bouquet of roses.

Eve stood on her tiptoes and held the bouquet to her chest. "For me?"

Linc sidestepped her. "Actually, no," Linc sounded apologetic. "Joe gave me orders to deliver a dozen roses to his wife."

Eve pouted at Linc, but handed CJ the flowers. "For the wife."

CJ inhaled their scent. "Thanks, Linc." She would rather have had Joe be there.

"I don't suppose you bought a second dozen for me?" Eve fell into her coquette role.

He leaned over and gave Eve a peck on her cheek. "CJ gets roses, but you get the man."

"Is that to make up for the roses?" she asked.

Ruth took the roses from CJ. "No matter whose roses they are, they deserve a proper vase." She walked off to the kitchen with the entire entourage following.

CJ pulled Linc back; she rested her hand on Linc's arm. "Have you heard anything from Joe?"

"We'll talk later," Linc said.

CJ's stomach tightened. "Later is never good news."

"He's fine."

"Where can I unload these treasures?" Parker held up the bags.

"Follow me." Jane led him into the kitchen and they both set their haul on the kitchen counter.

Jane peeked in one of the bags. "What goodies did you bring?"

Parker bowed and took the floor, waving his hand over the bags like a magician. "Ta-da!" He lifted a First Aid kit out of the bag.

"Is it really a First Aid kit?" Eve asked.

"It is."

Eve groaned.

Then Parker reached in the bag and held up a bottle of Scotch. "But I also brought a medicinal potion."

"That's more like it." Eve clapped.

"And I brought other less potent blends." He lifted a bottle of gin.

Jane grabbed it and held it to her chest. "Be still, my heart."

Next, Parker pulled out four pairs of sunglasses.

"Essential for sunbathing?" Eve asked.

Eve put on a pair and mimicked a Hollywood star, flipping an imaginary scarf over her shoulder.

"My dear Eve, you were the one complaining to me about how bright the lights were in training," Parker said.

Jane tried on a pair and twirled an imaginary mustache. "The better to see you with, my dear."

"The role fits you," Eve joked.

While Parker and Eve went on with their vaudeville show, CJ pulled Linc into the living room. "Come on, Linc. Not later. I want to know what you've heard."

Linc complied. "All I know is that he's stuck on Maui for another few weeks."

"Through Christmas?" CJ asked.

"Most likely longer than that."

Another "Ta-Da!" bellowed from Parker.

"If he stays on Maui, does that mean he won't deploy to the front?" She already knew the answer, but she hoped just asking would make it come true.

"Nothing's a guarantee. You know that."

"But maybe this will postpone it."

She waited for Linc to say something, but he didn't.

When they stepped back into the kitchen, Eve was telling a story about Parker's magic shows when they were kids. She was acting out sawing someone in half with a bread knife when there was another knock on the door.

CJ heart jumped. Joe! But no, it was Jane's husband.

"I'm Buck Meade," he said. "Is Jane here?"

"Come on in." CJ welcomed him. "The party's just starting."

Buck stepped in, and Linc shook his hand. "Linc Armstrong." Linc pointed to the aviator wings on Buck's shirt. "What do you fly?"

When Jane heard Buck's voice, she dashed out of the kitchen. "Buck! What are you doing here?"

Buck looked around at everyone in the room. "I didn't mean to break up your party. I'm just here to drop the car off for you."

Jane led Buck toward her bedroom. "We need to talk," she began, but Linc interrupted and asked Buck what squadron he was with.

"I'm on the *Lex*," Buck said. "Air Liaison officers."

"Who were you with before?" Linc asked.

"The 46th Pursuit Squadron," Buck said.

Parker jumped in. "The 46th? Wasn't 'Parachute Guy' with the 46th?"

"What parachute guy?" Eve asked.

Parker laughingly explained that in the middle of the attack some guy jumped out of his plane because he said his parachute didn't fit. "The 46th was outnumbered 100 to one, and this guy was worried about his parachute." He snickered. "I'd say he was one confident son of a bitch."

"I heard his new call sign is 'Chutes,'" Linc said.

Shoots. Chutes. It was Buck!

Buck snapped, "I wouldn't know. I don't keep up with that kind of bullshit."

Linc raised his eyebrows. "I wonder what it was like the first day he showed up in the ready room after that."

"Like I said, I don't keep up with that kind of bullshit." Buck pointed at his watch. "I've got a ride waiting for me at the O'Club." He looked at Jane. "I just came to give you the car. You coming?"

As they stood in front of the car, Buck dug in his pocket for the keys.

"Is it true? You're Parachute Guy?" She felt her tears welling—anger? shame? pity?

"It's not how it sounds." Buck bristled. "It was a mess out there. You couldn't see a goddamn plane through the smoke. I was one of the first guys out there. Ready to go."

"Don't lie to me, Buck."

He threw up his hands. "You don't get it. The Zeroes were everywhere. They strafed us with every run. I was climbing the wing when I put on my parachute, but the damn thing was too small, so I ran back to the truck to get one that fits, and that's when Sterling cold-cocked me and climbed into my plane.

"He came out of nowhere, and the next thing I knew, I was flat on the ground, and Sterling was taking off. I looked around for another plane to fly, but there was nothing to fly."

Let him tell his lies. It's the only thing he's got.

"You don't believe me, do you?" Buck said.

There was no believing to be had. The truth was simple: He had a plane, and he was too yellow to fly.

"Don't give me that holier-than-thou look. You don't know what you would have done."

There was no question. "I would have been in the air!"

Buck twisted her arm. "You listen to me. Sterling died because he thought he was a hot shot—just like you. That's what got him killed."

Jane jerked her arm away. "You live with what you did."

"I'm not a coward, Jane."

"Keep thinking that!"

Buck raised his fist.

Jane clenched her jaw, ready for his punch. "Do it."

Buck's fist rose higher.

"Go on. Hit me." Her voice trembled. "Go on."

A soldier ran across the street. "Are you okay, Ma'am?"

Buck lowered his fist. He eyed the private. "It's all good."

The soldier turned to Jane.

"I'm okay." But her knees shook, and her voice trembled.

"Keep moving, soldier," Buck ordered him.

The soldier looked at Jane again and she nodded. "It's all right."

Buck panted and paced as he watched the soldier walk down the block. "I don't know what I ever saw in you." He came toward her.

She looked toward the house; she could yell for help, the boys would be out in a second, but she stood still, banking on him being a coward.

Buck stopped, flung the car keys on the ground. "You're not worth it." He spat out the words and stalked off toward the club.

Once he was out of sight, Jane exhaled. She closed her eyes and hoped it would be the last time she saw him.

She looked toward the house to check if anyone was at the window. They were loud, but maybe they were back in the kitchen—laughing—Parker putting on his show.

She was relieved she hadn't called for help—mortified that she'd wanted to. Jane Anderson, Texas aviatrix—she and Buck were going to be the next Earhart and Putnam. Instead, she was on her knees, raking the weeds with her fingers, trying to find her car keys.

CHAPTER TWENTY-SEVEN
DECEMBER 20, 1941

Lizard Tunnel, Fort Shafter

THE WARDS WOKE in the predawn darkness to the sound of crowing roosters and pounding rain. Two-by-two, the girls, collars up and shoulders hunched against the rain, sprinted out of their quarters to board buses to Little Robert.

The rain sleeted horizontally against the bus, and the girls were ordered to remain in their seats until a roll call was conducted before they boarded "sampans" to their tunnel.

CJ thought the "sampans" should have been called what they were—open bed trucks with wood benches and shredded canvas covers that poured rivulets of rain.

The girls huddled together, squeezing into the dry seats, as the trucks grinded into low gear, bouncing over ruts and roots. CJ pressed her arms against her bouncing breasts. She wished she had hiked her bra straps higher. She wished she had a raincoat.

The sampans stopped in front of a canopied walkway that led to a bunker door embedded in a hill. Had the canopy not been there, the bunker would have gone unnoticed. CJ held on to the rail of the sampan and cautiously took a step at a time, then trekked across wood pallets that teetered over mud.

The WARDs shuffled under the canopy, their caps dripping, stomping their saddle shoes, and they shook the rain off themselves like a brood of wet hens.

A solider led them into an anteroom lit with hanging bare lightbulbs and no windows.

An officer with a pencil-thin mustache, a round bald head, and a Humpty Dumpty silhouette addressed them. "My name is Major David Oliver."

CJ thought he looked like an ancient history teacher at some boys' prep school. He was neither the young age nor in the physical conditions she expected of a major.

He stared at the mud on the linoleum floor and eyed the recruits head to toe. He grunted. "I assume you have no rain gear."

"None was issued," someone answered.

"Hmm." He shook his head. "When you do get your gear, hang it here." He pointed to the rolling closet, like a hotel bellman's cart, lined up against the wall. Two of them were jammed with military jackets.

"And the boots go in the cubbies."

CJ counted ten rows and six columns of them—there were a lot more people in the tunnel than she imagined—far more than herself and other WARDs.

Major Oliver said, "The first order of business is a tour of Lizard."

CJ noticed stains on his tie. His shoes looked dull and scuffed. She couldn't imagine how this man could have reached the rank of major. Maybe he was a specialist in radar called up for the war? Certainly, he wasn't "regular Army."

Oliver led them down a narrow hallway with several doors coming off each side. He stopped at the first unmarked door. "You'll spend your down time off the plotting board in the Canteen." He opened the door and told them to step in; when they did, every man in the place stared at them.

"All the way in," Oliver said.

The Canteen looked like a Woolworth's lunchroom with red vinyl stools, a Formica counter cluttered with jars of pickled eggs and steel napkin dispensers, and it had the distinct smells of burned coffee with an undercurrent of bug spray.

"You will take all your meals here," Oliver said.

Cigarette and cigar smoke hung over the eight tables.

It was like walking into a boys' locker room. All eyes turned toward them. There was an echo of "Who the hell are they?"

Some of them gawked, a few winked. CJ sized them up—burly football players at some tables, math geniuses at others—but all of them looked like they just got out of high school.

Lining the floor of the back wall, soldiers were asleep on cots, and a few unlucky ones were curled on blankets on the floor.

"All your personal messages will be posted here." Oliver pointed to a corkboard next to a poster of an innocent young girl in a white blouse with a warning: "She may look clean, but good-time girls spread syphilis and gonorrhea. You can't fight the Axis if you have VD."

CJ thought "Victory Through Condoms!" would have made a better caption.

He continued down the hall, stopping to point at the men's room where a blank cardboard sign hung from a nail. He flipped the board to the other side. It read: This is now a LADIES' ROOM.

From there, they went to the mail room. A cardboard sign taped to the Dutch door posted its hours of operation. "You will use the address: Your Name, c/o 7th Army Air Command, Territory of Hawaii."

At the end of the hallway was a double door marked "Amphitheater." He didn't take them through it. Instead, he backtracked to the anteroom where he stood in front of double doors on his left.

"When we enter the plotting room, it will take your eyes a few seconds to adjust to the light."

CJ doubted him, but when he swung open the doors with a flourish, she felt like she had been blinded by hundreds of flashing cameras.

Lizard's plotting room was twice the size of Little Robert's. The map was identical, but there were four rows, not two, of chairs behind the plotters. On the perimeter of the room was a wrap-around balcony jammed with soldiers sitting at desks, leaning over the rail, making hand signals to plotters working the board. Soldiers jogged up and down the stairs. They pinned notes on corkboards, monitored teletype machines, and worked out mathematical formulas on blackboards.

"For the next week or so, you will continue to be monitored by a shadow. The shadow will report to the command when you are competent enough to be on your own."

Sixteen Army officers were lined up, four on each side of the map—CJ assumed they were the "shadows."

"The first group of WARDs, please take your place next to your shadows. The others sit in the folding chairs behind them."

CJ stepped up to the plotting map. Her shadow stood next to her, focused and silent. When he turned toward her, she expected an introduction, but he silently bent over and pointed under the plotting map. "You need to see this." He pulled a drawer out from under the map where the plastic arrows, numbers, and posts were stored.

When CJ crouched down to see, her shadow asked her where her non-combatant armband was.

"I didn't think I needed it." No one told them to wear it, and none of the other WARDs were wearing theirs.

"Why else would it have been issued to you?" No smile, no wink, no nod. "Make sure you have it tomorrow."

"Yes, sir." She heard Joe's advice: Just play the game, do your job, and keep your mouth shut.

"Let's get started," he said. "Put on your headset."

CJ put on her headset, adjusted all the toggles and dials.

The shadow sent the coordinates through his microphone. She listened so intently that she held her breath; she got through her session without a mistake, but second-guessed every move she made.

At the end of her shift, he dismissed her without a comment, and she went to the canteen. Her neck ached, and her shoulders were so rounded and cramped she was sure she cast a shadow like the Hunchback of Notre Dame.

Music in the canteen blared a country song. The fluorescent lights buzzed, and the cloud of cigarette smoke was so low it almost reached the top of her head.

CJ ordered a coffee and sat at an empty table. The ashtray on the table was full, and dead flies floated in abandoned coffee cups.

A blond soldier pulled out a chair, swung it around backward, and sat on it, his legs splayed.

CJ pointed to the empty chairs. "I have friends coming."

"So do I." He pointed toward a soldier making his way to the table. The soldier sat next to her. "How are you doing, gorgeous?"

"Doing married." She held up her left hand.

"Rings can come off." The soldier pointed to his own wedding band.

"Not this one."

The soldier scooted his chair closer to her and put his hand on her thigh.

She slapped it off so hard his hand hit the edge of the table.

He pulled it back and rubbed it where a welt was already reddening his knuckles.

"You must be drunk or stupid for trying a move like that with me." CJ glared at him. "Don't even think about again."

A lieutenant, who she recognized as one of the shadows, put his tray on the table and sat in the empty chair. "Thanks for saving the table," he said to CJ. "We've got a lot to discuss."

CJ was ready for another assault—this time by the officers.

A second officer was right behind him. He nudged the blond soldier with his tray. "Sorry, boys, this is a working lunch."

The young soldiers looked at each other.

"Time to go, boys," the lieutenant said.

Neither got up.

"Now."

"Yes, sir. Yes, sir," the blond said and mocked a salute. "Enjoy your working lunch."

When they left, the officers introduced themselves to CJ as Bill Flynn and Tom Martin.

"Gentlemen, I appreciate you being my knights in shining armor, but I assure you, I had things under control."

Tom said, "I like to think of myself as a guardian of damsels in distress."

"Some damsels are their own guardians," CJ said.

"But their virtues still need protecting." Bill had a no-question-about-it New Jersey accent.

"How's that?" CJ asked.

"It's like this," Bill said. "You're the only women here besides nurses—and nurses are off limits."

"And why's that?" CJ already felt comfortable with Bill. He had a familiar big brother attitude.

Tom explained to CJ, "The nurses are officers."

"The WARDs are officers, too," CJ said.

Bill tapped the lieutenant's bar on his collar. "Where's your rank?"

"Our bars haven't been issued yet."

"Until you pin them on, you're all free game," Bill said.

CJ had played in a man's world her whole life. But this was a different game—an inch of brass on her collar, and the power shifted.

At dinner that night, CJ told the girls about her conversation.

Ruth put down her fork. "I already took care of it. I told Lieutenant Connor he needed to put a rush on our insignias. The shadows would treat us with more respect if they were reminded that we are officers."

"Well done, Mrs. Elliott," Jane piped up.

"And told him we needed rain gear immediately," Ruth said.

Eve grinned at Ruth. "Look at you. Our own Eliza Doolittle. Who knows what you'll be doing next?"

Chapter Twenty-eight

December 25, 1941

Base Chapel, Fort Shafter

ON CHRISTMAS MORNING, CJ took the base bus to the chapel. She dipped her hand in the holy water fount, sat in an empty pew, and set down her musette and gas mask.

Christmas 1941 was not a celebration of joy or peace to men of goodwill. There were no Christmas lights and no holiday greetings. Santa's toys for children sat on docks in California because the ships that were supposed to deliver them were loaded with tanks and trucks.

Traditionally, CJ's family went to Midnight Mass at Saint Antonius and squeezed into a pew with the "Christmas and Easter Catholics." Altar boys processed in carrying silver crosses and swinging brass censors filled with incense, and the last altar boy carried a statue of the Baby Jesus and placed it in the manger at the side altar.

CJ always imagined she'd be married in that church. It would be a High Mass. The altar would be decorated with roses and lilies, and the organist would play *Ave Maria* as she walked down the aisle on her father's arm. He'd be in a tuxedo, and she'd be in a wedding gown that her Aunt Gloria made. Joe would be standing on the steps of the altar, gazing at her. And when Father Ambrose declared them "man and wife," her grandmother would cry. But, on Christmas Day, 1941, CJ sat in the pew alone, and when she stood for the Gospel, she could almost feel the touch of Joe's hand over hers.

At the end of Mass, the chaplain addressed the troops directly. He prayed that God would keep them safe in battle and hold them in the palm of his hand.

"*Pax vobiscum,*" he chanted. Peace be with you.

Quarters M-15, Fort Shafter

CJ walked through the housing area, smiling as she smelled bacon and imagined young junior officers trying to make breakfast. When she opened the door to her own quarters, she inhaled the welcoming aromas of biscuits and bacon.

"Perfect timing." Ruth stood at the stove. "Set another place for yourself." Ruth pointed to the dish cupboard. "How was church?"

"Interesting. I was the only woman, and—"

"Merry Christmas to one and all!" Eve pranced out of her bedroom. She was wearing her uniform and her makeup was perfect.

CJ checked her watch. Ten o'clock. "I didn't think you were on the board until noon."

"That's when I'm scheduled, but Jane's taking my shift for me."

"She's taking your shift? Didn't she just get home from a night shift?" CJ asked.

"Yes, but Linc called. He's taking me to the Alexander for brunch, so I asked her to take it, and she said okay."

"He's lucky to get Christmas off," Ruth said.

"They all did," Eve said. "It's something about the squadron. I think the radios are down again, so they all have a 72-hour pass."

Ruth took the sheet of biscuits out of the oven. "Here you go, Eve. Christmas stollen."

"Thanks." Eve waved her hand no. "I don't want to ruin my appetite."

CJ caught the flare in Ruth's eyes. She'd gone with Ruth to three different stores to get the ingredients for the stollen, and she read the directions to Ruth as she mixed them.

"Well, I'm ready for some!" CJ pulled a piece off and dropped it. "Damn, that's hot!"

"What a surprise? Straight out of the oven," Eve said it to CJ, but she was staring at Ruth. Something was going on between them and CJ planned on staying out of it.

"Where've you been dressed up so early?" Eve asked CJ.

"Church."

"Right. Catholic." Eve stood in front of the living room mirror and pulled a tendril of hair out of her cap. "What do you think?" she asked CJ.

"I think it looks absurd," Ruth answered.

"I was asking CJ." Eve picked up her musette and gas mask and headed toward the door. "I'm going to wait for Linc outside. There seems to be a chill in here."

❧

After Eve left, CJ asked Ruth, "What's going on?"

"You know how much work went into this—she 'craved Christmas stollen'—so I made it for her, and then she comes prancing out, ready for a date with Linc."

"It's just breakfast, Ruth."

"It's more than breakfast! It's Eve. It's towels on the bathroom floor, glasses that never get washed, and then she asks Jane to take her shift after Jane worked all night." Ruth was on the verge of tears. "It's Eve!"

"You're right," CJ said. "But Eve is Eve and you've known her a lot longer than the rest of us."

"I know." Ruth lifted the stollen onto a platter. "It's me." She looked at CJ.

It was like the armor cracked. Ruth never asked for comfort. She never exposed herself. Maybe this was her asking for help?

CJ poured Ruth a cup of coffee. "Tell me about Christmas when you were growing up."

"You don't have to humor me," Ruth said. "I'm fine."

"Sit." CJ pulled her to the table. "Tell me what your holiday traditions were."

Ruth hesitated.

"I'm ordering you, Miss WARD!" CJ kidded.

"Yes, Ma'am." Ruth smiled. "But you tell me first."

"Okay." CJ paused. "Let's see. First our family went to midnight mass on Christmas Eve, and then we came home and opened our presents. Then, on Christmas, we'd go to Rockefeller Center to see the tree, and we'd have hot chocolate and watch the ice skaters."

"Do you skate?"

"My parents couldn't afford ice skates for us, let alone lessons. We went to watch the skaters!" CJ laughed. "Your turn. What was Christmas like for you?"

"Different years, different bases," Ruth said.

"What was your best Christmas?"

Ruth put down her cup and glanced mid-distance as if

remembering the day. "I was fourteen. We were living in Newport, and my father was deployed to Cuba."

"And that was your best Christmas?"

Ruth explained, "We had Christmas in March when he came home. My mother kept the decorations up for three months, and the night before my father came home, we decorated the hedges and trees with Christmas ornaments, and my mother made gingerbread cookies."

"Sounds sweet."

"Whenever my father came home from a deployment, we always celebrated the holidays he missed."

"The military's a tough family life," CJ said.

"Actually, I loved moving around and seeing new places. It's all I knew, and when my father was home, it felt special."

"I couldn't do it," CJ said.

"What if Joe decided to make the Marine Corps a career?"

"Never happen," CJ said. "Whenever we talk about careers, we mean mine. Didn't you ever want a career?"

Ruth hesitated before she answered. "All I ever wanted was to be a Navy wife. When I was a little girl, I dreamed about being a Navy bride. I imagined my wedding, with my husband in his dress white uniform, and the two of us walking under an arch of swords held by fellow officers."

"That's a nice dream for a wedding. But I don't know if I

could give up my whole life to it. So, you never wanted a career of your own?"

"This is my career."

There was no uncertainty in Ruth's voice, and CJ picked up on the cue not to judge. "What about the children?" CJ asked. "Are you and Gordon waiting until he retires before you start a family?"

"Not really." Ruth paused. "We had a daughter. Grace. She was stillborn." Ruth looked down and stirred her coffee. Then she told CJ about her two previous miscarriages.

"I got to hold Grace," Ruth said. "I never saw the other two."

CHAPTER TWENTY-NINE

DECEMBER 25, 1941

Chinatown

THE ALEXANDER HOTEL was fully booked, as were the next two restaurants Linc and Eve tried.

When Linc suggested they go back to the O'Club at Shafter, Eve suggested Chinatown.

"For Christmas brunch?!"

"I know a place that serves the best smoked eel and drowned pigs' feet." She winked. "Stick with me and live dangerously."

Linc acquiesced, and they drove to the edge of Chinatown. He parked on Kukui Street across the street from the Cherry Blossom Saimin Stand. It was the first time Eve had been there since the attack.

She didn't get out of the car right away. The shop windows were boarded up with plywood warning "Do Not Trespass" in hand-painted red letters. Mr. Hirasaki's charred truck was still in the alley and a small folding chair where Shirley would sit and watch her grandmother string lei was untouched.

This wasn't the time to mourn. Eve got out of the car and pointed across the street. "How about the noodle shop?"

Linc read the sign. "'My Lucky Belly'? You're testing me, aren't you?"

"I am testing you." She flicked up her eyebrows and ran across the street.

"What if mine is an unlucky belly?" Linc said.

"Then I guess you won't be flying tomorrow either."

Linc swung the door wide, and they made a grand entrance, arm-in-arm, laughing. A table of old Chinese men playing Mah-jong looked up.

The "mom" of the mom-and-pop shop clucked her tongue and pointed them to a table under a "See Peking" travel poster. Then, the mom snatched stained menus from the counter, tucked them under her arm, and followed Eve and Linc to their table. She handed the menus to them. Eve took Linc's menu and handed the menus back to her. "We'll have B12, I28, and G7."

Mom scribbled on her order pad and disappeared behind swinging doors.

"I guess you're a regular here," Linc said.

"I've never been here before. I pretended I was calling Bingo numbers. I have no idea what I ordered."

Linc closed his eyes and shook his head.

"Do you think I'm too reckless?" She cocked her head.

"A bit."

"You flyboys are supposed to be fearless."

"But the cautious pilot lives to old age," Linc said.

"And you're cautious?"

"I play by the rules."

Mom returned with a tea set. Eve poured the tea and held up the celadon-colored cup. "If this were a real Ming Dynasty cup, it would be worth $200 easily."

"You know your stuff. I'm impressed."

"I was an art history major at Mills. After graduation, I planned to apply for an internship at the Palace of Fine Arts. I think I had a good shot at it. But all that's on hold until after the war." She put the cup down. "What about you, Dairy Boy? What's your plan for after the war?"

"First of all, I didn't grow up on a farm. My father is a professor at the university at Madison and my mother was a home maker.

"When it came time for college, I applied to the Naval Academy, much to my father's chagrin—he's a pacificist."

"That must have been interesting." Eve leaned back a bit to give "Mom" room to set down dishes of Sweet and Sour Soup, Beef Broccoli, Fried Rice, and Pigs Feet.

Eve looked over the feast. "Hmm. I didn't do so bad."

"You can have all my pigs feet."

"Deal." Eve ladled soup from the tureen into each of their bowls. "The law of the land is that you've got to slurp your soup."

"My mother never allowed slurping at the table."

"Observe the master." Eve shifted her eyes to an old man holding a bowl to his chin and slurping with great flourish then she held her own bowl to her mouth. "Ready. On three, we slurp together."

Linc took the quietest of sips, then set the bowl down. "I have complied with the order, as requested, Ma'am."

"You've complied with the letter of the law but not the spirit of the law," Eve said, dishing out the beef, rice, and pigs' feet on Linc's plate.

"I told you, I'm going to pass on the pigs feet."

"Fine." Eve split her wooden chopsticks apart and rubbed them together like a fly sharpening its hands together. "Are you a chopsticks man or a fork man?"

"Fork."

"I'll give you a reprieve." Eve scooped rice on Linc's plate. "So, finish your story, fly boy. Your father is a pacifist and you went to Annapolis. Does that make you a rebel in uniform?"

"At first it wasn't an easy sell, but both his brothers fought in the Great War, and they helped me convince him."

"Did you join to learn how to fly?"

Linc chuckled. "More like I believed the recruiter: 'Join the Navy and see the world.' Once I was there, I tried out for the flight program on a lark, and they took me. It's been a fun ride, but I'm not making it a career." Linc took a bite of his beef. "This was a good choice."

"What are you going to do after the Navy?" Eve asked.

"Go back to Wisconsin."

"Wisconsin, after you've seen the real world?"

"My sister wrote that my parents put indoor plumbing in the house, and Madison has a new feed store with a telephone and electricity."

Eve tossed a grain of rice at Linc. "Be serious."

"Actually, I've been talking to Parker about medical school."

"Well, if you're going to be a surgeon, you should practice with these." Eve reached across the table, unwrapped Linc's chopsticks, and pulled them apart.

"I have no intention of becoming a surgeon. I see myself having a small general practice in Madison."

"So, you'll be the Flying Doctor of Wisconsin?"

"Of Madison," he corrected. "I'll have my practice in my house, and I know just the one I'm going to buy. It's a Gothic Revival on East Gorham Street with nine chimneys and a carved cupola that overlooks the lake."

She imagined Linc's medical practice in a lovely stone mansion on an oak-lined street, and there would be a side door entrance for his office. Every Saturday, he and his wife would eat at one of the three good restaurants in Madison, and his patients would stop by their table to chat. Just thinking about a life like that suffocated her.

"You do know what you want," Eve said.

"As if you don't?"

"I do." And the last thing she wanted was to be a small-town doctor's wife.

Quarters M-15, Fort Shafter

When she got back to quarters that night, she replayed the date for the girls. She told them that Linc liked Impressionist painters and Cole Porter and that he had mailed a beach shell home to his little brother, who had never seen the ocean. What she didn't mention was the predictable and boring life he planned for himself in Madison, Wisconsin.

"He's a nice guy," CJ said.

"He's charming." He was a good beau to pass the war with. But not to marry.

Chapter Thirty
December 30-31, 1941

Lizard Tunnel, Fort Shafter

CRANSTON'S NEWS OF the Day delivery was more abrupt than usual: "Christmas Eve, a Japanese plane crashed in a pineapple field in central Oahu. It started a cane fire that destroyed five houses and wounded eight civilians. Because it was a solitary plane, we assumed it was one of ours on a training flight. We were wrong.

"We made the same assumption about a Jap plane flying over Wailua that strafed twelve citizens." Cranston folded his arms across his belly. "We just aren't learning, ladies!"

Cranston pointed to Jane. "Amelia, how close is Wailua to Schofield?"

"It's adjacent."

"Would you say any soldier at Schofield could have looked up and watched the son of a bitch fly in?"

"It's possible."

"Amelia, how can you tell the difference between one of our planes and one of theirs?"

"A spotter can identify the plane."

"And then what?"

"An air raid is sounded." Jane didn't know where he was going with any of his questions.

"Twice this week, someone dropped the ball, and two attack planes flew over Oahu. They gave Washington DC nay-sayers reason to question the effectiveness of a radar system.

"We have to start getting our calls right, ladies. If you are going to make an error, then err on the side of caution. We can tolerate a false air raid. We can't tolerate a second attack."

The WARDs answered in unison, "Yes, Sergeant."

❧

Jane pulled the 4 p.m. to 8 p.m. duty on New Year's Eve. It was an uneventful shift, almost boring, except for the letter from Cornelia Fort about the Women's Auxiliary Ferrying Squadron.

Dear Jane,

You've got to join up!

I'm flying in a squadron of women.

Nancy Love has been appointed Senior Squadron Leader by

the Secretary of War. She's a good pilot and has tremendous enthusiasm and belief in women pilots.

We get up in the dark and get to the base by daylight. We wear cumbersome flight suits and a 30-pound parachute. Your lipstick wears off, and you spend the day dreaming about a hot bath and a steak dinner. We usually get a bath, but seldom a steak. And sometimes, we're too tired to eat and go straight to bed to get up and do the same thing the next day.

We all know there are so many disbelievers in women pilots. We realize what a spot we're in, and Nancy knows she has to deliver the goods, or there won't be another chance for women to be in any service.

She's set strong qualifications for our experimental groups, and I'm enclosing an application for you. Fill it out today! We need you!

The most concrete moment of happiness for me was at our first review. We marched with men, and suddenly, I felt part of something larger. While we were standing at attention, smart in our uniforms, a bomber took off followed by four fighters. We knew the bomber was headed across the ocean, and the fighters were going to escort it part of the way. I could hardly see them for the tears in my eyes. It was the most beautiful emotion I have ever known.

I, for one, am profoundly grateful that my one talent, flying, happens to be of use to my country when it's needed. That's all the luck I hope to have.

Join us in the WAFS, Jane,

Cornelia

Jane read the application Cornelia sent. It was all good until she read the number of hours required to apply.

We shall consider your application dependent upon the completion of the following:

1. *Completion of Civil Service Form 57. (enclosed)*
2. *Completion of an Army Air physical examination for flying. Form 64. (enclosed)*
3. *Successful completion of the Aviation Cadet examination. Any Army Air Corps Command shall administer this examination.*
4. *A statement of your immediate availability.*
5. *The presentation of your Civil Aeronautics License.*
6. *Your logbook verifying 1000 hours of logged flying time.*

Very truly yours,

Nancy Harkness Love

All Jane saw was "1000 hours." She had only 850. That wasn't enough. Nancy Love was only taking the best. The WAFS was a good fantasy, but only that. A fantasy.

Quarters M-15, Fort Shafter

When Jane got home that night, the girls were huddled around a votive candle on the sofa table singing, "Auld Lang Syne."

"Grab a drink and celebrate with us," CJ said.

Jane tossed her musette and gas mask on the empty chair. "Look at you, all decked out," she said to Eve. "Cocktail dress and rhinestone barrette. Where did Linc take you?"

"Mais non!" Eve slid a hand down her sequined gown. "This is all for you!"

Jane lifted the bottle of champagne off the table and read the label in the light of the candle. "This is good stuff." She poured herself a glass. "I'm guessing it's from Parker."

"Of course," Eve said.

"What's new at the tunnel?" CJ asked.

"I got a letter from Cornelia."

"How is she?" Eve asked.

"She loves it. The flying. The squadron. All of it."

"Did it make you want to join up?" Ruth asked.

"She sent me an application." Jane ran her finger over the paper in her pocket. "That wasn't such great news." She handed the application to Ruth, who gave up reading it by candlelight.

"Give us the Reader's Digest version," Ruth said.

"They require candidates to have 1000 hours of flight time, and I'm short by almost 150."

"Can you get them here?" CJ asked.

Jane shook her head. "All civilian flying's been shut down."

"What about going back to your old job in Texas and get them there?" CJ asked.

"I thought about it, but the only flights I could get out of here are evac flights, and since I don't have any children, it could be months before I'm evacuated. There's no way around it." Jane plopped on the couch and put her feet on the table. "I played all the options out. It won't work. That's it."

"What if you applied anyway?" Eve asked.

"It doesn't work that way," Jane said.

"What have you got to lose?" Eve persisted.

She hesitated to explain—her pride, her reputation as an aviatrix, the arrogance in applying. She stared at the candle. All those hours and still not enough.

"You want this, right?" CJ asked.

"Of course."

"Then don't be a wimp. Go for it," CJ said.

Jane laughed. "Well, thank you, Mother."

"How long have you wanted to be a pilot?" CJ asked.

Jane sighed. "It's a long story."

"Amuse us." Eve poured herself another glass. "It's New Year's Eve. We need a good story."

"It's boring," Jane argued.

"Don't be so self-deprecating," Eve said.

"All right. But don't say I didn't warn you." Jane lit a cigarette, took a deep drag, and began: "Once upon a time, when I was eight years old, I was playing outside. I spotted a small yellow plane in the sky." She paused. "Are you sure you want to hear this?"

"Yes!" They all said in unison.

Jane continued, "When it flew over the house, I jumped up and down and waved to the pilot. I watched it fly lower. Then I heard the engine sputter. Then, the plane started circling, and I was sure it was going to crash so I hid under a tree and watched it skid in the grass and bounce to a stop." Jane took another drag and tapped her cigarette on the ashtray. "Now, here's the good part: I watched the pilot climb out of the plane and walk the wing. I expected him to be a strapping hulk of a guy, but he was small. Then he jumped to the ground, took off his helmet, bent over, and shook out her long, red curly hair. The pilot was a girl!"

Eve clapped. "Brava!"

"I couldn't stop staring at her, then she walked up to me and said, "I'm Neta Snook. Your Mommy or Daddy around?

"I remember staring at her lipstick and asking her if she really was a lady pilot, and she said, 'That I am, baby girl.'

"I brought her in the house and introduced her to my parents like she was a puppy I found in the pasture. My parents invited her to stay for supper, and Neta bartered a home-cooked meal and a warm bed for a plane ride for me and my Daddy the next morning.

"My brothers begged to go instead of me, but Neta said, 'I didn't invite you.'

"The next morning, Daddy and I climbed in the cockpit. Neta ran up the engine. The propeller turned, and we bumped over the grass, picked up speed, and we were off the ground. I remember leaning over and putting my face to the wind, and that was the beginning of my love affair with flying."

"And then?" CJ asked.

"Straight out of high school, I got a job at Friendship Creek Air Base. Mama wasn't so happy about a single girl living alone, but Daddy knew how much I liked flying. So, they let me go.

"I started as a Girl Friday, then I learned to fly, and I became an instructor. Two years later, I met Buck, and we got married."

"Friendship's a cute name," Eve said.

"It's a miserable dust bowl of a place. The airfield's the only thing that keeps it on the map," Jane said. "When I first got there, they trained crop dusters, but then the Army contracted Sam—he's the owner—to do primary training. So, he brought in World War I pilots as instructors. They were a bunch of has-been blowhards who didn't want any girl near an airfield."

Jane perched on the couch and crossed her legs, her voice

quickening as she continued her story. "On my first day of work, I showed up in a yellow and white polka dot dress and my hair tied back in a grosgrain ribbon. I was so naïve! When I walked by the old codgers, one of them spat in a coffee can and said, 'A dollar says she's gone in a week.'

"The next morning, they put a cow pie on my desk chair. I picked it up and dumped it right in front of them and said, 'I grew up on a cattle ranch.'"

"That should have taken care of it," Ruth said.

"It just riled them up more. They put calendars of naked women on every wall in the office and cursed as loud and nasty as they could when I was around. Then one day, they nailed the 'lady latrine' door shut. So, I marched into the men's toilet, smiled at the guy at the urinal, did my business, and winked at him on my way out. After that, they stopped their foolishness."

"How did you learn to fly?" Ruth asked.

"The old codgers taught me. One by one—but they didn't know it. From day one on the job, I read flight manuals during my lunch break. After a while, I snuck them home and read them at night. Then, when I delivered messages to the ground school instructors, I'd linger at the back of their classes until one day, I just sat down. Little by little, I got the mechanics to walk me through pre-flights, and finally, I got one of the instructors to take me up on a ride. And without telling any of the others, every one of them took me up and let me take the controls."

"A woman after my own heart," Eve said.

"A year later, I was a certified instructor, and they tossed me a party at Jawbone's Cantina. By then, I'd learned to drink like a man, fly like a man, and say 'no' to advances like a lady—I had a firm rule about not dating."

"Weren't they too old to date?" Ruth asked.

"Not the codgers! The air cadets," Jane said. "At the start of every class, the cadets had a pool to see who would be the first to date me. They bought me beer and chocolates and left flowers on my desk. One of them told me my hair was 'the color of a polished hand-planed propeller.' Poor kid, I laughed in his face."

"I wouldn't mind if Joe would bring me flowers and candy," CJ said.

"Another one told me I had Amelia Earhart's guts."

Eve groaned.

"But Buck was different. He brought me copies of *Air Trails* and *Popular Aviation*, and he sat in my office for hours talking about the future of air passenger service." She paused, almost smiling. "We talked about the future of commercial flight schools, cargo companies and freight service. And I broke my rule and went to Jawbone's for a beer with him. That first night, we talked until 2 in the morning. We met a few more times that week, then almost every night. We started talking about starting our own business." She shrugged. "I never met someone so vibrant talking about his dream. What can I say? He seduced me with a promise of starting our own company. It was going to be a flight school, cargo company, and eventually, passenger service. He said, 'We'll call it A & M Aviation for Anderson and Meade.'" Jane hesitated

"He knew your sweet spot. I'll give him that," CJ said.

"He was pretty good in the looks department too," Eve added.

"He was. Square-jaw, fine-featured, aquamarine blue eyes, and when Buck Meade walked into a room, the party started."

"He sounds like the perfect politician." CJ was only half joking.

"Now, here's the kicker. Our company was only going to hire girls!"

"Are you serious?" Ruth asked.

"Absolutely."

"What happened?" Ruth prodded.

"Buck talked a good game, but he didn't have any follow-through. We got married, and that's the end of the story."

"Is that when he joined the Army?" CJ asked.

"No. That was all my idea—probably one of my worst." She rolled her eyes. "We were still talking about the business, when I pitched the Army to him saying the bombers were like cargo planes and that if he did a two-year hitch, the Army would take him through advanced training for free, and he'd be making the right contacts to capitalize on later."

"That makes sense," CJ said.

"I had it all planned out. When Buck moved on to Intermediate School in Yellow Springs, I'd stay back at Friendship to log in more hours and make money to salt away for our company, but Buck wouldn't have his wife living away from him. So, I took a job as a supply clerk in Yellow Springs.

"It was in Intermediate School where the training got harder and Buck started drinking. From there, we moved to Beeville, Texas, for Advanced Training, where he was drinking first thing in the morning. The rest of the story reads like *Perils of Pauline*."

"So, you never flew again?" Ruth asked Jane.

"And I miss it every day."

"What the hell," CJ said. "Try for it. You've got nothing to lose."

Chapter Thirty-One
January 8, 1942

Lizard Tunnel, Fort Shafter

A WEEK LATER, Jane still hadn't decided what she was going to do about the Women's Auxiliary Ferrying Squadron. She went from one day to the next. Work. Canteen. Meals with the girls. Work. Sleep. Rotely repeat until the afternoon of January 8th, when Jane and Fluff Ford were on the board.

Fluff coughed, and Jane looked at Fluff. Jane shifted her eyes to the plane Fluff was plotting, then up at the liaison officers on the balcony. Not one of the liaison officers claimed it; they weren't even looking up.

Five minutes later, when Oscar reported the plane's path and Fluff moved the second arrow—no liaison officer claimed it.

Jane kept glancing at the officers. The plane must be a reported training flight, she thought. It had to be.

At the fifteen-minute point, Oscar relayed the coordinates—the plane was headed straight for Schofield Barracks. When Fluff plotted it, all hell broke loose.

A balcony officer yelled, "WARD!"

All the WARDs looked up.

He pointed at Fluff. "You!"

Fluff snapped to attention. "Yes, sir."

"You have an unidentified aircraft!"

Now it's a concern? Jane thought. What were they thinking five minutes ago?

The protocol called for Fluff to order an island-wide air raid, and Jane listened to her activate it with precision.

Officers bound down the steps, and clerks banged out teletype messages.

Phones rang. Soldiers took notes and flashed hand signals to each other.

Major Oliver ordered the WARDs off the board, and then let into Fluff with a string of curses that turned the air blue.

But Fluff was right. It was the exact situation in which a WARD was required to order an alert. Jane remembered underlining the procedure in her manual. She remembered Cranston warning them, "If you are going to make an error, err on the side of caution. We can tolerate a false air raid. We can't let the enemy in."

In minutes, the fighter planes from Wheeler were scrambled and the board was filled with arrows.

When a flurry of planes took off from Ford Island, Jane knew it was the PBYs on patrol.

Bomb Shelter, Fort Shafter

Outside the tunnel, the air raid was blasted all over Oahu. When the sirens sounded, pedestrians were to seek shelter in businesses, schools, and churches—anywhere under cover.

At Fort Shafter quarters, Ruth, CJ, and Eve scrambled to their assigned shelter. They ran with their shoulders hunched against the rain and covering their heads as if it would protect them against falling shrapnel.

The shelter looked like a baseball dugout to CJ. There were long wooden benches lining the dirt walls and load-bearing two-by-fours that supported a soaked plywood ceiling.

CJ sat on the bench with her shoes in three inches of stagnant water and her soaked blouse plastered to her skin. The soldier sitting opposite her zeroed in on her breasts and CJ wrapped her arms around her chest.

"Move over," Eve told CJ.

"I can't."

"Then trade seats with me," Eve said.

It was easy to figure out Eve's motive: Sitting next to her, thigh-to-thigh, was a soldier in his BVDs.

CJ ignored Eve's theatrical huffs.

At first, there was a lot of shifting and sorting, then the cigars and cigarettes came out, and the stench of their smoke mingled with the brackish water.

CJ listened as the old schoolers passed around flasks and pontificated on how to beat the Japs. If they had been in charge, the war would have been over. They blustered while most of the younger soldiers lowered their heads and caught up on sleep.

It seemed like they were in the shelter for hours.

All CJ could think about was Joe. It seemed absurd that he was 40 miles away, and there was no way to contact him. There had to be a way to get a message to him.

When the all-clear sounded, and the girls got back to quarters, they stamped their shoes to loosen the mud, then wiped them as clean as they could with yesterday's newspaper, and when Jane got home, they bombarded her with questions.

Jane told them about the unidentified aircraft and Fluff ordering an air raid and Oliver tearing into her.

"The WARDs were ordered off the board and we had to sit in our chairs like little schoolgirls."

"What happened?" Ruth asked.

"What were they saying?"

"No one told us a thing. The shadows muttered to each other, shaking their heads and glancing at us once in a while, but no one spoke to us. The only thing they told us was that every WARD not on duty has to be at the Amphitheatre at 6 p.m." Jane paused. "I heard they may be disbanding us."

⁂

Jane thought the Amphitheater in Lizard was bigger than the Bijoux Theatre in Crawford, Texas.

Major Oliver, Lieutenant Connor, and Sergeant Cranston stood on stage looking like the Roman Triumvirate.

Oliver stepped to the podium. "Women of the WARD, this morning, a false alarm caused havoc to reign on this island." He grunted. "The command expected errors."

Errors? Jane thought. Fluff did exactly what she was supposed to do. It was the liaison officers who were asleep at the wheel.

Oliver continued, "It cannot be a routine occurrence. You must become more effective as plotters."

What the hell was he talking about? Fluff *had* been effective.

"This will not be the last false alarm that is ordered. But each alarm causes businesses to lose revenue, traffic is halted, and hysteria and rumors fly.

"To become effective, you need to learn the principles of identification, response times, operations, flight priorities, how to handle a distress situation, divergent echoes, and how to interpret those echoes. You must be comfortable with all these to order an air raid."

Jane felt like she was tumbling down Alice's rabbit hole. None of what he was saying made sense. This must have been what it was like during the attack—Oscar reporting a squadron of unidentified planes coming in and liaison officers brushing them off.

Oliver lowered his voice. "During peacetime, radar plotting is a nine-month training, but we don't have nine weeks. We don't have one week. Time is short, and the enemy is handing us one defeat after another."

Were they disbanding the WARD and putting soldiers back on the board?

"To remedy this situation, General Davidson has arranged that four WARDs be sent to Washington, D.C., to train with British Women's Auxiliary Air Force members."

Jane got more impatient.

"Air Chief Marshal Dowding has graciously given us the loan of two WAAFs to train those girls. In turn, those four WARDs will train all current and future WARD operators.

"To quote General Davidson, 'It is the human element of the system that renders radar intelligence useable. Humans and machines must work together to collect data, interpret it, disseminate, and give orders based on it.'"

Exactly, Jane thought, and that morning proved a severe breakdown in communication.

Oliver stepped back, and Lieutenant Connor took the podium. "The following women are being considered for this training: Ruth Elliot, Kathy Cooper, Joy Shaw, Dottie Best, Maili Frost, Joan Poole, and Janet Slausen."

Jane waited for her name to be called, but it wasn't.

"Will you ladies please remain after dismissal," Connor said.

Jane was a pilot. She was more than a pilot, she was a pilot instructor. True, Dottie Best flew, but her experience amounted to a few months of mail delivery.

Ruth? OK, Jane thought. She was the senior officer's wife; she had paid her dues for years in the Navy. Maybe she had some connections with the brass? But Kathy Cooper? Joy Shaw? What could they offer? And the others? She'd never even met any of the other girls in training.

At the end of the meeting Jane cornered Sergeant Cranston, practically pushing him into the wall. "Did I do something wrong I don't know about?"

"Let's go outside, Jane." Cranston raised a hand to calm her, but she wasn't done.

"I didn't make the cut for training? I'm the best recruit in the unit." Her voice was rising.

"Yes Ma'am." Cranston escorted her into the hallway to a vacant office. "Listen—"

"To what?" she said. "I've got more savvy than all of them put together, and you know it."

"And that's exactly why I rejected you," Cranston said.

"You rejected me because I'm good?"

"Jane, just listen. Those four WARDs will be pigeon-holed into training recruits for the duration."

"And?"

"In the next few months, the Army plans to set up radar information centers on Kauai and the Big Island. They'll need station coordinators—*my* job."

"I don't want *your* job."

"Will you just listen, Meade? I can guarantee if I put your name in, you'll get the job, and it will be in the regular Army. Not a volunteer, not a civilian. Regular Army."

"And my rank?" As soon as she said it, Jane wondered why the hell she had.

"You'd be a buck sergeant, Meade," Cranston said. "Do you have a problem with that, or do you want to stay in the WARD and be a fairy tale lieutenant?"

She felt like one of the old codgers at Friendship was laying down facts. Cranston was a bulldozing mentor. He had his point. But the WARD paid her $120 a month. With that kind of money, she could salt away cash for her own plane. Sergeants were paid $55.

"I'm not sure I want to be a sergeant," she said. "I'm getting paid $120 a month. What's buck sergeant make?"

"Less than $40," he said. "But after the war, it might get you into air traffic control."

"In the tower, not in the cockpit."

"Wake up, Meade. No one's going to do that."

"Nancy Love? Jacqui Cochran?" she countered.

"This is a bird in hand," Cranston said. "Don't let your pride get in your way, Amelia."

"It's not pride." Maybe it was?

Quarters M-15, Fort Shafter

When she talked to the girls about Cranston's offer, she said, "It's a gamble. If I go with Cranston's offer, maybe by the end of the war, the Army will stand up a women's squadron and I'll have an inside chance to get accepted. If I stay with the WARD, I'll keep getting a big fat paycheck that could help me buy my own plane.

CJ gritted her teeth and sighed. "One more time, Jane, what do you want?"

"I want the WAFS. But I'm 150 hours short."

Ruth said, "When Gordon was on the Admission Board at the Academy, sometimes they'd let in candidates who didn't have the minimum if a boy wrote a letter from the heart and they saw he had potential."

"That feels like something Buck would do to skirt the rules. I want to get in on my own terms," Jane said.

"Comparing yourself to Buck is annoying," Eve said.

"Look," CJ said, "you went from secretary to flight instructor in a single year. Nancy Love needs women like you. Tell her what you did! Tell her why you want to fly!"

"That and a nickel," Jane mocked.

"I've had it with you." Eve reached for a cigarette.

"Jane, CJ's right," Ruth said. "Make her understand why you want to be a part of the squadron. Tell her what you can offer."

Jane shook her head. "The bottom line is that I'm not qualified."

CJ threw her hands up in the air. "Do you want this damn thing or not?"

"More than anything."

"Then do something about it."

Eve lit her cigarette and tossed the lighter on the table. "Either do something about it, or stop whining."

Eve's words cut to the chase. Jane hated damsels in distress. She walked on to Friendship a naïve high school girl and look what she did. But, she chided herself, that was before she was playing in the big leagues.

She was too dumb to know the rules then. But now?

The next night in the canteen, Jane filled out the application and wrote a personal letter to Love. She licked the envelope, pressed the seal for good luck and dropped it in the mail slot, telling herself not to hope, but she held out a glimmer anyway.

CHAPTER THIRTY-TWO
JANUARY 10-16, 1942

Quarters M-15, Fort Shafter

CJ TILTED HER alarm clock to read it. Five a.m.

The phone rang again. No one calls with good news at that hour. She looked over. Ruth was out like a light.

CJ sat up and tap danced her feet on the floor to scatter the roaches. The phone rang again. Were the rest of the girls deaf?

She felt the wall and hobbled her way in the dark. "Hello."

"CJ, it's Linc."

She gripped the phone. "What happened to Joe?" He couldn't be dead. "What's wrong?"

"Everything's fine!" Linc blurted. "Joe's fine. I'm trying to get hold of Eve."

CJ was still between sleep and wake. If Linc had to talk to Eve at this hour, it had to be important.

"Could you give her a message for me?"

"A message?"

"Don't wake her up. I was supposed to pick her up to go to Kualoa this morning, but I caught a zero dark thirty flight, and I can't make it. Can you let her know?"

"You got me up at five a.m. to be your messenger girl?"

"Come on, CJ."

Had it been anyone but Linc, she would have slammed down the phone and let him call back until Eve got jolted out of her beauty sleep. "You owe me, Armstrong."

"I owe you a lot more than this, CJ."

"Things are getting pretty hot and heavy with you and Eve."

"I like her."

"I'd say you passed the like stage."

"Just give her the message, would you?"

"Fine!"

"Thanks, CJ. I love you like a sister." He hung up.

But she didn't say when she'd give Eve the message. Since she was up, she wasn't going to wait until a decent hour to tell her. She barged into Eve's room and jostled her shoulder. "Eve."

Eve groaned.

CJ shook her again. "Eve, Linc called."

Eve opened her eyes.

"He's not coming for you. He has to fly."

"Wait." Eve stretched her back, arching like a cat. "What did you say?"

"Linc has to fly. Date canceled." She stomped into the kitchen.

CJ knew it was hopeless for her to get back to sleep. She'd been living with insomnia since the war started. She tried saying a rosary, then a second, but her mind darted to Joe. The war. How were her parents getting along without her?

She had asked the medics for sleeping pills, but they weren't allowed to dispense them. They could hand out copious amounts of caffeine pills to keep the WARDs awake on their shifts, but wouldn't give them something to help them sleep. "Not approved."

She lit the pilot light on the stove and poured water into the coffee pot.

Eve shuffled into the kitchen. "What did Linc say?" Eve tied her robe. Even at 5 a.m., Eve was dressed in satin.

"He caught a predawn flight and can't pick you up. That's all he said."

"We were going to spend the day at Parker's beach house." Eve sat at the kitchen table.

"Aren't you scheduled to work?"

"I got Mary Erdman to cover me."

Of course, CJ thought, Eve always managed someone to pick up her shifts.

"I think Linc and I may...you know..." She looked at CJ.

"We've come close a few times." Eve paused. "I've never done it before."

Against her better judgment, CJ asked, "You never?" She let the question hang in the air.

"Never," Eve said.

CJ had to sit down. *Bon vivant* Eve had never done it?

"And I don't know how." Eve sat up as if she were posing for a portrait instead a declaration of virgin embarrassment.

Never in a million years could CJ have imagined herself giving the "birds and the bees" talk to a Honolulu socialite while sitting in a blacked-out kitchen.

"The mechanics of it all confuses me," Eve admitted.

"But you do know the basics, right?" She had to! CJ thought.

"Theoretically."

"What about condoms? Do you know about them?" CJ asked.

"Ginger and I found a pack on the beach once. We figured it out."

"What about women's things? Like diaphragms?" CJ asked.

"I saw a picture of one, but I've never seen one in person."

CJ couldn't believe she was about to do a "show and tell."

"Dear God." CJ went into her room. It was late enough for a sliver of sunlight to show through the gap between the window-sill and the blackout curtains. She opened her dresser drawer and fiddled around with her lingerie until she felt the round plastic box, which she brought to the kitchen. "This is a diaphragm."

Eve opened the box. "My God! It's a lot bigger than it looked in pictures. Do they come in sizes?" She poked at it. "How do I put it in?"

There was no way in hell that CJ was going to demonstrate. "The doctor will show you how."

"Doctor? Can't I get one at the drugstore?"

"No. You see your family doctor, and he takes care of it."

"I can't go to my family doctor. He'll tell my mother."

"Eve, you're a grown woman."

"If he tells my mother, that will be the end of that," Eve said.

"What about Parker?" CJ suggested.

"You can't be serious! I'm not having Parker touch me like that!"

"I meant you could ask him if he has a friend to help you?"

Eve paused. "Do you think you could ask Parker for me?"

"Do you want me to have sex for you, too?"

CJ gave in. She made the call, and Parker gave her the name of a friend of his who worked at Kalihi Palama Settlement.

"His name is Doctor Stanley," CJ told Eve.

"The Kalihi Palama Settlement?" Eve sounded incredulous. It was a clinic where the Red Cross sent indigent women. "Am I even allowed to go to that kind of place?"

CJ bit her tongue. "Stanley is on staff at Queen's Hospital. He volunteers at the clinic."

"Can I see him at the hospital?"

"Sure. Make the appointment yourself. He already knows your situation."

"My 'situation?' I'm not some teenage harlot."

"No, you're a twenty-one-year-old who's scared her mother will find out she's having sex."

"I suppose no one my mother knows would be at the settlement." Eve sighed. "All right. I'll go there. But you're coming with me."

Kalihi Palama Settlement Clinic

The following Thursday, CJ and Eve scheduled themselves to have the day off to go to the clinic together.

"Then we can go to lunch," Eve said. "What about the Willows?"

"No lunch." CJ was firm, but it was Eve's car, and Eve was driving so God knew where they could end up.

As they turned onto Vineyard Boulevard, CJ said, "Look for a two-story white building with square columns over the portico and a bright red door. Parker said we can't miss it."

"Famous last words."

"There it is." It was next door to a shop with a handwritten sign, "Can't Bust 'Em Work Clothes. Guaranteed."

Eve pulled in the lot, parked, and checked her makeup in the rearview mirror.

"You look fine, Hollywood." CJ got out of the car.

Eve stepped in gingerly.

The waiting room was rectangular, with cinderblock walls, soot-coated jalousie windows, and lines of metal folding chairs filled with nodding-off mothers ignoring their rambunctious toddlers who were racing around. There was no plush upholstered furniture, no magazines, and no lithographs of Diamond Head on the walls. It was a crowded beige slab of a room—serviceable, free, and smelling of dirty diapers.

When Eve's name was called, CJ strolled Vineyard Boulevard, stopping in the "Can't Bust 'Em Work Clothes" store where she bought herself a pair of rain boots and a bag of clothespins to hang wet laundry on the lines they'd strung from the kitchen to the living room. Down the street, she couldn't resist stopping off at the malasada man's stand to pick up a dozen to bring home.

When she returned to the clinic, it was as if there were a shift change of patients. Most clients were young white women, primly dressed and perfectly coiffed.

The blonde sitting next to CJ inhaled loudly and smiled. "Malasadas?"

CJ nodded. "Bringing them home for my roommates."

The girl looked like a model for Ivory soap. She had fair skin and blue eyes, as innocent as the day was long. "Where do you live?" the girl asked.

"On the other side of Pearl Harbor." She tried to be as vague as possible.

"Well, these will be cold when you get them home." She pulled a malasada out of the bag. "Can I have one?"

Since she already had it halfway to her mouth, CJ said, "Sure."

The girl put out her other hand. "My name is Jean O'Hara."

From her saccharine-sweet drawl, CJ guessed she was a fine Southern girl. "Where are you from?" CJ shook her hand.

"Kind of all over." The girl leaned over and cupped her hand to her mouth to catch the powdered sugar. "My mother was in the entertainment business, so we traveled a lot." A veil of sugar dusted the floor. "But mainly, I lived in Oklahoma."

"What brought you out here?"

The girl looked at CJ as if it were a question she shouldn't have had to ask. "I'm an entertainer." She waved her hand at the other young women sitting around them. "We all are."

"Do you sing?"

The girl put the malasada down. "Sweetheart, we're working girls at the Boogie Houses. I'm at the Rex."

The redhead beside her said, "I'm at the New Senator Hotel."

A few others smiled and waved.

CJ took in their scrubbed faces and blue eyes. These all-American girls worked in lace-curtained brothels like the Ritz, the Anchor, and others. A brunette said, "We came out here to serve our country. All our customers are sailors."

There wasn't the slightest tinge of irony in her voice. CJ imagined an *Advertiser* headline: "Patriotic Prostitutes Doing Their Bit For the War." It was too bad that the Hawaii censors would never approve it.

After a bit, Eve came back out to the waiting room. She stood at the counter waving a small paper bag to CJ.

CJ nodded.

The receptionist said, "We ask for a donation of two dollars and fifty cents."

Eve handed over three dollars. "Please keep the change to help pay for as many families as possible."

The receptionist opened a drawer and pulled out a Mason jar labeled "Boogie Girl Fund" and said, "Without you girls, I don't know how we'd keep this place going."

"My pleasure." Eve beamed with *noblesse oblige*, and CJ restrained herself from explaining to Eve who the receptionist thought she was.

Chapter Thirty-three
January 18,1942

Quarters M-15, Fort Shafter

JANUARY 1942 WAS logged as the rainiest month on record. Roads flooded and souls grew moldy.

On the fourteenth straight day, CJ announced that in twenty-six days, they could officially board the ark.

Then, on the morning of the 15th, the rain stopped. Seeing the sun again seemed like a hopeful sign.

WARDs lounged on lawn chairs like newly blooming flowers, faces to the sun. They basted themselves with a potion of olive oil and iodine until they were blistery brown. But the war news was continued to be dire: The Japanese took Singapore, Thailand, the Philippines, Guam, and Burma. At the Battle at Wake Island, 12 U.S. aircraft were lost, nearly 1200 civilian workers were taken prisoner by the Japanese, and over 450 Marines surrendered.

Nancy West's husband, Bill, was a fighter pilot on the *Enterprise* at the battle at Wake. During an intense dogfight, Bill spotted a squadron mate surrounded by Japanese.

According to the incident report the Navy sent Nancy, *"Ensign West dove into the fray driving off the enemy fire aircraft enabling his squadron mate to escape. In doing so, Ensign West's plane was shot up, and he was seriously wounded in the right shoulder. He will be transferred to the hospital ship* Solace, *where he is expected to recover completely."*

Upon hearing the news, every WARD celebrated as if Bill were her own husband who made it through a bad scrape.

Within a few weeks, Bill was back flying; he was on a reconnaissance mission on the *Enterprise*. The wind conditions weren't the best, and the ship couldn't get enough speed.

The CO of Squadron Six took off first, and as his wingman, Bill was second in line. His plane lifted, stalled, and careened off the bow.

Ruth was having lunch when she spied Lieutenant Connor and Father Estabrook approaching the house.

As soon as she saw the chaplain, she knew Gordon was dead. She didn't answer the door—if she didn't answer the door, they couldn't deliver the news.

Connor knocked again.

She told herself that they were probably coming to talk to her about some administrative duty.

But why would they come to her house? In person? On her day off? Why wouldn't they just call?

"Hello?" Connor called from the porch.

Ruth opened the door, holding on to the doorknob for dear life.

Connor must have read her terror because his first words were, "It's not Gordon."

Nothing he said after that mattered.

"Come in." Ruth pulled Eve's blouse and cap off a living room sofa and motioned for Father Estabrook and Lieutenant Connor to sit.

Ruth sat on the couch, cautious, anxious.

Once they were all seated, Connor announced, "It's Nancy West's husband."

Ruth closed her eyes and took in a deep breath, and along with it a guilty relief that it wasn't Gordon. "Then, why are you here?"

Father Estabrook said, "We would like you to accompany us on the condolence visit."

The condolence visit—the chaplain, the condolence officer, and the CO's wife knock on the door—and life is never the same.

"Why me?" Ruth asked.

"You're the senior wife. You must have experience with this."

She had no experience at all. Gordon was in Intelligence. He had never lost a man in his command. Besides, Ruth was not the "senior wife," she was simply a WARD just like any other recruit.

You have a presence about you, Ruth," Father Estabrook said, "A kind of grace."

Grace? How ironic. She had heard the compliment before: "Ruth Elliot buried her daughter and handled it with such grace." What an ironic choice of words.

"What happened to him?" Ruth asked.

Connor handed her the incident report:

"Ensign West's aircraft crashed off the bow of the USS Enterprise. *West managed to free himself and make it out onto the wing. Just as the plane started to sink, West's boot became entangled in the radio antenna wire. He was unable to free himself in time, so he went down with the plane. Air Crewman Milton Clark, his radioman/gunner, cleared the aircraft. Clark was picked up by the USS* Conyngham.*"*

Ruth read it and handed it back to Connor. "Nancy doesn't need to know the details."

"She's entitled to an explanation," Connor said.

"The explanation will be that Bill died a hero," Ruth said. "All right. I'll come with you."

⚘

Lieutenant Conor knocked on the door and Nancy opened it. Her eyes widened. Her glance moved from the chaplain, to Connor, to Ruth. She gripped the door's edge. Her mouth opened, but no sound came out.

She took a step away from them.

"I'm sorry," Ruth said.

"Bill?" Her lips trembled. "Are you sure?"

Nancy staggered into Ruth's arms and Ruth stiffened, holding Nancy upright, feeling Nancy's sobs. Then Ruth closed her eyes and told herself not to take in Nancy's grief.

Ruth guided Nancy to the couch and instructed Connor to call Jean Knight, Nancy's best friend.

"Did anyone else go down?" Nancy asked.

Ruth shook her head. She was sure Nancy hadn't even begun to absorb what had happened. Nancy asked about other pilots, but no questions about Bill.

Then she paused, hesitated, and asked the chaplain, "Are they sure it was Bill?"

Ruth answered for him, "He had an accident on takeoff."

"Bill always said taking off from a carrier took brass balls." She smiled through her tears. "What happened?" she asked Ruth.

Ruth chose her words carefully. "He was seen after the crash, but his parachute was off, and he went down. "

"And the crewman?" Nancy asked.

Lieutenant Connor answered, "His gunner was picked up alive."

Nancy nodded. "You know Bill was wounded at Wake?" She asked Connor. "And they put him right back into the fleet."

Nancy looked down, twisting her wedding band.

"Maybe something happened with his shoulder?" Her jaw clenched and she repeated, "They put him right back into the fleet."

Jean Knight threw open the bungalow door. "Nancy!"

Nancy whispered, "Bill's gone."

Lizard Tunnel, Fort Shafter

Ruth knew it was going to hit Nancy, maybe not that night, or the next, but there would be that one moment she would realize that she'd never see Bill again. She'd never hear his laugh, feel his arms around hers, have his hand reach out to hers. Never make love with him again, have children, or grow old together. None of it would happen.

From that moment, her life would be marked as "before" or "after" Bill died—as Ruth's was marked by before or after Grace.

Ruth knew efficiency was a distraction from grief. Take on tasks. Immerse yourself until you are exhausted.

That afternoon she shuttled between Little Robert and Lizard

Tunnel to get permission for Nancy and Jean to have a 96-hour pass and she arranged for a "rest and relaxation" stay at one of the Waikiki hotels taken over by the military.

She coordinated all the admin requirements and notified the other Squadron Six pilots' wives of about Bill's accident. By the end of the day, she established a "meal tree" to have dinners delivered to Nancy's quarters and a Motor Corps car available to her. Then she took the sampan to Lizard Tunnel for her shift where Lieutenant Connor pulled her aside to tell her how grateful General Davidson was for her efforts.

This mixed blessing of recognition caused Davidson to remove her name from consideration for training in Washington, D.C.

Connor said, "The general feels we need a compassionate woman familiar with military protocol for condolence calls."

All Ruth wanted out of the WARDs was anonymity. No Officers' Wives Boards, no privileges or obligations of her husband's rank. She wanted to be applauded for her own work, and when she was a candidate to go to D.C., she couldn't help but already imagine herself there.

She planned shopping trips with her sister. Lunch at the Smithsonian café, a weekend trip to visit old friends in Norfolk, and, perhaps, an appointment with the gynecologist at Georgetown Hospital.

Connor droned on, "This is only the first of fatalities that will be suffered and there is no Commanding Officer's wife to accompany the chaplain on these visits."

Ruth knew exactly where he was going.

"General Davidson wants to designate you as a stand in for a Commanding Officer's wife."

It was everything Ruth wanted to avoid.

"He wants everything in place before the second class of WARD recruits graduates."

"Let me think about it," she said.

"Ruth, you know you're the only choice."

It was already a done deal. She took a deep breath. "Of course."

Once more Ruth rose to be the "good officer's wife," the dutiful Admiral's daughter, stepping up to do her part for God and country.

Chapter Thirty-four
February 2, 1942

Quarters M-15, Fort Shafter

IN FEBRUARY, THE rain came back with a vengeance. It pounded the quarter's roof, trickled down the bedroom walls, and puddled on the windowsills.

CJ was making her bed, grimacing as she propped her pillow against her bedspread. Everything in her world was turning into mold and mildew. Her sheets were damp, towels never dried, and she was constantly ducking under wet clothes strung from lines in the living room.

It was endless, like Chinese water torture. Drip. Drip. Drip. Eve's wet towels on the bathroom floor and Ruth cleaning up after her. She was sick of Eve's selfishness and Ruth's proper order. And Jane? Why the hell couldn't she make a decision about what she was doing?

Then there was Joe. It was two weeks since he left for Maui, and she still hadn't heard from him—not a letter, a postcard, or a V-mail message. For God's sake, on a clear day, she could see Maui on the horizon. Joe could have floated a message in a bottle, and she'd have had it already.

Moving to Paradise might have been a mistake.

"Good morning, sleepy head." Ruth opened the door carrying a cup of coffee. She looked like a poster girl for the Women's Air Raid Defense with her hair pulled back in a tight chignon, her uniform pleats pressed to knife-edge creases, and her double-strand of pearls.

Ruth set the coffee on CJ's bedside table.

"Thanks." CJ smoothed her damp bedspread and plumped her damp pillow.

"You okay?" Ruth asked.

"Why?" CJ asked.

"You were tossing and turning all night and muttering a bit."

Oh Lord. Coffee, sleepy head, commenting about how she'd slept? Ruth was in maternal mode. CJ would be fine if everyone, especially Ruth, left her alone. "I have a lot on my mind."

"A penny for your thoughts?" Ruth asked.

She wanted an answer, so CJ gave it to her. She dropped to the edge of the bed. "I'm thinking of going home."

Ruth didn't push or ask any questions, but by now CJ was spoiling for a fight.

"I think it's best," CJ said.

"If you've given it thought," Ruth was noncommittal.

Of course, she'd given it thought, and she wanted Ruth to hear every one of them. She got to her feet, and launched into her litany of complaints. "I came to Hawaii, got married, got a job…not the greatest job…but a start…and then—"

"Then the war happened?"

"I just want things to go back to the way they were."

"Don't we all?" Ruth said.

Ruth's dismissive tone infuriated CJ. "I just got married. It wasn't fair."

"It'll be four months before you're evacuated. What are you going to do until then?" Ruth asked.

Her abrupt switch to practicalities stayed CJ's pique. "I'll stay in the WARD." But then…

"Joe will be happy about that," Ruth said.

What right did Ruth have to tell her what Joe thought?

"I don't care what he thinks! I haven't heard from him since he left for Maui. How do you live like this? Your husband's gone. Your husband's home. You get settled at a new base. You move to a different base. You can't have a career. You've given up your entire life!"

CJ knew she had crossed the line the second Ruth's eyes widened and her nostrils flared.

"Let me tell you what I think." Ruth's tone sounded like a fed-up teacher who had just slammed a book on her desk. "Nancy West's husband died. Karly Herr's husband had his legs amputated. The Japanese invaded the Dutch East Indies and forced General MacArthur to withdraw from Manila. Thinking about a career isn't first on my mind these days."

In that instant, CJ hated Ruth. Hated her calm, her certainty, her ability to keep everything in line. But even as the thought formed, guilt crept in. It wasn't Ruth she hated—not really. She hated the silence from Joe. The not knowing.

Yes, there was a war, but damn it, why did that make it wrong for her to want Joe to call her?

Lizard Tunnel, Fort Shafter

When CJ got to the tunnel that morning, the teletype report was tacked to the corkboard. A Japanese sub sank a freighter 400 miles off the coast of Maui. Two other subs had been spotted east of Molokai.

CJ recalled Ruth's words, "I don't have time to think of a career right now."

She walked to the mailroom to check for a letter, where she found one from Joe. After her morning rant, she felt ashamed for being a whiny asshole. Joe's letter was postmarked ten days previously. After the "snip and snoops" had their way had with it, the letter it looked like a grade school snowflake.

Dear CJ,

I love you. I'm sorry I didn't get a chance to say goodbye. Things moved so fast.

CJ, I'm so sorry I brought you here. I know what you're going to say, it was your decision, but it was my idea that got you started. I …… not trying to tell you what to do, but I'm asking you to consider going home as soon as possible. I don't want you getting stranded ……….

You know I can't tell you where I am or how long I'll be here. The weather is cooler here and more people live in kiiiiiii than all of …… I haven't heard a horn honk since I got here!

I miss you, babe, and I think of you all the time.

There's a place here where you can go to watch the sunrise. They say it's beautiful, but work is …. and it'll be a long time before I see the rising sun.

Last week I was in …… stopped in a bakery to check it out. Your father would have loved it. His daughter helped him run it, and her daughter was running around the counters singing nursery rhymes.

I got daydreaming about our kids stopping by the bakery after school to see your parents.

It's .... here. Write to me, babe. I got to go.

I love you,

Joe

P.S. Put a dab of your perfume on your letter.

CJ traced her fingers over the holes in Joe's letter. She wished for a Captain Marvel Ring to decode what Joe was saying. *It'll be a long time before I see the rising sun.* She assumed the "rising sun" was Japan, and she hoped that *a long time before he saw it* meant he wasn't going to the front for a long time.

"*Pazienza e coraggi.*" She heard her grandmother's words. Oh, Nonna, patience and courage.

When she walked into the plotting room, she noted how little air traffic there was over the island. Maile Frost told her there was a poison gas drill going on in Honolulu.

It was so slow on the board that CJ didn't plot in an aircraft for the first two hours. The monotony was deadly.

Quarters M-15, Fort Shafter

It wasn't until she got back to quarters that she found out the reason. The afternoon edition of the *Advertiser's* headlines read: Gas Drill Cripples Honolulu! in three-inch letters.

Front page photos showed tanks driving down Bishop Street, soldiers in full gas mask combat gear marching down the street, and hundreds of people jammed on the bridge from Chinatown to Iwilei.

Eve looked up from polishing her nails. "It was just a drill. I don't know why everyone had to evacuate."

CJ and Jane exchanged glances and shook their heads. Neither of them explained the point of the drill to Eve.

"Where's Ruth?" CJ asked. She needed to apologize.

"Commissary. Grocery shopping," Jane said.

"Thank God for Mother Ruth." Eve blew on her polished nails.

Yes, thank God for Mother Ruth, CJ thought. She hoped Ruth would understand and forgive her for being a self-consumed ass earlier.

"I have news." CJ held up her letter, fluttering it in the ceiling fan breeze showing off all the holes. "I got a letter from Joe."

"Give us the details," Jane said.

"Or what's left to read," Eve quipped. "The censors certainly did their job."

CJ read most of it, then repeated the line about the rising sun and not being able to see it for a while. "It's got to mean that he won't be going to the front, right? I mean he says rising sun twice." She waited for Jane and Eve to agree.

"It makes sense," Jane said.

"Probably." Eve didn't look up from painting her toes.

"It can't mean anything else," CJ said, knowing she was hanging on to every thread of hope she could.

The only sure thing about the letter was Joe's return address.

She went to her room and started a letter to him. She told him how she thought of him in the morning when she heard the soldiers march in cadence, about a letter from her mother saying she was praying a novena for Joe, about Eve and Jane and Ruth and life on base. She wrote faster, and her handwriting got bigger. She wrote about the rain, the mud, the feral cats.

"How rainy is it?" she wrote. "The cockroaches are following us into the house to get dry."

She hated the roaches and the spiders and centipedes.

She moaned about missing her family and fumed that Maui was so close that she could see it on the horizon when it wasn't raining but when the hell was that going to be? She was sick of rice, craved pasta, wanted a pizza, a bagel—but most of all she wanted Joe, damn it. She re-read her letter, wiped her tears, and tore the letter to shreds.

CHAPTER THIRTY-FIVE
FEBRUARY 14, 1942

Kualoa Ranch

ON VALENTINE'S DAY, Linc pulled up in Parker's convertible. Eve watched him from her bedroom window. The Dairy Boy had gone native sporting an Aloha shirt and khaki shorts; but he needed a tan. His legs were glowing white.

Linc raked his hand through his hair before he opened the screen door. When he stepped in, he glared at Eve's three suitcases. "This is for the weekend?"

"I need every bit of it to look good," Eve answered.

Linc loaded the luggage in the car while Eve slid in the front seat.

"You look lovely, Miss Garbo," he teased as she wrapped a white silk scarf over her head.

"I know." Eve slipped on her wrap-around sunglasses, completing the Greta Garbo look. She flipped the sun visor down and adjusted her scarf and glasses. "Too bad there can't be a Valentine's Day party at the ranch. It's quite the event. The food is fabulous, and everyone takes a turn at the piano. The boys annihilate Broadway tunes with tawdry lyrics."

Eve smiled as she continued to reminisce. "When I was a kid, Mother would take me and Ginger to the ranch for the summer. To be precise, Mother would drive us up there and drink away the summer with Mrs. Holt while the three of us ran wild.

"Parker was our cohort. We played pirates a lot," she said, her voice light and animated. "One time, Parker convinced us to pretend we were castaways 'hiding out from the law.' We slept in a cave on the beach that night, shivering our patooties off and scared half out of our wits. The next morning, we ran up the hill for breakfast, and our mothers hadn't even noticed that we were gone." Eve rolled her eyes. "They were both so attentive."

"It sounds idyllic," Linc said.

"It was pure innocence." Eve stared past Diamond Head. It was mid-February and a few breaching whales were beginning their pilgrimage back to Alaska.

"Pull over!" Eve motioned Linc toward a gravel parking lot.

"Yes, ma'am." Linc gave her a smart salute.

When they got out of the car, Eve took Linc's hand and ran to the edge of the cliff. From there, they looked down on the

Makapuu Lighthouse. "This is my favorite spot on the island." She twirled with her arms in the air. "Look at it!"

The Koolau Mountains dropped into the ocean and small islands dotted an ocean striped azure, teal and navy.

Eve pointed to a patch of gray on the horizon. "That's Molokai. On a clear day you could see Maui. I wish you could see it!"

"There's nothing like flying over these cliffs," Linc said.

"What's it like?"

"You're totally alive, then it's like you're falling, but you pull up just in time." Linc stood at the cliff's edge, and Eve noticed his silhouette framed against the sky, a gust of wind lifting his shirt.

Linc wrapped his arms around her waist. "If I had one place to be in for the rest of my life, this would be my paradise."

An albatross drifted on the wind, wings still as it skimmed the air above them, then disappeared down toward the water with barely a ripple.

"You mean with me, of course?"

"With you." He kissed her lips, her cheeks. He nuzzled her neck.

"So, you'd leave Wisconsin to stay here?" Eve fluttered her eyelashes so deftly, they could almost be heard.

"I can't let my guard down one minute with you."

"Never."

As they drove to the ranch, Eve was lost in memories of her summers spent there with Ginger and Parker.

"It's the next left. It's right after the bend," Eve said.

Linc shifted gears to make it up the hill.

Before Eve got out of the car, she took in the sight of the ranch. She climbed the gravel path, hands in her pockets, her long strides making it up the hill.

Mrs. Holt's wicker swing still hung in the gazebo. The Adirondack chairs were lined up on the porch to face the ocean, and the hand-carved "Aloha" sign was still tilted over the front door. "It's just like I remembered it."

⌘

When she stepped inside, a bouquet of anthuriums was on the table and the house smelled of Lysol and bleach. "I haven't been up here in years."

Eve ran her hand over the bamboo print upholstery on the couch. "Even the curtains are the same."

As Linc carried in the luggage, Eve said, "The first bedroom on the left was always mine."

Linc set her bags in the room, then put his in the room across from it.

She felt foolish. And presumptuous. She thought this was going to be "the weekend."

"Do you want a beer?"

"I'll get it." Eve inventoried the food: strawberries, steaks, champagne. For sure, this had to be "the weekend," or at least Parker thought so when he stocked the fridge.

Eve grabbed two beers, and Linc opened the screen door. He pushed two Adirondack chairs close to each other. "Come sit."

The sun was beginning to set, and the vista from the porch overlooked the ocean and the thin ribbon of road along the coast.

"What would you be doing in Wisconsin for Valentine's Day?"

"We wouldn't be sitting outside, that's for sure. If it was above zero, we'd think it was an early spring. But one year on Lincoln's birthday weekend we went to Star Lake."

"We?"

"My parent, grandparents, aunts, uncles, cousins and at least three dogs."

"In one cottage?"

"It's more like a camp," Linc said. "The main house has eight bedrooms. The bunkhouse sleeps ten and the boathouse has a loft—that was my favorite place to sleep during the summer. I'd pretend I was in Scotland and the loons were wailing in the fog, warning me about an invading clan."

"So, you do have an imagination, Dairy Boy."

Linc snickered. "That was in summer. During the winter, we'd have snowdrifts up to the second-floor windows. One year, my cousin and I got in trouble for jumping into it and our dads had to dig us out."

"It sounds like it's straight out of Currier and Ives."

"You'd love it," Linc said.

Eve pulled out a cigarette, and Linc lit it. "It sounds lovely for someone else."

"So says the cosmopolitan dilettante."

"I'm holding off for my San Francisco dream," Eve said. "Do you know that Parker's been offered the Chief of Surgery at San Francisco General after the war? And," Eve turned to Linc. "By the way, San Francisco has good medical schools for you to consider."

"So does Wisconsin."

Eve patted Linc's hand. "Can you imagine what it must be like to fly over San Francisco at night? The Golden Gate all lit up. It must be wonderful." She leaned forward. "What's it feel like to fly at night?"

"It's like floating. You feel like you can close your eyes and let yourself fall until your wheels hit the ground."

"That doesn't sound prudent."

"You rely on your training and trust your instincts.'

"I couldn't do that. I need more control."

"I know."

※

After a leisurely dinner of grilled steak and potatoes, Eve brought out a tray of strawberries and Linc popped the bottle of champagne.

"Happy Valentine's Day." They toasted each other.

"I've forgotten how much I crave being alone," Linc said.

Eve reared her head. "Excuse me?"

"Alone, without the 'greatest pilots in the world'—the constant banter and the stink of jet fuel."

Eve put down her champagne. "Actually, I was wondering how you were able to catch a 48-hour pass."

"The whole squadron's off. There' a safety stand down. We're having trouble with our radios."

"That sounds troublesome," Eve said.

Linc reached for her hand. "Are you worried about me?"

She curled her lip. "I'm worried about the war."

By the time Eve finished her sentence, a winter "pineapple shower" broke, and within minutes, a fine mist was a pelting downpour. Linc grabbed the strawberries and champagne and Eve ran in the house with the glasses.

They set down their things, laughing, whisking rain off their arms and faces.

"The Hawaiians consider rain a good omen," Eve said.

Linc brushed a wisp of hair from Eve's forehead.

"It's a blessing," Eve said. She looked into Linc's eyes, waiting, expecting that first kiss of the night. Maybe this will start it, she thought—our first night together.

Linc lifted her chin and gently kissed her.

Yes, this was it. It was going to happen, and she was prepared. She wondered if a diaphragm moved during sex, or if Linc would be able to feel it.

Linc took her in his arms and carried her into the bedroom. He laid her on the bed, sat and unbuttoned her blouse.

Eve wanted to tell him—warn him—this was her first time.

He brushed his lips against her shoulder and slipped off her blouse. She wasn't sure she knew how to do this right, let alone do it well.

He unhooked her bra and kissed her breasts.

Pay attention to what he's doing, Eve chided herself. Just do what comes naturally.

He took off his shirt, his trousers and tossed all his clothes to the floor and she breathed in the scent of his sandalwood cologne.

"Linc…"

He unzipped her skirt and glided it down her legs. He kissed her belly, and Eve was grateful it was dark. She had that scar from her appendix being removed, she angled her left hip up to his mouth, hoping he wouldn't notice the scar.

Dear God, she thought. Pay attention!

He traced his fingers around the band of her panties, and Eve began to give in to his touch. She put her hand over his. "This is my first time," she said.

He paused; she thought she saw his eyes widen.

Linc sat up. "We can wait," he whispered. He stroked her cheek. "It's up to you."

She knew her answer—she wrapped her arms around his back. She drew him close, buried her face in his chest then glided his hand down her hip. Then, she moved his hand between her thighs and gave in to the rhythm of his stroke. She squeezed her legs tightly, felt buckle of his watch against her thighs, and then opened herself up to be loved by him, submitting to every pleasure, every unexpected shiver and surge of warmth. She pushed her hips against his, and their bodies fell into a gentle rhythm. She reached to draw him into her.

"Wait," Linc whispered.

It was too late.

She thrust against him, and they came together—shuddering breathlessly, flushed with the scent of sex.

And when they both collapsed, consumed and spent, he took her face in his hand and said, "I love you, Eve."

Eve didn't answer.

"I love you," Linc repeated.

Eve knew what she was supposed to say, but she'd never said I love you to anyone before—anyone besides her parents and Ginger.

"Thank you," was the best she could commit to.

⌘

The next morning, Eve wrapped herself in a sheet and watched Linc shave in the bathroom mirror. Eve had never been with a naked man before, and she examined him like an artist appreciating her model. There was a curve to his back, and at the top of his thighs, there was no hair where they joined his hips.

He lathered his brush, swirled soap over his face, and angled his cheek to the mirror.

Linc caught her looking at her in the mirror and smiled. Then he winced when he nicked his chin. A pink streak blossomed in the soap. Eve got out of bed, tore off a piece of Kleenex and pressed it against his cut.

"Will you marry me?" he said.

Eve laughed. He was probably joking, but his words caught in her chest. "I haven't even told you that I love you," she said.

"You can pretend until you do."

Later that morning, they trekked down the steep trail to the beach, and she hoped the breeze would clear his head. Marriage? He was her first lover.

When they got to the beach, Linc spread a blanket on the sand. Streamers of seaweed tangled in the barbed wire—even sleepy Kualoa was girded against the enemy.

Linc lounged on his side, his elbow bent and his head in his hand. Eve struck the pose of a Vargas pinup. "Want to take my picture?

"Sorry, the F.B.I. took my camera," he joked.

"How about now?" She dropped one of the straps of her suit and posed with one hand on her head, the other on her hip and let her hair fall over her face.

"That's one to put in my cockpit." Linc pretended to take her photo. "Marry me."

She sat next to him and coyly sifted sand through her fingers. "I don't think so."

"We can go to Waikiki right now and buy a ring."

"I can buy my own rings, thank you."

"I'd make love to you forever." He winked.

Eve leaned over and gave him a peck on the cheek. "You don't have to make an honorable woman of me. Now that I'm tainted, I'm fair game."

Linc started to speak but then fell silent. He traced the wing of her eyebrow, twined a strand of her hair around his finger, and pulled her close.

"I want to make you my wife." He glided his finger against the edge of her lips. "Marry me." He kissed her, and she gave in and sank against him to make love in the heat of the midday sun.

Chapter Thirty-six
February 17, 1942

Lizard Tunnel, Fort Shafter

WHEN JANE SIGNED in for her afternoon shift, Dottie Best pulled her aside.

"It's on the board," Dottie said quietly.

Jane's stomach dropped. "How did it happen?"

"It was a mid-air."

The accident report was tacked on the board next to one announcing the Seabees' arrival in Samoa to build an airfield.

Jane unpinned Nancy Love's statement.

At 6 p.m., February 16, 1942, Cornelia Fort was killed in a routine ferrying flight.

Her hand trembled.

Lieutenant Fort was ferrying a bomber from Long Beach, California to Love Field in Dallas when she had a mid-air collision with another WAFS plane.

Cornelia was solid. Careful.

While flying in formation, the left wing of her bomber was struck by the landing gear of flight officer Frank Stamme Jr.'s plane. Stamme had been flying too close to Fort's plane, approaching her and then pulling back…

What the hell was he doing?

…breaking off the tip of her wing and six feet of leading edge, causing Fort to go into an irreversible dive and crashed. The accident occurred ten miles south of Merkel, Texas, in Mulberry Canyon, Texas.

Cordelia hadn't had a chance.

Fort's body will be sent home to Hawaii where she will be buried. Donations to pay to transport the body are to be sent to Lieutenant Colonel Nancy Love, Commanding Officer of the squadron.

Quarters M-15

Jane dreaded sharing the news with the girls that night. She paused on the porch, gathering her thoughts.

She opened the living room door; CJ and Eve were sitting on the couch.

"Sit. Relax," Eve said.

"You looked bushed," CJ said.

"It's been a tough day," Jane answered. "Cornelia's dead."

The silence among them held for a moment.

CJ put her hand to her mouth, then she crossed herself.

Eve remembered Cornelia at the Debutantes' Ball at the Pacific Club. She had stunned everyone in a satin slip of a gown.

"What happened?" CJ asked.

Jane knew they didn't need details. Neither of them was a pilot. They wouldn't understand. She answered, "It was a routine flight gone bad."

"Routine?" Eve creased her eyebrow. "Cornelia was anything but routine. How the hell…?"

"It happens more than you think," Jane answered.

Eve scoffed. "Well, that's not comforting."

Dear God, CJ thought. Where have you been during the News of the Day? Routine flights crashing, mid-airs, friendly fire!

CJ turned to Jane. "Are you reconsidering joining the WAFS?"

"It makes me want to fly with them more than ever."

Chapter Thirty-seven
February 22, 1942

Quarters M-15, Fort Shafter

RUTH BROKE OUT laughing. "I'm afraid to ask!"

Linc and Parker stood at the front door in their dress white uniforms, resplendent with medals, ribbons, Groucho Marx eyeglasses, noses, and mustaches, each holding a box stenciled "Property of USN."

"We are magician assistants." Parker scooted around her and headed to the kitchen.

Linc followed him, carrying two small boxes.

Parker laid his loot on the counter. "Master Chief Harry Houdini Delaney can make anything appear or disappear."

"Translation?" Ruth asked.

Parker took off his disguise and laid it next to the sink. "Master Chief Houdini can make anything appear from steaks, to champagne, to Jeeps that got 'destroyed' during the attack."

Parker waved his hand over the booty. "What we have for you here, ladies, are the remains of an admiral's change of command reception."

Eve bustled out of her room. "Did I hear Lieutenant Armstrong's voice?"

"You missed the grand entrance," Ruth said.

Parker and Linc got back in their Groucho Marx disguises.

"It's a good look for you, Park," she mocked.

"What about me?" Linc wiggled his moustache.

"You, my dear, are infinitely more handsome without them." Eve took off Linc's disguise and kissed him.

Parker explained, "The outgoing admiral's call sign is Groucho, so all the officers were given these to wear during the roast."

"How very dignified," Eve smirked.

"You won't be so sarcastic when you see the booty!" Parker opened the box. "London broil, gin…and more gin…and lettuce!"

"Fresh lettuce!" Ruth cradled it to her chest. "Be still, my heart."

Eve cradled the gin. "Be still, mine!"

"And some Grade A hooch." Parker held up a bottle of Glenlivet.

"The only catch is we've got to get the boxes back to him pronto." Linc looked at Eve. "Want to go for a ride?"

Parker turned to Linc, "If you don't mind, I need to talk to Eve. It's Holt-Russell family stuff."

Linc raised his eyebrows. "Should I be jealous?"

"Feel free to stay if you want an update on our mothers," Parker said.

Linc pointed his index fingers in the air. "And those are the magic words that will make me disappear."

After Linc left, Parker led Eve out to the porch.

"What's up with the dowager queens?" Eve asked.

"You've been hijacked," Parker admitted. "I want to talk about Linc."

Eve cocked her head. "This should be interesting."

"Linc's in love with you," Parker said.

"That's no news." Eve raised her eyebrows. "Most men are."

"He's talking about marrying you, Eve."

"I know."

"And…"

"I'm not the domestic type, you know that. I'm Eve Russell."

"Don't be glib with me."

"Don't be glib? A bit hypocritical coming from the master of glib."

"Point taken," Parker said. "But this is serious. Linc loves you."

"Can I help it if I'm irresistible?" Eve leaned back, taking a starlet pose.

"Quit the *dame fatale* bit."

Eve's eyes hardened. She pointed to the pack of cigarettes on the porch table, and Parker handed it to her. She lit a cigarette, took in the first drag, and blew one of her trademark smoke rings to the ceiling, all the while staring at Park, waiting for his next assault.

Still nothing from Park.

Eve broke the silence, "What's your point, Park? We're having a good time for now."

"He's talking about—"

"I know."

"Then stop acting like you don't care."

"I'm not interested in being Midwest Annie."

"Be serious." His voice had an edge to it.

"Park, I'm honestly not sure I want to marry anyone." She resorted to ingenue wit. "I'd like to just date forever."

"Your face and figure aren't going to last forever," Parker said.

His words stung, but she wasn't giving in to the barbs. "Maybe I should marry a plastic surgeon?" Eve picked a piece of tobacco from her tongue and stared at it.

"What are you going to do when you're 30, Eve? And don't tell me you're walking up Lombard Street with a satchel of wine and roses."

"I'll have a job at the Fine Arts Museum. I'll spend my weekends at Half Moon Bay and have dinners at the Cliff House every Tuesday night." She sounded like an insolent adolescent.

"At 40?"

"The same thing, except I'll be a gallery curator and wear conservative suits, probably Chanel."

"You'll quit the first time they refuse your request for an extended vacation."

"I can always live off my trust."

"Will your trust love you?"

"You're being melodramatic, Park."

"Pansy Parker and his melodrama!"

Eve shifted in her seat.

"You act like love is a joke," he said.

"Maybe it is."

Parker's tone sharpened. "Do you have any idea what I'd give to share my life with someone I love? To go to dinner? To dance in public?"

She tapped her cigarette against the ashtray, not looking at him.

"I wish I could share my life with someone," he whispered.

"What if you moved to San Francisco and married me?"

"Don't insult me, Eve."

Eve stubbed out her cigarette. "I like Linc, but…"

"But what?"

"I wouldn't mind strolling the streets of San Francisco with him, but marrying him? Can you picture me in Madison, Wisconsin? Weekends at the lake house, an annual weekend in

Chicago, every other year in Europe? That would be grand, but the time in between? Unfathomable."

Parker rubbed his forehead. "Then let him know that now."

Her face softened. "Park, I'm honestly scared the hell out of anyone needing me. I don't know how—"

"You need to take a risk, Eve."

She held up her cigarette and retreated into her charade. "I want to be adored." Then an unbearable sense of vulnerability crept through her and she looked away so Parker couldn't see her mask drop. "I don't want to get it wrong."

Chapter Thirty-eight
February 26-March 2, 1942

Lizard Tunnel, Fort Shafter

"SOMETHING'S GOING ON," CJ said, and whatever "it" was, it was big.

All leaves were canceled. Stretcher-bearers were ordered to advanced first aid training, and no off-base phone calls were allowed.

Those were the facts, but they were eclipsed by the rumors: WARDs were being issued pistols. A secret tunnel in Lizard warehoused 30 days of food and water. Suicide pills were being stocked in the clinic—just in case.

Those were the rumors—mostly not credible. But the truth was that MPs who used to joke with the WARDs in the canteen were now demanding straight answers to the question, "Who goes there?"

One night after their shift, CJ and Jane went for a midnight stroll. They passed a group of sentries. An MP who CJ swore she recognized yelled, "Halt. Who goes there?"

The official answer was "Friend." But Eve waved to the fellow and said, "It's just me, honey."

Metal clicked. The bolt of his rifle retracted. "Who goes there?" he repeated.

"Friend," Eve answered. Too late. Too hesitant.

"You know us. We're WARDs." CJ's voice faltered.

The MP didn't lower his rifle, and Eve repeated, "Friend. We're WARDs."

When they got back to quarters, they told Ruth and Jane what happened.

"Everybody's getting jittery," Ruth said.

Jane said she heard Army engineers were building runways on Kualoa. "I figure that means we're ready to send planes to Japan."

"Why not build them on Midway Island?" CJ asked.

Midway was over 900 miles closer to Tokyo than Kualoa.

"Too many Japs subs there?"

Whatever was going on, no one was giving a clue. The only thing the WARDs knew was that they were plotting B-25s night and day on runs from Honolulu to Midway.

Oscar passed on scuttlebutt that the bombers were practicing short-field takeoffs once they got to Midway.

The WARDs were double scheduled, sleeping in shifts. While

a full shift was on the board, each WARD had two backups in the tunnel. On February 26th, the shadows were back, taking over some shifts and bumping WARDs off the board.

Bill Flynn and Tom Martin showed up on the second day.

Tom was attacking his stack of fried egg sandwiches with such vigor that Eve hesitated before asking if he knew anything.

"Not a lick," he mumbled through his mouthful.

Bill answered for him. "They've got us triple-timing it. We're at Little Robert training the recruits and flying back and forth to Kauai and the Big Island to help set up remote stations."

"I heard they're building up Midway." CJ's reporter's gut was sure Midway was where the action would be.

Tom squirted his fried eggs with catsup. "All I know is that something's going on."

On February 28th, Ruth had the morning shift when the WARDs plotted out a squadron of sixteen B-25s flying north. The bombers didn't return that day, nor did they return the next day. This was it.

By the third day, the rumor mill went silent, and all conjecture ceased as if any speculation about the mission would cause bad luck.

∾

For two days, any out-of-rhythm breath, any suspicious tone in a greeting, any glance held too long caused speculation. No one was talking.

On March 2nd, CJ and Ruth were working the board when enough Army brass entered the plotting room to sink it. WARDs exchanged glances. What the hell was going on?

The entourage climbed the stairs to the balcony. They moved in huddles, leaning over junior officers who were measuring maps with rulers. Mathematical formulas were scribbled on blackboards, and the liaison officers pressed their headsets against their ears.

CJ's hands moved automatically, tracking the same predictable training flights, but her eyes stayed locked on the balcony. Papers rustled, voices whispered, and fingers jabbed at maps.

Then, the Navy brass paraded in, led by a two-star admiral.

Ruth coughed. CJ looked up, and Ruth darted her eyes toward the balcony. The admiral and general were wearing the headsets of the liaison officers.

Twenty minutes passed, and then one of the generals came to the rail of the balcony.

"Ladies and gentlemen," he announced, and every head snapped toward him.

"This morning, sixteen B-25s under the command of Lieutenant Colonel James Doolittle bombed Tokyo. This was the first time in history that Japan was attacked on its sovereign land."

The room exploded. Cheers went up, boots pounded the floor, fists slammed desks, paper was tossed in the air. Some whooped, some laughed. They hugged and thrusted their fists in the air.

The general cheered them on, "We did it."

In spite of the jubilation around her, Ruth froze, knowing the Japanese would retaliate with a swift vengeance.

Then, the general put his hands up to calm them. "The inflicted damage was minimal, but the psychological impact was devastating." The general read from a teletype report: "Of the sixteen B-25 crews, one is reported landing in Russia, the other fifteen have either landed or crashed in China." Cheers burst from the room.

The mention of China slammed the breath out of Ruth.

"Until the Intelligence units in China dispatch information, we have no other news."

The Intelligence units in China.

Gordon.

CHAPTER THIRTY-NINE
MARCH 10-16, 1942

Quarters M-15, Fort Shafter

CJ TORE OPEN the letter from Joe:

Dear CJ,

It's definite, my sister's baby is due on St. Patrick's Day. I wish I could be there with them to celebrate at O'Toole's, but I suppose I'll have to satisfy myself with raising a beer at Murphy's.

I can't wait until we can have our own baby.

Love you,

Joe

She didn't need a decoder ring to figure out that letter. Murphy's and O'Toole's were Irish pubs across the street from each other in Chinatown, and in a few days, Joe would be back on Oahu.

From the day she got Joe's letter, CJ lathered her face with skin cream. She bought a new dress, a black lace negligee, and heels that actually fit her. She shaved her legs and put on her "good" makeup every day, just in case Joe turned up unexpectedly.

On March 13th, CJ pulled a double shift, covering for Fluff Ford. She had a headache from eight hours under fluorescent light, and the only meal she'd had was a hard-boiled egg. All she wanted was a shower and a bed.

When she got home, Ruth, Jane, and Eve sat, almost posing, on the living room couch, grinning like Cheshire cats. The girls kept smiling. They kept staring at her. Something was up. Then she noticed her luggage lined up next to the couch. "Did we get a 96 to go somewhere?"

"Well, one of us did," Ruth said.

Joe stepped out of the kitchen.

She did a double take. It was him!

She clamped her arms around his neck. His Old Spice. The starched smell of his uniform. His five o'clock shadow. "It's you."

"In the flesh."

She nuzzled her neck in his chest and heard his voice resonate. She stepped back and cradled his face in her hands. "You're real."

"100%." Joe kissed her, and she wiped the tears from her face. "I love you, Mr. Delano."

"Ha. We're married, and she still calls me by my last name!"

"And I'm Mrs. Delano!" She held his hands in hers, as if she let go, he would disappear.

"And with a few fairy godmothers, you're going to have the honeymoon you never had," Eve said. "You've got an unofficial 96-hour pass at a Waikiki beach house."

CJ turned to Joe. "Were you in on this?"

"Nope." Joe shook his head. "The girls have your shifts covered, and…" He bowed to Eve. "Someone coerced Parker to give up his beach house."

Jane said, "And Linc stocked it with champagne and a few of your favorite records."

"Is there anything you didn't take care of?" CJ asked.

"The only thing we can't guarantee is the weather," Jane said.

"Don't worry," CJ said. "We're never leaving the bedroom."

Even Ruth cracked a smile.

Parker's Beach House, Waikiki

When they got to Parker's beach house, Joe carried CJ over the threshold. "I should have done this at the Royal."

"There's lots we should have done at the Royal." CJ grinned.

"Then let's get to it."

Joe kicked the door closed, and CJ had his tie off and was unbuttoning his shirt before they staggered into the bedroom. They tangled and sweated, and made love until they were exhausted, and they made love again, and tried again, but Joe's failed attempt had CJ giggling.

"Give me a chance," Joe said, but in minutes, he was snoring.

CJ traced her finger down Joe's spine.

"Be a good wife, Carmela," her mother's words came to her. But how?

That afternoon, CJ and Joe basked in the sun. CJ wore the red polka-dot bathing suit the girls bought her, and Joe was in his G.I. boxers. He lolled on a hammock strung between two coconut trees, smoking his cigar and resting his beer on his belly.

The beer was cold and the sun was hot. CJ rolled her bottle against her cheek. She listened to the rhythm of the waves and breathed in the ever-constant perfume of plumeria.

Don't ask him, she told herself. She swore she wouldn't. Why ruin the day?

But the words came out, "How long are you home for?"

"A couple of weeks."

"And then?"

"Who knows?"

"But, what do you think is going to happen?"

"Can we not talk about it?"

CJ saw Joe's grip on his beer bottle tighten, but she couldn't let it go. "You must have some idea when you're deploying."

"I won't know until that day."

She heard the tension in his voice but tried one more approach. "Maybe they'll keep you on Maui?"

He chugged his beer and tossed the bottle on the sand.

"Maybe?" She couldn't help herself.

"We've got two weeks together. Let's not waste it talking about what may happen."

Joe got out of the hammock and sat next to her. She was ready for him to take her in his arms, but he reached for her hand instead.

"You have to face facts," he said. "It's coming, and we've got to be ready for it."

Now it was CJ who did not want to waste time talking about what may happen.

"There are a few things we need to talk about."

She refused to hear any burial plans.

Instead Joe said, "Do you think you should get pregnant?"

Pregnant? She was dashing down images of herself in a black dress at a cemetery. Pregnant? Where the hell did that come from?

"What are you talking about?"

"If I die, do you want a baby to remember me?" He was serious.

"If I die, do you want to have a baby?" She snatched her hand away. "You've lost your mind!"

"I don't know. Maybe you'd want to have a career and not be saddled with a kid?"

"I'm not listening to you!"

"I love you, CJ. I want to make you happy."

"I am not listening!"

"Babe, please."

"No!" She held up her hands, signaling him away.

"If I died, I'd feel so much better if I could leave a part of me with you."

"You're insane."

He reached for her. "Hear me out."

Flight or fight.

"Do not follow me, Delano." Her warning was clear. "Go away." She ran.

He wants a baby so I can remember him? Like buying saltwater taffy from Atlantic City?

She kept running until her breath was ragged, then she slowed, walking, digging her feet in the sand, kicking it up with every step.

I'll remember him! I'll go to Atlantic City on the anniversary of his death and buy a triple-size box of taffy.

She hated seeing barbed wire strung on the beach, seeing Pearl Harbor on the horizon. Her vision blurred, but she refused to cry, trying to unhear Joe's words.

She should never have come to Hawaii. If she'd stayed home, she would only know that Joe was on Maui, safe from the war.

It didn't take long before she heard Joe call her. She knew he'd catch up. She wanted him to catch up.

Joe held her by her shoulders. "I love you, CJ."

Love was never a question.

"I only want the best for you."

She heard the pleading in his voice. She knew he wanted the best. She knew what he meant about a baby. "I love you" was on her lips, but before she could say it, Joe asked her again.

"CJ, do you want to have a baby?"

Whether he was going to be there or not, he wanted it all—the house in New Jersey, their kids in the yard and her in the kitchen.

God forbid, what if he does die? What was the harm if he died with a dream?

He was deploying. Just give it to him.

"Let's have a baby."

And each time they had sex, she slathered her diaphragm with medical cream and inserted it so high that Joe would never feel it. Hell, there had to be a patron saint of liars to pray to.

CHAPTER FORTY
MARCH 17, 1941

Chinatown

THE SUN BOUNCED off shop windows and cobblestones slick with spilled beer on Merchant Street. The street was crowded with "Irish" cops who looked away at drunken sailors.

They were a motley crew—Eve, CJ, Ginger, Linc, and Parker—all in their uniforms, locking arms, weaving through the revelers.

Ginger tipped her paper mâché hat to a vendor selling jade trinkets. Parker adjusted his shamrock tie, while Linc darted back to the jade vendor's booth. "Go on. I'll catch up," he told them.

Bell-bottom sailors danced jigs and belted out "Galway Bay."

"If I didn't know better, I'd think we won the war," Eve said.

A sailor tugged at the green satin bow tied at Eve's waist. Linc put his arm around her, shielding her. "You may want to ditch the bow."

"Like hell." Eve retied the green satin bow even bigger. "When I commit, I commit."

"Are you trying to tell me something?"

"That no one tells Eve Russell what to do," she shot back.

"None of us needs that lesson," Ginger mocked.

"Joe!" CJ spotted him standing in front of Wo Fat's.

They made their way to the door.

"Hurry up!" Parker held the door open, and they bulldozed through the crowd and claimed a booth.

A waitress slammed down two pitchers of beer. "Glasses are at the bar. Grab 'em yourself or wait…" She glanced at the crowd. "A lifetime."

Eve swiped the tabletop and looked at her finger, and cringed. "Park, could you ask her to clean the table?"

Joe snorted. "The doc doesn't have combat training to take her on."

"Fine, then you do it," Eve said.

Joe stood. "I'm going to the bar to get the mugs. It's safer."

"Sit down, Marine," Park said. "There are other ways to get this done, chap." He held a five-dollar bill over his head and waved it. "Five bucks to the first guy to get us five glasses and another full pitcher."

Three sailors reached for the bill.

Parker snatched it away. "When you deliver."

An Asian kid wearing a "Kiss Me I'm Irish" pin on his apron delivered a platter of corned beef and cabbage and a wire basket of forks, spoons, and napkins.

"We didn't order anything," Ginger said.

"No ordering tonight. Everybody's getting the same thing."

The two sailors set five coffee cups and a pitcher of Guinness on the table. "They ran out of glasses, sir," one of them said.

"Good enough!" Parker handed over the five.

Joe hoisted his coffee cup in a toast, "To the dear sister I don't have." He pulled CJ closer. "To family. The one we have and the one we hope is on the way."

She hadn't planned to tell them like this—hell, she hadn't planned anything. But Joe's toast hung in the air. It was impossible to pull back.

Eve swiveled her head toward CJ. "What?"

CJ shook her head slightly, mouthed, "I'll explain later," and then gave Eve a *let it go* glare.

But what was there to explain? That she was sending Joe off to war hoping that she was pregnant, or worse yet—him thinking she wanted to be. Joe had to know the odds of it working so fast were slim. She'd write him a letter in a month, telling him how disappointed she was that she wasn't pregnant, but as soon as the war was over, they'd go back to New Jersey and fill the house with beautiful dark-eyed, dark-haired children.

❧

"Band leader!" Linc shouted to the fiddler. "I have a request." Linc stood up.

"Please, God, not *Danny Boy*," Parker yelled.

Linc pulled a small burlap bag out of his uniform pocket.

"What'd you get me?" Eve coaxed.

"The prize at the end of the rainbow." Linc slid out of the booth and took Eve's hand.

When they squeezed into the crowd, Linc cued the fiddler, "Now." The band played, "Love, will you marry me, marry me, marry me? Love, will you marry me and take me out of danger?"

Linc got down on one knee.

"Oh, no. No. No. You are not doing this."

Linc held up a ten-cent jade ring. "Eve Dorothea Russell, will you marry me?"

"This isn't fair." Eve glanced at CJ, her eyes wide, like she'd been pushed onstage without her lines.

The crowd chanted, glasses slamming tables. "Say yes! Say yes!"

Linc held the ring higher, unwavering. "Say yes."

Eve's lips parted—then closed. Then opened again. What was she doing?

"Yes."

Linc kissed his fiancée, and the bartender rang a brass bell, "Drinks for the newly betrothed on the house."

They settled back in the booth.

Eve held out her ring. "Who told you I like jade?"

"That would be me," Ginger said. "But I told him it had to be from Gump's."

"And who told you my middle name?"

"Your father told me," Linc said.

"Pops?"

"When I asked him for your hand, and he gave us his blessing."

"They know?" Of course, Mother would know. She always knew everything first. "Mother's probably already planning the wedding."

"I wouldn't go that far," Ginger said.

Right, Eve thought. First, she'd have to investigate Linc's family's pedigree.

Quarters M-15, Fort Shafter

For the next few days, whenever Eve was in quarters, she sketched wedding gowns and debated what font to use for her invitations.

She was standing in front of the mirror playing with her hair when she asked Jane, "Maybe a barrette of pikake? What do you think?"

Jane raised an eyebrow in Ruth's direction and answered Eve, "I'm not sure."

Then Eve pulled her hair off her face. "And emerald earrings?"

"Emeralds may be ostentatious." Ruth came out of the kitchen.

"I suppose." Eve twisted into her hair into a severe chignon. "Or I could go very regal and wear a diamond choker."

Ruth suggested the obvious. "What about pearls?"

"I don't know." Eve sighed. "There are so many decisions."

The only thing Eve knew for certain was that she was not getting married at Central Union Church.

Her mother argued that the Russells had been getting married there for generations. But since the rose garden at Central Union had been replaced by a vegetable Victory Garden, Eve was adamant that she would not take her first steps as Mrs. Lincoln Armstrong "strolling through a pea patch."

Chapter Forty-one
March 20, 1942

Quarters M-15, Fort Shafter

RUTH WAS IN the backyard lounging on a wicker chaise lounge. She jiggled her glass of iced tea and drank the last bit, too sun-lazy to go back to the kitchen for a refill.

She was dropping the straps of her bathing suit to avoid a tan line when she heard, "Is anybody there?"

It was Paul Hastings. She yanked up her straps and covered herself with a towel.

"Anybody?"

When Paul saw her, he dragged a lawn chair over the grass and set it next to her. He sat down, slowly, timidly.

He could have news about Gordon. She'd have to tolerate him to find out.

Paul leaned in. His leg bounced. "Ruth, about the other day—"

She didn't move. "Don't mention it again."

He stammered. "I'm sorry about what—"

She pulled back her shoulders. "If that's why you're here, let it go. If you're here with news about Gordon, tell me."

Paul nodded. "He's back in Australia."

"I heard some of the Doolittle pilots landed in China." She paused, waiting for him to reply. When he didn't, she was direct. "Was he part of the Doolittle operation?"

"I can't say," Paul said.

"I'm not an idiot, Paul. I know he was in China. What was he doing there?"

"He was living in a Catholic mission in Nencheng Village, and he was safe."

"*Was* safe?" Ruth's fears peaked.

"*Is* safe," Paul quickly corrected.

"What happened?"

Paul hesitated.

"What happened? Tell me. Now."

"How much do you want to know?"

She said, "All of it," but she already knew she would regret it.

"When the Japanese found out which village helped the American pilots…they wiped them out." He sighed. "One of them, Linchwan, had 50,000 people…almost all Catholic converts, that's why there was a monastery where Gordon was." Paul looked away.

"When the Japanese hunted out which villages helped our pilots…they killed every man, woman and child. And every animal from livestock to dogs."

Ruth felt the words like a blow to her chest.

"Girls as young as ten were raped."

She didn't want to know anymore.

"Intelligence estimates that 250,000 Chinese were killed in retribution."

"250,000? Did they go from village to village?"

He shook his head. "They poisoned the water with bubonic plague and sprayed anthrax over the province."

"And Gordon is fine?"

Paul lowered his voice. "He's fine, Ruth, honestly." And he slowly told her what happened in Gordon's village.

"The priests at Nencheng were able to rescue dozens of orphaned Chinese infants and children. They tried to place them with other Chinese families, but no one would take them fearing retribution from the Japanese. So, when the Americans evacuated, they took the children with them to Australia. It was a tough trip all around.

"As of now, the Red Cross is working out transporting the orphans to the U.S., and Gordon's accompanying them."

"Do you know when they'll arrive?"

"It's a hospital ship. So, the route is uncertain."

"And the Red Cross is the liaison agency?"

He nodded.

If it was a Red Cross operation, she knew Mrs. Russell would have all the details first.

Chapter Forty-two
March 24, 1942

Parker's Beach House, Waikiki

THE NIGHT BEFORE Joe left, he and CJ danced on the lanai to *Stardust* and *Moonlight Serenade*. The phonograph needle hissed. A record would drop, then the next, and when the music ended, they kept dancing.

CJ buried her face in Joe's chest; his shirt was damp with salt air. Joe clasped his hands low on her back with his fingers splayed as if to anchor her to him.

They held each other tight, and their lovemaking was soft and sweet, not desperate, as if they were pretending the morning wouldn't come.

CJ stared at her sleeping husband. She memorized the rhythm of his breath, wishing she could cast a spell on him to keep him safe. The sun set, and the sun rose on the day Joe was to leave. Their morning was quiet as if speaking would break the spell.

Joe's dog tags jingled as he fastened his belt. CJ's hands trembled as she buttoned her shirt.

The coffee between them went untouched.

When they got to his base, there was no tearful farewell. Joe scooped CJ into his arms. He grazed her lips with a soft kiss.

He whispered a simple "I love you" and walked toward the hangar, never looking back.

CJ wrapped her arms around herself, forcing herself to not run after him, to tell him to be careful, to wish the war away.

Be strong, she told herself. Be a good wife. But how, Mamma?

She stared at the back of his jacket as he walked away, heard the click of the sentry gate, saw Joe return the salute. She watched Joe get into a waiting Jeep and drive away.

The scene ended, the curtain dropped, and she got back in the car. She had half an hour before her shift, and with so few cars on the road, she could make it with ten minutes to spare.

But when she got downtown, there was a detour, and she could smell smoke.

Not again. Whatever it was, not again.

A Jeep pulled up next to her, and the MP leaned out of his window. His voice was too calm. The news was too routine. "Mid-air over Kalihi," he said. "Training flight."

She didn't ask questions, but he told her anyway. "About 12 civilians dead."

CJ felt compelled to ask, "And the crew?"

"No survivors."

"PBYs?"

"Bombers."

Thank God it wasn't Linc. She was becoming so numbed by war that she barely noticed she was moving from terror to getting on with her day.

"I've got to be at Fort Shafter." She looked at her watch. "In twenty minutes."

"You're looking at 45 minutes, an hour tops. He shook his head. "You should turn off your engine."

Yes. Don't waste gas. Don't waste sugar. But lives…? For a second, she thought she was talking to Joe.

Lizard Tunnel, Fort Shafter

By time CJ got to the base, she was two hours late. She was ready to explain to Major Oliver, but before she could continue, he said, "You weren't the only one caught in traffic." He told her the basics of the incident. "The report's on the board."

She unpinned it and read: "A B-25 bomber collided with a PBY mid-air over Kalihi. Eight military personnel, including all the PBY crew members, were killed, as well as twenty civilians."

Jesus, the MP was wrong? It was a PBY! She skimmed to the

bottom of the page for the list of the dead. Linc's name wasn't on it, thank God.

She wanted Joe. She wanted him to hold her.

The report went on: "Twelve homes were destroyed. The first report of civilian damage was the home of Mr. Chin Ho Kelley. At the time, Kelley was working at the Navy Yard.

His wife Esther. Dead

His four-year-old daughter. Dead.

His two-year-old son. Dead."

CJ imagined Chin Ho Kelley welding, mask down, metal arcing when a Navy officer approached him and put his hand on Kelley's shoulder as he gave him the news, and Kelley's life was irrevocably changed.

His wife and children would be reduced to a two-inch column report on page 21 of the paper. She could predict the coverage. "Tragic incident…lives lost," but their stories would go untold.

Major Oliver told her to go home; she willingly did. She wasn't sure how much information had been released and wanted to make sure Eve knew Linc wasn't involved.

When CJ told her, she expected Eve to be relieved and grateful, but instead, she brushed off the news, flicking her hair over her shoulder. "I knew it wasn't Linc. Jane told me."

CJ hoped Eve was hiding behind her well-practiced façade.

CJ looked at Jane.

It was horrific," Jane said. "We all saw it. Fluff Ford plotted them in. And we watched them heading straight for each other."

"In broad daylight? It doesn't make sense."

"The PBY's radio was out," Jane said.

"But they still had eyes on each other, didn't they? They must have seen each other!"

Jane's voice was barely above a whisper. "Sometimes, it's too late."

CHAPTER FORTY-THREE
MARCH 28-29, 1942

Quarters M-15, Fort Shafter

RUTH SAT ON her bed and opened Gordon's letter. It was four pages, censored with blacked-over lines, paragraphs spliced out and a few photos: a kangaroo mid-hop, a koala curled in the crook of a tree, and men from his unit—each holding an infant.

Gordon's handwriting was like him: neat, controlled, precise. But his first words shocked her. *"I love you, Ruth. I miss you. I'd consider any life after the war—even life as a civilian."*

She had never asked him to leave the service. Navy life wasn't difficult for her It was all she knew. It was all she expected. Gordon loved the Navy, and he had only four more years to retire.

Civilian life? Why?

He went on to write at length about infants the unit snuck

out of China, and Ruth assumed they were the babies the men held in the photo, Then, he wrote about one in particular infant.

"It's such a blessing to have an innocent life in the middle of this war. When I kiss Song, she looks up at me and smiles. Not since Grace have I felt such joy and i iii. ii i. ii.=i ii.

I love you, Ruth."

Not since Grace have I felt such joy? He was replacing his daughter with some refugee infant?

He wants…then words cut out. What could a censor find that was offensive? Was it some secret of war that her husband was taken with a child he rescued?

What did the next line read?

She had to let her question go and focus on Gordon coming home. Maybe they'd try for another baby.

⁂

The next morning, CJ staggered into the kitchen. "Good morning, Eve."

Eve rattled every cup, saucer, and spoon in the kitchen, complaining about the coffee, slamming drawers, grumbling, muttering, turning toward CJ.

"What's with you?" CJ asked.

"Linc wants me to write a letter to his mother to introduce

myself. She wants to put an announcement about our engagement in the *Square Dance Country Herald*."

"It is probably time you 'met' her," CJ said.

Eve slammed the cupboard door and looked around. "There's not one decent cup or saucer in the place. And not one of you can make a decent pot!" She stomped out toward her room as Ruth walked into the kitchen, tying her bathrobe belt. "What's all the fuss?"

"Linc asked Eve to write to his mother. She wants to announce their engagement in the Madison newspaper."

Ruth arched her eyebrows. "The plot thickens."

CJ passed the coffee pot to Ruth. Ruth poured herself a cup, stirred it, and stared at the pack of Lucky Strikes. "Do you mind if I have a cigarette?"

CJ slid the pack to her. "When did you start smoking?"

"This morning." Ruth lit a cigarette.

"Mrs. Commander's wife with a cigarette dangling out of her mouth? So, what's up?"

"Nothing."

"Is that why you have mascara flakes dripping down your cheeks?"

"I got a letter from Gordon. He's due in Honolulu soon."

CJ pulled a chair up next to Ruth. "You should be dancing!"

"He's coming home with orphans. About 20 of them. From China." Ruth took a shallow inhale of her cigarette.

"I thought Gordon was in Australia."

"They're refugees." Ruth exposed as few details as she could. "In the letter, he mentioned a baby girl named Song."

"What a beautiful name," CJ said.

It sounded like a siren's call to Ruth.

Ruth took his letter out of her pocket and read, "*Not since Grace have I felt such joy and* i iii. ii i. ii.=i ii.

"I counted out the letters in the words trying to figure out what he wants. One. Four. Two. Two. Five. Three. I'm sure it says, 'I want us to adopt her.'"

CJ felt like she was walking in a minefield. "I'm sure there are lots of words that would fit."

Ruth shook her head. "I'm not."

CHAPTER FORTY-FOUR
APRIL 1, 1942

Quarters M-15, Fort Shafter

GORDON'S NEXT LETTER confirmed Ruth's fears.

My dearest Ruth,

The atrocities of war that I have seen defy the fury of hell. I have witnessed the true manifestation of evil. I lost hope in the nature of humanity, but in the midst of this despair, these Chinese children became my whole purpose.

I'll be bringing 17 of the surviving children home with me, and I am ardent in my mission that each will be placed with a loving family.

Ruth, you should see them. Each one of them is a gift, and Song is my gift.

I've enclosed a photo of me holding her. Look how she curls her fingers around mine.

Ruth, Song changes every day. Yesterday she cooed when I rocked her to sleep, and when I see her smile, I pray to God that she'll never remember the horrors she has seen.

I want to watch her grow. I want her to fill our lives with joy.

Ruth, Song may be God's way of giving us a baby.

I love you,

Gordon

Ruth couldn't stop staring at Gordon holding this Chinese baby—dark hair, a round face, and Oriental eyes.

This may be God's way of giving us a baby?

It wasn't God's way. It was Gordon taken with his own heroism.

I rock her to sleep.

You had your own baby to rock.

Give us a baby?

Ruth turned the photo over.

My Song. Sydney. 1942.

She let the letter fall to the floor.

His Song?

She felt the heat in her chest. The bile rising. Panting, she ran into the bathroom and slumped over the toilet, holding back her hair as she retched.

He wants to replace Grace with Song.

A Song for Grace. She almost laughed.

A Song: melodic and haunting.

And Grace: God's love bestowed on man to console him through despair. At least, that's the definition she remembered from Sunday School.

Ruth hunched over the sink and wiped the vomit off her face. She peeled off her clothes and stepped into the shower.

How could he even write to her about a baby? After two miscarriages, Grace was their miracle. She let the water run over her body and pressed her back to the wall. Then slid into the tub and sat with her knees pressed to her chest and her arms locked around her shins.

Maybe he gave up on her having a baby that would live? He never made any accusations, whispered or implied, about it and she knew that if she asked Gordon the unspoken question, he would have told her none of this was her fault. But she knew he blamed her. How could any man forgive a woman who lost his children?

During her first pregnancy, Ruth fell. She was sure that caused the miscarriage. With her second pregnancy, she stopped playing tennis, riding horses, and even going into the ocean. But it still ended in a miscarriage.

When she was pregnant with Grace, she was obsessive. The

iron pills. The raw egg in wine. The 8 ounces of milk each day. She may as well have stopped walking under ladders for all the good it did, because it didn't protect her. Grace died the day she was born.

She knew it was her fault.

Maybe she didn't want a baby, and this was her body's way of showing it? That was ridiculous! All she'd ever wanted was a baby.

Maybe it was God's will?

She watched the water from the shower pour down her legs.

"Anybody home?" She recognized CJ's voice but didn't answer.

Ruth was afraid that CJ had been in their room. She probably would have seen Gordon's letter on the floor, and she knew CJ couldn't stop herself from reading it.

"Hello? Ruth?" CJ rattled the doorknob and stepped inside. "Ruth?"

She pulled back the curtain.

Ruth squeezed herself into a ball. "Go away!"

"Ruth, what happened?" CJ knelt next to the tub.

"It's Gordon… He wants to replace Grace."

CJ hiked her uniform and stepped into the tub, water pouring down on her.

"He wants to forget her."

CJ sat next to Ruth, soaked to the hips in water.

"I can't do this." Ruth shook her head.

"Talk to me." CJ cradled Ruth in her arms.

"He wants to adopt some Chinese baby." Water dripped from Ruth's hair onto her face.

"I can't abandon my daughter."

"But, Grace—"

"Leave me alone!" Ruth buried her face in her hands.

"I'm sorry." CJ let go of Ruth.

"You don't understand." Ruth sobbed. "I don't want anyone else's baby, I want Grace."

The two of them sat, with the shower raining down.

"I can never love another baby," Ruth said. "If I did, it would be like Grace died again."

CHAPTER FORTY-FIVE
APRIL 4, 1942

Quarters M-15, Fort Shafter

THE GIRLS WERE lazily lounging in the living room. Jane was buried behind an issue of *Popular Aviation* while CJ painted her toenails and Eve leafed through wedding magazines she had strewn all over the sofa.

"Take a look." Eve held up a centerfold spread of a wedding reception at the Hasting Gardens at Half Moon Bay. "That would be a divine place for a wedding."

Jane lowered her magazine and offered a half-hearted smile.

"Where is it?" CJ asked. Her voice belied her lack of interest.

"About an hour south of San Francisco," Eve said. "Linc's going to love it."

"For the fairy tale wedding?" CJ held her nail polish brush in mid-air.

"No, for weekend picnics. It's glorious in the fall." Eve stared in the mid-distance as if remembering a time there. "There's an inn where we could go in October." Eve perked up. "We'll be able to pick our pumpkin and take it home to carve."

Jane put down her magazine. "Are you planning on living in San Francisco?"

"Linc's going to medical school," Eve announced as if it were common knowledge.

"San Franciso?" CJ asked. "It thought he was going to school in Wisconsin."

"Parker's going to convince him that Stanford is the place to go."

"Does Linc know about the plan?" CJ wanted to get the record straight.

"Not yet." Eve dismissed the question.

Jane glanced at CJ, then slunk down, hiding herself behind her magazine.

"Do you plan on telling Linc your plan before the wedding?" CJ asked.

"He knows Parker is thinking of moving to San Francisco after the war. And when he hears us out, he'll agree."

"When he hears you out?" CJ's brows rose. "So, he doesn't know?"

Eve reached for her "Wedding Plans" notebook and showed CJ a gown she cut out from *Hawaii Brides*. "Isn't it gorgeous?'

CJ nodded.

"I want the wedding to be perfect! So, you two tell me the most memorable moments of your weddings. Jane, you go first."

Jane dropped her magazine to her lap. "I don't remember," she huffed.

"Nonsense," Eve insisted. "Tell me. There must be something that stood out."

"It's not good."

Eve ignored Jane's warning to stop asking. "I insist!"

And almost as an act of vengeance, Jane said, "Here's my memorable moment: My father paused when we were halfway down the aisle and said, 'Janie, we've got a hootin' band and plenty of booze. We don't need a groom to have a party. Are you sure you want to go through with this?'" She paused. "And I told him I knew what I was doing."

"You're right. That wasn't so good." Eve turned to CJ. "Are there any plans of the wedding you were supposed to have that I could use?"

CJ fingered her grandmother's pearl earrings. "My Aunt Amelia was going to sew my gown. I remember my mother and aunt talking about how long the train should be."

As her words left her mouth, her mind drifted back to the Saturday after Thanksgiving, standing on the platform at Newark railroad station. Her mother pulled her aside and slipped a scuffed blue velvet box in her hand. CJ recognized the box immediately—as a kid, she would sneak into her mother's room and play dress-up with her mother's jewelry. There was the cameo from Rome, the coral necklace from Capri, and her grandmother's pearl earrings in the blue velvet box.

"My mother wore these on her wedding day," she'd told CJ.

She opened the box. "Oh, Mom. I'll wear them when I get married."

"Be a good wife, Carmela." CJ's mother patted her hands.

"I promise." CJ snapped back to reality when Ruth opened the front door without a smile or a greeting.

"What's the matter?" CJ knew Ruth well enough by now to sense when something wasn't right.

"Kak Hamlin." Ruth pressed her lips together and paused. Her husband's been captured. He's in a Japanese prisoner of war camp in Java."

Jane put down her magazine.

Ruth continued, "There's a signup sheet in the canteen to take her shifts."

"How is she?" Jane asked.

"Suzanne Samuels said she was near comatose."

Ruth picked up her mask and musette. "If you'll excuse me, I'll be in my room."

Ruth shut her bedroom door. Her hand shook as she reached for a clothes hanger.

CHAPTER FORTY-SIX
APRIL 8, 1942

Quarters M-15, Fort Shafter

RUTH WOKE TO the slow whirl of the ceiling fan and watched dust motes swirl in the light. It was that numb moment between sleeping and waking before she remembered Grace.

She could still see the white walls of the Maternity Ward. The white sheets. She could smell the antiseptic and feel her body cramping. She remembered Gordon's face when he told her that Grace died, and she saw the nurse carrying Grace in.

For months after, Gordon would reach for her in bed, and she'd pull away, get up, put on her robe and pace the living room with her arms folded. There were some nights she wondered if she had imagined it all—the pregnancy, Grace, the funeral. Then she would caress her hands over her belly, remember when it was swollen, remember Grace stretching as if she were yawning, and knew it wasn't a dream.

It was over a year that Grace was gone. She needed to keep going—needed to get out of bed. Shower. Get dressed.

When she got to the bathroom, she leaned over the sink and stared in the mirror. Her hair was matted where she slept, and the pillow had left deep creases on her cheeks.

By the time she showered and dressed, Jane and Eve had already left, and CJ was working an early shift. It would have been easy to go back to bed, feign illness, and wallow in grief.

Instead, she poured herself a cup of coffee, stood on her tip-toes, slid the bottle of Scotch to the shelf edge, and poured it into her cup.

CHAPTER FORTY-SEVEN
APRIL 11-12, 1942

Quarters M-15, Fort Shafter

WHEN CJ GOT home from work, there was a note propped up on the telephone: Call the *Advertiser*. Mr. Russell would like to speak with you.

When she called, it was Maude who gave her the news. There was an opening at the *Stars and Stripes,* and Mr. Russell wanted to offer her his endorsement for the position. But before they spoke, he wanted her to meet with Liz Townsend.

The Honolulu Advertiser Building, Honolulu

The next day at the *Advertiser*, Liz was relatively cordial to CJ, but she still managed to get in her digs. "Sarah Miller wasn't interested in the *Stars and Stripes* job, so it was down to you."

CJ kept her face blank. So, they were down to the bottom of the barrel, and that's where they found her?

Liz offered CJ a cigarette. CJ didn't want anything Liz was offering.

"Mr. Russell wants to recommend you for the job." Liz's tone was flippant. "It's in Australia." Liz lit her cigarette and waved the match out. "War correspondence work takes a special kind of grit."

It took a special kind of grit to tolerate a meeting with Liz, but CJ forced herself to ask Liz how war correspondence is different, then braced herself for a self-aggrandizing monologue.

"It takes the life out of you. It'll kill you if you let it."

CJ tapped her foot against the floor.

"I'm not sure you have it in you," Liz said.

Keep your mouth shut and listen, CJ told herself. Liz may have something of value to hear.

"You have to weigh the odds. Decide if you really want it," Liz said. "It's a chance very few women get, and you don't want to be my age and have any regrets."

"Would you do it again?"

"Me? Yeah." Liz tapped her cigarette against the ashtray. "The prize isn't being a war correspondent. You just survive that. It's what comes after." She glanced at CJ. "It gets you off the Society Page. You pay your price, and you get to move on."

CJ noticed the subtle tremor in Liz's hand, the mottled age spots. At her age, CJ didn't want to be chasing a combat story.

Liz leaned over her desk. "It doesn't matter who you work for—*Colliers, Life, Stars and Stripes*, it's all the same. Before your piece gets back to the States, censors will twist your facts, manipulate your numbers."

"And if you try to correct them?" CJ asked.

"You look the other way, or you're on the next ship home." Liz exhaled smoke through her nose. "If you really want to write the truth, you sit on it," Liz said. You keep two sets of notes—one to hand in, one to hide under your mattress—and you wait until the world is ready to read it. And you try not to make things up or to steal from the other reporters. And when that fails, you drink yourself into oblivion with the other liars."

"It's not a pretty picture," CJ said.

"You wanted the truth."

"Anything else I should know?"

"You'd be one of the first females in the Pacific theater. If you keep your head down and play the game right, you'll have doors open to you after the war. You'll be quoted, courted, and interviewed. You will have 'arrived.'"

"Do you think my writing has what it takes?" The second it was out of her mouth, CJ regretted it.

Without breaking eye contact with CJ, Liz crushed out her cigarette. "I do. I read your piece on the Nuuanu burial. Do you know what I remember about it? One thing…the girl who sang the solo for her deceased father. The rest of it…the numbers of dead, the politicians, the stale speeches. Who cares? But everyone who read that piece knew what it was like to bury a loved one, and very few of them would have the guts to do what that little girl did. Now, that's a story. Human interest is your strength."

"I'm not interested in human interest," CJ said. "I want to walk by the newsstand and see my byline on the front page."

"Front page? *Merde.*" She spat out the words. "You've got the gift to tell a good story."

"It's not what you did."

Liz nodded. "*Touché.* You're right. And if someone offered me human interest, I would have run the other way. I wanted the big story, so I went with the *Washington Post.*

"At first, I was the paper's darling—the hotshot girl straight out of the trenches. But, after a while, it was the same good old boy network. I had to fight for every assignment and still got the occasional pat on the ass, but I made a hell of a lot more money.

"Then, one day, I caught a matinee of *Waikiki Calls,* and Hawaii looked as far away from D.C. bullshit as I could get. So, I sent my resume to the *Advertiser* that night, and two weeks later, I was sitting at this desk." Liz lit another cigarette.

"CJ, I read Graham's letter to the *Stars and Stripes* about you. You could walk into the job after a letter like that," Liz said. "It's all up to you."

Quarters M-15, Fort Shafter

That afternoon, while taking clothes off the line, CJ laid out her options to Ruth.

"The WARD is safe. The money's steady and I feel like I'm at the forefront of what's going on in the world." She folded a pillowcase, in half, smoothing the edges. "The *Stars and Stripes,* on the other hand…" Her voice rose a pitch. "The money's not as good, but there's a pot of gold at the end of the rainbow. So, those are my two options." She tossed the pillowcase into the laundry basket.

"You've got a third option." Ruth stepped toward CJ holding two corners of a sheet. "You could go home."

CJ stepped forward to meet her. She knew going home was always an option, but it was going back to what was safe. "I don't know."

"Is it the WARD money?" Ruth asked.

How could she explain to Ruth that running home felt like she couldn't handle the world outside her cocoon. "It feels like running away."

"Running from what?"

She wanted to say failure, but she answered, "I don't know."

Chapter Forty-eight
April 18, 1942

O'Club, Fort Shafter

EVE AND LINC took the corner booth at the O'Club. Eve pressed the Gump's brochure flat on the table. "This one." She pointed to a ring from Tiffany.

Linc's eyebrows went up when he saw the price.

"It's the one!" Eve beamed like a child.

Linc took a breath. "It's expensive."

"It's a wedding present from my parents." Eve put her hand firmly on Linc's; then, she gave him the worse option. "Either that or they'll buy us a house up the street from them."

Linc withdrew his hand. "Eve, a small-town doctor won't be able to afford to have his wife shop at Tiffany's."

Eve smirked. "There'll always be Christmas and my birthday."

"I'm not comfortable with this." Linc's voice was calm, but there was no question of its intent.

Eve put her hand up to stop him. "Wait." She turned the brochure around to face him. "There." She patted the illustration of men's wedding bands. "Just look at these."

Linc twisted his Annapolis ring. "I wasn't planning on wearing one."

Eve's voice rose. "Why not?" She stared at him fidgeting with his academy ring. "Are you married to the Navy?"

"That's not it."

She slapped the brochure on the table. "You're not thinking of it as a career, are you?"

Linc crossed his arms on the table, hiding his Annapolis ring in the crook of his elbow.

"You're going to medical school, right?" Eve demanded.

"I am."

"Stanford? University of San Francisco?"

"I've already had a family friend look into Wisconsin for me. You know that."

"Parker says Stanford is the better medical school."

"Madison has an excellent reputation," Linc countered.

"If you went to Stanford, we could spend weekends in San Francisco."

"Medical school is intense, Eve."

"What was the name of that hotel on Nob Hill?" Eve snapped her fingers. "The Mark Hopkins! That's it."

"We won't be staying at the Mark Hopkins Hotel on a medical student's salary."

"If we live in San Francisco, I can work at the Fine Art Museum."

"Eve, I want to raise my family in Madison."

Family? Another hurdle.

"Of course! We can settle down in Madison. Buy that house with the side office for your practice, but why not give me San Francisco for a few years—it won't be long."

Eve was certain that once Linc was through medical school, an internship, and maybe a residency, San Francisco would be home, and there'd be no more talk about Wisconsin.

Linc sipped his beer. "Let's get through the war first."

Chapter Forty-nine
April 22, 1942

Lizard Tunnel, Fort Shafter

JANE CHECKED THE mail room after her night shift ended at 3 a.m. She had to skim the letter twice to make sure she was actually reading what she thought. She skimmed it a third time:

Dear Mrs. Meade,

Welcome to the Women's Auxiliary Ferrying Squadron. I admire your determination. I can train anyone in multiple aircraft, but I can't teach grit. Jane, you proved to me you're a pilot that I want on my team.

Your passion for flying and willingness to do your part in the war convinced me that we can deal with the 150-hour deficit. You've got solid experience, and a few flight checks should take care of that.

Then the shocker:

In all the years I've known Gus Cranston, I know he's never one to gild a rose. He thinks you were born to fly. That's a glowing endorsement from a man I can only remember saying that women have no place in the air.

Damn. She smiled to herself.

You will report to New Castle Army Field, Delaware, by May 15, 1942. An Army transport plane departing from Hickam will be scheduled accordingly. I look forward to serving with you.

Lieutenant Colonel Nancy Harkness Love

Commanding Officer

Women's Auxiliary Ferrying Squadron

Quarters M-15, Fort Shafter

As soon as Eve heard the news about Jane getting in Love's squadron, she got on the coconut wireless to Linc and sparked a shopping spree to Mossman's Jewelers and a Chinatown lei shop.

CJ baked a cake and picked flowers from the Palm Circle Gardens. Ruth went to the O'Club to scrounge any decorations she could, and then stopped by Lizard Tunnel to convince Major Oliver to double-shift Jane, telling him about the surprise party.

By noon, the stage was set. A hand-drawn banner of a bi-plane with a pilot waving from the cockpit was hung from the ceiling. Crepe paper streamers were tied to the Papasan chair and Parker was poised to pop the champagne.

By the time Jane got home, the five of them had polished off two pitchers of Bloody Marys and were at least three, maybe four sheets to the wind.

Jane opened the door to them singing 'Congratulations to you' to the tune of 'Happy Birthday.' "Y'all are unbelievable!" she said.

Linc took Jane's arm and led her to her Papasan throne. Parker popped the champagne and Eve toasted to "the best damn pilot the Army will ever have!"

Jane Anderson Meade, rancher's daughter and Texas aviatrix, laughed through her tears.

"This is from all of us." Linc presented Jane with a pair of flight gloves. "Ignore the 'Property of the US Navy stamp.'"

The gloves were a perfect fit.

Then Eve presented Jane with a black leather box. Jane immediately recognized the Breiting logo on it. "This is too much!"

"Open it!" CJ leaned over to get a look at the watch.

It was an orange-dialed Breitling Pilot watch with a miniature dial capable of tracking her flight time.

"Put it on," CJ said. "We want to see how it looks."

Jane lifted it out of the box. The band gleamed, the orange dial almost glowed.

"It's got three dials," Eve pointed out. "The little one's for GMT." She beamed, as if she was proud to remember what Jane had taught her.

Then Parker draped a jasmine lei on Jane and her tears turned to sniffing. "Get me a handkerchief!" She laughed. "I'm not wiping my nose with these new gloves!"

Jane put the watch on. "No one has ever done anything like this before."

"And no one's deserved it more." Parker kissed her cheek and readjusted the lei to drape over her shoulders.

"You're getting sentimental on me, Park." Jane raised an eyebrow.

He took her hand in his. "You truly deserve it."

The celebration stretched through the late afternoon, when Parker walked Jane out to the porch.

"If you're going to propose to me, I'll have you know I'm a married woman. At least technically."

"In a way, it's about that." His tone was serious. "About Buck, really."

She braced herself.

He hesitated. "Buck's name is on the list of injured from the Coral Sea."

"How bad is he?"

"The chart says 'extensive injuries.' He's slated for stateside rehab."

"Stateside? Does that mean they're sending him straight to the mainland?" It would be easier if she never had to face him.

He shook his head. "They'll dock here for a few days first."

"When?" She twisted her wedding ring.

"My guess? Mid-May."

That was the same week her flight to WAFS training was scheduled. If she could arrange an earlier flight, even by a week, she could be gone before Buck came back.

"Jane," Parker said gently, "his leg's been amputated." Parker's face softened. "He'll need a rehab companion. The Army usually brings in the spouse for that."

Later that night, when the girls were sitting in the dark on the porch, Eve asked Jane, "What was the big secret Parker had?"

"Buck's been injured. His leg's been amputated." Just repeating the words made her throat tighten. "Parker said the Army sends the wives through rehab to learn how to care for the wounds. They'll probably try to set up rehab for us in Pittsburgh."

"Us!" Eve reared her head back. "You aren't really thinking about staying with him?"

"I may have to."

"Why?" CJ asked.

"Because I married him?" She was trying to make the decision the obvious and only reaction.

"You would have been divorced if it weren't for the war," CJ said.

"And he would have had both legs," Jane said.

"He's still the same man!" Eve erupted.

"I forced him to join the Army. If it weren't for me—"

"That's horse hockey and you know it." CJ talked over her. "I doubt Buck Meade does anything he doesn't want to do. Besides, if he didn't sign up, he would have been drafted and carrying a rifle in the mud somewhere."

"I owe him," Jane said.

"You owe him nothing," Ruth said.

Jane agreed, but why did she feel guilty admitting it?

CHAPTER FIFTY
APRIL 23, 1942

Lizard Tunnel, Fort Shafter

CJ READ THE report:

Singapore: Alexandra Barracks Hospital

Among the deaths reported were 50 soldiers in the Alexandra Barracks Hospital. The first to be shot was a British doctor who emerged from the hospital carrying a white flag. Upon entering the hospital, the Japanese killed patients, doctors, and nurses—some of them in surgery. They forced another 400 patients to walk to an unventilated room where they were held overnight, then bayoneted the following morning.

Dear God, CJ thought. If she were with the *Stars and Stripes* that would have been one of her stories.

It was hard enough for her to read it, let alone write it. If she took the job with *Stars and Stripes* she'd have to focus on the facts. Just numbers. Stay detached.

But she couldn't stop seeing faces of the wounded at Ford Island.

Focus on just the numbers? Who the hell was she kidding?

<h1 style="text-align:center">CHAPTER FIFTY-ONE</h1>
<h1 style="text-align:center">APRIL 26, 1942</h1>

Lizard Tunnel, Fort Shafter

CJ WAS PLOTTING Linc on a routine flight to Bellows past Honolulu toward Hawaii Kai.

She wished Joe were in Hawaii; she would have asked him to talk to Linc. She was afraid Linc was making a mistake marrying Eve. Eve was looking for a fairy tale life where she was the golden princess.

She plotted Linc toward Makapuu Lighthouse, then Oscar repeated the same coordinates.

She'd worked the board long enough to know the fog and rain over Makapuu were probably giving a false reading. Linc was a good pilot, and this was a routine flight.

But Oscar repeated the coordinates again and she slid a third arrow to the same spot. A Liaison Officer stood next to her, but he didn't relieve her.

She looked at him, as if asking if he knew anything. Maybe the cliff had blocked Linc's signal? Maybe Linc ditched? He was a good swimmer, and the Coast Guard station was right there.

She kept plotting her other planes thinking if Linc had crashed, someone would have reported it already. She held on to that hope until Major Oliver rested his hand on CJ's shoulders and took her off the board and the Liaison Officer stepped in.

CJ stared at Oliver, unable to take in his words. "Low altitude… crashed into the hillside…200 yards south of the lighthouse. Witnesses said there was an explosion followed by a ball of fire. There were no survivors.

"The bottom line," Oliver continued, "is that the visibility was zero, and their radios were out."

The goddamn radios!

Russell Estate, Nuuanu

Eve stopped by the house to raid the liquor cabinet and to pick up a few throw pillows for quarters. She hadn't expected everyone to be home.

"Hail, hail. The gang's all here." Eve fluttered in and tossed her gas mask on the telephone table. But when she walked in the living room, it looked like a tableau from the Grand Inquisition, with her mother poised like Torquemada. The first words out of her mother's mouth were, "Mrs. Holt told me you're trying to force Linc to move to San Francisco."

Eve readied herself for battle. "Good afternoon, Mother. How are you?"

"She said you're coercing him to go to medical school in California."

"Coercing?" Eve snorted a laugh.

"It was mortifying for me to hear it."

Eve and Ginger exchanged glances.

"Mrs. Holt should get her facts right," Eve snapped.

"According to her, Linc has no idea what you're planning."

Eve looked toward her father, buried behind the newspaper.

"It's a good plan," Eve said. "Eventually, I'm sure he'll agree."

Mr. Russell lowered the paper. "Eventually? Does this mean he doesn't know anything about it?"

Mrs. Russell answered, speaking as if from a judge's bench. "It means his plans are to go back home to Wisconsin, and Eve's plans are to live in San Francisco in another one of her fantasies."

"Linc will be far better off in the long run," Eve defended herself.

"He told Mrs. Holt that it was his plan to settle in Wisconsin." Her nostrils flared. "Could it be that you don't want to play at being Midwest Annie?"

Eve tilted her head. "You always said I was good at horseback riding."

"Listen to me, young lady! This marriage doesn't have a chance in hell of surviving with your antics."

Eve looked at her father expecting some support, but he just sat there.

Her mother ranted, "This pretense is not fair. Not to Linc and not to me."

"You? Everything's not about you, Mother." Eve grabbed her car keys. "I'm going back to quarters."

"Eve, you will not leave until we are finished discussing this."

"I have to get back to the base."

"Listen to me, Eve, when this marriage fails, don't show up on my doorstep expecting me to rescue you."

"Don't worry, Mother. You are the last person I expect to rescue me."

The doorbell rang. "Who on earth?" Mrs. Russell flared.

The doorbell rang again and Mrs. Russell motioned to Ginger to answer it.

Ginger opened the door to Ruth, Father Estabrook, and an officer she didn't know.

"Come on in. Ruth, Father." Ginger smiled and waved them in.

"Is Eve at home?" Ruth wasn't smiling.

"She's in the living room."

Ruth stepped in, cautiously, almost tentatively. The chaplain and the officer followed her, nodding to Ginger as they passed her.

Eve knew the protocol for a condolence call: The CO, the chaplain and the officer came in person to deliver the news in person.

Linc.

Ruth stepped toward Eve.

Eve shook her head. "No." She stepped back.

"Eve." Ruth held out her arms.

"No!" Eve put up her hand, pushing away what she knew was coming.

Ruth said, "It happened this afternoon."

Eve staggered to the sofa behind her and sat, staring at the rug.

Ruth looked at the rug, finely woven, intricately patterned. she gazed at the carved coffee table, the crystal drink glasses, The perfectly appointed room—and she was there to destroy it all.

Ginger sat next to her sister and put her arm around her.

"Linc's a good pilot." Eve white knuckled her car keys.

Ruth proceeded gently. "There was cloud cover over Makapuu. They came in low to land and crashed into the cliff…they probably thought they were already at Bellows."

"What about the radio?" Eve asked.

"It was out," Lieutenant Connors said.

Eve glared at Connors and hurled the keys across the room.

He took the slightest step toward her.

Eve put her hand up. "Do not take one step closer!"

Father Estabrook looked at Ginger as if asking if he should approach. Ginger shook her head.

Eve sat up straight and challenged her mother—Proper Loretta Russell, standing with her hands folded at her waist, the portrait of maternal concern.

"Are you happy now, Mother? You won't have to rescue me anymore?"

"How about you, Pops? Do you have any consoling words?"

He looked helpless, tears in his eyes.

Eve stood. "You did your duty, Ruth. Now, go home," she commanded, as if Ruth were a servant.

Ruth stepped back for her to pass and Eve walked up the stairs and closed the door to her room.

Eve stood at her dresser, took off her jade ring, and wrapped it in a tissue. Then she put it in a sandalwood box and closed the lid.

Quarters M-15, For Shafter

That night, CJ sat on the porch and wrote in her journal by the light of the moon. She wrote about Linc and Joe's parents sitting at the same table at the Academy's Honor Dinner. About them cheering from the bleachers at graduation. She remembered taking photos of the two families posed on the south lawn.

Linc and Joe. Mutt and Jeff. She smiled through her tears. She hated that Joe would find out about the crash in a random report: "Lieutenant Lincoln Armstrong, USN, was killed in a routine flight off the coast of Oahu."

She wanted to write to him that Linc's radio wasn't working. That there was a dense cloud cover and zero visibility. But did any of it matter? Maybe it did. Maybe it was part of Linc's story, because it wasn't about five men dying, or fifty or five hundred. It was about one man, one woman, one child. The stories of war belonged to Ruth, to Nancy West, to the civilian dead, and to the military pilots who died in routine training flights.

Sitting on the porch in the moonlight CJ made a promise to Linc. She would tell his story.

CHAPTER FIFTY-TWO
APRIL 28, 1942

Quarters M-15, Fort Shafter

THE FOLLOWING DAY, Ruth was the only one home when Ginger came by to pick up Eve's things from quarters.

When Ginger told Ruth that Eve was quitting the WARD, Ruth said. "It's not a good time for her to decide about anything."

"I agree," Ginger said. "She has to do something. All she's does now is sit in her room alone, and if anyone goes in—off with their heads."

"It's to be expected," Ruth said.

"I know, but it's like dealing with a wounded animal," Ginger said. "Mother's suggesting she study at University of Hawaii, so you know she'd die before she did that."

"She needs time," Ruth said.

"And a visit from you."

"I'm probably the last person she wants to see right now," Ruth answered. "When she's ready, she'll reach out."

Pearl Harbor Hospital

Jane refused Parker's offer to drive her to the hospital. "I need to do this myself."

"Are you sure you don't want me to come? I know a lot of the docs there if you wanted to know information about Buck."

"I'm really fine."

But she wasn't fine. She had no idea what was going to happen.

She drove into the hospital entry, under the black wrought iron arch. Tied to it was a hand-painted canvas banner reading: U.S. Army 147th General Hospital covering the lettering of the former Saint Louis Hospital sign.

The hospital's foyer was grand. The marble floor gleamed, the windows were spotless, and there wasn't a speck of dust in the robes of the plaster saints.

Jane asked a nun in a white habit for Buck's room; the nun told her he was in the fourth-floor solarium. The line in front of the elevators was four-deep with wheelchairs, so she opted for the stairs. She took the steps slowly, noticing where fifty years of footsteps had worn down the marble.

She wasn't ready to see Buck, wasn't ready to see his leg. What would she say? What would he say?

They were divorcing? They were staying married?

She spotted him in the corner of the solarium. His silhouette was framed by the afternoon sun. She approached slowly, relieved he didn't see her. When he did, she wanted to run.

"Hi." With each step Jane wished Buck had never come home. She didn't want him dead—no, he could still be fine flying. He looked like he wished he was anywhere than sitting in a wheel-chair, stubbing his cigarette on the ashtray perched on its arm.

"I didn't think you'd show up," was Buck's greeting.

She wished she hadn't.

"How are you?" She realized how stupid she sounded.

"How do you think I am?" He flicked open the blanket that covered his leg—or where his leg was. "This is all your doing. You and your hotshot ideas," he said, loud enough for everyone in the solarium to hear. A few heads turned.

She wasn't going to do this in public. "Is there a place we could talk privately? I could wheel you there."

"Wheel me? Like the cripple I am?" He snorted a laugh. "If I wanted to go somewhere, I could wheel myself."

Jane wasn't going to fight. Buck lost a leg. His life would never be the same.

Buck flicked his cigarette lighter. Jane hated when he did that, and he knew it. "Do you know where they'll be sending you for rehab?" she asked.

He flicked the lighter again. "What do you care?"

"I do care about you, Buck." She stared out the hospital window. In the garden, There was a monkeypod tree that must have been 50 feet across.

"Wives care," he said. "You never were a real wife."

Jane refused to take the bait.

"No love and marriage and a baby carriage." He flicked the lighter.

"That's not who we are, Buck," she said. "You said that romance was for fools. We were going to be aviation giants. Bigger than Putnam and Earhart, remember?"

"Until you forced me to join the Army and I got blown up."

"It has nothing to do with the war."

"You're right. It's got everything to do with you. If it weren't for you, I could have spent the war at home. My father has connections." He waved his arm over his hip. "And not ended up like this."

She wasn't going to argue. "I got accepted into the Women's Auxiliary Ferrying Squadron."

"Well, that little plan's been scrubbed." He locked his eyes on her. "Because we'll both be going to Pittsburgh." He lifted the stump of his legs. "Where I'm getting fitted with a wooden leg and you're going to learn how to take care of it. I'll strap it on in the morning and unstrap it at night." He mimicked putting it on. "They tell me I'll have welts for months. But don't worry, they're going to teach you how to massage the ointment on it."

He forced her decision. "I'm joining the WAFS."

"New plan." He flicked his goddamn lighter at her. "You get a lifetime of taking care of me."

"You want revenge," she said.

He snickered.

"I can't do this, Buck."

"Oh, but you will."

Had he been the slightest bit different, had he given her the slightest reason to stay, she would have.

She drew in every breath of courage she could, stood up and slung her gas mask over her shoulder. Her throat was tight. She almost didn't say it. "I'm leaving you, Buck."

"You wouldn't dare," he yelled.

"We can work out the details later."

She walked away, not looking back, nor quickening her pace.

Quarters M-15, Fort Shafter

It was late by the time Jane got back to quarters. she told Ruth and CJ her decision. There was no jubilation or disparagement of Buck.

Ruth whispered, almost respectfully, "You can do this, Jane. You're strong."

"I'm not sure I can actually do it," she said.

CJ, never holding back, said, "For God's sake, Jane, you're a pilot, you shoot like Annie Oakley, and you're smarter than anyone I know."

"And I'm the wife of soldier who lost his leg."

"Stop it, Jane. We've been through this already," CJ said.

"Could you leave Joe if he were wounded?"

"If Joe treated me like Buck treated you, I'd be out the door."

"Don't soften your opinion," Ruth said to CJ.

"I'm sorry," CJ said. "That didn't come out right, but Jane, you can't give up your life to him. You're a pilot. A gal pilot!"

"I am a pilot," Jane conceded.

"Imagine a life of flying." CJ paused. "Now imagine a life taking care of Buck."

Jane exhaled.

"You told us why you love flying," Ruth said. "Remember? New Year's Eve?" She put her hand on Jane's shoulder. "I'd never seen you smile like that."

Jane shook her head. "Then the fairy tale ended."

"But it doesn't mean there isn't a new story waiting to be told," Ruth said.

CHAPTER FIFTY-THREE
MAY 2-3, 1942

Quarters M-15, Fort Shafter

IT TOOK SERGEANT Cranston two days to call in a few favors to get Jane scheduled early for the WAFS. He arranged a flight out faster than Jane thought possible—she had 24 hours to pack and clear her things out of Wheeler Housing.

She didn't have much, and she wanted even less. She had already boxed up all her wedding gifts to be shipped to Buck's family and she left everything in the house that belonged to him, even the old issues of *Popular Aviation* that he had given to her at Friendship.

When the MP came to pick Jane up, she and CJ had already said their farewells. They shed a few tears, teased each other, and promised to stay in touch, and Jane hugged CJ for the last time.

"Watch your sixes," CJ quipped.

"Watch your sixes?" Jane laughed. "Who taught you that?"

"Linc did." CJ winked.

It was "watch your six," but there was no need to tell her.

Jane winked back and pretended to lift a glass. "To Linc."

❧

CJ stood her 8 a.m. to noon shift, and when she got home, Ruth was sitting on the porch. There was an empty glass on the armrest. CJ hovered over it for a beat. The drink looked like water—but she had a gut feeling it was vodka.

"Hey," she said, her voice lighter than she felt. "You doing okay?"

Ruth answered without looking up. "Fine."

CJ glanced at the glass again. "Can I get you something? Iced tea? Water?"

Ruth reached for her Lucky Strikes. "Iced tea would be wonderful."

As soon as she got in the kitchen, CJ smelled Ruth's glass. Nothing—but vodka doesn't smell. She returned with iced tea for herself and set Ruth's on the armrest. "Anything else new in your life?" She was acting so chirpy that she made herself nauseated.

"Loretta Russell called." Ruth shook the glass, the ice tinkling. "The orphans are due in next week."

CJ kept up the chirp. "That's great. So, Gordon is coming home."

"And Song."

She dropped the chirpy cheeriness and let a moment pass before she spoke again. "Then you'll get to meet her."

Ruth lit a cigarette. The tip of it flamed orange. "Why would I do that?"

"Because she's a baby? Because Gordon wants you to?"

"Because she's a baby?" Ruth's eyes narrowed. "She's not my baby."

CJ should have kept her mouth shut.

"There's something else."

What more could there be?

"With Jane gone, it makes sense for you to move into that room."

"Of course."

"Maybe today?"

"I understand," CJ said, but she now understood that Ruth was drinking—a lot—and having her own room would make that so much easier.

Ruth took a sip, then casually added, "Oh—by the way. A girl from the *Advertiser* called. She said Mr. Russell wants to meet with you."

"Did she say what about?"

"It was something about *Stars and Stripes*." Ruth flicked her cigarette ash. "She said it was important. I think her name was Mary or Maude, or something like that."

CJ called Maude to arrange an appointment. The bottom line of their conversation was that the *Stars and Stripes* job was there for the taking. Front page reporting—straight from the Pacific Theater. All she had to do was say yes.

It was the dream she thought she owed her parents—their little girl would be an international journalist. It was what all the female professors at Columbia drilled into her. Shoot for the top men's job.

It was a good job. Besides, she'd be in Australia—closer to Joe—as if she would ever get to see him.

There was only one person she really had to convince, and that was going to take some soul searching.

The Honolulu Advertiser Building, Honolulu

The next day, on her way to the *Advertiser*, CJ picked up a dozen donuts.

The shopkeeper tied the box with blue-and-white striped twine. How many times had she wrapped the pastries at her family's bakery?

When she handed the box to Maude, Maude asked, "Are you going to take it?"

CJ was ten minutes from her meeting with Mr. Russell, and she still didn't know.

"It would be foolish not to," she said.

Maude flipped the box open. "That sounds like an 'I don't want to do it, but it's the right thing to do kind of answer.'"

CJ smiled. "You know it's the right thing."

"Oh yeah?" Maude said. "Why?"

"It just is," she answered.

Maude offered the open box of pastries.

CJ passed. She didn't want to show up in Mr. Russell's office with a dusting of powdered sugar on her uniform.

"Just is?" Maude echoed.

"I owe it to my parents."

CJ walked into Mr. Russell's office and told him at the start that she was declining the offer.

He looked at her from under his heavy eyebrows. She didn't want to disappoint him—and there was the guilt of him putting her name up for the job at the *Stars and Stripes.*

He took off his glasses and pinched the bridge of his nose.

CJ held her breath.

He nodded, then said, "You can't shake off the dead."

Her face must have telegraphed her confusion.

"It would have been a waste of your talent to take it."

"Some people might say it's a waste of my training not to," CJ said.

Mr. Russell opened the bottom drawer of his desk. CJ knew a bottle of Scotch and two glasses would soon appear.

"Well, let's put those folks out to pasture." He placed the bottle on his desk.

"It was drilled into me at Columbia: Don't write about dog

shows, don't make coffee, and never bend over. Human interest is for those who can't report."

"It's bad advice. They should have been nurturing your talent." He poured them both drinks. "Some reporters *can* shake off the dead. Reduce them to a headline in tomorrow's fish wrap. But you, you dig deeper. It's your talent—seeing the story behind the headlines." He handed her a glass. "There's no shame in human interest."

But there was—she owed every other woman trying to be a hard-boiled reporter.

"If you're really good, you can make a name for yourself," Mr. Russell said. "CJ Delano. Man or woman."

He lifted his glass in a toast. "To a quick end to the war."

She raised her glass. "To a quick end to the war."

Quarters M-15, Fort Shafter

That night she wrote a postcard to Joe:

Dear Joe,

I'm going home. Details to follow.

I love you,

CJ

Chapter Fifty-four
May 25-26, 1942

Pistol Range, Fort Shafter

THE SCUTTLEBUTT WAS that something big was about to happen. A few days ago, CJ would have been hungry on the trail to find out what it was, but now she dreaded knowing. "Something big" meant a major confrontation, casualties, the risk of defeat, and the possibility of Joe being wounded.

On May 25th the WARDs were ordered to pistol training. A truck shuttled them to the Boy Scout Lodge. The walls were painted stark white, and steel bars covered the high windows. The only lights flicked from ceiling bulbs, and the only color was the red bull's eye targets pinned to hay bales.

The morning session of pistol training consisted of assembling, disassembling and cleaning their weapons. During the afternoon session, they practiced shooting stances and eye and hand movements before they finally were allowed to fire their weapons.

Each girl had a soldier as her shadow, cueing her, adjusting her stance. The girls shot—mostly badly. CJ scored marksman.

The next day, the WARDs lined up for immunizations—typhoid, dengue, and malaria—and copies of the Geneva Conventions were distributed to them. Lieutenant Connors read out loud, "You have the right to be treated as officers in the event of capture."

Oh God. If she hadn't taken her name off the evac list she might have been on a train to New Jersey right now instead of holding a copy of the Geneva Conventions.

Quarters M-15, Fort Shafter

That afternoon, CJ found Ruth on the porch, sitting on the glider, with her feet tucked under her legs.

"We missed you at pistol training," CJ said.

"I'm going tomorrow."

CJ knew the only training scheduled was that day.

"Have you been out here all day?" There was an empty coffee cup on the armrest.

"Mostly." Ruth dug her cigarettes out of her robe pocket and lit one after another.

"Ruth, I'm worried about you."

"I'm fine."

"Your 'fine' worries me. You skipped pistol training. You know it was the only day, and you're dropping your shifts."

"Gordon's home." Ruth didn't make eye contact with CJ. "He wants to take me to meet Song this afternoon."

"If he's coming, don't you think you should get dressed?"

"If I'm dressed, he'll expect me to go to the hospital."

And as if on cue, a Navy car pulled up to the quarters.

Gordon climbed the stairs. He opened the screen door, but Ruth didn't get up.

Gordon nodded to CJ.

He looked like he had lost thirty pounds. His uniform hung on him like a little boy wearing his father's suit.

"Hello, Ruth," he said it quietly.

CJ knew her place. "It's good to have you home, Commander," she said, "but, I've got things to do," and went inside.

As soon as CJ left, Ruth spoke quickly, not giving Gordon a chance to interrupt. "Between Mrs. Russell and the Chinese Aid Society, we're certain we can find good homes for all the orphans."

"Even Song?"

"She's an infant, that's to her advantage, and I assume she's healthy."

"She's beautiful, Ruth. You should see her. She's bright and happy, and already babbling."

"Stop it, Gordon. You're talking about her like you're her father."

"She makes me feel alive again."

"Gordon, you saved her in the middle of that godawful place. But you're home now."

"I want you to meet her."

"There's no reason for me to."

"I'm asking you. Isn't that enough?"

Ruth didn't answer right away. She looked down at her cigarette. "Gordon, I don't want somebody else's baby."

"I know I'm pushing too fast. But once you meet her…"

"I want to give you our own baby, Gordon."

"It may not happen."

"I've wanted two things out of life: to be a good wife and mother. Is that so much to ask?"

"I love you, Ruth." He sat next to her.

She ground her cigarette in the ashtray. "And now you want to replace our daughter."

"Dear God, I don't want to replace her."

"Then why adopt? There must be plenty of Chinese families who want her."

"Just meet her."

"I don't want to." She wanted her own baby. "I miss Grace."

She broke down and Gordon took her in his arms. "No one will replace her, Ruth. but nothing will bring her back."

"I'll see the Georgetown doctor, and everything will be fine."

"And if we have another baby, will you love that child?"

Ruth imagined herself looking down at the newborn infant, but she could only see Grace's face.

"You've got to get back to living, Ruth."

"I am living!"

"You're not happy."

How could he be happy? Our daughter died.

"We both deserve happiness, Ruth."

But she was closest to Grace in grief. It was her comfort and she would never let go of it.

CHAPTER FIFTY-FIVE

MAY 30, 1942

St. Francis Hospital, Honolulu

MRS. RUSSELL CALLED RUTH to tell her that she had designated Ruth as the liaison with the Army for the care of the Chinese orphans. She had done most of the assessments, but she needed Ruth to do the last four. And, she had arranged for an MP to pick her up and take her to the St. Francis Hospital.

Then she thanked Ruth and disconnected the call, before Ruth could refuse.

She was frustrated at being caught in Mrs. Russell's web, but she knew she had to go. She vowed it would be a quick visit—a twenty-minute administrative nuisance—and asked CJ to go with her because she didn't want to be alone.

As they drove up to the hospital parking lot, a line of Army ambulances jammed up the entrance.

"What do you think's going on?" CJ asked Ruth.

"I'm not sure."

Patients on gurneys were being carried into the hospital by medics. CJ stopped one of them. "What's going on?"

The medic glanced at the lieutenant's bars on CJ's uniform. "We're moving some patients to dispensaries, Ma'am."

"Freeing up hospital beds?"

"Yes, Ma'am,"

The medic proceeded and CJ turned to Ruth. "Has Gordon said anything to you?"

"He wouldn't even if he knew," Ruth said.

CJ kept walking; Ruth held back.

"I can't do this," Ruth said.

"I'll be right with you. All you have to do is fill out forms." She put her hand out to Ruth.

"What if one of the babies is Song?"

"Then I'll do that assessment and you finish up the rest," CJ said.

"You're not Red Cross," Ruth said.

CJ rolled her eyes. "I can fill out papers."

The nursery was on the second floor, just past the maternity ward. It was just over a year since Ruth had been in a maternity ward, but she left the hospital without a baby.

A nurse met them in the corridor. Her name tag said: Nurse Louise Silva, and her uniform and cap were starched as stiff as her posture.

"It's good to meet you, Mrs. Russell." Nurse Silva hovered over Ruth.

"Oh, I'm not Mrs. Russell." Ruth explained she was just filling in, as was CJ who she introduced as a Red Cross liaison volunteer. "We're just here to fill out the remaining forms."

The nurse escorted them into a closet-sized office with an interior door to the nursery. She handed clipboards to Ruth and CJ. "Let's get started." She walked them into the nursery.

The nursery was jammed with white bassinets lined up like laundry carts. At the window, a man tapped the glass, waving at a baby.

Nurse Silva stood at the first bassinette. "This is Song. Her paperwork needs a bit more input."

Ruth turned her back.

"She's wheezing," CJ said.

Ruth heard it too—shallow, rattling breath. Babies weren't supposed to wheeze.

"We're watching her," was Nurse Silva's only response.

Ruth checked herself from asking any questions. This wasn't her baby. Song was the nurse's charge. They would take care of her. It was their job, not hers.

Chapter Fifty-six
May 31–June 1, 1942

Lizard Tunnel, Fort Shafter

RUTH WAS IN the canteen, standing at the counter, asking for some aspirin, when CJ walked in. "Are you okay?"

"Headache." Ruth rubbed her temples. "I've got a double-shift replacing someone on your crew." She turned toward the jukebox. "And if they play *Back in the Saddle Again* one more time, I'm going to rip the plug right out of the wall."

CJ knew it was more than the music.

They settled at a table.

"I'm overwhelmed," Ruth said. "I've got to finish the hospital visit for Mrs. Russell by tomorrow, and I still have some questions about a few of the babies."

"I'm right here in front of you." CJ pointed to her own face. "I can do some of this stuff."

"Did you hear her wheezing?" Ruth asked.

"You mean Song?" CJ nodded.

"And that nurse's answer, 'We're watching her.' What kind of answer is that? She's an infant with obvious respiratory issues."

"I can go out there this afternoon."

Ruth shook her head. "If any notifications need to be made, it should be me."

"Notifications?"

"I'm probably overreacting." Ruth stirred her coffee. She couldn't stop hearing Song's breathing—so labored. She'd be damned if she'd watch another infant die.

Song needed care. She needed an advocate. Then she caught herself. Song wasn't her child. She was another woman's child—a woman who gave up her daughter to keep her alive.

What did she owe to that mother? Another woman who'd never see her child grow?

Quarters M-15, Fort Shafter

The next morning, Nurse Silva called Ruth. The Office of the Military Governor and the Department of Immigration needed an additional set of forms for the infants. They had to be submitted immediately. Could Ruth come to the hospital?

"I've got a noon shift today. I can't make it. Maybe Mrs. Russell can—"

CJ waved her hands in front of Ruth and Ruth put her hand over the receiver. CJ said, "I can go."

"You're not Red Cross."

"You told her I was." CJ reminded her. "And do you think Immigration's going to care?"

Ruth went back on the phone. "The friend I brought yesterday—the other Red Cross volunteer. Could she fill out the forms?"

Ruth listened. Nodded. "I understand… Yes, I have that authority… No, I don't believe the other volunteer does." She looked at CJ.

"Go!" CJ mouthed. "I'll take your shift."

"Yes, Nurse Silva," Ruth said into the phone. "I'll be there by ten."

Saint Francis Hospital

When Ruth arrived, Song's bassinette was missing. Her stomach turned.

"You have good timing," Nurse Silva said. "Your husband is in the private room."

"Commander Elliott?" Ruth asked.

"He comes in every day to be with Song," Silva said, almost fondly. "Miraculously, he leaves with his uniform still perfectly pressed."

The nurse's tone softened. Maybe yesterday Ruth hit her on a bad day.

"Come on in," she led Ruth into the nursery where Gordon sat in the rocking chair, feeding Song from a bottle.

Her tiny hands curled around his.

"How is she?" Ruth asked.

"I thought she'd be better by now," Silva said.

"Fever?"

The nurse nodded.

Gordon looked up. His face showed no emotion.

"I'm just here to fill out immigration forms for the infants," Ruth explained.

"Do you want to hold her?" He offered Song to her.

Ruth shook her head. "I'm only here to sign some papers. I've got to get back to my shift."

She would never hold Song. It would feel like she was betraying Grace.

"I'll call you later," Gordon said.

"Don't bother. I told you, I'll be on the board tonight."

CHAPTER FIFTY-SEVEN
JUNE 2-4, 1942

Lizard Tunnel, Fort Shafter

ON JUNE 2ND, the WARDs were sequestered on base. They couldn't use the phones, and the recruits who trained as litter bearers were ordered to sleep at the dispensary. At midnight, sixty B-17s flown in from California headed for Midway Island.

At 8 a.m., CJ was sitting in the front row in the amphitheater when Major Oliver announced, "In the event of an invasion, there will be no assistance available to you. All WARDs are on your own to handle injuries and casualties."

What the hell was he talking about?

"And you will prepare to seek shelter in caves above the base. No medics will be assigned to you." Major Oliver turned to Lieutenant Connors, "Have they been issued their pistols?"

"Not yet."

CJ took in the facts—but absorbing them was a different story.

On June 3rd, the Japanese attacked Alaska. On June 4th, PBYs spotted four Japanese carriers 470 miles from Midway and the U.S. fleet was sailing in to engage.

The battle of Midway had begun.

Ruth had stayed past her shift, sitting on the floor with tens of other WARDs and soldiers who waited and listened.

Four hours into the battle, reports came in that Navy bombers had sunk a Japanese carrier. After the announcement, the room was silent. One carrier was not a battle victory.

More soldiers came in, squeezing on benches and perched on metal cabinets.

Soldiers rolled out chalkboards and pinned maps to the walls.

During the fifth hour, CJ took her shift on the board. Her hands trembled as she adjusted her headset. She switched the toggles, picked up her rake, and prayed for courage. "Oscar, this is Rascal. Can you read me?"

"Rascal, I can read you."

"I can read you," CJ said. "What's happening?"

"It's a shit farm." Oscar's transmission was garbled.

"Oscar, could you repeat?"

"A shit farm, Rascal. It doesn't look good."

Midway!

CJ remembered Cranston screaming at her. "The Japs know where it is."

Dear God, there was no room for error. thought, make him wrong.

"Oscar? You there?" CJ asked.

"I'm here, Rascal. I'll keep you appraised."

An hour passed.

"Oscar?" All she got was static. "Oscar?" She looked up at the Liaison Officers, shrugged, and put up her palms to the air. "I'm not getting anything."

One of them mouthed to her. "Wait."

Wait for what?

Nothing was moving. Nothing being transmitted. She kept looking up at the Liaison Officer, but he was head down, his hands pressed to his earphones. What the hell was he hearing?

What the hell was going on?

At 8:03 p.m., the Pacific Commander in Chief arrived. He climbed the steps to the balcony and tapped the microphone. "Ladies and gentlemen, all four of their carriers are out of commission."

CJ wasn't sure what that meant.

"We have victory!"

Caps were tossed. Soldiers hugged and jumped and shed tears. Shouts. Cheers. A sergeant on the far bench let out a screeching pig call.

CJ had to keep her eyes on the board ready to plot in any planes, but she cocked her head and watched it all with a reporter's eye: A soldier hugged the chalkboard. Another fell to his knees and prayed.

There was hope they could win the war.

"We did it, Linc," CJ whispered, fighting back tears for the cost they had all paid.

Chapter Fifty-eight
June 6-7, 1942

St. Francis Hospital, Honolulu

THE VICTORY OF battle rang hollow for Ruth.

She went to visit Song the morning after the battle. Song's condition was worse, and her survival was in question.

She knew this wasn't her fault. She hadn't carried Song. She didn't fall while she was pregnant with her, or play competitive tennis. She was a stand in for a mother who would never hear Song talk. Maybe she'd never even seen Song's eyes.

In that moment, Ruth refused to let Song die.

Nurse Silva placed Song on Ruth's lap and Ruth rocked Song. She kissed her burning forehead, she sang a soft lullaby. This baby would not die. Ruth pushed the thought down.

She wiped Song's forehead with a cool cloth. She prayed for her recovery—not to a distant God who called children to him, but to every mother who had buried a child. They knew grief no one else did, and they knew how precious life was.

Nurse Silva pumped drops of medicine in Song's mouth, and Song looked like a baby bird. Live, little girl. Ruth willed Song to hear her thoughts, but the baby remained lethargic.

She waited an hour past when Gordon usually arrived, but she knew the day after Midway, he'd be shuttling from Admiral, to code breakers, to the Intelligence Office.

She needed to talk about Song. So, she drove to Babies' Cemetery to visit Grace.

Schofield Barracks Babies' Cemetery

Ruth unrolled a mat and sat in front of Grace's headstone. She traced the letters in Grace's name. "You never were going to be the only one. Your father and I were going to fill the house with children … It's not happening the way we planned… There's a baby…a sick baby…" Ruth pressed her hand against the stone. "She may die." Ruth pressed her hand against the stone. "Her name is Song and I want her to live." Ruth felt tears running down her cheek.

"I wish you could help her," Ruth said.

I wish you could help me.

When she got back to quarters, she called Gordon to asking him to come by quarters.

Her thought when she hung up was simple: God give me the courage.

When he arrived, they sat on the porch.

"I went to see Grace," she said. "I told her about Song…about how I was starting to love her…and I wanted her to be ours."

Quarters M-15, Fort Shafter

The next morning, CJ shuffled in from a six-hour shift.

She heard the shower running and headed for the kitchen—then froze.

Gordon, barefoot and wearing Ruth's robe, was pouring coffee.

"Good morning." CJ tried to sound casual.

He lifted the pot. "Fresh cup?"

She raised an eyebrow at the robe. "Bold fashion choice."

"Ruth's in the shower."

CJ nodded, laying her purse on the counter.

"And yes," he said, confirming the obvious. "I spent the night."

"I kind of guessed that," CJ said.

"To be clear, I spent the night. With my wife." a smile tugged at the corner of his mouth.

"Mm-hmm." CJ smiled.

"So why do I feel like a teenager sneaking in my girl-friend's house?"

Ruth walked in, towel-wrapped, and put her arm around Gordon. "Because that's exactly who you are."

"Well," CJ said, "I guess I'll try to find somewhere else to be."

"No need to rush off," Gordon said. "We're heading out."

"To see Song," Ruth added.

St. Francis Hospital, Honolulu

Gordon took Ruth's arm as they walked in the nursery.

"You're here together." Nurse Silva seemed surprised. She wiped down the rocking chair and handed Ruth a small blanket. Then she placed Song in Ruth's arms.

Ruth kissed Song's forehead. "She feels cooler."

The nurse said, "She's a tough little fighter. Her fever broke last night."

Gordon stood behind Ruth, his hands on her shoulders, lean-ing over, smiling as Song, asleep, curled her finger around Ruth's thumb.

"She's so small." Ruth smoothed Song's hair.

"And beautiful," Gordon said.

Ruth hummed as she rocked her.

Can you love me Song? Can I learn to love you?

Song opened her eyes. They were brilliant onyx.

Ruth kissed Song's forehead. "You have a sister. Someday, I'll take you out to meet her."

Chapter Fifty-nine

June 10, 1942

Downtown Honolulu

CJ WROTE TO Joe that she was scheduled to be evacuated on June 11th.

She was downtown shopping for gifts to bring home to her parents when she spotted Eve across the street.

Eve waved; she was dressed to the nines.

It had been almost two months since Linc died. Eve hadn't returned a single call—not from CJ, not from Ruth.

"Fancy meeting you here," Eve said in the bored socialite voice CJ knew so well.

They hugged—tentative, cautious. Shared practiced kisses beside each other's cheeks.

"How are you?" Eve asked.

"Very well," CJ replied, matching Eve's practiced smile. "Parker said he saw you at the Halekulani last week."

"Zachary Dillingham's birthday luncheon," Eve said, fiddling with her bracelet. "It was…festive."

"His family is in shipping. Did I remember that right?"

Eve nodded. "Zach was headquartered in San Francisco before the war.

So Eve still had San Francisco in her sights.

"I've been shopping for my mother," Eve said breezily. "I thought she needed a pearl bracelet." She held up her arm toward CJ. "And you?"

CJ almost told her she was going home. But that would have dragged things out and CJ wanted to move on as quickly as possible.

"Tell me about the new recruits," Eve said too brightly. "Did you get lucky with a good roommate?"

"I haven't been assigned one."

"Well," Eve said, her voice light and practiced, "once things settle down, I'll have you and Ruth over for brunch."

"Sure." CJ smiled. "When things settle down."

"Great," Eve said—another shared kiss of the air next to each other's cheek. "I'll call."

"Great." CJ repeated, and she watched Eve walk away.

Chapter Sixty
June 11, 1942

Honolulu Dock

THE DAY CJ left to go back to New Jersey, there were no hula dancers on the pier. No Royal Hawaiian Band or lei sellers pushing through the crowd. "Boat Days" was a ghost of the past.

Aloha Tower was camouflaged green, and the water where local boys dove for coins in the harbor was guarded by soldiers with bayonets.

It had been six months.

Had she failed? Had she learned anything? It didn't matter, she was going home, back to New Jersey, to help in her family's bakery, to write to Joe each night and run to the mailbox each day to see if he'd written to her.

She was going back to the *Newark Star-Ledger* where she'd be covering fashion shows and Junior League teas, and she'd push Mr. Spina to let her run a human-interest piece. Maybe she'd write an essay about Hawaii? Or the war? It didn't matter. The truth was, she wasn't that good at hard-boiled reporting, nor did she want to be. It wasn't much more than writing obits. You wrote down the facts, names, dates, and places. There really wasn't much to mess up, or much to be good at. You just had to be assigned to the right place at the right time. She was going home to be who she always was. And she would tell the stories.

Epilogue
1995

CJ FINGERED THE engraved invitation. Fifty years. She was unsure if she would go to the reunion. It had been a long time since she had seen the girls. Was it Eve's second wedding?

The girls had promised to keep in touch, but frequent letters had ebbed to birthday and Christmas cards…and then nothing.

She thought about their days together, but there were some memories that should remain in the past.

When CJ's daughter Sophia read the invitation, she encouraged her, "You know Dad would have already booked the flight."

Sophia was right. Joe would have booked first-class tickets the day the invitation arrived. Then he would have called the Royal Hawaiian Hotel and reserved the Honeymoon Suite—if the Royal still existed. But CJ didn't want to go without him.

It had been four years since Joe died, and there were days she still expected him to walk in the door. And there were mornings she could almost see him hit the alarm clock and stumble to the bathroom—then the click of the lighter and his first cigarette of the day.

She missed him on big occasions like holidays and celebrations and the times when her friends took her dinner and there was an empty fourth chair.

But those weren't the hardest times for her. It was when she stubbed her toe and he wasn't there to laugh at her for swearing. It was when the car needed fixing and the mechanic treated her like an idiot, or when she couldn't find the insurance papers and the premium was overdue.

She thought about Jane making good on her threat to hang Eve's lingerie from the porch if she didn't take shorter showers. About the night Linc and Parker showed up looking like the Marx Brothers. She thought about Joe and their wedding night at the Royal Hawaiian.

CJ had a vague idea of where her WARD cap and wings were. Her uniform was long gone. She let Sophia use it as a costume for Halloween one year. After that, she donated it to a high school drama club.

She rooted around the attic until she found the Rubbermaid bin labeled "Hawaii" and pried it open. There were menus from drive-ins, warped 78 vinyls, a bus schedule, movie tickets, and a packet of Joe's letters from the front.

Then, at the bottom, were her marble cover composition tablets. The ones where she wrote the stories that censors wouldn't allow. The civilian dead. Iwilei evacuations. The constant looming of submarines. She smiled when she saw her sketches of nuns in their habits digging trenches around their schools and all-American-looking prostitutes walking a picket line.

She'd found her career telling the stories of the unsung, and for the last ten years of it, she had her own syndicated column.

❧

The day Ruth received the invitation, she had just returned from the commissary. When she read it, she shook her head. "Fifty years!"

What had she done? Traveled, worked, almost divorced, forgave, fell back in love. Accepted her grief, raised a daughter.

She was unsure about attending, but she was a good officer's wife to the end and called to RSVP that day. Her WARD wings were in a pink quilted box she kept in her top dresser drawer. The only other thing she kept in the box was a glassine envelope with a lock of Grace's hair.

§

Eve kept her WARD badge and wings in a tarnished silver cigarette case with a ten-cent jade ring. She wasted no time reserving a first-class ticket to Honolulu.

It had been seven years since she had been in Hawaii. After her parents died, she and Ginger sold the family home, and Ginger moved to D.C. with her husband.

The day before the reunion, Eve drove out to the Makapuu Lighthouse and stood at the same spot where she and Linc stood on Valentine's Day, 1942.

The trail to the lighthouse was one mile, paved, with no shade or restrooms. She didn't remember the trail being so steep and the sun so hot. Her knees ached and she panted.

She stopped at a crowded overlook facing Hawaii Kai. She didn't remember so many tourists either. Eve smiled at a young couple taking photos and pushed on.

The thought rose of St. Patrick's Day when Linc proposed to her in front of their friends. What else could she have said?

She said yes because that was what you were supposed to do at moments like that.

She must have smiled thinking about it because a young girl passing her turned and said, "That must be a good memory!"

"It is," she answered.

She kept climbing. Her new athletic shoes, "guaranteed to give full support to older athletes," were not jettisoning her up the hill. She stopped at the overlook facing Molokai and Maui and remembered asking Linc to take her flying. She remembered their drive to Kualoa and the first time he made love to her. She could almost feel his finger tracing her lips.

Could she have been the Madison doctor's wife? Wisconsin was closer to Paris than San Francisco was to Hawaii. And if they had children, she could have hired a nanny to teach them French.

She continued to climb.

Typically, older women were invisible. But hiking a trail in the blazing sun, with her shirt glued to her back from sweat, she found herself the object of stares that screamed out judgments that she was either stark raving mad or an inspirational role model.

One more switchback and she'd be there.

The landmark had to be close. The guidebook stated that it was located at the bottom of the lighthouse.

When she saw it, she was disappointed. She expected it would be grander than the modest brass plaque on the ground. The wind had worn down the letters, but the names were still legible:

Lieutenant JG Lincoln W. Armstrong, Ensign George Doll, Ensign William Howe, AMM1c Orren Roberts, Amm3c Harvey Hayman, ARM2 Jack Parrish, AMM2c Billy B. Herring, AM3c Delbert Berchot, RM3c Charles Andrews.

She crouched slowly, wishing she had something to lean on, and ran her finger over Linc's name.

Lincoln W. Armstrong. She smiled at reading the "W." How strange. She was to be the future Mrs. Armstrong, but she never knew he had a middle name. Maybe it stood for William? Or Wade? Or Warren?

She reached in her pocket, opened the sandalwood box, and placed the ten-cent jade ring next to his name.

Could she have been Mrs. Lincoln Armstrong?

❧

The first day CJ was in Hawaii, she drove over the new bridge connecting Pearl City to Ford Island. The ferries were gone. The golf course was gone, replaced by a park. The new dispensary was a slick black glass clinic.

When she saw a Marine in a maternity uniform, she almost heard Joe grouse, "The whole damn military's gone soft." But Joe wasn't there.

The hangars were still there, and the tower loomed over the abandoned airstrip. Corrugated tin roofs were pitted with rust from the salt air; windows had been shot out. Some junior housing bungalows, battered and abandoned, had been placed at the entrance of "Historic Housing" as if they would eventually be an exhibit.

In the "Historic Housing" neighborhood, mothers still pushed babies, although the carriages were jogging strollers, and the moms weren't wearing dresses and heels. In front of each quarter were hand-carved placards with the names of the men who lived there on December 7, 1941. The sign in front of Quarters 31B still read "Commander Gordon Elliott, USN."

On the morning of the reunion, Ruth pinned her WARD wings on, measuring the placement on her lapel with a ruler.

She took a last look at herself in the hallway mirror and adjusted the silk bow of her blouse in the hall mirror. She checked the clasp on her double-strand pearl choker. *It's been a good life,* she thought.

✑

One hundred twenty-six WARDs came back for the reunion. Their hair was silver or tastefully-dyed champagne. Their eyes clouded with age, their skin leathered by years of golfing, gardening, or raising children. Some were stooped over, and a few used walkers.

They approached each other timidly as if they were searching for their friend among faces that had succumbed to time.

"Nancy?" A woman furrowed her brow.

"Betty, is that you?"

A touch of an arm, then an embrace, and the years faded away.

Mary Jane Buckingham wore her WARD cap over her still-red hair. Shannon Solomon wore her wings on a necklace, and Irene Cope was still slim enough to fit in her uniform.

CJ and Ruth spotted each other at a distance, and the two of them worked their way through the crowd. When they reached each other, they stood in silence, smiling, their tears welling up.

"It's been too long," Ruth whispered.

"All those years."

Ruth stepped back and examined CJ from head to toe. "You don't look a day older."

"Than Methuselah?" CJ quipped.

❧

Eve stopped at the O'Club foyer and looked through the crowd. She wondered if she would recognize the girls. She expected Ruth to still be wearing her pearl choker and suit, and assumed CJ had gained weight after having all those children. And Jane.

Oh, Jane! She might be in a flight suit or boots crusted with cow manure.

She spotted them! "Ruth! CJ!" Eve sashayed toward them.

"You looked wonderful!" Ruth told Eve, and CJ had to agree.

Eve raised her chin and stretched her hand down her neck. "My husband is a plastic surgeon."

"Number 3?" CJ asked.

"I stopped at three." Eve twisted her lip into a smile. "And I'd be insane to divorce him."

"Are you living in San Francisco?" Ruth asked

"Of course," Eve answered.

"What about you?" Eve asked CJ. "Still in New Jersey with your children?"

"The children are all married and gone."

"I forgot." Eve tossed her head in that offhand manner CJ remembered so well. "How many do you have?"

"Four." CJ knew Eve wasn't interested in the details, but she named them off intentionally. "Joe named our first son Raphael, but we call him RD. Then came Joe, Jr., Sophia, and Vincent after my father."

"Joe must be retired by now," Eve said.

"Joe died four years ago. Lung cancer." CJ paused. "We had forty-nine good years."

"I'm sorry," Ruth said.

"And Gordon?" CJ asked.

"He retired from the Navy, worked as a consultant for the governor for a while, then sometime in 1976, he bought a new set of golf clubs and hasn't worked a day since—except on Friday when he takes Grace to the zoo."

Ruth saw Eve's eyes widen at the mention of the name Grace.

"Grace is Song's little girl—that is Doctor Song! And the family lives twenty minutes from us in Kailua."

"You're still in Hawaii?"

"It was the perfect place to raise Song." Ruth turned to Eve. "Still in San Francisco, I assume?"

"I have a home on Nob Hill and a *pied-à-terre* in Paris, and I get to have dinner with Parker at least once a month. He's got a 'friend' that lives with him—a tax lawyer—but his friend gives me my time to be with Park."

CJ caught Eve's eye. "Is Parker still the love of your life?"

"As close as I've come." Her tone was wistful, then she bounced back to her *bon vivant* façade. "Well, where's our fourth?" She looked around the room. "Have you two seen Jane?"

Ruth held up the envelope addressed to all of them and started to open it. "She left us a letter at the reception desk."

They settled at a table. Ruth unfolded the letter and scanned it before reading it out loud.

"It's from Sam Horn." She looked at Eve, then CJ. "Jane passed last year. Heart attack."

Ruth read Sam's words aloud.

After the war, Jane left the WAFS and went back to Friendship, and we were married in six months.

Jane loved my two girls like they were her own, and before they were twelve years old, she taught them both to fly cargo planes. By the time she was in high school, my oldest, Jean, had her pilot's license, and now she's running the cargo company. The other girl ended up a school teacher.

Jane and I had a son named Harrison. If you can believe it, he's already retired from the Army. Jane could never forgive him for not going Army Air, but he retired as a Lieutenant Colonel, and we're so proud.

Between my girls and our son, we have seven grandchildren. Our Thanksgiving table is long and loud.

I know Jane would have loved seeing you girls. She told so many stories of your time together. So, when the invitation came, I thought I'd dig up some photos for you to have, and I had a copy made of her WAFS reunion in '65. I thought you'd want to see her in her flight suit and helmet.

If any of you ladies ever make it to Friendship, Texas, there's a place for you at our table.

Sorry I never got to meet you,
Sam Horn

The photos were cracked and curled, faded to sepia, and grainy, but still could be made out: Jane riding bareback at Shafter Stables, Eve showing off the first chicken she cooked, Ruth getting a citation from General Davidson,

When CJ found the photo of Eve's panties hanging on the front porch rail, Ruth recounted the story of Jane's retaliation against Eve for using all the hot water.

"They were Lady Marlene lingerie!" Eve protested.

When Eve saw the photo Linc took of them in their bathing suits and gas masks, mocking a salute, she smiled wistfully. "I'd like to have that one." She immediately put it in her purse.

"And this one's mine!" Ruth picked one up of her changing a tire on a Jeep. "Gordon will never believe it."

Eve took one of herself with her prize chicken dish and the girls retold their stories. They talked about getting together once a year—a plan each knew would never happen.

Then the announcement was made for the WARDs to process into the ballroom. They were the first class of female radar plotters—at the crossroads of their lives—patriots, heroes, young wives, and lovers.

A Hawaiian priest chanted them in.

CJ, Ruth, and Eve marched down the aisle and filed into the second row, leaving an empty chair for Jane.

It was a missing man formation.

History of the Women's Air Raid Defense

ON DECEMBER 15, 1941, Brigadier General Howard C. Davidson, Commander of the Seventh Fighter Command, was informed that all soldiers serving as air traffic plotters at the Army's Information Center were ordered to combat duty. Davidson had one month to replace them. His solution was to establish a women's civilian unit based on the British Women's Auxiliary Air Force he had observed in London.

At four a.m. on December 16, General Davidson called Mr. Alexander Walker to ask if he and his wife Una could recruit fifty women for a secret war mission. He told them that the women must be between twenty and thirty-four years of age, trustworthy, and free of family responsibilities. They would be required to pass a physical examination, an intelligence test, clear a security investigation, be willing to be live sequestered in military quarters, and must not be subject to evacuation.

The next day, Mrs. Walker provided him with a total of fifty-four names. However, with the expansion of Oahu's radar aircraft warning system and the planned establishment of radar stations on the neighboring islands, General Davidson realized he needed twice as many recruits as he anticipated. It became apparent to Davidson that it was necessary to draw from the pool of military wives and daughters to meet his staffing quota. The problem was that military dependents were under orders to evacuate Hawaii unless they were in an "essential job." So General Davidson had to convince the U.S. Army that service in the WARD was essential to the islands' defense. The Army agreed, and on December 26, 1941, at the first meeting of the Women's Air Raid Defense (WARD), half of the applicants were military dependents.

On New Year's Day, 1942, the volunteers began their training at Iolani Place in the former Senate Chamber. They trained for two weeks under the direction of Lieutenant Ardie Konkle; they were given the code name "Rascal." They were issued gas masks, helmets, non-combatant arm bands, and measured for their uniforms. They took classes in the techniques of aircraft plotting, meteorology, military protocol and technical orders.

On January 12, 1942, the first group of women went to "Little Robert" to relieve the men for a day shift. "Little Robert" was the temporary Information Center at Fort Shafter. It was the "penthouse" of a ramshackle wooden building hidden amid abandoned warehouses at Shafter Flats. A new center, a series of tunnels dug out of a mountainside on Fort Shafter, was under construction and opened on May 12, 1942. Tradition has it that the WARD named the tunnel "Lizard" in honor of all the geckos living there.

After the defeat of the Japanese at the Battle of Midway in June 1942, most islanders considered the threat of invasion over, and their lives began to take on more normalcy. As a result, recruiting for the WARD became more challenging. Some of the original WARD members returned to their families, former careers, or interrupted studies. The attrition rate was high—some women left due to pregnancy. Military wives left when their husbands were transferred, sent to the front, killed, or captured. At the same time, the Army was ready to establish units on Maui, the Big Island, and Kauai. Every new station meant one woman for each of the four shifts. During the summer of 1942, recruiting hit rock bottom—the employment situation on the island was critical, and salaries for women soared for office jobs that didn't carry any of the restrictions or obligations of the WARD. The Army dropped the recruitment age for WARD to 17, special shift arrangements were made for University of Hawaii students, a pool of reserve women who lived at home was developed, but still, the number of women needed to staff the stations far exceeded the number of recruits.

To meet the staffing quotas of the radar centers, the Army began recruiting on the mainland. In January 1943, Colonel Lorry Tindal was assigned to work with the U.S. Army Air

Defense Recruiting Office in San Francisco. On February 13, 1943, the first thirty-four candidates from the mainland arrived in Hawaii. After that, four to eight women each month were sent from that office. These women signed a contract for one year with transportation furnished to and from California.

Over the course of the war, more than 650 women served in the WARD. In May 1945, General Davidson wrote to Kitty Coonely, the WARD Chief Supervisor, "I have seen many information control centers, I have several under me now, but the one in Honolulu manned by the WARD is the best I have seen. I understand that the war has moved on and left Honolulu behind, but you can take great pride in the fact that while it did threaten Hawaii, you maintained the best Air Raid Defense system in the world."

The Women's Air Raid Defense stood their last shift in September 1945.

Note: I used the real names of three WARDs: Nancy West, Kathleen Hamlin and Fluff Ford. Nancy West continued to operate as a plotter after the death of her husband as portrayed in the novel. Kathleen Hamlin stayed in the WARD throughout the war knowing her husband was a Japanese Prisoner of War, and Fluff Ford plotted out her husband as he flew to Midway; he never returned, but she continued on.

Author's Notes

WHAT YOU HAVE read is a labor of love that took over twenty years to write. It started innocently enough with a lecture about the civilian dead of World War 2—that's where I found out about the tragedies of Gussie Ornellas's daughters and the deaths at the Cherry Blossom Saimin Stand.

I told Gussie's story as close to the truth as I could. I could not imagine her grief in burying two daughters and a nephew. Then I found out about the Hirasaki family and so many other civilian families that suffered deaths and loss of their homes. I wanted to understand how these women got up the next day and went on with daily life.

I started researching the period. If you are interested in Hawai'i during the war years, I encourage you to read Gwen Allen's *Hawaii War Years*.

I read newspapers, archival materials, oral histories, and conducted personal interviews. The circle of women I interviewed kept growing. One woman introduced me to the next, and eventually, I met several members of the Women's Air Raid Defense through that network.

Most of my research was conducted at the Hawai'i State Archives, the Hawaiian and Pacific Collection at the University of Hawai'i, the University of Hawai'i Archives, the War Records Depository, the Center for Oral History, and the Hawai'i and Pacific Section of the Hawai'i State Public Library. And as a librarian myself, so many of my colleagues assisted me in this project. The "librarian circle" became a network of people who introduced me to even more resources, references and World War 2 survivors.

Among the women I met were members of the charter member of the Women's Air Raid Defense. I owe special thanks to Ruth Cope and Kathy Cooper who generously shared their stories. I met Sister Ruth Schroeder, a retired nun living at the Sacred Hearts Convent. Ruth was the German nun I described as being interned.

One of the reasons it took me so long to write this book is that I suffered from hero worship of these women, and one of my biggest heroes was Shimeji Kanazawa. In the book, there is a character with her name who is the wife of the Hongwanji Buddhist Mission. Shim was not a bishop's wife; she was a young Big Island teacher who moved to Honolulu and during the war, when the Vice Consul of Sweden needed a representative to assist him with his overwhelming duties, he asked to meet "a girl with a Red Cross heart." Shim took over many of the responsibilities of the Vice Consul of Sweden including overseeing the treatment of Japanese POWs. After the war, she championed the rights of the aged and was recognized by President Clinton for her work.

Most of the events in CNR are factual, however, I did shift a few dates and locations. (For example Operation K and the bombing of Roosevelt High School occurred in March 1942, not December 1941) I've tried to maintain the spirit of the time and I encourage you to research any incident you find interesting.

As for my journey as a writer, I must thank Tim Storm—teacher, mentor, editor, and, if I may, friend. He took me from stories of a boy talking to a dog to this.

I owe thanks to the many critique groups who allowed me to share my writing. Thank you to Anne Keller who walked and talked with me for hours about the stubborn characters of *Code Name Rascal*. And to Elaine Schroller, my editor, who was the doula.

Thank you to every person who told me not to give up and who supported me through this project. It took a long time, but now, at seventy-five years old, I feel I am old enough, mature enough, and have lived long enough to tell the stories of these women with accuracy and dignity.

So many have helped me on this journey—I can't even imagine the number. If I mention one name, I will egregiously omit hundreds of others. So, I thank you now—if it was one email, a text, a reference—anything—Thank you. Some of you will find your names used in this book. I used names of actual WARD members to thank them for their service. I used names of the military members involved in the formation of the unit, but the characters who I named were all fictious and have no bearing on the actual persons.

From day one, my husband has been my first and last reader, editor, book coach, chef, therapist, and partner of over fifty years. He deserves writing credit. And, on the way we did a historical photo book of World War 2.

(*Images of Hawaii: Hawaii the War Years*. Arcadia Press.)

God bless my husband for keeping me together through it all. I hope we have at least another twenty on this marvelous ride.

About the Author

Dorothea N. Buckingham (better known to all as Dee) has called Hawai'i home for over 30 years. Following her career as a librarian in the Hawaii State Library System and the University of Hawaii, she was able to pursue writing full-time. Her published titles include: "The Essential Guide to Sumo a complete guide to the Japanese sport" (Bess Press, Inc., 1994) which was very popular during the height of the American sumo wrestlers. "My Name is Loa" (Sydney Press, third printing 2022), her first young adult novel, is still a consistent backlist book and was on the Kamehameha Schools' reading list for over ten years. "Who Murdered Jane Stanford?: An Answer Imagined" (Sydney Press, 2022) is a historical novel about the mysterious death of Jane Leland Stanford in Hawaii in 1905.

Dee has a deep fondness for both the young adult and historical fiction genres and has received numerous regional and national reviews for her young adult works. In fact, "Staring Down The Dragon" (Sydney Press, 2003), was an American Library Association's "Best Book for Young Adults." Writing the story of Rell DeMello, a high school sophomore returning to school after nearly a year of cancer treatment, was a daunting challenge. However, she felt strongly that it could offer a meaningful portrayal of a teen dealing with a realistic crisis. "Delicious Tidbits – The Recipes and Stories of Sackets Harbor" (Sydney Press, 2007) is a historical, pictorial cookbook developed around the unique characters, organizations, events, and anecdotes surrounding the beautiful village of Sackets Harbor, New York.

During the course of her writing career, Dee became a certified book coach and helps new writers bring their books to fruition. She is a talented speaker, has appeared on west coast radio and television in Hawai'i, and has presented book talks and workshops to governors, school children and fellow authors. Her passion is to teach and share. If you'd like to arrange for Dee to meet your group, or Zoom with your book club, please contact her directly at buckaloha@gmail.com or deebuckingham96744@gmail.com.

If you would like to know more about Dee and her other works, check out her website at: DorotheaBuckingham.com